TINA LEONARD

Frisco Joe's Fiancée

Laredo's Sassy Sweetheart

Harlequin®

TORONTO NEW YORK LONDON
AMSTERDAM PARIS SYDNEY HAMBURG
STOCKHOLM ATHENS TOKYO MILAN MADRID
PRAGUE WARSAW BUDAPEST AUCKLAND

Recycling programs
for this product may
not exist in your area.

ISBN-13: 978-0-373-68827-2

FRISCO JOE'S FIANCÉE & LAREDO'S SASSY SWEETHEART

Copyright © 2011 by Harlequin Books S.A.

The publisher acknowledges the copyright holder
of the individual works as follows:

FRISCO JOE'S FIANCÉE
Copyright © 2003 by Tina Leonard

LAREDO'S SASSY SWEETHEART
Copyright © 2003 by Tina Leonard

This edition published by arrangement with Harlequin Books S.A.

For questions and comments about the quality of this book
please contact us at Customer_eCare@Harlequin.ca.

® and TM are trademarks of the publisher. Trademarks indicated with
® are registered in the United States Patent and Trademark Office, the
Canadian Trade Marks Office and in other countries.

www.Harlequin.com

Printed in U.S.A.

TINA LEONARD

is a bestselling author of more than forty projects, including a popular thirteen-book miniseries for Harlequin American Romance. Her books have made the Waldenbooks, Ingram and Nielsen BookScan bestseller lists. Tina feels she has been blessed with a fertile imagination and quick typing skills, excellent editors and a family who loves her career. Born on a military base, she lived in many states before eventually marrying the boy who did her crayon printing for her in the first grade. Tina believes happy endings are a wonderful part of a good life. You can visit her at www.tinaleonard.com.

CONTENTS

Many thanks to the readers who keep me laughing,
keep me enlightened, keep me writing.
I can never thank you enough for what you
give to me. In this book I would like to extend
a special thank-you to the following wonderful people:
Latesha Ballard, Katie Jenkins, Candy Gorcsi,
Barbara Goodell, Ken Lester, Marina Tatum,
Gill Hopkins, Crystal Partin, Rita Rondeau,
Diana Tidlund, Cryna Palmiere, Beth Woodfin,
Chere K. Gruver, Melissa Lawson and Georgia Haynes.

As always, thanks to the wonderful editors
at Harlequin. And big kisses to Lisa and Dean
from the proudest Mumzie on the planet.

FRISCO JOE'S FIANCÉE

PROLOGUE

"YOU NEED HELP," Mimi Cannady told Mason Jefferson as they peered at each other with some distrust. Outside, a storm brewed over Union Junction, Texas, crackling and vicious. "You'll thank me for this later, Mason. I just know it."

He turned his head to stare at the want ad she'd typed on the glowing computer screen. The room was dim, almost dark, as the February night had fallen swiftly, obliterating the cold light of winter. Mimi was right: he did need help at the ranch. Woman help.

His family: the Jefferson brothers of the Jefferson Ranch, better known as Malfunction Junction. Twelve men, each on a mission of survival in a family that loved each other, but like an old piano, had become woefully out of harmony.

Still, he wasn't sure Mimi's unconventional idea was the way to get the help he—or the family—needed. "I don't like it," he said for the tenth time. "What if the woman we get is…" He searched for a word that wouldn't irritate the woman he'd known ever since their childhoods on neighboring ranches. Mimi was spunky, witty, a veritable handful of laughter and quixotic temperament—always into everything. As the daughter of the town sheriff, she'd made a habit of skirting the law, just for fun. "What if the woman we get is not useful to my situation?"

Mimi's gaze turned from the computer screen to his face, touching every feature, it seemed, in a strangely searching manner. This childhood friend of his had gotten him into trouble more than once—he'd desperately like to know what was behind her blue eyes now. Thunder rumbled, ever closer to Malfunction Junction, the only home Mason and his eleven brothers had ever known.

Eleven wild, almost Grizzly Adams–types.

From Mimi's point of view, Mason was little better than his younger eleven.

I need help.

"The ad goes through the agency, you can always send her back," Mimi said, her tone reassuring. "It's like using a nanny service. If you don't like her, you let the company know. But my friend, Julia Finehurst, who runs the Honey-Do Agency, has made a reputation matching up the right people to the right situations. I'm sure you'll get exactly what you want."

Mimi had told him many things over the years, and, infrequently, she was right on the money. But *infrequent* was the operative word. He read the overly specific, purposefully careful ad one more time:

Middle-aged man requires live-in housekeeper to cook and clean for family of twelve cowboys on a thousand-acre ranch. Must like ranch living, not be offended by occasional swearing, not be afraid of snakes, large animals, extreme heat, insects, loneliness. Applicant must be forty-five or older, mature, able to cook real well. Best time to interview after nightfall.

"I don't like the part about me being a middle-aged man," he protested. "You've always said thirty-seven was just right for the picking."

Mimi cleared her throat, clearly trying to think of a rebuttal. Mason raised a brow, curious to hear what she came up with.

"No female is going to come all the way out here if she suspects she's going to be man prey. At least no *serious* job applicant," she stressed. "We don't want anyone to misunderstand what kind of position you're looking to fill." For a half second, she examined her fingernails, seeming to consider other points of argument. "Besides, that was my only line in the ad, Mason. You added all the other drawbacks that are sure to run off good women. You practically want her to be a goddess."

"Maybe you should put in something about law-abiding. I don't want any wild women on the property," he said, eyeing Mimi's long blond tresses. Her hair hung to her waist, hardly ever curled or styled, though occasionally she tortured it into a braid so that she could pull it through the back of a baseball cap.

It was hard to believe she was thirty-two.

It was harder to believe that he was the sole caretaker of younger brothers and a family ranch. There was simply too much to do, and while everyone pitched in with the ranch work, the three houses with four brothers each pitifully lacked a woman's touch to make them homes.

An *older* woman's touch, as Mimi had pointed out. A calming, settling influence.

An older woman, even a motherly figure, was fine with Mason, because none of the Jefferson males had expressed the least desire for a wife—mainly because they were all satisfied to continue sowing their wild oats. A younger woman might prove a distraction to their work, and they had enough of those. Plus, a young woman would want a family eventually, and they had more family than they could handle.

"It's now or never," Mimi said softly as the trees whipped around the two-story house. "It's going to take Julia some time to find appropriate applicants."

Strong wind cried through the branches, and lightning lit the room, showing Mimi's gaze on him. "Though I've attached a picture of you to this email, it's going to be tough to find a decent woman to want to come out here and live in hard conditions. The cattle sale is in two weeks, and I'm not coming over here to cook and clean up after your crew while you're gone. I've got enough on my hands as it is."

"I wouldn't want you to. You might lead my brothers into avoiding their duties."

The last time Mimi had gotten a harebrained idea, they'd all gone picnicking at the lake. Mimi had brought along some cousins of hers from Idaho, and four of his brothers had proceeded to fistfight over the two girls. Mason had never been so ashamed of his family—a female was no reason to fight! But then Mimi had jumped into the fray, and he'd had to pull her out before she got herself hurt—and she'd slapped him soundly before she realized it was only her good friend rescuing her as a gentleman should. She'd apologized, but on certain days, he was certain his head still rang from the blow she'd landed on him.

His head was ringing now as he stared at her, and he decided maybe it was the storm. "This won't be the first goony thing you've talked me into, Mimi."

"And it may not be the last. But I promise you this is a guaranteed winner of an idea. You couldn't do any better if you were betting on a champion thoroughbred on race day." She smiled at him. "Press Send, Mason. Help will be on the way before you know it."

It had fallen to Mason as the eldest to rear the unholy bunch of brothers—and lately the situation was about out of control. Frisco was surly. Fannin was talking crazy about packing up and heading out to find out whatever happened to their dad, Maverick, who'd been gone since Mason had turned eighteen nearly twenty years ago. Laredo had mentioned he was thinking about moving east to ease his wandering feet, while his twin, Tex, was cross-pollinating roses with the contentment of an early settler. Calhoun had been eyeing riding the rodeo circuit. Ranger had briefly mentioned enlisting, while his twin, Archer, had taken to writing poetry to a lady pen pal in Australia. Crockett was painting pictures of nudes—from memory, as best as Mason could tell—and his twin, Navarro, was considering going with Calhoun on the rodeo circuit, which would mean the wild boys wreaking havoc on themselves and every female within eyesight. Bandera hadn't slept in a week and was spouting poetry like Whitman, and Last, well, Last was bugging Mason about when they were going to get some womenfolk and children at the ranch. Lord only knew, with the way Last adored women—and they returned his affection—it was a wonder there wasn't a small city's-worth of children at the ranch already.

Something had to be done. The weight of responsibility bore down on Mason, urging him to stay at the helm and not jump ship the way Maverick had. Mason was the father figure, the decision-maker, the authoritarian.

Only with the woman sitting next to him did he relax from the pressure of his life. She gave him other things to go crazy about, giving him a break from thinking about his family's problems. If he was the captain of the Jefferson ship, she was the storm breaking over his bow, threatening to send him to unknown destinations—and sometimes, her storm seemed safer than the fraternal quicksand under his feet.

He always felt on the edge with Mimi, Mason acknowledged, as he reached out slowly toward the keyboard. Frankly, she scared him just a little, always had. There'd been stitches in his head when he'd fallen from a tree she could climb better than him; there'd been a scolding from his dad when she'd skipped school and he'd gone looking for her. More times than he could count, he'd gone along with the schemes she conjured—and he'd always rued them. Every time, he thought, but like a piper's music calling to him, he could not resist Mimi's sense of fun and lightheartedness. His finger trembling, knowing there'd be hell to pay for listening to her, he hesitantly reached out to touch the send key.

Fierce lightning burst over the house, cracking as if it was striking the old stone chimney. Mimi screamed and grabbed for Mason, flattening his hand against the keyboard. Message Sent flashed briefly on the screen as the computer died and the electricity went out, but Mason didn't notice. It felt so good to have Mimi in his arms—under cover of safe, secure darkness—that he just grinned to himself and held her tight.

CHAPTER ONE

Home is what a man feels in his heart

—Maverick Jefferson to his second son, Frisco,
when Frisco had boyhood nightmares that the
ranch might blow away like Dorothy's house
in the Wizard of Oz

"I WANT YOU TO get your butt over here right now and fix this problem," Frisco Joe Jefferson said to his older brother, close to cursing before deciding the heck with keeping his anger to himself. He had a crisis on his hands, and Mason could darn well share the misery. "Damn it, Mason, these women say you put up an advertisement for a housekeeper. If you did, then I suggest you come pick one out."

A moment passed as Frisco listened. Furious, he hung up the phone, turning to stare at his ten younger brothers, all of whom were close to the window in the kitchen of the main house so they could spy on the approximately twenty women gathered shivering on the front lawn. The women were all shapes and sizes, all races, all ages. Luggage dotted the frozen grass. Frisco, as eldest during Mason's absence, was supposed to be in command. "Mason said to call Mimi."

"Typical," Bandera said. "What's Mimi supposed to do about it?"

Frisco shook his head. "Unless she can make all those ladies disappear, I'm not sure."

"I'd hate for *all* of them to disappear," Fannin said, his gaze longing. "Most of them are pretty cute."

"And one of them has a baby," Last said. "I'll take that one."

"We're not taking *any* of them," Frisco said with quiet determination. From the window, he could see Shoeshine Johnson's school bus rumbling back to the bus depot after depositing his travelers. "I'm calling Mimi."

The brothers went back to their surreptitious peering through the window while Frisco dialed Mimi Cannady's number.

"Mimi," Frisco said abruptly when she answered, "I need your help."

"Uh-uh," she responded automatically. "No. I told Mason before he left on this two-week business trip that I unequivocally could not be responsible for his responsibilities. It takes up too much time, Frisco. I have my dad to think about."

What bull-malarkey. Sheriff Cannady was as fit as an untried rodeo rider. So what Mimi had told Mason, then, was best put as "Wake up, buddy. I'm not just the girl next door. I've got a life of my own, and I'm not content to be treated like a convenience anymore."

He sighed, unable to blame Mimi. "Listen, Mimi. I certainly understand how you feel. Mason just seemed to think you might be best able to pick through the housekeepers, in order to choose one he might like. He mentioned you helped him write the advertisement. I've got to admit, the rest of us are in the dark about what you two were thinking."

"Housekeepers?" Mimi echoed, clearly dumbfounded,

much as Mason had been. Mason had sounded as if he hadn't known what Frisco was talking about—initially.

"I guess they're wanting to be housekeepers," he said. "There's about twenty of them out front. It seems as if they came together."

"Oh, my stars," Mimi breathed. "Twenty?"

"I'm just estimating. *Did* you send out an ad for a housekeeper? Because I gotta be honest with you, the rest of us don't think we need woman help on the ranch."

"Woman help," Mimi murmured. She fully remembered writing that ad with Mason. She'd typed the email address to her friend at the Honey-Do Agency. But Julia would have called her before sending out applicants to the ranch, and she would never have sent twenty. Twenty!

Something was wrong. "I did type an ad for Mason, but we never sent it. That bad storm came, the one that toppled the old oak tree, and the lights went out—" She blushed, remembering clutching Mason and loving the feel of his muscles beneath his crisp denim shirt, and the smell of him, and the sound of his heart pounding against her ear.

After that momentary let-down in her facade of just-friends, Mimi had vowed to stay clear of Mason. One day he just might figure out how she felt about him, and then, most certainly, she'd lose his friendship.

Friendship was all she had of him, and she was going to keep it. "We must have accidentally sent it out somehow." Dimly she remembered one of them hitting the keyboard before the electricity went out, but at the time, she'd blindly grabbed for Mason and forgotten all about housekeepers and other trivial things. Obviously, one of them had smashed incorrect letters, and sent the email to the wrong address.

Now they were all sitting square on top of a huge dilemma. And yet, it would be good for Mason to see that he needed her…in spite of what he said to the contrary, his life would be so much better with her in it.

But he'd have to learn that on his own. It was said that one could lead a horse to water but couldn't make him drink. Lord only knew, she'd waited so long on Mason that it felt as if her watering can was nearly dry. "Can't you interview them, Frisco?"

"Seeing as how none of us here think we need a lady at the ranch, I'm not interested in that job," Frisco said.

"I think you could use a housekeeper. The place is never clean. Or tidy."

"Then it's our job to clean our houses better," Frisco said sternly. "When there's as much to be done as a property this size requires, we're not too worried if the dishes stay in the sink an extra day."

"Precisely my point. You could use the help."

"But not the aggravation a woman brings. We have you, Mimi, and that's enough."

Laughter, not unkind, in the background nettled her. "What does that mean?"

"It means when we need something, you're kind enough to help us out."

That was the problem. Mason and all his brothers had the luxury of her jumping whenever they needed something. No wonder Mason saw her as an extension of his family. Not that it was a bad thing to have the Jeffersons looking out for her—it had come in handy over the years.

But it was now or never. The tie that bound them had

to be cut on both ends, or she'd always be little Mimi Cannady, almost-sis, tomboy-next-door, for-a-good-gag-call Mimi. Toilet-papering houses, tying cans on goat tails, painting rural mailboxes with smiley faces—they'd done it all.

Together.

"Not this time, Frisco," she said. "I have a lot going on in my own life right now. Thanks for calling."

She hung up the phone and went to check on her father.

"SHE'S NOT COMING," Frisco said, hanging up the phone.

"Mimi is abandoning us in our hour of need?" Last asked, his tone surprised.

"See if we ever go fix her sinks when they back up again," Laredo grumbled.

"She'd be over here in a snap if it were Mason calling for help," Ranger grumbled. "That woman's a jill-in-the-box when it comes to him, popping up like crazy whenever he decides to wind her crank."

"I've never known exactly which one of them was winding whose crank," Navarro commented.

Calhoun laughed. "She's been real prickly ever since you drank too much champagne at the Christmas party two months ago and sang that stupid Mimi-and-Mason, sitting-in-a-Christmas-tree—"

"Shut up," Archer said loudly, the author of the musical ditty.

"Yeah, she has been different since then," Last said. "Maybe if you'd act your age and not your hat size, we wouldn't be struggling with this right now. She'd be over here—"

"No." Frisco shook his head. "No, this is our problem. We can take care of it ourselves."

The brothers glanced at each other, then huddled around the window. It looked like a garden party on the lawn. There were more women than the ranch had ever seen on the property at one time, and considering there were twelve brothers in the family, that was saying a lot.

Frisco cleared his throat and drew himself up tall, realizing that the mantle of family was clearly on his shoulders. He was determined to bear it well. "I'll explain that this is a simple miscommunication problem."

Laredo looked at him. "Do you want us for backup?"

"I think I can handle this. The ladies might be intimidated by all of us." He was somewhat intimidated by all of *them*—he hadn't expected twenty anxious women to show up today. No doubt there would be some initial disappointment that there was no position available, but he could get money out of the Malfunction Junction Ranch's petty cash to give them for the return bus trip.

"You go, bro," Bandera encouraged. "We'll be cheering you on from in here."

"That's right," Tex agreed.

"Couldn't we keep just one?" Last asked. "Maybe the little blonde over there, holding the baby?"

Frisco peered out, immediately seeing what made Last pick her out of the crowd. "She's not a puppy. We can't just 'keep' her. Anyway, she'd get lonely out here. Even Mimi gets lonely, and she was born in Union Junction." He frowned for a second, thinking that the petite blonde would be more tempting as a date than a housekeeper. In fact, he wasn't certain he'd get any work done at all if he knew she was in his house, cooking his meals, making a home for him.

His mouth began to water at the thought of home-cooked food, prepared by caring hands. A strange humming buzzed in his ears as he watched her press the baby's head against her lips in a sweet kiss. The baby was crying, probably cold from being outside in February's brisk chill, despite the bunting encasing the small body. "What would we do with a baby out here, anyway?" he murmured.

They all looked dumbfounded at that.

Fannin shook his head. "Definite drawback. I guess."

"Maybe we could have them in for a cup of cocoa before we take them to the station," Last suggested, his tone hopeful.

"No!" Frisco knew exactly where his youngest brother was heading with that idea. Once the ladies were in the house, maybe Frisco would soften his stance…. Last had a sensitive heart where other people were concerned. He had reason to be a bit delicate—too young to really remember when their mother, Mercy, had died; too old not to question why their father, Maverick, had left them for parts unknown. He would sympathize with a single mother and her child.

But this was no place for a woman, a baby or soft hearts. "We can't, Last," he said firmly, meeting his brother's eyes. "I'll go tell them."

He went outside, his shoulders squared. "Ladies," he said loudly, "I hate to be the bearer of bad news, but we're not looking for a housekeeper at this time. We'll be happy to pay your return bus fare to wherever you came from."

A middle-aged, not-unattractive woman stepped forward to be the spokeswoman. "How come you placed an ad, then?"

"It was a mistake. We're terribly sorry."

"You're not the man who placed the ad. We saw his picture." She crossed her arms over her chest. "We came all the way to apply with *him*. Where is he?"

"He's gone for the next two weeks," Frisco said, determined to be patient, not meeting the blonde's gaze, though he realized she was staring up at him as he stood on the wide porch. Trying not to look back at her made his scalp tighten and prickle as if he were sweating all over his head. "We've contacted our brother, and he said the email was sent in error. As I said, we are happy to take you to the bus station in town. Now, if you all will load into the trucks my brothers will be bringing around in a moment, we'll get you started on your way back home."

They didn't like it; grumbling rose among them, but there was nothing he could do about that. A mistake was a mistake, an honest one.

But he'd handled it, and handling twenty women was easier than he thought it'd be, he decided, opening truck doors and helping them into various seats. He didn't see the little blonde and the baby; they weren't among the passengers who jumped into his cab, but he'd be willing to bet Last had eagerly escorted the two of them to his vehicle.

Better him than me.

It was a motley, somewhat sad procession as the brothers drove six trucks to the bus stop, but it was the right thing to do.

They left them in the station, having paid for tickets and making sure they had enough money for snacks. He handed the clump of tickets to the woman he dubbed the spokeswoman, tipped his hat to their silent faces, and feeling guilty as hell, slunk out with his brothers.

"I'm gonna kill Mimi and Mason for this stupid stunt," he muttered to Fannin. "Reckon they planned this?"

"What for?" Fannin glanced at him as they walked through the parking lot.

"I don't know. I just know that when those two get together, there's always hell to pay."

"I know. That's why they can't stay together in one room very long. It's spontaneous combustion."

"I'm going home to have a beer," Frisco said. "And then I'm going to bed."

"No poker tonight?"

"Heck no. I'm all played out." That baby wasn't going to enjoy a long bus ride back to Lonely Hearts Station, he knew. And the little mother had looked so tired.

Damn Mason and Mimi anyway. "See ya," he said to Fannin, surly again. Then he got in his truck and drove home, deciding to skip the beer and go right upstairs.

He'd been up since 4:00 a.m., and a lot had happened. If he went to sleep now, maybe he could forget all the events of the day.

Stripping to his boxers, he left jeans, boots and his shirt on the floor, crawling quickly between the sheets to escape the slight chill in the room.

His bare skin made instant contact with something small and soft in the bed. "What the hell?" he murmured, flipping on the bedside lamp in a hurry.

It was the baby, no longer wearing her white bunting and sound asleep in the middle of his bed, peacefully sucking her tiny fist.

CHAPTER TWO

"HOLY SMOKES, FRISCO," Navarro said as Frisco came barreling down the stairs. All ten of his brothers glanced at him. "Your drawers on fire?" Navarro asked.

"There's a baby in my bed!" Frisco shouted. Remembering that a baby could be loud when it was awake, he lowered his voice to an unnerved whisper. "That little blonde put her baby in my bed!"

"Are you sure?" Fannin asked.

Frisco looked at him as if he'd gone mad. "I think I know a baby when I see one!"

"How do you know it's hers?" Fannin said patiently.

"Because she was the only one who had a child that young with her." And the picture of her kissing the baby's head was still fresh in his mind. "I know it's hers."

"Dang." Bandera threw his cards onto the round den table. "I'm certain she didn't know it was your bed, Frisco. No woman would give your surly butt her sweet, fragile angel."

His brothers laughed heartily. The instant fear, which had sent Frisco running down the stairs, began to turn to bad humor. "Where is she?" he demanded of Last.

"How would I know?" the youngest Jefferson shot back. "I thought she was getting in your truck."

"My truck? Oh, no, she definitely was not getting into my truck," Frisco insisted. He would have noticed that for certain. "I told you we couldn't keep her, Last. You go find her, and take her and her baby back. *Now.*"

Last stood up, angry. "I don't know where she is."

Tex sighed. "Maybe she's not here."

"What?" Frisco stared at him. "Why do you say that?"

"I'm just saying maybe we'd better search the three houses and have a look for her," Tex said evenly. "And hope she's not far from her baby."

"I'm not," a woman said quietly, as she stepped into the den from the hallway.

The entire roomful of men rose, half for the sake of good manners and half because she'd startled them.

"I'm sorry to be the cause of so much trouble," she said, her voice soft and gentle, almost shy. "I was changing Emmeline's diaper when everyone left."

Frisco's mouth had dropped open when she walked into the room, holding a baby bottle. Up close, she was even more adorable. He loved worn blue jeans on a woman; he loved blond hair that hung straight to a woman's chin. He loved sleepy eyes that stared right at him. There was some silent communication going on between them; there was something she was trying to tell him—

Her gaze averted from his, and Ranger coughed. "You might want to go throw on a pair of jeans, Frisco."

ANNABELLE TURNBERRY knew what a man looked like without his clothes on, of course, or she wouldn't have two-month-old Emmie. She'd just never seen a man like the one the other men called Frisco—the boxers only hid enough to keep her from being totally mortified.

And fascinated. She almost couldn't stop staring until his brother reminded him he was sans jeans.

This was a household of men, and it seemed to be a normal routine to move about the house wearing whatever. She frowned. Her ex-fiancé had taken his clothes off in the dark the one time he took her to bed; she wasn't sure she knew what he looked like. The fact that she'd just seen more of a stranger than she'd ever seen of her ex-fiancé wasn't comforting.

Frisco shot up the stairs, muttering an apology. He looked just as good from the backside, she thought, taking a fast peek only because…because—

Well, there was no good justification for it. No excuse. It almost seemed wrong to look at another man, especially since she'd recently given birth, but it wasn't as if she'd been looking out of lust, more out of admiration. After all, if a man who looked like Adonis took off running suddenly, wouldn't *any* woman have to look?

She dropped her gaze, thinking that she was in a houseful of Adonises, and maybe therefore in a precarious position. They didn't know her; she didn't know them. Maybe she was guilty of breaking and entering or something else that concerned the law.

"It's okay," one of the men said, standing up to come over to her. "Next time you see Frisco, he'll be fully dressed."

"Oh. Well. I'm so sorry for the—"

"Don't worry about it."

The man smiled at her, his gaze full of compassion. Annabelle was relieved because she hadn't known what to say first, or even what she was going to say. There were so many things to apologize for!

"You're tired. Why don't you go lie upstairs with

your baby until we can get you back to…where was it, again?"

"The Lonely Hearts Salon in Lonely Hearts Station, Texas." She swallowed. "My name is Annabelle Turnberry."

The kind man slapped his forehead. "We have manners, we really do. I'm Last Jefferson."

He put out his hand to her, and she took it, noticing that his grip was gentle.

"These are my brothers, going from the top to the bottom, not counting Mason, who isn't here." They stood when he pointed to each one, as he recited, "Frisco's upstairs, Fannin, Laredo, Tex, Calhoun, Ranger, Archer, Crockett, Navarro, Bandera, and me."

"Last," she repeated.

"But never least."

His smile was devilish, inviting her to join in the harmless repartee. She could easily see that he never allowed himself to be outdone by his older brothers. "I'll remember that. Last but not least."

He smiled. "Good girl. Go upstairs and get some rest."

"No. I don't think so," Frisco said, his voice deep as he came down the stairs. He tucked a denim shirt into jeans, he was barefoot, and Annabelle thought he might be the most handsome man she'd ever seen. But he was obviously a bad-humored rascal, and falling for that kind of man was what had landed her in her current predicament.

Or had given her a baby, anyway. Her predicament of being at the ranch with eleven men was her own fault, a direct result of deciding it was time to take charge of her life, stand on her own two feet. Move away from all things familiar and start over.

My life is more out of control than ever.

"She can't make a bus now, Frisco," Last said, his tone reasonable.

"And she can't stay here."

Annabelle stared at the tall cowboy, her misgivings growing. As far as he was concerned, she was an imposition, which, to be fair, she was, but it wasn't all her fault. It was his brother who'd put the ad out over the internet. She'd just thought to apply for a job where her baby would grow up safe. And in a real house, not a room over the beauty salon. Or at least that's what Delilah had encouraged her to try for. Emmie would be very safe on a ranch with twelve men, the biggest danger probably being teaching her daughter that cows weren't big doggies.

"Why not?" Last demanded, having appointed himself her champion. The other brothers began a protest that started out, "Come on, Frisco, lighten up," but Frisco raised his hand to silence them.

"Because she's a woman, and it wouldn't be appropriate for her to stay with eleven bachelors," he snapped. "Do I have to spell everything out for you lunkheads?"

"Yes. Sometimes," Last said on a sigh. "So now what?"

"It's late. The baby's asleep. I hate to wake her now just to put her in a truck to get hauled off," the blonde said. Frisco put his hands in his pockets and looked at her.

The dilemma was painful for all. Annabelle realized she was more of a problem than she'd thought. She couldn't match his nearly-black-eyed stare and glanced at the baby bottle in her hand.

A knock at the front door made everybody turn.

"We expectin' anybody?" Fannin asked, going to the door.

"Nope," Frisco replied.

But the door burst open before Fannin could open it, a woman making herself at home as if she always did. "Girl in the house. Everybody decent? Or at least got clothes on?" she called out.

No one yelled back the standard We-got-clothes-on-but-we're-not-decent line. The newcomer latched a curious gaze on Annabelle.

The room fell silent.

"Two girls in the house, maybe?" Annabelle said. "Decent and fully clothed?" She'd wanted to be light and airy to make a situation that was turning increasingly uncomfortable more easy for all. But by the look on the woman's face, maybe not.

"Mimi, this is Annabelle Turnberry. Annabelle, Mimi Cannady, our next-door neighbor," he said.

"How do you do?" Mimi asked politely.

"Fine, thank you."

"Annabelle's applying to be our new housekeeper," Last said cheerfully.

"Housekeeper?" Mimi's gaze turned worried. "She can't."

"Why not?" Annabelle knew she wasn't in the running for the job—if there was one, Frisco had made it clear she wasn't under consideration. But maybe Mimi could explain it better, and then Annabelle wouldn't feel as if she'd simply made another silly mistake in her life by taking off for parts unknown to become a housekeeper.

"You're not forty-five," Mimi said. "That was in the ad, if you recall."

"Forty-five?" Last said. "Why so old?"

"You'd have to ask Mason," Mimi replied, her tone bright. "He was adamant on the age requirement."

Annabelle caught the glance that passed between Mimi and Frisco, Mimi's chin up, Frisco's gaze narrowed suspiciously.

"Well, Mimi, it seems we agree on one thing," he said softly.

"Will wonders never cease?" she shot back, her tone too sweet. Yet somehow strong underneath.

Annabelle's eyebrows raised.

"She'll have to come home with me," Mimi said, with a put-upon sigh. "One of you can drive Annabelle back into town tomorrow."

"Thought you weren't going to help us anymore," Last said helpfully. "We sure don't want to put you out any."

"That's okay," Mimi said, in the voice of a Good Samaritan. "Annabelle will be more comfortable at my house, I feel certain."

From upstairs, Emmie's wail floated down, loud and miserable.

"What's that?" Mimi demanded.

"It's my baby," Annabelle said hurriedly. "She suffers from colic and doesn't sleep well at night. Excuse me."

She ran off up the stairs, almost glad to be away from whatever unspoken conversation was going on downstairs. One thing she was certain of, Frisco didn't want her there—and neither did Mimi.

"NICE OF YOU TO GIVE us a hand, Mimi." Frisco tossed her a wry grin. "We'll think about you listening to sweet baby tears all night."

Mimi was about fit to be tied. She'd nearly not come in time! What if these over-eager Jefferson brothers had hired the attractive little blonde? Mason would be back in two weeks, after all, and the last thing she wanted him to find upon his arrival was a dainty housekeeper.

"I've never seen you jealous before, Mimi," Frisco said lazily. "You sure do put on a good show."

"Shush, Frisco." Mimi rolled her eyes at him. "If you were only half as smart as you think you are, you'd still only be thinking on a third-grade level."

"Mimi and Mason, sittin' in a tree—" one of the brothers started.

She whirled around. "Cut it out, guys, or I leave the lady—and the baby—with you. And *none* of you will get a wink of sleep tonight, I'll bet."

It would be more because of Annabelle than the baby that they might not sleep tonight, but Mimi wasn't going to let any of them know they'd scored with their baiting of her. She knew how to keep this group of bad boys in check.

It was Mason who threw her for a loop. And she wasn't about to have him come home to a ready-made family scenario. She didn't like the fact that her house-keeping scheme had nearly backfired on her.

"We're just yanking your chain, Mimi." Frisco grinned at her, eager to make peace.

"I'll go help Annabelle pack up the baby," she said with a long-suffering sigh.

A loud pounding sounded on the door, and this time, Fannin waited to see if it would burst open again, with someone else making themselves at home.

No one came in, so he got up and jerked the door open. To Mimi's horror, what looked like a sorority stood on the porch, before silently filing into the den. A middle-aged woman stepped forward.

"Annabelle didn't get on the bus with us," she announced with grave determination. "And we're not leaving without her."

CHAPTER THREE

DESIRE TO GET ALL these women off his property swept over Frisco. "Annabelle and the baby are fine," he said, somewhat annoyed that the spokeswoman seemed to think some type of transgression might be wrought upon his two short-term house guests.

"We have a right to be concerned. We don't know you," she replied.

"Yes, but did all of you have to come back for her? I paid for those bus tickets." Good money, he could have added, but thought better of it.

"Busses aren't running."

Voices murmuring behind her told him that all the women were concurring with her statement. Shock began to spread through his tired brain. "They were running when I left."

"Apparently, there's ice on the roads out of Union Junction. Storm on the way in, too. They shut down the station and canceled all outgoing routes. Even Shoeshine Johnson's school bus-taxi service was closed."

"How'd you get here?" Bad luck seemed to swirl around him. If the busses weren't running, he could wind up with a bunch of females—and a colicky baby. The thought was enough to chill his bones. He sent a belligerent glare Mimi's way so that she'd know this was all her fault. And Mason's.

"We hitched a ride with the driver of an eighteen-wheeler who loaded us into the back of his truck. He'd stopped across the highway at the truck stop."

He stared at her, trying to imagine that.

"Twenty minutes in the truck wasn't bad. Any farther than that and we'd have had to spend the night in the bus station," she admitted. "That would have been miserable. But Jerry made certain we were comfortable."

Frisco blew out a breath as he looked around at all the women. He wouldn't have wanted them spending the night in a bus station, especially not since they'd come to Union Junction to apply for a job at the ranch. There was some responsibility involved, he admitted to himself, if not chivalry.

"There's plenty of room here," he said begrudgingly. "We have three houses on the property that the twelve of us share. We'll divide you up…" He hesitated at the black look in the spokeswoman's eye. Clearly there'd be no dividing.

"On the other hand, Navarro's house should sleep all of you just fine."

Navarro straightened but wasn't going to disagree with the pointed look Frisco shot him. "I'll go pack."

Three of his brothers went out the door with him, fairly peacefully for four men who'd just given up their home. Frisco was suspicious about the lack of protest. He watched Last shoot a smile toward the ladies and realized he had a bigger problem on his hand.

His brothers saw an advantage to all these women being stuck on the ranch for the night.

He'd have to keep a tight eye on them to make certain there were no shenanigans.

Navarro came back inside, escorting a stranger. "The truck driver was still outside."

"Hey, Delilah, ladies," he said to the spokeswoman

and her companions, astonishing Frisco, who hadn't even thought to ask her—or any of them—their names. There were simply too many women, and he'd never remember them all. Nor had he expected to see them again.

Delilah clapped a hand to her forehead. "I forgot all about you, Jerry! I'm so sorry! Come on into the kitchen, and I'll fix you a nice cup of whatever Mr. Jefferson's got on hand."

"Miss, er—Ms. Delilah—" Frisco began.

She gave him a straightforward eyeing that said she didn't think much of his manners. "It's Ms. Honeycutt."

At this unspoken verbal wall that was suddenly erected, all the ladies seemed to straighten their backs.

"Delilah," Jerry said, taking off his cap, "these men haven't done anything to offend you, have they?"

Frisco shook his head, realizing his brothers had already gained their feet. The females crossed their arms.

"I can take you right back into town. There's bound to be a place where all of you can hole up. I was under the impression that this was where you wanted to be," the stocky white-haired-and-bearded Jerry said.

"We merely wanted to come back and rescue our Annabelle and little Em," Delilah said, her gaze on Frisco. "But we know when we're not wanted."

"Now, wait a minute—" Frisco began, then halted as he wondered why he was bothering to argue. He really didn't want them here. But a look from his brothers hinted that his manners had somehow aggravated a delicate situation. "We were not expecting guests, that's true, but there's plenty of room for the girls here at the ranch."

He was proud of his offer. Jerry gaped at him. "These are not girls, son," he said sternly. "Haven't you even made proper introductions with these fine ladies?"

Proper introductions before what? Frisco wanted to demand. He'd wanted them gone. What difference did the niceties make?

"This here's Delilah Honeycutt," Jerry said, undertaking the duty of explaining Frisco's lack of manners to him. "And the rest—first names only, since you don't seem too interested, and alphabetical, to make it easy for you—are Beatrice, Carly, Daisy, Dixie, Gretchen, Hannah, Jessica, Julie, Katy, Kiki, Lily, Marnie, Remy, Shasta, Tisha, Velvet, Violet. And you apparently already know Annabelle and baby Emmeline, or we wouldn't be standing here right now."

His expression gave no doubt that he figured Frisco and his brothers were up to something heinous.

"How'd you do that?" Frisco demanded.

"Do what?"

"Memorize all their names so fast?"

Jerry looked at Delilah apologetically. "This may not be the brightest light on the truck, Delilah. You might want to think over your options for the night." He sighed. "I'm a truck driver, son. A good memory helps me when I'm driving transcoastal. And memory games keep me from being bored."

"That boy appears to be the surly one of all these gentlemen," Ms. Honeycutt said. "If you were my boy, you'd approach company with much better deportment. Come on, Jerry," Delilah said, with a slight sniff Frisco's way. "It's time you were given a cup of cocoa."

Frisco's jaw dropped as the tougher-than-cow-hooves truck driver docilely followed her into *his* kitchen, some of the ladies following.

"Good going, big bro," one of his brothers said, but he didn't pay any attention to the snickers and general laughter. His brain felt short-wired.

For the short term, it appeared that life as he'd known it was going to be very different.

He needed a plan, and some organization. Glancing at Mimi, he saw her trying not to giggle. Well she might laugh, since this was yet another one of her schemes with combustible results.

Vowing not to let it bother him, Frisco realized there was only one thing he could do while he was playing host.

For the first time in his life, he was going to have to be a good sport.

ANNABELLE WAS GLAD her friends had returned, even though Frisco looked very grim about it. Frankly, she'd been afraid when she'd discovered she'd allowed herself to get left behind. Frisco didn't want her here, and she'd been happy for Mimi's invitation—even though she sensed Mimi's invitation wasn't because she was anxious to get her hands on a baby. There was something else going on with Mimi.

Yet as long as Annabelle had all her friends, she'd be fine. They'd been her support ever since Tom had left her.

Her friends were the reason she hadn't hesitated to come out here, at the urging of Delilah and the other ladies of the Lonely Hearts Beauty Salon. Darn Dina at the Never Lonely Cut-n-Gurls Salon anyway.

But no, it was Tom who had left her, and that couldn't be blamed on Dina. Annabelle knew she'd picked the wrong man to fall in love with, if he could be so faithless.

"I'll never let that happen again," she said against Emmeline's soft head. "I always heard three strikes and you're out. I only intend to strike out *once*."

In Fort Worth, Mason had a lot of time to think. One of the things he couldn't stop thinking about was Mimi. She'd been in his thoughts long before he'd told Frisco to call her to solve the minor problem that had cropped up at the ranch.

Mason wondered if he missed Mimi, hellion that she was. He'd as surely miss an ingrown toenail, right?

Fortunately, he had this unwelcome thought while he was sitting in a beer joint, listening to old country tunes on an out-of-whack jukebox. The proper antidote to thinking weird stuff like he was thinking was another beer and a two-step with a cute, obliging regular.

Otherwise, he'd have to start riding rodeo again to knock some sense into himself. He'd been alone way too long if he thought he was missing Mimi Cannady.

Of course, if he wanted to play devil's advocate with himself, there *was* the night of the big storm. Remembering the feel of Mimi as she jumped into his arms made his chest spread with warmth. Shaking his head, he swallowed some more beer.

Mimi would drive him crazy sooner or later.

At least for now, things were under control at the ranch. He'd thank her for that later. And the cattle auction had gone better than he'd hoped. Another week, and he'd be home.

His blood picked up as Mimi's face appeared in his memory. She was laughing at him, the way she always did.

Another beer, another dance, and then surely he'd be tired enough not to think about his nutty little neighbor.

"WE NEED A BATTLE PLAN here," Frisco told his brothers as they conglomerated in the kitchen of the big house. "We gotta get these women out of here tomorrow."

"Shh," Laredo said. "They might hear you."

They'd long since said good-night to the ladies and sent them down to the third house on the property—the one farthest from the other two and his brothers. Mimi had gone down to see to the ladies' comfort—except for Annabelle, who was upstairs with Emmeline, sound asleep in *his* bed.

How that particular arrangement had passed Ms. Delilah Honeycutt's military-style sensibilities, he wasn't certain. For a moment, he'd thought she might stay herself, but then she'd apparently decided the other group of women needed her chaperonage more. But she'd given him a severe stare that had said, Don't even think about it. If he'd been hot for Annabelle, the good Ms. Delilah and her icy stare should have cooled him off.

Annabelle and the baby, upstairs in his bed. Sleeping soundly, he hoped. She'd probably pulled off her blue jeans to sleep in…what, exactly? His mouth dried out. He'd never brought a woman home to sleep in his bed. The nice thing about willing women was that they were always willing to take him home to their houses. The upside to this was that he didn't have to shoo anyone out of his house, didn't have any messy reminders of the night before, such as makeup in the bathroom, earrings on the side table or perfume in his sheets.

There was a baby—and a woman—in his sheets now. He couldn't figure what she might be wearing to bed. Something. Maybe nothing. He couldn't identify the sudden surge of emotions he felt at that thought.

"Why?" Last asked. "Why do they have to go? What are they hurting?" The other brothers murmured, as well.

Frisco decided his brothers needed a cold bucket of water upside their heads. But then, they didn't have a pile of diapers and a bottle on their bedside table. "We've got a lot of work to do, and if a storm is coming in, they need to get back to their families. They don't want to stay here for a week until the back roads clear," he said sternly, as much to be sharp with them as to clear his head from the realization that he heard water running upstairs. He held his breath, waiting for the water to shut off, but it didn't.

Water running upstairs meant Annabelle had helped herself to his shower.

She was now definitely naked.

Chills ran all over him. "Don't ask questions," he snapped. "Just help me think how we're going to transport them all back to where they came from!"

"They might be worth keeping," Tex suggested. "Have you ever considered that?"

Frisco shook his head, ignoring the butterflies he suffered at the suggestion. "Out of the question."

Suddenly, the sound of a baby crying drifted to the kitchen. Frisco stiffened.

"Sounds like Emmeline's colic has started back up," Ranger said. "That poor little baby doesn't give her mother much of a break, does she?"

Frisco glanced at the stove clock. Annabelle had been naked for approximately three minutes. *Showering* for approximately three minutes, he amended.

"I'll go see what's going on," he said.

ANNABELLE SIGHED, unable to remember the last time she'd been able to enjoy ten minutes to herself. Em was a wonderful baby and she loved her dearly, but the colic kept her so upset that it was hard to snatch a moment alone.

Even though Tom left me for a Never Lonely Cut-n-Gurl, I've still got Em, she thought.

It was worth it.

The pediatrician had said Em would grow out of her colic—these things just took time. She just needed a lot of love and comforting, and reassurance that she didn't have to suffer alone.

Annabelle completely understood her daughter's needs, because she felt the same way sometimes herself.

Anyway, Tom was, as Delilah called him, a louse. She had a family of women to rely on now, and she had Em. Life was so much better than it had ever been for her.

Turning around for an extra stolen moment of bliss, she let the hot water pour down her back. The truth was, she didn't want Tom back.

He hadn't wanted Em, and she'd never forgive him for that.

Never.

To FRISCO'S SURPRISE, the baby had managed to worm a piece of blanket over her head as she flailed. "That's easy enough to fix," he said quietly to the infant, with a hurried look at the bathroom door. The shower was still running, so it was safe. Annabelle wouldn't come out in a state of undress he was certain they'd both rather avoid.

He was pretty sure the petite blonde looked good in a towel, though.

"Hey, baby, don't be so upset," he said, reaching out to stroke the tiny back. "You're not alone anymore."

Baby Emmeline—had Annabelle called her Emmie?—seemed to hesitate in her wails, either at the sound of his voice or the human contact. "Hmm. I barely know what to do with an angry woman, but maybe it's something a man has to work up to. Starting small might be the way to go." Gingerly he reached to cradle Em in his fingers, and then balanced her in his palms until he was certain he had her positioned properly. Then he lifted her to his chest, cradling her as he hummed.

The crying completely ceased.

"Like falling off a log," he sang to her to the tune of a low country song. "A man never forgets how to make a woman feel good. At least not if he's smart."

She snuffled against him.

"You like my singing, huh? You're the only one who likes it, then. My brothers show no respect for my vocal attributes."

Em didn't object, so he hummed to her and stood, about to leave the room in case Annabelle should put in a towel-clad appearance. "Since you're obviously a lady who likes late-night excitement, let's go watch some Classic Sports Channel. I bet if you learned young enough, you'd love football."

But when he slid into his leather recliner and turned the TV on softly, he realized Em was asleep. "You just wanted to know you're not alone," he murmured. "We all feel like that sometimes, little baby."

LAREDO AND TEX STOOD beside the recliner, staring down at Frisco. The chair was tipped back, his mouth was open, his boots were pointed tips to the ceiling, and there was a baby on his chest. The remote, which would usually lie where the baby was, had fallen to the carpet.

"Are my eyes lying to me?" Laredo whispered.

Tex shook his head, dumbfounded.

"Where's the camera? Get me the camera. I need a picture of this! No one will ever believe that my foul-tempered brother actually let a baby crawl onto his person."

Tex handed him the camera and Laredo squeezed off a shot.

"You wake that baby, and Frisco's gonna chew your head, Laredo."

They both froze for a second as the baby sighed. Neither brother nor infant awoke, however.

Laredo gestured to Tex to follow him back into the kitchen. "I just had a brainstorm."

"I'm wary of storms, myself."

Laredo eyed him wryly. "I'm thinking about all these women."

Tex raised a brow. "You and all the rest of us. Glad to hear you're normal, Laredo."

"I'll ignore that for the moment, in the spirit of brotherhood."

Tex grinned.

"I'm serious here. Give me a listen before you shoot this down, Tex. What if a woman was the way to get Frisco in a better frame of mind?"

Tex gave him his most sober look, which was nearly ruined by the twinkle in his eyes. "Frisco's frame is bent. Totally. I do believe there's not a woman alive who can make him hang on the level."

Laredo sighed, used to his brother's clowning. "But maybe some womanliness is the way to get Frisco to act like a human being."

"Like a shot of instant female hormones to counteract his overload of testosterone?"

Laredo shook his head. "No, I'm talking flesh-and-blood woman. Like sweet Annabelle."

Tex burst out laughing.

CHAPTER FOUR

TEX STOPPED LAUGHING as he took in Laredo's focused expression. "Frisco has women all the time, or at least he could, if he'd pay them any attention. They practically fall out of the pew in church on Sundays."

Laredo shrugged. "That's pretty much a chain reaction to all of us walking in. When twelve men walk in, I'm sure the testosterone quotient in the room shoots up appreciably. You don't know that it's because of Frisco. He's been so foul lately that I doubt any woman would keep him for long, anyway."

Tex scratched his head. "I thought he was being a pain in the rump on principle."

"I'm suggesting that maybe it's been a *while* since he's had a woman."

Long while was embedded in the way Laredo stressed the time frame. Tex frowned. "I don't think any of these girls are going to sleep with our brother just to get him out of a bad mood. And even if they wanted to, Mother Delilah would freak. She's going to keep her flock safe from us wolves."

"I don't know that it has to be a sexual thing, exactly. Maybe he needs his own woman to balance him out." Laredo's expression turned thoughtful. "And apparently, we were looking for a housekeeper."

"Are you hinting that we should hire one of these women?" Tex shook his head. "If Mason was here right now and could see Malfunction Junction-turned-Petticoat Junction, he'd be figuring out a way to get rid of them, not keep them."

"But then Mason's got Mimi keeping him all ginned up. How much excitement can a man stand, anyway? So all I'm saying is that having a woman around might make Frisco happy."

"Frisco being ginned up all the time does not sound like a recipe for happiness."

"But this Annabelle girl isn't like Mimi," Laredo pointed out. "She's not the type to keep Frisco in a knot just for fun."

"Annabelle's your choice for a housekeeper? Mimi's going to eat your heart. I distinctly got the impression that the new housekeeper was supposed to be elderly. Not a sweet young thing living here with me, you, Frisco—and Mason."

Laredo rubbed his chin. "It could be dicey," he admitted. "The unknown factor in this is Mason."

Sudden pounding down the stairs alerted the men that Annabelle had discovered her baby was missing. "Quick! Intercept her before she wakes the baby!" Laredo commanded, jumping to his feet.

"She's not a football, damn it!" But Tex shot out of the kitchen, no more anxious to have baby Em awakened than Laredo was.

Their jaws dropped as they realized they were too late. Annabelle stood staring down at the sleeping man cradling her baby. Her expression was one of amazement. Maybe even wonder.

Best yet, Annabelle's hair was wet, she'd thrown her robe on over her towel so it had caught, and the legs that had previously been concealed by jeans and boots were totally exposed. She had wonderful legs and sparkly pink toenail polish on dainty toes.

Laredo and Tex backed up slowly into the kitchen.

"Last had it right," Laredo said, his blood pressure darn near shooting out of his head. "We *gotta* keep her. For Frisco's sake."

Tex swept a hand across his brow as he leaned up against the pantry. "Oh, God, yes. She's too adorable to send back. I don't care how cranky the baby is. We'll all take turns holding her. But to save my brother from himself, I gladly volunteer my services."

"To rock the baby," Laredo said pointedly.

"Just to rock the baby," Tex agreed. "But damn, if any of those women are hiding such charms under those frumpy country dresses, I get first dibs on the next one we see undressed."

Annabelle peeped around the corner, the robe fully pulled down over the towel now. "What are you guys doing in here?" she asked. "And why does Frisco have my baby?"

Laredo jerked straight. He arranged his face in a Boy Scout expression. "Frisco just *loves* babies, Annabelle. Loves them beyond anything you can imagine. I think he misses having young'uns in the house, if you want to know the truth. And when he heard your little Emmie up there wailing, why, he just raced to comfort her."

She looked at him uncertainly. "That was nice of him."

"Yes, ma'am," Tex said. "And right before he dozed off, he said he hoped you'd help yourself to anything you need in the house." His Adam's apple jumped as he swallowed. "And furthermore, he said not to bother moving Em. He said you're to get the rest you need, and he'll watch her tonight. Since she's so colicky and all."

Annabelle's lips parted, which Laredo thought was an expression Frisco would surely have to appreciate.

"That's awfully nice of him."

She didn't sound certain. Laredo nodded enthusiastically. "Yes. That's what people say about Frisco. He's such a…nice…person."

He held his breath.

"I suppose I'll head back upstairs, if you're sure about this?"

The two brothers nodded quickly.

"Well, all right. Come knock on the door if Frisco changes his mind."

They nodded again. Annabelle left the kitchen, and the brothers high-fived each other.

She poked her head back around the corner, and they stiffened guiltily. "I'll leave the diaper bag in the hall. I doubt Em will sleep much longer, and he can bring her to me when she wakes up."

"Excellent. We'll be sure to see that Frisco gets it," Laredo said. "Don't you worry about Em. She's in good hands."

Annabelle didn't look all that likely to agree, but with a last glance at the man holding her content child, she went back up the stairs.

"Frisco's gonna whup your hide."

"No, he isn't," Laredo said with a grin, "because you're not going to tell him. In the morning, she'll thank him for watching her baby, and he'll puff up with pride and say it was nothing, they'll see each other in a rosy light, and boom! Instant happiness for Frisco."

Tex shook his head. "I don't remember you being so good with relationships, Laredo. Since when did you become the inventor of the mysterious perfect match?"

"I'm not looking for a woman, Tex, so shut up. In fact, never try this on me, because I won't fall for it. But then, I'm a pleasant person in general." He glanced out at his brother. "It's Frisco who's had a problem. Unless I miss my guess, it's well on its way to being fixed."

"You've missed more than your guess before," Tex mumbled as he cracked open a beer.

But Laredo ignored him. "There's just two things that worry me," he murmured.

"Can't imagine that it's just two." Tex sighed. "They must be big, combo worries."

Laredo looked around the corner to check on Frisco and Em. "One," he said thoughtfully, "we're going to have to figure out how we talk Mother Delilah into leaving Annabelle here. She distinctly said she wasn't leaving without her—and there's a reason she's being so over-protective."

"I knew this wasn't going to be easy," Tex said with a sigh. "And, two?"

"Em is only two months old." He came and sat down across the table from his brother. "And that means that somewhere, there's a father who just might show up any time."

Tex swallowed. "Suppose he doesn't?"

Laredo shook his head. "Think of Annabelle in that towel, and then ask yourself how long you'd stay away."

"Five minutes, tops."

"I'd last three. Not that she's my type, but all things being equal, you know, three minutes. I'd want my baby and my woman all to myself."

"Maybe he's married."

Laredo shook his head. "I don't think so. Annabelle doesn't seem the type to fall for a married man, and Mother D didn't strike me as putting up with monkey business."

"Could be she dumped him, I guess."

"Or he dumped her."

They stared at each other.

"That would explain Mother D's protective stance." Laredo considered his beer for a moment. "There is a father involved, but he wouldn't be the first man in history who turned tail and ran at the thought of commitment."

"Witness the twelve of us."

"Precisely. Except we'd live up to our responsibilities," Laredo said sternly.

"And wear condoms," Tex agreed easily. "Don't get your dander up. I'm just saying none of us have been keen to marry anyone. Possibly, neither was Annabelle's boyfriend. As I mention, this is the problem. No matter how much we might think occupying Frisco with a woman might be just what he needs, the fact is, we don't know anything about this girl. She could be a real disaster. And even if she's not, even if we discovered she was the sweetest thing since Southern tea, Frisco might resist her just on principle."

"He's that ornery." This was something none of the brothers would deny. Not that Frisco had ever been an easy brother to live with, but he had been known to lighten up occasionally. These days, it seemed a pattern was set: Mason rode Frisco, and Frisco rode anyone within earshot.

It made for damn unpleasant living conditions. With it being winter, and them cooped up more than usual, Frisco's mood needed a shot of sweetness.

"Does it really matter who she is or what her problems are?" Laredo mused. "We're not looking for her to be Frisco's dream woman. We would hire her as the housekeeper. Whatever happens after that would have nothing to do with us."

Tex nodded. "Mason apparently thought we needed her."

"Well, someone. Preferably middle-aged, though I'm not sure why he'd feel that way. Annabelle would be much easier on the eyes than Delilah. Not that Delilah's unattractive, but Annabelle's kind of hot."

A cough escaped Tex. "I'd agree with you there."

"Annabelle might get lonely here, but she has the baby to keep her occupied."

"And all of us."

Laredo eyed him. "In a brotherly sort of way."

"Exactly. And the minute she's unhappy, we'll personally take her back to her home."

"Think we can get Frisco to buy it?"

"Hell no," Tex decreed. "That's why you're going to have to go around him on this one."

"Me?" Laredo straightened. "Am I the twin with the brains?"

"I'm the twin with the good ideas. You merely execute them."

"I was born first."

Tex shrugged. "Technically, only because the doctor reached in and grabbed you first. It doesn't give you leverage or bragging rights. You figure out a way to convince Frisco that Annabelle is just what he needs."

"In a manner of speaking."

"Yes. She just might be what we all need, but since that sounds kinky, we'll say she's for Frisco."

"You know," Laredo said slowly, "this isn't a half bad

idea. In a way, Annabelle is perfect for us. None of us are interested in settling down. But the ad Mason wrote clearly illustrates his belief that we need a housekeeper, a woman to set things straight around here. You can figure that Annabelle is no more interested in us than we are in her, simply due to the fact that Em is about two months old. That means Annabelle's been through some difficulty recently, and more than likely another man is the last thing she needs!" He sat up, snapping his fingers. "It's a win-win situation!"

"Do you know how few of those there really are?" Tex warned. "Think about it. Every time someone tries to manipulate us into a so-called win-win, it's usually when someone wants something from the Union Junction ranch."

"This time, we're doing the negotiating. Piece of cake." Laredo got up, peering out the kitchen at his brother. "If that baby's father walked out on her, she'll have twelve men to make up for it."

"Probably scare the little angel into permanent colic."

"I don't think so," Laredo murmured. "It's the stomachache Frisco's going to give me that's gonna hurt." He went out into the den to stare down at his brother. Frisco was sleeping like a baby with the baby. "It's just as cute as two vines curling into each other," he murmured.

Behind him, he heard Annabelle's feet on the landing. She came to stand beside him, her light eyebrows raised in question.

"She's fine," Laredo said. "Neither of them have moved."

"I don't understand it," Annabelle said. "Emmie doesn't do that for me."

"Ah, well." Laredo gestured toward his brother. "Frisco has that settling effect on people."

"Really?" Annabelle eyed the sleeping giant. "I would never have guessed."

"Don't let his gruffness fool you. He's had a lot on his mind the past few...months."

"Oh, I see."

Laredo could tell Annabelle didn't see, but she was trying to be sympathetic in spite of herself. He brightened. Sympathy boded well for Frisco. "So, I suppose you were interested in applying for the position of housekeeper?"

She looked at him. "I thought Frisco said you weren't looking for a housekeeper. That it was a mistake."

"Frisco's not looking for one at the main house," Laredo said hurriedly. "We're looking for one at house number two."

"House number two?"

"Four brothers live in one house. We built two to match the original family home. Your friends are all staying in house number three."

"Who stays where?"

Depends on who's got company, he started to say, but bit that back quickly. "Well, in this house, it's Mason, Frisco, me and Tex."

"You're twins, right? I'm having trouble telling you apart."

He could tell this unnerved her. "I'm nicer than Tex," he told her kindly.

"That doesn't help much."

"I'll smile when I look at you, and that'll be your clue, okay?"

She smiled back at him, relaxing a little. "How can

you hire me if you live in the main house with Frisco and he said he wasn't looking for a housekeeper?"

He hesitated, his plan stuck. Frisco slumbered on, blissfully unaware of the matchmaking being planned on his behalf. "I don't know," Laredo said honestly. "It was Texas's idea. I'm just supposed to execute it."

Annabelle laughed a little, a quick, quiet sound, as if she wasn't used to being lighthearted. "You're both being sweet, but it's all right. I don't want to cause problems. No more than I have, anyway."

He shook his head. "You're no trouble, Annabelle."

Her brows raised. "Laredo, can I ask you something? Are you…flirting with me?"

"Oh, yes, ma'am," he said. "But only out of force of habit."

"You're not…"

"No, I'm not. Absolutely not." He gave her his most earnest look. "Neither is Tex. I've got an itch too big to scratch, and Tex is deep into rose-growing and putting down roots. You'd be bored to tears if the smell of manure didn't get you first."

"So you're trying to hire me behind your brother's back because…" She waited for him to fill in the blank.

"We could use help at the Union Junction ranch."

"What kind of help would that be?"

He gestured expansively. "Cooking, for starters. We're kind of tired of our cooking, though some of us have gotten pretty good at it. I'm just about sick of Crock-Pot dinners."

"Crock-Pot?"

"We throw it on in the morning and forget about it until we get home at night. And it's hot food."

"Can't complain about hot food." She wrinkled her nose at him. "I can't cook."

His jaw dropped helplessly as his plan suffered a grand crack. "You *can't?*"

"Just pancakes." She smiled at his crestfallen expression.

Laredo glanced at Frisco, who had begun a gentle, rhythmic breathing. Frisco didn't like pancakes. "You could learn…."

"If you think you and your brothers cared to be guinea pigs. It could be rough for a while."

"It very well might." Maybe the Crock-Pot was a miracle invention after all. He could still put food in it in the mornings, and then Annabelle could serve it at night, and Frisco might be fooled.

Doubtful. Laredo didn't have any new recipes. Frisco would recognize his handiwork.

"Do you sew? Clean? Garden?"

"I could try."

Executing this idea was turning out to be harder than he thought it would be. Laredo could almost hear Tex snickering in the kitchen. Annabelle had no selling points for housekeeping. She was pretty, petite, sweet.

She was a woman with a man maybe not too far out of the picture and a colicky baby. Not to mention that she and Frisco hadn't exactly taken to each other like lint on Sunday clothes.

Annabelle looked up at him, her expression kind. "The problem that you're running into, Laredo, is that I didn't come out to Union Junction Ranch to apply for the position of housekeeper with all my heart. Keep my secret?"

Frisco opened one eye to stare at Annabelle balefully. "Then can I have my money for your bus fare refunded?"

CHAPTER FIVE

"FRISCO!" LAREDO AND TEX exclaimed sternly, but Frisco only had eyes for the little blonde as she flounced away.

"Well, heck, if she wasn't a sincere job applicant, she shouldn't waste my time. She shouldn't waste the ranch's money," he grumbled, fully aware that he was being churlish. He'd made her mad, and he wished he'd kept his mouth shut. He was going to hear about this from his family for days—and the worst part of it was, he'd sort of been teasing. But with his voice rough from snoozing, it had come out as a complaint.

Annabelle had good reason to be annoyed with him. He was pretty annoyed with himself.

His brothers eyed him belligerently. "Aw, heck," he began, just about the time Annabelle flounced back down the stairs, snapping a crisp hundred-dollar bill at him.

"Bill repaid."

He stared up at her. "Now, there's no reason to be all huffy about it—"

"I'm not huffy."

She tried to give him the money again, but he dodged it, pretending his hands were too full of sleeping Emmie.

"Look, I shouldn't have said it—"

"True, but the fact is, you're right, and I should have already offered to pay my own freight."

Well, he had to admit she was darn appealing when she was in a snit. That was something admirable in a woman, because very few looked appealing when they were fussing. Mimi managed to look somewhere between spitting-cat-outraged and Heather-Locklear-saucy, and he suspected that's what kept Mason on his toes: His brother probably wasn't certain if he was dealing with a hellcat or an erotic dream.

At this moment, Frisco wasn't certain what he was dealing with, either. "Tell you what, you pour juice in the morning, and we'll discuss all this then. I really want to go back to sleep," he lied, because he actually wanted to mull over the way Annabelle looked in the long, silky white robe. Like a madonna, for one thing, and maybe a pinup for another. He liked a woman a little rounder than was fashionable, a bit lush, and she was just right, no doubt thanks to the bundle of joy snuggled on his chest—

"Can you cook *any*thing?" he demanded.

"Only popcorn. Occasionally toast, but it's risky."

He tried to school his face not to show dismay, but it hardly worked. "What good is a housekeeper who doesn't cook?"

Annabelle laid the money on the coffee table in front of him. "I shouldn't think she'd be much good at all." She smiled at him and then the brothers. "Well, since you've got everything under control, I guess I'll go back upstairs. I never knew my baby could sleep so hard. It must be this good country air—"

Frisco held up his hand to halt Annabelle from leaving. "I know this is a rhetorical question, probably, but if you weren't applying for the job, what are you doing here?"

"Is there a rule against bonding with your sisters?" She looked at him with wide eyes.

"Those women are your sisters?" Frisco asked, dismayed.

She sighed. "Really, for a grown man, you are very naive. Sisters, as in emotional sisters. Good friends."

"Sounds like an Oprah-thing to me."

"It is not an Oprah-thing. It's the same thing you and your brothers have, I would assume, a brotherhood. A family," she said stiffly. "Well, that's what those women represent to me."

"They're your family."

"Exactly." Her gaze went to Emmie, lingering with a loving touch. "They may not be blood relatives, but I prefer their company."

"Prefer? As in, rather than your own family?"

She gave him a bland look, indicating that she was through being interrogated. "Unless you want me to take Emmie, I'm going to try to get two hours of sleep."

"No!" Tex said.

"Sleeping babies need their sleep," Laredo added.

Annabelle smiled at them. "You two are sweet. What's wrong with you?" she demanded of Frisco.

"Hey, I've got your baby asleep, don't I?" he asked, wounded.

"Yes, but you're just so…lordly about everything."

"Oh, Frisco's definitely lordly," Laredo agreed. "There are days when we just pray the Lord will get him out of our hair. Not that we want anything to happen to him, you know, just maybe a runaway calf or two for him to chase for a couple of hours, days—"

"C'mon," Tex said, shoving his twin back toward the

kitchen. "You must be hungry, 'cause you're gnawing on your foot again."

After his brothers left the room—which was a good thing, because they were getting on Frisco's nerves—he looked at Annabelle. "Of course, you never gave me a straight answer about what you're doing here. And since I'm soothing your baby, I deserve at least a stab at something resembling an answer."

She reached to turn the ceiling fan lights down a bit, dimming the room. Then she went to sit in front of the fireplace, where a couple of logs were in the process of burning down to shimmering coals.

He sure did admire the way she moved. Graceful, quiet. Feminine.

"It's a long story, Frisco, and I'm not sure which chapter of it you want."

"Meaning?"

"Meaning that there's my reason for being here, and then there's the Lonely Hearts Beauty Salon's reason for being here en masse."

"Start with whichever you want to. I've got until your darling wakes up." He grinned at her, to show he didn't mind Annabelle, nor Emmeline.

"Well," Annabelle said slowly, "I'm the receptionist at the Lonely Hearts Beauty Salon."

"And all these women came from that salon?"

"Yes."

"I imagine the exodus closed down the shop, didn't it?"

She nodded. "We've had some…tough times in the salon, so Delilah, who owns and runs it, decided she was due a one-week vacation. None of the women with us are married. They may have been married at one time, or had significant others, but there was nothing in their way of enjoying a trip out to the country."

"This had everything to do with Mason's email."

"Yes. And his photo was attached. He looked reasonably trustworthy, and some of us are going to need new jobs soon. Delilah decided we could start here on our vacation-slash-opportunity hunt. We're taking buses through all of west Texas checking out small towns."

"Once you leave here, you mean."

"Hopefully tomorrow."

"This is just a fun hiatus, a lark, to see if we'd hire one of you?"

She shrugged. "No. As I said, the shop isn't doing all that well lately. Delilah's going to have to cut back staff. We thought you were looking for help. Your ranch seemed as good a place to start as any."

Scratching his chin, Frisco said, "I didn't realize there were employment issues. All I knew was that we'd been descended upon by a herd of females."

"And your standard reaction is to run females off?"

Her brow was quirked at him, kind of sassy. He knew she was teasing him, and he wanted to put her in her place, but he couldn't think how. "Generally we don't respond too well to women coming our way without warning," he said drily. "We prefer to have our visiting hours elsewhere."

"Mmm. Leaving you free to hit and run." She looked down at her fingers, which were free of rings. "Well, that seems sensible."

"We were talking about you," Frisco reminded her a bit tersely, since he didn't like her reference at all. He was pretty certain he saw pain on her face, and he didn't want her lumping him in with a possible woman-snaking weasel who "hit and ran." "So, you're on vacation…"

"Oh, yes. Well, I didn't really want to come. Delilah and everyone talked me into it. They didn't want me to stay there and…be alone."

Okay. There *was* a weasel—he was still close to the poultry, near enough to bite, and Delilah was guarding the chicken house.

He looked at Annabelle's smooth blond hair, the way it fell over her shoulders as she stared down at her fingers. It was like gazing at an angel. Even if the angel had a fast tongue on her, she was still a nice girl. His heart shifted as he thought about someone bruising her heart.

This is why I don't get involved with girls like her. They get their feelings hurt so easily when they want promises instead of a good time.

Emmeline shifted, then sighed. Frisco glanced down at the baby. He wanted to know why Annabelle had fallen for someone who'd broken her heart, a loser who didn't care enough to take care of his own child, but he didn't dare. It was none of his business. "And now that you're here? Still wish you hadn't come on vacation?"

She wrinkled her nose at him. "I feel like I'm working."

He looked at her. "What does that mean?"

"That talking to you is kind of hard. You want answers but you don't offer any of your own."

A shrug would have been nice, but he was afraid to joggle Emmie. "Ask anything you want to."

"I don't have any questions. I just thought you might want to offer some conversation. Some minor details about yourself. Like why you say you don't want to have women around, but then pick up a baby the first chance you get."

"She was crying—" he began defensively.

"And I would have gotten her."

"You were in the shower. I wanted you to be able to finish."

"Thank you."

"You're welcome. I didn't know Emmie would fall asleep for me. But once she did, she kind of put a warm spot on my chest and it relaxed me and I dozed off. And now I don't want her awakened because she'll start crying again. What's wrong with that?"

"Nothing. I just wonder why you're working so hard to be a tough guy when you've got a soft heart."

Frisco snorted. "No one says I've got a soft heart."

"I do."

She gave him that don't-argue-with-me look, and Frisco rolled his eyes.

"Would you hire me for the job?" Annabelle asked.

"No. Well, not for my house. If I was hiring, maybe for Fannin's crew."

"Why?"

"If you needed a job, why not?"

"You said you weren't hiring."

"That's when I was annoyed."

"I think you're annoyed now, and yet you'd still hire me for Fannin's house."

"I didn't say that. I said *if*. And that's a big if."

"You're letting me sleep in your room."

"You made yourself at home!"

"I think you're more softhearted than you care for anyone to know."

"Well, I'm not an evil weasel. I wouldn't abandon a woman—" He stopped, catching himself. "I didn't mean that the way it sounded."

She drew a deep breath. "You couldn't mean it in a bad way, Frisco, because there's no way you could guess the truth. Tom left me for a Never Lonely Cut-n-Gurl."

"A what?"

"A rival beauty salon employee. Across the street from our shop, Delilah's own sister set up shop, determined, I guess, to put her out of business. There's some feud between them that I don't know everything about, but it's pretty all-consuming. For the last three years, everything Delilah has done Marvella somehow manages to do one better."

His jaw dropped. "You're painting an awful picture. Two bossy beauty queen sisters at each other's throats."

She gazed at him steadfastly. "It's really hurt Delilah, both emotionally and financially. She's devastated. And then when Tom walked out on me for Dina, I think it was all Delilah could bear. She treats me like a daughter, and to Delilah, Tom was the one thing Marvella should have kept her mitts off."

"Tom left you for Dina. How did Marvella have anything to do with that?"

"Oh. The Never Lonely girls are pretty good at stealing our customers. We get all the ladies who won't suffer to step foot in a place where they suspect their men are getting more than a close shave. And we get the old men whose wives don't want them getting their bald heads shined by a—"

"Whoa. Stop. Back up." Frisco shook his head. "You're scaring me."

"Don't like haircuts?"

While his hair did hover pretty much along the back of his neck, straggling inside and outside of his shirt collar depending on the wind and working conditions, Frisco couldn't say he was scared of a pair of scissors.

"I'm a little surprised that a man who was having a pretty baby like Emmie would do business elsewhere, if you'll excuse the bad choice of words." He eyed Annabelle and decided for the tenth time that she was lacking just about nothing to make a man happy—at least outwardly. "And you're not exactly hard on the eyes," he said gruffly.

She lowered her gaze. "Thank you. We've never been quite certain what they're doing over there to steal our clientele, but my ex-fiancé must have liked whatever it was enough to…"

"Desert. Like a petty coward."

"I don't know. I don't want to be too rough on Tom, because I did fall in love with him. But fatherhood must have spooked him, and I guess he needed a trim and instead of facing me, he went to the Never Lonely—"

"Have you talked to him since Emmie was born?" he asked, his heart hammering roughly in his chest. What a loser, what a pathetic sidewinder she'd picked to fall in love with! Poor Emmie. Frisco settled into the chair more comfortably, reclining as if he were relaxed, determined to conceal his disgust.

"No. I left a message on his answering machine that we'd had a daughter. Six pounds, seven ounces, blue eyes, heart-shaped lips, perfect set of lungs." Slowly, she shook her head. "Of course, I never heard from him."

He'd heard some lowdown things, but that took the cake. "Don't think about it," he said roughly. "I shouldn't have asked so many nosy questions. It's not like me."

She cocked her head at him. "I believe you're the caring type. But you play a good game of emotional hide-and-seek. I probably recognize it because I do the same thing."

"What?" He didn't like her thinking she could see inside his head.

"I'm very careful of my feelings, too." She smiled at him, sweet and knowing as if they shared a secret. "I learned that from Tom."

"To hide your feelings?"

"No. He sprayed feelings everywhere like they were pennies easily spent, and then when it came to something meaningful, he had empty pockets." She winked at him. "I think you're just the opposite. Deep, hidden pockets."

He didn't like this little lady looking at him so directly. Her big eyes were taking him in as though she knew him, as if he were some kind of big-hearted man, and her gaze was making a part of his body swell to the point where he was going to need deep pockets to hide what was going on. "Go to bed," he said sternly. "You're getting on my nerves."

"Call me when Emmie wakes."

"I'm sure you'll hear her. She's showing early signs of growing into her mother's big mouth." He closed his eyes to indicate that he wanted to be left alone.

He heard feet on the stairs and breathed a sigh of relief.

Tomorrow couldn't come soon enough. These Lonely Hearts ladies were more trouble than he needed.

Lonely Hearts ladies and Never Lonely girls having catfights in the center of a small-town street. What nonsense.

And yet, Delilah had struck him as a no-nonsense woman. What kind of woman tried to run her own sister out of business? And encouraged her employees to steal customers—and fiancés? Surely Annabelle had been yanking his chain. Family didn't act that way.

Or at least they shouldn't. It had been mighty restless around Union Junction for a while—these ladies with their sad stories just might be the fuse on top of the powder keg the Jefferson brothers had become.

But they would still love each other. They'd never act like Delilah's sister supposedly had. Family stuck together through thick and thin.

He'd brain all his younger brothers if they ever tried any tricks like Marvella's.

And then he chuckled to himself. Delilah. Marvella.

Annabelle had just blown so much smoke into his eyes with a sob-story fairy tale. And like a big dumb slob, he'd fallen for every word. She'd sized him up as a caring guy, and gone for his heart with her baby and her jerk ex-fiancé story. After all, hadn't she gone straight to make herself at home in his bed?

Maybe she knew more about what the Never Lonely girls were peddling than she was letting on.

And he'd just about bitten the bait, hook and all. She'd left the hundred-dollar bill on the table at his feet. It was a lot of money for a woman who supposedly had very little; he didn't know many single mothers who carried around unbroken Ben Franklins. Shoot, he rarely had an unbroken Ben in his own wallet because they were difficult for small stores to change.

The money wasn't necessarily a giveaway, but he wouldn't be the first man in history to fall for a pretty face and good storytelling ability; kings and mortal men alike were known to have feet of clay when it came to such a fatal combination.

He'd been seventeen when Maverick had abandoned the ranch, leaving Mason to care for all of them. As a boy, he'd dreamed of his family being whole.

He was thirty-six now, too old for fairy tales. And too damn old to be deceived by a fiction-spinning female. He shifted the area between his jeans pockets uncomfortably.

Annabelle had nearly gotten to him.

"Close only counts in horse shoes and hand grenades," he whispered to Emmie. "You're a cute little grenade, but I've got your mother all figured out, and you're going home tomorrow."

Delilah would be very nervous if she knew what he'd been thinking about Annabelle. He was guilty, and guilty with her baby lying on his chest, this baby she'd birthed only two months ago. He was pretty certain that made him something of a schmuck. Probably a big schmuck.

Tomorrow, he'd say goodbye to their unexpected company, and then maybe head into town for some willing female fun. If Annabelle Turnberry could make him feel something that might have been lust, then it was way past time to cool down the horsepower in his engines.

Safe from listening ears, Mimi made a phone call. "Julia, I need to ask you a favor. I sent out an email for housekeeping help, but the help that arrived here isn't exactly what I had in mind. Did you get my email?"

"I haven't had an email from you since the one you sent me two months ago saying you thought Mason was an unromantic donkey. Wasn't that around Christmas? He gave you a lead rope for your horse because you'd broken yours using it for... I remember. You used it to drag a goat across to Mason's and tied it to the post on the porch to make a point about goats being easy to keep. Of course, the goat chewed through the lead rope and ate the front shrubbery before Mason caught him.

Why was it again you were making the point about goats? Or trying to?"

"Never mind that!" Mimi took a deep breath, annoyed to be reminded about her scheme taking an unforeseen turn. Luckily, Mason had been forgiving—she'd even seen a twinkle in his eye when he handed her the chewed-up lead rope. But he'd given her a new one for Christmas, probably to make his point that goats were more trouble than they were worth—and she'd been annoyed that he'd gotten the upper hand on her, again. "I didn't say anything about romance. I just said he was a donkey."

"Ah. I'm putting words where they don't belong."

"Yes, you are. There never was, and never will be, romance between the two of us. Mason is like my overbearing older brother. We rub each other the wrong way. Anyway, I—that is, Mason—wants a housekeeper."

"Why doesn't he call me?"

"Because he doesn't know you, Julia, and we sent out an email to you about the matter, which he participated in typing, I might add," she tacked on, so that Julia would know this wasn't just a scheme. "Only the email went haywire, and we ended up with eighteen inappropriate candidates, instead, plus their den mother and a baby."

"Oh. Inappropriate," Julia said, clearly trying not to giggle. "Are they beautiful?"

"Some of them," Mimi said begrudgingly. "Don't you have any big, strong women over fifty named Olga that need a great place to work? Mason and I were thinking of grandmotherly candidates for the job."

Julia laughed so hard it sounded as if she might faint from oxygen deprivation. "I fail to see the humor in the situation. Do you laugh at all your clients' needs?" Mimi demanded.

"Just yours, Mimi. And I'm not laughing meanly. I'm laughing at how your brain works."

"I'm only trying to save Mason the trouble, since I got him into this."

"Again."

Mimi sniffed. "He does need a housekeeper."

"And you're afraid he might find a wife, instead."

She straightened. "That thought never occurred to me."

"Uh-huh. Has a…candidate…applied for the post?"

"One. Actually I don't think she's really applied, but I'm afraid that when Mason gets home, he might hire her."

"Since you're not in love with him, what difference does it make? Wouldn't that be a good thing? Poor Mason might like being tied down."

"Not to this girl!" Mimi shook her head. "No, she's all wrong for him. She has a baby, and she's too busy with the baby, and—"

"Mimi. Are you ever going to admit that you just might have a tiny crush on Mason?"

"Absolutely not."

She thought she heard another giggle. "Honestly, Julia, we'd fight too much under the same roof. But that doesn't mean I want someone taking advantage of his loneliness."

"If there's a bunch of women on the ranch, he won't be too lonely. When's he getting back?"

"They won't be here then," Mimi said. "And if you're any good at your job, a very efficient Olga will be."

"A grandmotherly type."

"I think that would be appropriate, under the circumstances, don't you? These men would probably enjoy a bit of mothering."

"You might could stand a bit of it yourself. It might keep you from going off the tracks all the time, Mimi."

"We don't discuss mothers. You know we don't even say that word when it applies to me." Hers had left her father and her for the bright lights of Hollywood, and as far as she was concerned, all the best to her. A mother was not what she was looking for. "I turned out just fine as a single-parented child."

"Yeah, but it's made you unable to seek emotional attachments."

Mimi gasped. "Attachments are for vacuum cleaners! If I ever met the right man, I'd know it. Now, let's get back to what Mason needs."

"What Mason needs is a swift slap on the head for letting you run his life so inefficiently. But I happen to have the perfect person to suit your—Mason's—needs. When are the eighteen ladies, den mother and baby leaving?"

"As soon as the roads unfreeze," Mimi said, wishing the sun would bring a miraculous fifty-degree day.

"Many people have waited a long time for hell to freeze. It could be a long time before Union Junction unfreezes—and the guests go home."

She didn't even want to think about Mason coming home to find pretty, petite Annabelle and adorable Emmie in his house. Not that she wished them ill— she just didn't wish them for Mason. "Listen, Julia. You send Olga before Mason returns home. I'll take care of everything else."

"Including thawing the deep freeze?"

"I'll think of something." She eyed her pink-and-white bedroom with the four-poster bed. "I think Emmie would be very soothed by my bedroom. I'm sure my old crib is in the attic, too. Dad never throws anything away."

It was her mom who'd been unable to hang onto anything. No attachments, emotional or otherwise, for her. Mimi was determined to hang onto the one thing she considered hers: Mason. Maybe not hers as in a husband, but definitely hers as in a…as in a…best friend.

"Whatever happened to the goat, Mimi?" Julia asked.

"Oh, I've still got her," she replied, not really paying attention. "Actually, she had a baby not too long ago, a bit out of season but healthy nonetheless. I named it Mason's Folly, because Mason named my original goat Mimi's Dolly. He said I'd been such a tomboy growing up that I never had any dolls, but why would I? The Jefferson brothers would have made a sport of looking up my dolls' dresses." She rolled her eyes; not a whole lot had changed for the Jeffersons. If gossip held true, they managed to get under lots of dresses. "Mason was being a butt when he said that my goat was the closest thing to a doll I'd ever had. He said maybe I could sew it a dress and put ribbons on its horns."

Julia laughed again. "You've spoiled him for other women, I'm sure."

"Speaking of other women, which has nothing to do with the conversation at hand, did I tell you Dad's expecting a lawyer from Dallas to come visit the ranch soon? He says he's about my age and well off and from a good ranching family in East Texas. I can't imagine how a man from a good ranching family becomes a lawyer."

"Dad bailing you out of something?"

Mimi rolled her eyes. "Dad's going to redo some contracts and his will. I'm supposed to show Brian the town, though Union Junction is now iced over in a big way. Maybe he won't make it after all." Mimi looked at her nails, which she realized might need filing after she had mopped all afternoon. "I have to go, Julia. Union Junction's on the verge of disaster, and I want to be wherever Dad needs me to help."

"I'll send Olga as soon as she can make arrangements to be there."

"Great! Mason will be so pleased."

"Sure he will."

Julia hung up, and Mimi switched the phone off with a smile on her face. If she could get rid of the chaos on Mason's ranch before he got home, he wouldn't have reason to say *I told you so. As usual.*

Well, he wouldn't say *as usual,* but she knew he'd think it. After all, the goat incident was fresh in both their memories. In the spring, she'd replant the hedges by Mason's porch, something bright and blooming that would impress him with her gardening expertise. He'd forget all about the goat then.

Unfortunately, numerous females plus a baby would be so much more disastrous than one little ol' lead-rope-chewing, hedge-eating goat.

Mason would *never* let her live it down. And for her birthday, he'd probably give her a book on how to avoid your well-meaning, disaster-prone neighbors.

She touched the lead rope he'd given her, which she kept hanging by her mirror with all the other Christmas presents he'd given her over the years. And corsages from homecoming. Cartoon paper valentines that read *You're my best buddy.* Joke birthday cards.

All non-sentimental.

That was Mason, though. At least, it was the Mason she knew, and she really didn't want another woman to know him that way. Or any way at all.

CHAPTER SIX

"Sun's up! You should be, too!"

A woman's voice roused Frisco from the comfort of his leather recliner. Emmie had awakened only once last night, but for some reason, she'd let out a little cry, decided she was too sleepy to insist on anything more energetic, and gone back to snoozing.

He kind of liked feeling he had the power to make the little baby content. He really liked her smell, all sleepy-soft baby-powder-and-shampoo.

"Sorry, Frisco," Delilah said, as she closed the front door and began unwinding a scarf from her head. She peeled off a big coat and put her things on the entry-hall table. "Did I wake Emmie?"

"No. She must have worn herself out yesterday from crying. She's been quiet."

"Reckon she's sick?" Delilah came over to touch Emmie's forehead and feel her neck.

"I wouldn't know," Frisco said with some alarm. "I just thought she was as tired as I was."

"She feels fine to me." Delilah looked up at him, her eyes bright with laughter. "I think she likes being around a man. Good thing you had your hands full with Emmie, or I would have had to put my foot down about Annabelle staying here with you. I can tell you're a bit of a charmer."

She winked at him, and Frisco felt himself heat around his neckline.

"I'd offer to take her from you, but I'm about to cook you some breakfast. Unless you'd rather I hold Emmie, instead—"

"She's fine where she is," Frisco said hurriedly.

Delilah laughed. "How do you like your eggs?"

He nearly sighed with anticipation. "Any way you're fixing them."

"I make them with hash browns, whatever meat you've got in the fridge and maybe salsa on the side. How long's it been since you've had huevos rancheros?"

"Too long."

She laughed and went into the kitchen. "All right, sleepyheads, everybody off the table. Good grief, you'd think that was a princess sleeping in a tower upstairs. I can't tell you two apart, so if you don't mind, tell me again which is which."

"Tex." He let out a head-splitting yawn before he could stop himself.

"Laredo, ma'am. I've got the longer hair."

"And better manners," Delilah observed, with a sly wink for Tex that Frisco caught as he came into the kitchen.

"Emmie is awake," Frisco said, announcing what didn't really need to be mentioned as Emmie's cries filled the kitchen.

"Her breakfast is in the fridge. Warm it up in the microwave for about eight seconds, Laredo."

Laredo shot out of his chair, anxious to do whatever he could to appease the screaming baby. "Shh, shh," Frisco told Emmie, but the red face didn't unscrunch long enough to listen. "Hurry, dammit, Laredo!"

Laredo had his head in the fridge. "I don't see a baby's breakfast."

"It's the bottles on the side door," Delilah instructed. "Just take one out, take off the cap, put in a glass of water to warm— Never mind. Watch this. You'll know how to do this next time." She got out a glass, filled it with water part-way, then set it in the microwave for a few seconds. When the timer dinged, she took out the water and dropped the baby bottle into it.

"How's she supposed to drink it like that?" Frisco asked, ready to surrender the aggravated baby. "She wants it now!"

"Patience," Delilah told him. "Are you going to feed her?"

"Not if she's going to be mad like this."

She raised a brow at him. "If you big strong men think you can handle this baby, either as a pack or individually, I can cook breakfast. If you can't, then I can feed Emmie myself, and breakfast can wait."

"We've got it under control," the men agreed, Frisco eyeing the eggs that were set out on the counter and the butter already melting in the skillet.

"Excellent." She tested the bottle, then stuck it out toward the brothers. "Which one of you wants to be Emmie's best friend?"

"I'll take her," Annabelle said, walking into the kitchen. "Thanks, everybody."

"Are you feeling better?" Delilah asked.

Frisco looked at Annabelle with surprise. "I didn't know you weren't feeling well."

He really was a handsome man, Annabelle had to admit. She felt much more comfortable around him in her blue jeans and sweater than she had in a bathrobe, non-descript and modest as it was. When he looked at her with those brown eyes, staring out from under dark brows and nearly-black hair, it was enough to make her heart beat a little faster. His expression was intent, as if he truly cared about her well-being. But she was wary enough to recognize how much she needed that sense of someone caring right now.

"I only needed some sleep," she said, taking Emmie from him. "Thank you so much for looking after my daughter. Delilah, you're doing my job."

"Didn't you say you can't cook?" Frisco asked.

"That's right. But I can kick three grown men out of the kitchen and set the table after I feed Emmie." She sat down on the plank bench, making sure she didn't disturb the baby from her bottle.

Delilah turned to the counter, stirring some canned chili. The three men hovered in the doorway, as if uncertain as to how they should react to being evicted from their own kitchen. "It's okay," Annabelle said, looking up. "It's our way of earning our keep."

Frisco drew his brows together. "We don't charge for one night's lodging."

Annabelle smiled at him. "Well, there were nineteen of us, plus Jerry. So we must earn our keep."

"Where *is* Jerry?" Frisco asked, with a quick glance at Delilah.

"He bunked with the other men at house number two. Isn't that how you have the addresses set up? House one, two and three?" Delilah answered.

"Somewhat."

Frisco didn't look certain, and Annabelle decided the Jefferson men had never had need for addresses before the Lonely Hearts women had come along.

That was all right. They'd be gone soon enough.

The front door blew open, then slammed as Jerry

came into the hallway, stomping his boots on the entry-hall rug. "Gosh-a-mighty, it's cold out there!"

"Come get a cup of coffee, Jerry," Delilah called. "It's on the entry table."

"Just what a man needs after chopping logs!" He came into the kitchen, offering red, chapped hands to Frisco and the twins to shake.

"Chopping logs?" Frisco asked.

"Yep." He took the towel that Delilah handed him with a wink and a smile of thanks for her thoughtfulness. "Delilah said it looked like that pile of wood out by the fence needed splitting and so I did it."

"You'll be ready for a hearty breakfast," Delilah said with approval. "I'm sure you're starved."

"Starved for whatever you're cooking." He sent a nod Annabelle's way. "No better way to get your blood moving in the morning than chopping logs in twenty-degree weather."

Frisco shot her a funny look. Annabelle wondered why he'd looked so odd. But then, he looked uncomfortable around her a lot. She stroked Emmie's cheek and decided there was nothing she could do about a man who was kind one moment, and burr-tempered the next.

"You didn't have to split those logs," Frisco said, his tone conveying his surprise.

"Gotta earn my keep," Jerry said. "At least that's what Delilah said, and goodness knows, I'm trying hard to impress her."

Delilah blushed clear up her neck, Annabelle noted with a smile. She'd suspected that the beefy truck driver might have had his eye caught by Delilah, but she hadn't imagined the interest might be two-sided.

Delilah wouldn't fall for a man who would always be on the road.

Then again, opposites sometimes attracted, as she knew too well from falling for Tom. She'd been thinking hearth and home, and he'd clearly been thinking bed and back door.

"What's the sigh for?" Frisco asked, coming to sit across from her.

"Did I sigh? I didn't mean to." She could barely meet his gaze when he looked at her like that, intense and focused as if her every emotion was of great importance to him.

"You sighed. I know what a sigh sounds like. I just don't know what it means. Are you feeling okay? Delilah mentioned you hadn't been—"

"I'm fine," Annabelle insisted gently. "You have no need to worry about me."

He rubbed the back of his neck as he considered her words. Her stop sign clearly threw him, and he wasn't certain how to proceed. But that was the problem: she wasn't sure how to proceed around him, either. One minute, gentle, the next, prickly—she'd go crazy around a man like that.

She didn't want to think that his concern meant anything more than his sharper moments did.

"You're my guest. I do have to worry about you."

She shook her head at him. "Not much longer. I've called a taxi."

"A taxi!"

"Shh!" She indicated that she didn't want Delilah and Jerry involved in their conversation. Laredo and Tex had left the moment Jerry went over to talk with Delilah by the stove and deftly chop peppers for her.

"Why did you call a taxi?" he demanded in a hushed but urgent tone.

"Because I want to go home, of course."

"I'm not letting you go home in a taxi. I can drive you back myself."

"No need, thanks. They'll have the outgoing roads sanded by now, I'm sure." She shook her head at him, not wanting to feel her heart tremble at his concern for her. "Frisco, you held my baby all night, and I got the best night of sleep I've had in well over three months. I feel rested enough to go home and face my life."

"You mean the chicken-hearted weasel."

"What?"

"Never mind." He looked away, ran a hand through his hair, turned back to gaze at Emmie, then looked Annabelle in the eyes. "What about the vacation with the other women? The hunt for jobs?"

She shrugged. "I'm being selfish. I'm being inconsiderate of Emmie. I thought that going with Delilah and all my friends would be a nice change, but I realized several things during the night." Shyness crept over her, but Frisco was listening intently, so she continued. "I can't run away from my problems. It's not fair to Emmie, when she could be home in her comfy crib."

"She slept on my comfy chest just fine, thank you. Didn't you say that was the first time you've been able to sleep all night? And that she usually cried no matter what you did for her?"

"Yes, but she can't sleep on your comfy chest every night, Frisco." Annabelle lowered her gaze, thinking that comfy chests were hard to come by and Frisco's was a great place for any woman to lie. Steadfastly, she went on with her points. "I can't run away from Tom."

"Does he care where you are?"

"Thank you for pointing that out, but no, he doesn't. My point was that I *am* running away from him, and I can't, because he is Emmie's father, and so she is always going to remind me of him. Leaving town isn't going to solve that."

He took a deep breath. "Are you still in love with him?"

She shook her head. "I got over that a long time ago. But Frisco, it doesn't change the facts of my life."

He drummed his fingers on the table, which fascinated Emmie because she stopped sucking long enough to glance his way before resuming.

"Let me take you back," he said gruffly. "A taxi is going to be expensive as hell."

She smiled. "It's all right. Thanks." Frisco was so handsome, and he seemed determined to look out for her. She'd be blind not to recognize why the Lonely Hearts women had returned for her last night: They knew that she, of all of them, had the most vulnerable heart. They'd been determined that she would not be left in a place where so many temptations roamed. So they'd come back for her.

She really didn't want everyone to have to keep looking out for her. A broken heart didn't make her unaware; in fact, it made her stronger in some ways. "Thanks all the same, Frisco. But I've got to do this on my own."

The front door burst open, and though she'd expected to see more brothers pile in for breakfast, Mimi and what looked to be the county sheriff strolled in.

"Hey, Mimi," Frisco said. "Sheriff Cannady."

"Hi." Mimi barely glanced at Frisco, Annabelle noticed. She indicated the sheriff standing next to her. "Dad says they just closed the roads out of Union Junction on all sides for today. The entire day, at least."

Annabelle sat up straight, her heart pounding.

"What's up, Sheriff?" Frisco went to shake his hand.

The sheriff nodded at Delilah and Jerry. "This constant deluge washed out the old pipes coming down from the dam. They burst in the night, flooding highways and roads. In fact, they flooded Union Junction square. There's not a store in the town that's dry."

Delilah gasped. "Is anyone hurt?"

"No, but there's a lot of damage. I don't think the feed store or the general store's gonna see their floors for a while. I'm afraid of more ruptures if we have another hard freeze tonight."

Frisco was already shrugging into a jacket. "I'll go into town and see what I can do."

The sheriff nodded. "Be honest with you, Frisco, Mimi told me you had guests at the ranch. I was hoping maybe you could haul the ladies—forgive me, ma'am, for asking this while you're on your vacation, but since you can't leave town, I'm going to beg for your help on this matter—into town so they can help with the clean-up. It's going to take probably two days to sweep out all that damn water."

"I've got plenty of hands to bring with me," Delilah said. "Let me feed this crew right quick, and we'll hop in the trucks."

"No need," Jerry said. "I can haul all the women into town in my rig. That way we can load into the trailer anything you need hauled out, like trash and ruined flooring. And the men can get themselves and their trucks wherever they're most needed."

"I was hoping you'd say that." He shook Jerry's hand gratefully. "Then I'll take the Jefferson brothers out to the dam with me and see if we can lay enough bags and such to keep the water back if it comes up tonight."

"And I can haul bags for them to lay down." Jerry tossed the peppers into the sauté skillet and grabbed plates. "Frisco, call your brothers and let's get this crew fed. Annabelle, call the ladies and make sure they're dressed for extremely chilly weather."

"You can't go, Annabelle," Delilah said, turning from the stove even as she swiftly stirred eggs into the peppers.

"I know. I'll stay here and clean up the kitchen."

"That'll take a couple of hours with just you doing it. I don't want you getting tired out."

"I'll be fine," she told Delilah. "And then I'll make dinner."

Everyone turned to look at her. "I can read a recipe," Annabelle insisted. "Don't look so horrified. Truly. I'm happy to do it."

"I'll pull out something easy," Delilah murmured. "It's a good plan, Annabelle. I'm sure you'll do fine."

Emmie had finished her bottle, so Annabelle put her up on her shoulder to burp as she walked out toward the den. Frisco was piling logs beside the fireplace. "Don't let this fire go out," he told her. "You and Emmie stay warm." He scribbled a number down on a piece of paper. "This is my cell number. If you need anything, call. I can be here in twenty minutes."

She took the paper, her fingers touching his so that she practically snapped her hand back as if static had sparked between them. "Frisco, you don't have to take care of me."

He looked at her as he shoved wool-lined gloves into his jacket. "I don't have to help take care of the town, either, but I will."

So she was a responsibility, a guest in his home he

had to care for as host. "I see. Well, consider me fully cared for."

His lips twisted at her in a wry smile. "You're the most difficult woman to understand I have ever met. Besides Mimi."

She raised her brows. "And I never met a man before who made a study out of being hard-headed."

He filled a thermos with hot coffee from the entry table. "Eleven of my brothers fit that description. I'm the gentle one. If I don't get a check-in call from you in four hours, I'm coming back."

"I'll call you!" she agreed hastily. "Goodness, Frisco. You don't have to worry about me so much!"

"I'm worried about you burning dinner. You may need instructions for turning on the stove." With a mischievous wink, he went out the front door.

"Devil!" she said under her breath to Emmie.

"But you've gotta admit," Delilah said as she refilled the coffee pot, "he's a handsome one."

"I don't have to admit that at all." And she wouldn't, either. The disaster that had hit Union Junction didn't deter her from her course of action. She might not be able to leave, but she sure wouldn't let her heart get away from her again, either.

She crumpled up the paper with Frisco's number, and then remembered his words. She put it carefully into her pocket.

Four hours. She glanced at the clock, marking the time so that she'd call at the right hour. No way was she giving Frisco any reason to come back to check on her.

Emmie protested a little when Annabelle laid her on the bed, but it was such a sweet sound that she smiled down at her baby.

Tom had never called to check on his newborn daughter, and he'd never called to see if Annabelle was feeling all right during her pregnancy. As soon as she'd told him about the baby, it seemed his heels had caught on fire with his rapid departure.

"He doesn't know how adorable you are," she told the baby as she removed the wet diaper. "He doesn't know how precious."

But Frisco seemed to know it. And he had no reason to care.

Yet he seemed to.

"Can I get you anything, Annabelle?"

She turned to see Mimi looking around the door. "No, thanks, Mimi. You go ahead and help with the clean-up. I'll hold the fort here."

Mimi blinked at her, then glanced at the baby in Frisco's bed. "If you want to stay at my house tonight, you know you're welcome."

"Oh. Thank you. I may do that." She'd planned on leaving; maybe going to Mimi's house would allow Frisco to stop feeling as if she was his guest, and therefore, his ward.

"I'll leave the back door open in case you find there's something you need for cooking dinner that Mason doesn't have here."

"Is that safe?"

Mimi smiled. "No one messes with the Jefferson brothers. Too many hair-trigger tempers."

"Oh, dear." Annabelle wasn't certain if she was comforted or worried by that piece of information.

"Besides, the ice is going to make it impossible for normal vehicles to travel. It's going to be trucks and sanding equipment on the road today. But if you need anything, you just go out the back door, walk across the stone steps—be careful of the ice—and the steps lead right to my back door."

"Thank you."

She wondered why sadness seemed to flash over Mimi's face, but the blonde recovered, smiling brightly. "Well, I'm off to mop up."

"It's going to be a cold job. I don't envy you."

"And I don't envy you the stacks of dishes in the kitchen. I estimate thirty-four people grabbed something to eat here, including my father, who's never passed up good huevos rancheros in his life." She raised her brows with a teasing smile. "Hope you like washing dishes."

"It's fine. Emmie's going to take a nap, and then I'll get started. Aren't you going to nap, sweetie?" She sat on the bed, rocking the baby as Emmie's eyes began to close.

"What is it like?" Mimi asked softly, her body arrested in the doorway.

"Heavenly." Annabelle smiled at her. "The best thing that ever happened to me. Emmie's all I've got, actually, but she's everything I could ever have dreamed of."

Mimi jerked her head in a nod of recognition. "I would have liked a baby."

She left before Annabelle could reply, but it occurred to her that Mimi was expressing a wish that she didn't seem to think would be fulfilled.

CHAPTER SEVEN

"I NEVER DID FIGURE out how Annabelle ended up in your bed," Laredo said as he heaved a bag of sand down from the back of Jerry's rig.

Frisco tossed the sandbag onto the dam they were trying to build before looking at his brother. "I think she simply picked the room closest to the hall."

"It wasn't that she had designs on you?" Laredo asked with a grin.

Frisco shrugged, knowing nothing could be further from reality. If anything, Annabelle seemed to avoid him. There was certainly a firm wall there, firmer than this sandbag wall they were laying. "If she has designs on me, it's a design I don't recognize."

"I wish she'd chosen my bedroom to move into."

Frisco gave him a steady eyeing and took an extra minute before accepting the heavy sandbag his brother was trying to hand him. "Why?"

"She's cute. And I like her."

"Don't waste any time thinking about it."

Laredo grinned. "Why? You staking a claim?"

Frisco refused to let Laredo's dig get to him. "She's still talking about Emmie's dad. I don't think either of us has a chance."

"Don't tell me she's still in love with him. Let me guess, he got what he wanted, left her high and dry, but she thinks he's coming back any day now. Once he figures out his little daughter needs him."

"I don't think she's that delusional. Or that she wants him back. I think she's trying to figure out being a new mother and a single parent, though. She's not really thinking about another man. Seems the one she had was enough for a while."

"It's such a shame when bad men mess up women for the rest of us."

Frisco gave him a narrow stare. "I don't remember you being a helluva catch yourself, bro. Weren't you the one blabbering about moving east? Hearing what your name sounded like from the mouths of girls in Tennessee, North Carolina, South Carolina, New York? All those different accents you wanted to study in the flesh?"

Laredo coughed. "I might have been bragging a bit."

"Just a bit. Considering I never thought the girls in all those states would be dumb enough to let you experiment on them. Only way I figured you'd hear their accents was when they said, 'You gotta be kiddin', cowboy.'"

"Anyway, so what about Annabelle? Is it a hands-off kind of thing?"

Frisco quit heaving sandbags altogether to stare up at his brother. "You're serious, aren't you?"

Laredo shrugged. "She's sweet."

Frisco stared at him for a long moment. Then he went back to work. "Knock yourself out."

"I don't want there to be any hard feelings or anything."

He shook his head. "There wouldn't be. I'm not in the market for a woman. A wife doesn't interest me, especially not with the added responsibility of a baby. I've got enough on my hands with the ranch. If I'm lucky, Mason won't saddle me with buying the new cattle in the spring."

"What's up with you and Mason, anyway? The two of you have been at each other all winter."

Frisco declined to reply.

"Is the ranch doing all right?"

"It's doing better than we expected with the last two summers being so hot and beef prices being low. We were lucky corn and wheat prices stayed high enough for us to make a profit."

"So what's the deal with you two? You're always quiet, and he's always annoyed with you."

"He's got a lot of responsibility on him," Frisco said mildly. "I understand that. There are twelve of us, and though everyone's old enough to take care of themselves, he considers himself the father figure and trustee."

Mason *had* been the father after Maverick left. Taking his place had made Mason more authoritarian. In a way, Frisco was the first-born child, then, ready-made to want everything to go just right. He wanted to make changes, make the ranch better if possible. Mason wanted everything to stay the same, the way they'd always known it, under control.

Frisco wanted to do some things his way. Make his own mark. It made for instant conflict.

"Mason might like it if we all started settling down," Laredo pointed out.

"Be my guest. I'll throw rice at your wedding."

Laredo held back the next sandbag so that Frisco had to look up at him. "You really aren't interested in her, are you?"

Frisco shook his head.

Laredo sighed, handing him the bag. "Guess trying to make you jealous won't work."

"No."

"I kind of thought Annabelle had a little shine in her eye for you."

"That was a fleck of baby powder. The last thing Annabelle wants is a man. She's trying to sort out her own life. And the last thing I want is a woman. I have enough fun watching Mimi and Mason try to survive each other. There's enough vicarious pleasure in that battle to put me off marrying for good. I mean, it just shows that no matter how many years you know a woman, you really don't know her."

Laredo laughed. "Mimi's just Mimi. Different."

Frisco grunted, going silent as he worked. Once upon a time, he'd wondered if he would ever find the right woman. He turned thirty-six and realized he was too old to be a real father. Just thinking about being a father turned his stomach inside out anyway. His role model was basically Mason, and they argued too much for normal sanity. He loved his brother, but they had two different ways of seeing life. Mason was careful. Frisco wanted to branch out some, test his mettle.

Yet, like the pipes that had burst, everything could change in a matter of seconds. He supposed Mason was right to be careful. There were ten younger brothers to think of, and though none of them were kids, they didn't dare squander the family fortunes on experimentation. In his mind, he knew Mason was probably right, but the caution grated on him. "So, what about going east? You still thinking about it, Laredo?"

"Sure. I want to do something big in my life. I can't really do that with three older brothers. If Mason doesn't clamp me into place, you or Fannin will."

"Not clamp exactly."

"Clamp exactly. The Jefferson ship is a pretty tight one."

Tightly run where the business was concerned; wild as wolves where everything else mattered. It was as if they all came together to run the business and fell apart when personal matters rose to the surface. They womanized. They caroused. Sometimes they drank to excess. They'd been known to hold a grudge and sometimes to exact revenge.

"Tight ship maybe, but we are not Texas's most wholesome family. There's plenty of room for you to do whatever you want to do, Laredo."

"I didn't say I needed to sow more wild oats. If I sow any more oats, my field's gonna get harvested." Laredo laughed at Frisco's wry expression. "I said I wanted to do something big, and I don't think I can do that in Union Junction. I figure I'm gonna have to go away to do it."

"Come back a hero?"

"I don't have to be a hero for anyone but myself."

Frisco snorted. "Then what's the point?"

"The point is that I'd know. I would know that I had reached a higher potential."

It was no different from his chafing about expanding the business, Frisco supposed. All the brothers had wandering feet to some extent. His own grouchiness was due to the feeling of being penned-in.

Glancing at his watch, he realized it was nearly time to get the call from Annabelle. He did think Annabelle was cute, though he'd told his brother differently. He just didn't want to think about her too much. Until she left the ranch, he felt responsible for her and Emmie, but after that, life would go back to normal for him.

Pausing as he bent over, he realized she had put a crack in his boredom. He'd been a trifle relieved when the roads had been closed, though he'd been careful not to show that he'd welcome an extra day to get to know her.

That was a heavy admission for his conscience.

"What the hell are you doing, Frisco?"

Laredo was looking at him strangely. Frisco tossed the bag down and stood, glaring.

"I was laying a bag. What the hell did it look like I was doing?"

"I don't want to say, but you being stooped over and stuck like that was kinda weird. It looked like you'd gone into a trance. Is your back going out?"

"Why would my back go out?" Frisco demanded, becoming supremely annoyed.

"Because you're thirty-six. Let's switch. You hand me the bags, and I'll lay them."

"I'm fine! Mind your own business." It wasn't a pain in his back that had hit him; it was the pain of realizing Annabelle was on his mind for the thirtieth time that day, and it was still early.

"I'm getting down. You come up here." Laredo hopped down from the trailer.

"Get your butt back up there! I said I'm *fine*."

"Quit being stubborn. It's time we changed places. You're going to be sore as all heck tomorrow, and we're going to have to keep laying for some time. Don't be pigheaded."

"I'm not. If you don't get back up in that truck, Laredo, I'm going to squash you like a bug."

"I don't think so, since you're the one who can't stand up straight." Laredo did a fake boxing, punch counter-punch in the air. "I could go rings around you, bro."

Frisco could no longer contain his irritation. "I *am* going to squash you, Laredo. You've been needing a good hammering all winter, and I'm—"

Laredo landed a soft punch to his chest, by gosh, it was a baby one, just playful, Frisco knew, even as he felt himself slipping on an ice patch and falling toward the river. A little tap like that shouldn't have thrown him, but the next thing he knew, he was tumbling down the embankment, rolling over rocks and boulders on his way to the rushing water. A sharp pain went through his leg, and the next thing he knew, he was flat on his back and a white-haired, red-cheeked Santa Claus in work clothes was staring into his face.

"You all right?" Santa asked him.

"I'm fine, Santa, sir," Frisco said. "Where's your sleigh?"

"Oh, hell," Santa said.

"You're not supposed to swear. The elves might start using bad language, and then what would Mrs. Claus say?" Frisco said.

"Mrs. Claus… Uh, okay, Frisco. Hang on, buddy. My name's Jerry. You remember me, don't you?"

Frisco thought so, but he wasn't sure. There were stars in his head and blinding pain in his leg, and suddenly, he didn't care if Santa cursed anymore or not because he was probably going to let out a good-sized string of dictionary-excluded words himself.

"Frisco! What the hell happened?"

He opened his eyes to see Laredo staring down at him. Now that was a mug he recognized. "Laredo, you dumb-ass. You pushed me down the dam."

"Can you move your arms?"

"Of course." Frisco tried to show him, but he felt awfully weak.

"All right. We'll call Doc Gonzalez. He'll be here in a minute, and you'll be all set up good as new. Don't move, okay, Frisco?"

Frisco wanted to shrug, but he was tired and cold. His phone rang and he remembered Annabelle was supposed to call him to tell him she was all right.

"Guess I should have been the one to call and tell her I was all right," Frisco said to no one. "She's fine, and I'm not."

"Who do you want to call?" Santa-Jerry asked him.

"No one. She's bad luck. I should have known she was bad luck. Women are, you know."

"Uh, that's right, Frisco. Whatever you say. Did someone get ahold of Doc Gonzalez?"

Why did Laredo sound so worried? He felt someone pull the phone from his pocket.

"Hello?" he heard Laredo say. "Hey, Annabelle. Glad to hear things are fine. Sandwiches if we want them? Well, you know what? We might be coming back to the house in about thirty minutes or so, so if you've got sandwiches and coffee out, that would be great. Frisco's had a little, um, fall. I think he's fine, but unless Doc Gonzalez says he needs to get checked out at the hospital, we may leave him at home with you. Would you mind having two babies to take care of?"

"Shut the hell up, Laredo," Frisco said, his head clearing enough to realize he was the butt of a joke.

"Thanks, Annabelle. We'll see you soon."

The phone was shoved back into his pocket. "I like a woman who does what she's told. She called right on time," Frisco said.

"Oh, boy. Come on, Doc."

"If women did what they were told, this would be a peaceful society," Frisco continued.

"Oh, my Lord. It's going to be Armageddon at the ranch. I hope Doc's got something that'll shut your stupid mouth, Frisco, 'cause you're sure as hell going idiot on me." Laredo leaned down to feel his hands. "Are you cold?"

"I've got moving blankets in the back of the truck," Jerry said. "Hang on."

"My leg hurts," Frisco complained.

"We know. Just lie still."

A heap of blankets landed on his chest, and Frisco decided he felt much warmer. Of course, Emmie had felt better, but she wasn't here right now. She was at home, nice and toasty, where she belonged.

"You coulda broke my arm, Laredo. And then how would I hold Emmie?" he wondered.

"Jeez" was all the reply he got. He heard boots stamping, and then the pain in his leg hurt so bad he suddenly went lights-out.

ANNABELLE GASPED WHEN Laredo, Tex and Jerry brought a barely-cursing Frisco inside. "Is he all right?"

"He's fine. Just ornery and unhappy and maybe a bit cold," Laredo told her. "Is it easier to keep an eye on him upstairs or downstairs?"

"The baby sleeps upstairs. Might as well put him up there, too. Maybe Frisco will feel better in his own bed." She watched as the brothers gingerly carried Frisco, mosh-pit style, up the stairs and turned to the left. Gently, they laid him down next to the sleeping Emmie.

"Don't you dare wake that baby, Frisco," Laredo commanded in a soft voice. "No grunts, no groans."

"We're going to need a baby monitor," Tex said, "so

that Annabelle doesn't have to run up here every two seconds to take care of Frisco. The baby will give her less trouble than him."

"Shut up," Frisco said, but his voice was weary and Annabelle was pretty certain he was hurting more than he let on.

"It's okay. He'll be fine," she said. "Won't you, Frisco?"

"Annabelle, Annabelle, my country 'tis of thee," he sang. "Shake your groove thing, I'm your boogie man!"

She shot Laredo a questioning glance.

"The doc gave him a shot at his office. I think it went non-stop, direct flight to Frisco's head," Laredo explained.

"Something for the pain," Tex clarified. "The X-ray showed a clean break in his leg, so that was easily addressed. We're not too sure, but he might be a bit scrambled upstairs. He's been behaving a bit oddly."

"Oh?" Annabelle said, worried that maybe Frisco needed more medical attention than he'd got.

"Yeah, he keeps babbling about Emmie. And you. And burned dinner," Tex explained. "We think that's all pretty extraordinary behavior for our brother."

Tex shot him a warning look. "Not extraordinary that he'd be talking about you and Emmie, of course. Frisco's just not the most talkative man on the planet," Tex clarified, his tone a definite override to Laredo's slip. "Doc Gonzalez would like Frisco to rest tonight and see if he's still addled tomorrow. If he is, we'll take him in for a CT scan. We'd take him now, but the hospital's overrun with outpatient care from the flooding and hypothermia from the cold."

"Actually, we've all been stupid at one time or another," Laredo said with a shrug. "We always come out of it in a few hours."

"Except the time Last got kicked in the head. Remember that? We thought he was going to time travel permanently."

"That dummy. He shouldn't have been at the business end of that bronc like that. I still say Last was just yanking our chains, the freaky little garden gnome. It never takes any of us very long to shake off a little bump or bruise." Laredo rolled his eyes, his expression somewhat haunted, as if he didn't quite believe his own denial of Last's condition.

"How is the sandbagging going?" Annabelle interrupted, all the while keeping an eye on Frisco. He glanced at Emmie sleeping next to him, pulled the blanket closer to her head and seemed satisfied with the adjustment.

"We'll know tonight. We're just going to keep laying sandbags and praying." Tex nodded at his brother. "You gonna be all right with him?"

"We'll be fine," Annabelle assured him. "Grab some sandwiches on your way out."

"Thanks, Annabelle. We don't know what we would have done without you and the other Lonely Hearts ladies. They sure have been a big help in town." Laredo tipped his hat to her. "If he gives you any trouble, smack him."

"He'll be fine." She went to the door and watched them go down the stairs. "Be careful."

The men raised their hands in parting. She went back inside the bedroom just in time to see Frisco scoot the baby nearly up under his arm.

"Come here, soft Emmie, and lower my blood pressure," he crooned.

The baby never batted an eye at the adjustment, but Frisco had Annabelle blinking. She went to the side of the bed to stare down at him. "Do you want another pillow under your leg?"

"I'm fine. Thanks."

"How do you feel?"

"Not as bad as when I got my leg caught in a chute at the rodeo, thanks. I'll live."

"Glad to hear it."

He looked up at her. "Laredo did this to me."

"You look capable of defending yourself."

Frisco snorted. "He took a cheap shot at me."

"Maybe you're just feeling sorry for yourself? Pity-party psychosis brought on by the pain injection?"

"Maybe." He closed his eyes before opening them to look at her steadfastly. "Come here and kiss me, Annabelle."

CHAPTER EIGHT

ANNABELLE'S LIPS PARTED. Kiss Frisco? No way. Not while he was lying in a bed and medicated to the max. Kiss him? Never. Not while she was trying to get her life together. What a very bad idea.

She decided to ignore him.

"I'm sure a small kiss is all the medication I'd need, Anna-Anna-Bella-Bella. Bella Anna."

Her brows puckered. "Frisco, you obviously don't handle medicine very well. Maybe I'll have the doctor splint your mouth to match your leg."

He squinted at her. "Just a quick one, to make my ouchy go away."

She rolled her eyes at the big man, trussed up, helpless, with a baby under his arm, spouting nonsense. "Pathetic, Frisco. Really. You won't want to remember this conversation in the morning."

"I think you like me. Don't you, Annabelle? Emmie sure does."

"Emmie's designs on you are not the same as mine," she said starchily. Sitting down in the rocker across from him, she pulled out a book. "I have to wash some things, so go to sleep."

"I'll only be helpless one day. I want my kiss now, while I'm half-anaesthetized."

"What good does that do?" Her heart beat harder as she considered his silly pleading.

"It makes me brave enough to ask a woman I know I shouldn't ask for anything. Under normal circumstances, that is."

"So you're saying that a quick, sisterly kiss is something we could both forget when the drugs wear off." Her brow quirked.

"I don't know. Do drugs work like alcohol?"

"Do you often kiss women while you're alcohol-impaired just so you won't have to remember your behavior?"

"I don't think so. I've always had to be fairly responsible." His brow furrowed. "Maybe that's why I'm so tempted now."

"Well, I'm not impaired. And I'd remember." Likely, she'd never forget it. He was a very appealing man.

He brightened. "We could get you impaired. Maybe Doc Gonzalez could give you a shot, too."

"Thanks, no," she said hastily. "I had enough of those in the hospital having Emmie."

"Oh. Well, then, I guess I'm just going to have to do without." His expression turned sad.

"Yes, I think you are."

"Maybe it's better that way."

"I'm sure it is."

"I probably wouldn't like kissing you."

Now he was heading from pathetic to whiny manipulative. Two could play that game. "I *know* I wouldn't like kissing you."

"Betcha a hundred bucks you would," he said confidently.

She laughed. "I don't need a hundred bucks."

He frowned. "I'll bet you your hundred-dollar bill back that you'll like kissing me."

"Really, Frisco, you have nothing to prove, and I don't need the money."

"Why not? Emmie might need a new dress some day."

"I'm financially able to take care of Emmie. Don't worry about her. And I owed you for the bus ticket. Why don't you go to sleep now? You have to be tired."

"Strangely enough, I feel strung like a bad guitar string."

Great. She had to babysit the only six-foot-four male who went hyper on pain medication. Heaven forbid he should fold like a tent the way most people would.

"I changed my mind," Frisco said suddenly. "I don't want you to kiss me." The fog had left his mind for just a minute, long enough for him to know he was making a royal ass of himself. She smelled good, like roses in his mother's garden. Blond hair pushed back by a white headband fell smoothly in a gleaming curve to the edge of her chin. China-blue eyes, fringed by long black lashes, regarded him intently, stripping him of his bravado. She had full supple lips which were slicked with some kind of clear gloss, lips which Frisco thought would be fabulous for kissing and soothing other parts of his body, as well.

He stopped those thoughts in a hurry. Miss Annabelle and her dainty dress were a nightmare to a man who should want nothing more than to get her the hell out of his bedroom in a hurry. She was testing the limit of his strength—and worse, she'd made it clear she wanted no part of him. Had he really thought she would?

"I'd like a blanket, please. There's one in the bottom of that dresser." Emmie could probably use a blanket, too. All she had was her baby blanket over her, and he didn't want her catching a chill.

Annabelle got up, walked to the dresser, bent down to open the drawer. The white eyelet dress slid up a good three inches, revealing strong white legs, despite her quick tug at the hem to keep it in place. A sudden nurse fantasy ran all over him, making him hotter than a branding iron in a fire. But this was Annabelle. He couldn't indulge in a nurse fantasy about her!

Closing the drawer, she turned, the cotton blanket in her hands.

Too late.

"Oh, my," she said.

He groaned, unable to hide the erection making a tent of the sheet.

The front door slammed downstairs. Boots sounded on the stairwell.

Annabelle's gaze met Frisco's, then flew to his predicament. In a reflex action that caught him completely off guard, she flung the folded blanket across the five-foot distance between them.

The heavy cotton landed on his lap with a thud, whooshing the air out of him and flattening whatever pride he had left.

"Annabelle, here's a bottle of painkillers Doc Gonzalez thought Frisco might need," Laredo said, stepping into the room, talking quietly until he saw that Frisco was awake and the baby was still asleep. "Dang, it's hotter than hopping toads on summer cement in here, Frisco. Whaddya need a blanket for? Should I get you a fan?"

"No," Frisco said between clenched teeth, his ears ringing.

"Perhaps he needs a pain pill rather than a blanket," Laredo told Annabelle. "The doc said the shot wouldn't last more than four hours or six, maybe. But Frisco's so darn big, maybe it already wore off."

"We'll give him a while longer. Thanks."

She smiled demurely at Laredo, and he smiled back, clearly taking a second look at the delicate woman. Frisco allowed his head to fall back against the pillow as he closed his eyes. Laredo's boots thumped down the stairs, and the front door slammed.

"You did that on purpose," he complained.

"Should I have left you sticking up? Seemed awkward to me." Annabelle jerked open the bedside drawer to toss the bottle of painkillers inside.

"I would have thought of something. It wasn't necessary for you to…crush me."

"I suppose thanking me for saving you from humiliation would be too much to ask for."

"I'd rather be slightly embarrassed than—"

"Oh, hush. You'd argue with the devil himself." Annabelle glanced in the drawer. "If I give you a pain pill, do you think you'd O.D.? I don't want that on my conscience, but I would love for you to go to sleep. How are you feeling in general?"

"I think the stars have faded from my vision. I'm only seeing black dots now."

"Fine." She started to slam the drawer shut, but something caught her attention.

Frisco's breath caught in his throat. Surely she wouldn't say anything about his stash.

"Is this what the well-dressed man wears nowadays?" She held up a condom in a bright package. "Striped with fluorescent colors," she read. "And this one says it has stars and an interesting device on the tip for maximum pleasure."

He'd take back the part about preferring humiliation to pain.

"I had no idea these things came in any other style besides plain old, plain old."

"Now you know." He wasn't going to say anything more than that. He wanted her out of his drawer. "Would you quit rummaging around in there?"

She closed the drawer. "Sorry. But a guy who dresses to impress shouldn't be upset if a gal looks at the suits." Rising, she straightened the blanket briskly. "Did you really want this, or did you just need camouflage?"

"I'll keep the camouflage."

"I think that's best." She settled into the rocker across the room. "Go to sleep. Please."

"You sit there and be quiet, and maybe I can."

Shrugging, she opened a book, placing it in her lap as she curled up in the rocker. The dress slid to her knees and Frisco closed his eyes, shutting out the alluring picture she made.

If Laredo had ever wanted to punish Frisco for anything he'd ever done to his younger brother, he'd picked an excellent method.

Torture.

ANNABELLE RECOGNIZED at once that taking care of a newborn was a piece of cake compared to a male who was used to independence and overriding everything in his path.

Gently, she moved Emmie to a pallet on the floor, covertly studying the big man who was just as studiously ignoring her. His eyes were closed so she couldn't see the dark-brown irises. Ebony brows complemented black hair which lay unruly against the pillow. He still had an obvious dilemma, which fascinated Annabelle. Surely it should have deflated by now? She thought about Tom and frowned. His hadn't lasted so long. Nor had it been so...

"What are you reading?"

She started a little at the brusque question and hoped he hadn't seen her staring at the blanket. "A romance."

"Isn't that a little racy for a new mom?"

"Happy endings are good for me."

He was silent, looking at her with those dark eyes. Annabelle went back to staring at a page. She did feel a bit isolated now that she was a single mother. Her relationship with Tom had left her wondering if there was any kindling left to start a fire with if she ever met a man she might like. Tom had sucked a lot of the heat from her life.

She certainly hadn't felt with Tom the way she did right now. Frisco's laserlike focus on her made her feel as if she might burst into flames any second. It was best to quit pretending he didn't affect her—she was pretty sure he'd figure out her secret soon if she wasn't careful.

"Since you're not going to fall asleep, I'm going to go downstairs and do some things. Call me if you need me."

He was silent.

"Frisco, I'm just not interested in testing the water with anyone."

"I know. I'm not, either." He shook his head. "I don't know why I wanted to kiss you. I'm sorry."

"I was tempted, you know." It wasn't necessary to beat his ego to smithereens.

"If that was tempted, you made Eve look bad."

She smiled at him. "If things were different, if I didn't

have a newborn, I might be up for a quick kiss with a man I barely know."

"I lost my mind for a minute, Annabelle. It won't happen again. I sure didn't mean to make you uncomfortable."

She smiled slightly. "Your leg's broken. It levels the playing field quite a bit. I can resist from five feet away."

"I wouldn't want you unless you wanted me."

"Okay."

"Do you?"

She laughed. "No," she told him, aware that the hopeful expression on his face was due to the painkillers scrambling his brain. Frisco and drugs were not a successful mix.

"Damn."

"I could get Laredo to find you another nurse. There're other Lonely Hearts ladies here."

"No, thanks," he said hurriedly. "I like you. But not in *that way,* of course."

"Of course. Go to sleep."

She left the room, her heart practically pounding in her ears. Too much man, too much temptation for her damaged ego to resist. Tom had never wanted her that way. Being the focus of Frisco's intoxicated interest was way more flattering—and sensual—than anything she'd ever known.

It would be so nice to give in. He probably wouldn't have remembered it tomorrow. Just a kiss. What would it have hurt?

Everything, of course. Because sometimes kissing was the start of something bigger.

And that was a risk she simply couldn't take.

CHAPTER NINE

"SO RUN THIS THING about the big-haired beauty queens across the street by me one more time. The... What'd you call them? The Snip-n-Snarls? Brush-n-Babes?"

Frisco's voice in the dark startled Annabelle. She'd come in to sneak Emmie out of Frisco's room. "I'm skipping storytime right now, Frisco. Go back to sleep."

"I just want to know what makes your customers desert Ms. Delilah."

Annabelle reached inside the bathroom and flipped on the light before closing the door. Just a crack of illumination shone into the dark bedroom. "We've long wondered ourselves. Delilah and her stylists are very good with hair, and the customers seem satisfied—until they find out about the shop across the street. One try over there, and the men never come back to us." Including Tom, but that fact was redundant, no need to mention it again. "They attend church with nicks out of their hair, though, and it's easy to tell where they were Saturday night. It's almost like a visual roll call." She lowered her voice. "To be honest, I'm not certain all those Cut-n-Gurls have beauty-school training. Delilah says she doesn't know when Marvella would have gone to school." She shrugged. "Of course, there's not so much to cutting a man's hair, I suppose. Their tool of choice appears to be clippers. You'll notice the men who frequent their salon tend to sport short, uneven silhouettes, which has always reminded me of a golf course with divots missing here and there."

"There has to be something you're not telling me. And since I can't sleep, I'm in the mood for a story."

She was pretty tired. The men and women had all returned from sandbagging, sweeping out water, and whatever other duties they'd been assigned. She'd cooked dinner, had it hot and ready—a recipe from an old file she'd found in the kitchen—and fed what seemed like an army of people. Chicken soup, a monster-sized bowl of green salad, and King Ranch casserole. She'd given herself an A for Edibility, but it had meant a lot of cleanup time in the kitchen. Everyone was gone now, except for Laredo and Tex, who'd showered and gone to bed in their own rooms. Right now, she could fall asleep on the floor.

"I can't tell you a story because I have to get some sleep. But I'll give you a bit of gossip I've mulled many times since I heard it. Supposedly—and this is just gossip, I certainly don't know for sure—on the wall of their salon is written in big, sparkly gold letters: Save a horse, ride a cowboy."

"I can see where that might be appealing."

"Frisco!"

He chuckled. "I've been needing a haircut for a while now—"

"Frisco, I think I'd consider that desertion at the minimum and disregarding my confidences at the maximum. Now I'm going to bed." He wasn't supposed to have been amused, and he darn sure wasn't supposed to be interested!

"Come on. I was only playing."

"Playing dumb?" How could he joke after what she'd told him about Tom?

"Trying to keep you in here a while longer."

"Not like that, you aren't. Friends understand where the line shouldn't be crossed."

"I guess I didn't realize we were friends, Annabelle. I'm happy to hear you say that."

"I have to help you to the bathroom, don't I? Surely assisting you makes us more than acquaintances."

"You're real antsy about that salon, aren't you?"

She rolled her eyes in the dark. "To say the least, especially for Delilah's sake. Anyway, how do you think you'd feel, if someone made a joke about someone you'd once cared about?"

He thought about Laredo teasing him about Annabelle. "I'd probably want to squish his head."

"Lie real still so I can use your brand of revenge on you."

"I wouldn't really be interested in a woman who compared riding me to riding a horse."

Her brows shot up; she could feel her face pink. She and Tom had made love once. It had been nothing like riding a horse. In fact, it had been more like…riding her first bike. One second she'd been on; the next second she'd tumbled to the ground.

"Annabelle, have you noticed how much this baby's been sleeping?"

His soft voice shifted her away from her disheartening thoughts. "She's obviously joining you in your lazy habits."

"Hmm. Maybe she's decided to give me a second chance."

"To do what?" Ever since Frisco had held Emmie, she'd been charmed into sleeping better.

"To get to know her."

"Frisco, my daughter is innocent. I no longer am.

And I really don't want to get to know you, if that's what you're implying. You're a big, ornery male. I want peace and quiet in my life. I will never get that with you."

"No, you won't. I readily admit that."

They were both quiet for a moment. Then he said, "Might as well lie down on the opposite side of the bed, Annabelle. There's plenty of room. I promise not to even breathe on you."

She was so tired. The alternative was finding another bed somewhere in the house, and frankly, she didn't want to root through bedrooms in case she opened a door where one of the other brothers was sleeping. She wasn't even certain there was another bedroom.

"I snore," she told him.

"That will be annoying. I'll toss this blanket over your head. The one you used on me."

She giggled and edged cautiously to the side of the bed. "You should have seen your face."

"You should have seen yours. You looked like you'd never seen a man in that condition before."

Her smile melted away. She hadn't—at least not like Frisco. But she wasn't going to tell this irritating cowboy that. He was cocky and conceited, and she'd be embarrassed. Besides, that was all more private than she cared to share. "Shut up, Frisco," she said, instead. "If I'm sleeping in here with you for the sake of convenience, you have to be quiet. You're going to wake Emmie."

"She's used to my voice by now. She doesn't even stir until she wants a bottle or a diaper change."

Annabelle sighed to herself and slid into bed with her dress on, but decided that was uncomfortable. The little bit of light was necessary, but it left her having to sleep with her eyelet dress on. Dare she slip it off and doze in her underthings?

No. "Is the light bothering you?" she asked.

"I'd rather it be dark, but I didn't want to suggest it. You're awfully tense about us sharing a bed."

"I'm tense about you in general," she said, getting up to flip off light. "Goodness knows, I can't imagine why I feel that way."

"I can't, either," he agreed, way too cheerfully for her liking.

"Good *night,* Frisco," she stressed so he'd cease his teasing.

"Good night, Annabelle."

She sighed as she hit the pillow. For a moment, she wondered if she would really be able to sleep in the same bed with Frisco, but in a way, she felt oddly comforted with him in the same room.

Even in the same bed.

"Dinner was good, Annabelle," he said, sounding sleepy.

"Thank you." She felt warmed by his praise. Okay, maybe he wasn't all that bad. Cranky, sure. The truth was, she didn't know what kind of man she could trust anymore. Tom had been all blond hair and blue eyes come-on, and she'd desperately needed that at the time. Her world had turned dark after her father died, and there was Tom, light and airy and interested. She had fallen like a sack of potatoes from a truck.

It would be textbook cliché now to turn around and fall for Tom's total opposite. If she'd figured nothing else out about herself, it was that she was still grieving, still running—and sooner or later, a girl had to slow down.

"Annabelle?" Frisco said.

"Yes?"

"You sure are the prettiest housekeeper we've ever had."

"I wasn't aware you'd had any before."

"I want you to focus on the compliment and not the comment."

Her eyes snapped open in the dark. A shiver ran over her. Was he making a pass at her? Surely not. Certainly he seemed to like Emmie, but more often than not, he seemed out of sorts around Annabelle. "Um, thank you," she murmured uncertainly.

"Annabelle?"

"Yes?"

"I've been wanting to kiss you ever since I first laid eyes on you. I wouldn't, of course. But I did think about it."

Her breath caught for an instant. And then she dove in wearing only courage. "I've thought about kissing you, too," she whispered. She squeezed her eyes tightly shut.

To her surprise, Frisco rolled over to face her. She couldn't see him, but she knew he was close to her face. He smelled good, and his nearness touched her skin with warmth. Instantly, she wanted to get closer to him, pull him to her.

When he brushed her hair away from her face, she sighed with longing.

"I shouldn't, Annabelle," he murmured. "It would be ungentlemanly to take advantage of you."

She thought she'd already had a man take advantage of her—and it hadn't felt like this. Just Frisco's voice made her shiver inside. She wanted him to touch her.

And then he did, with his lips. First, brushing against her forehead, and then along her cheeks. Then her eyelids. Annabelle's insides seemed to contract, as if her inner soul knew exactly what it wanted from him. In spite of his size and his gruff exterior, Frisco was soft and gentle and not scary at all.

His lips touched hers suddenly, and Annabelle realized he'd been going slowly with her, gentling her. His patience made her relax so that she melted against him.

Frisco felt Annabelle give into him. It was a surrender.

He hadn't expected it. She was so delicate and ethereal, like mythical magical moonflies beating their wings at night. He wanted desperately to catch her, to hold her, to rub her magic all over him.

Caught off guard, his whole body afire, Frisco forced himself to pull away.

"Good night, Annabelle," he said hoarsely.

IN THE NIGHT, the sandbags held back the water. Though the temperature struggled up above the freezing mark, the ice stayed on the roads.

"I'm hauling the ladies into town. They're going to do some mopping and other things," Jerry told Annabelle. "Will you be all right here? Or do you and Emmie want to come with us?"

Emmie was behaving so much better that, as much as Annabelle would have loved to leave, she decided it was better for her baby to stay put. Frisco had a wonderfully comforting touch for Emmie's colic. Helping out here was a small price for Emmie's welfare. But just for tonight. "I'll stay and cook. Jerry, when are you heading back?"

"Good Lord willing and if the creek doesn't rise, tomorrow, little lady. Why do you ask?"

She looked into his cheery blue eyes. "I need to get going myself."

"Ah. Cabin fever?"

"Something like that."

"Frisco fever?"

"Close enough to be right on the mark." She sighed. "I'm just ready to move on."

"Delilah says you'd been 'moving on' for a couple months before you came into her shop. That she hired you right off the street because you looked tired and haunted. Something eating you, Annabelle?" He gave her a kindly smile, his cheeks rosy from cold. "I got real big shoulders to cry on."

"No. No, thanks," she said hurriedly. "I'm fine. I just need to get back."

"To the salon? I don't know yet that the ladies are going back tomorrow. They may head farther east. They're still on vacation, you know."

"I'm not going back to the salon. Don't tell Delilah, Jerry. I want to tell her myself, please."

"Fair enough. We roll at 8:00 a.m. Can you and Emmie be ready?"

"We'll be ready, Jerry. Thanks."

He touched his cap and walked across the yard toward his truck. She headed into the kitchen, hurrying upstairs to retrieve Emmie before the baby began a full-scale assault for her bottle.

Frisco lay on the bed, sound asleep, his leg awkwardly propped up, his body turned uncomfortably. He was beautiful when he slept, dark and masterful. Emmie, unaware that she was sleeping next to a giant, had scooched up under his arm, her diapered rump in the air, her fist in her mouth.

Annabelle wished she had a camera. She'd like to

remember Emmie having this moment with a man, nearly a father figure. Maybe the only man who would ever nap with her like that. Her eyes clouded. Maybe *I've just made a total wreck of my life and Emmie's,* she thought. The last thing I ever meant to do was hurt her.

The blanket she'd thrown at Frisco was on the floor. Picking it up, she folded it, then knelt to put it in the bottom drawer. What she couldn't see last night caused her to hesitate now. A framed picture of a man, a woman and twelve ragamuffin-looking boys stared out at her. The picture was eight-by-eleven, black-and-white, taken by a real photographer on the grounds of the Union Junction ranch. Though the boys looked ragtag, it was clear that they were loved and happy. Everyone wore jeans, except the lady, who wore a Jackie Kennedy–style dress and gloves. She reminded Annabelle of Audrey Hepburn, with her big eyes and delicate frame.

If this was the Jefferson brothers' mother, she'd been quite a looker. She'd also been slightly built. Annabelle wrinkled her nose. She hadn't lost ten of the pounds she'd gained with Emmie. Multiply ten pounds by twelve kids.

And all the boys had that wiry, lean frame. "It's not fair. At least one of you could have been a mutant," she muttered. If the man in the picture was the father of the clan, he was tall, lean and handsome. Like all his offspring.

You'd think the Union Junction women would be throwing panties at the ranch windows every night.

Still, why waste a good pair of panties when none of the brothers was inclined to settle down? It was a little unsettling, because she knew Frisco had started knocking edges off her hard heart, softening it into a penetrable organ once again. If anything, this picture told her why she couldn't fall for him, even if she wanted to. She couldn't live up to the family frozen in time, captured in a perfect moment.

She put the frame away and stood up.

Frisco was leaning up on his elbows, watching her intently. "Find everything you need?"

"Not yet," she said, her nose in the air. She hated getting caught snooping and he darn well knew it, so he could just temper his sarcasm with a little sweetness today. "Have *you* found everything you need?"

"Not yet," he replied.

She crossed her arms. "I don't have to wait on you hand-and-foot. It's not a royal right ceded to you just because you were dumb enough to roll down a hill."

He scratched at the stubble on his face. "Calm down, Sparky. I apologize. I'm a little sensitive about…what's in that drawer."

"Fine. I'm a little sensitive about being snapped at."

His gaze roamed over her long skirt, boots and red sweater. "How'd you sleep?"

"Just like Emmie."

"I seem to have a beneficial effect on you Turnberrys."

That she wasn't about to debate. "Do you want some orange juice? Breakfast?"

"I'm not very hungry. Thanks."

"Call me if you need something." She went to scoop up Emmie, who was starting to flail restlessly beside Frisco, a sure sign a bottle was needed.

"I'm sorry I teased you last night about the rivals across the street."

"It doesn't matter anymore."

She bent to pick up the baby. He reached out with a hand to halt her in mid-bend.

"I'll feed her. I've got nothing else to do, and I might as well be useful."

Her heart turned over. "Why are you being so nice about my baby?"

"Why not?"

"Because I really don't need your pity, and neither does Emmie. We're fine, Frisco, really fine on our own."

"I don't pity you. I'm feeling sorry for myself."

She stared into his dark eyes. "Because?"

"I don't really know. But I haven't held a baby in years, and I'm not ever going to hold one of my own, and the experience is far from killing me."

She couldn't say that yes, he would hold one of his own. He was pushing forty—slowly, but pushing it all the same—with no apparent inclination to do anything about getting babies. Her gaze slowly dropped, then returned to his. "Is it because of the picture? Is that why you keep it hidden?"

His eyes hooded suddenly. "I just want to feed Emmie, Annabelle. That's all I'm asking for. I have a strange feeling you're not going to be here much longer, and after that—and after my leg heals—I'm going to be back to work. Back to being myself. All this will be out of my system."

She wondered how he could know exactly what she'd been thinking. "Okay," she said, her arms hesitantly offering Emmie to him. "I'll bring you a bottle."

"And flip on that TV, if you don't mind. Emmie and I are going to watch something intelligent like football, aren't we, Emmie?" he cooed to the baby now curled into a tucked position on his chest. "Football strategy is good for you. Teamwork is key to a well-run home and business."

"Good grief." Annabelle left the room to hurry downstairs for the bottle. The man was a bit unhinged, even in an undrugged state.

"I THINK YOUR LITTLE birdy might be about ready to fly the coop," Jerry said to Delilah as they perched in his truck for a quick lunch break. "Not that I'm supposed to be giving you any info, mind you."

"I was afraid of that." Delilah sighed. "Annabelle's my rolling stone. The only reason she hung around the salon as long as she did was because she felt guilty about Emmie. Figured it was best for the baby to have a chance to know her father. Annabelle's real sensitive about that type of thing since she lost her father last year."

"Is that why she looks so uncomfortable all the time? Like she can't light for more than five minutes?"

"She's still grieving, that's for certain. And trying to figure out her place in the world. Annabelle doesn't really belong in a small town, I'm afraid. She's a big-city girl, the daughter of Jason Turnberry, wine magnate. She's got a ton of money, though she's refusing to touch much of it right now while she's trying to figure out where she fits and what she could make of herself without family money. I've often been thankful for her decision to live more simply, because I believe if that pond scum, Tom, had ever figured out who she was, he'd have stuck on her like a leech. And he didn't love her. Not even a little, so I'm grateful she's smart enough to try to find her own way."

"It's good to know who one is in life."

"Yes." Delilah nodded. "And Annabelle never had the chance to figure it out. Her mother was some society dame who didn't want her, so Jason Turnberry raised her. Only he became ill in the last ten years of his life, starting about the time Annabelle would have just about graduated college. She came home and spent the last years of her father's life nursing him. He was her best friend, her only family, and he left Annabelle his company." Delilah shrugged. "So when she lost her father, she lost her whole person."

Jerry sighed. "It's too bad she won't find herself in time. I do believe I saw a twinkle in Frisco's eye for her."

"Well, if he twinkled, she'd sure put out the flame. Besides, she doesn't belong here, Jerry. And if I'm not mistaken, these boys are somewhat emotionally devastated themselves. No bonding ability at all. A lot of cock, a bit of bull and too much story, if you know what I mean. No feminine touch to rein all that in."

"I don't reckon you put two people in the same boat unless they both know how to row."

"And how to swim if the boats tips over." Delilah stood, brushing crumbs from her jeans. "I'm just learning a few new strokes myself since my sister came to town."

"You'll outlast her."

She shook her head. "I have no idea what makes Marvella tick. But if grit gets me any points, I'll be standing no matter what she does. You don't happen to know where I can find a cowboy who can stay on the meanest bull in Texas, do you?"

"I'm well past my youth, Delilah, though you know I'd sure try to stick in the saddle. Why do you need a cowboy?"

"Every year the town holds a big fair, and one of the draws is bull-riding. The cowboy with the best time wins the purse. I sure could use the purse, now that Marvella's managed to draw my business down so much. We've always won, and I've always been able to give the purse to charity. This year, I'm sorry to say, my business is the charity." She looked at him sadly. "If I want to keep these girls on, I'm going to need some cash."

"Delilah, I'd be happy—"

She held up a hand. "Thank you, Jerry, but it's a resourceful woman who rides the waves of luck, be it high or low tide. If it's time for the Lonely Hearts Salon to go out on ebb tide, so be it. But I plan to pay my girls something."

He pursed his lips. "What kind of riding is it?"

"Ugly. Because you have to have a bull that doesn't just dance around like a youthful grandma. You have to have one that's full of fire, as that's what draws the audience. And my bull is Bloodthirsty Black."

"Oh. And Marvella's?"

"Bad-Ass Blue. She just got him last year—bought him from the best-scoring cowboy at the Fort Worth rodeo."

"She really does have it in for you, doesn't she?"

"Every bit, every step of the way."

"Ever think about getting out of her way?"

"Nope." She shook her head at him and grinned. "I was there first. I'm older. It's my town. If one of us goes, it ain't gonna be me."

"That-a-girl." He squinted toward the dam where the Jefferson brothers were busy replacing sandbags in the shoring that had slipped in the night. "You know what sticks in a saddle the best, Delilah?"

"What?"

"A tall tale. Every word bigger and braver than the

last. A lot of cock, a bit of bull and too much story, as you put it."

"The Jefferson brothers?"

"I heard one of them mention he was thinking about trying the rodeo circuit."

She watched them for a few moments. "Nah," she said after a while. "They've already got one man down. Whoever rides Bloodthirsty Black is likely to get busted up. I couldn't do that to them."

"You just don't want to ask them because you'd be asking for something for yourself. These men know what it means to try to keep a business afloat, Delilah."

"I know. But I'm admiring Annabelle these days, Jerry. I'm going to figure out something on my own."

CHAPTER TEN

AROUND NIGHTFALL, Laredo and Tex went to town with Jerry to pick up the ladies and haul them back to the ranch for dinner.

"They sure have been good sports about their vacation getting screwed up," Laredo said.

"I may miss them when they go," Tex agreed. "A few of them, anyway."

Jerry grunted from his place at the wheel. The brothers looked at each other.

"Maybe this means we need a woman or two at the ranch. Liven things up a bit," Tex said.

"We could get some dogs if all we wanted was to liven things up a bit," Laredo pointed out. "Although that Katy Goodnight gal kind of caught my eye. I like the way she mops."

"Oh, now there's a proposal. 'Hang out with me at the ranch so I can watch you mop.'" Tex and Jerry had a good laugh at Laredo's expense.

"I like the way she moves her tush. Back and forth, side to side. Then north and south. Her dark hair flops around in that long ponytail and— What?" Laredo stopped as both men were staring at him incredulously.

"You've got the hots for her," Tex said.

"Uh-uh. Liking to watch a woman mop is not having the hots for her," Laredo argued.

"He may have a point. It sounds more like he has a fetish for clean floors."

"And even if I do have a fetish for clean floors, which I do not—is it a crime to like the way a woman moves, I ask you? Is that any better or worse than having an over-excited enthusiasm for manure and buds that never open for you?"

Tex stiffened, insulted. "Any day now, one of those roses is going to open, Laredo. It's going to be lush and beautiful and fragrant—"

"Jeez, Tex, why don't you just get a woman?" Laredo couldn't explain why he was so annoyed, except that he hadn't liked being teased. That didn't make him a chauvinist or anything. She could have been wiping tables and he probably would have been just as—

An unpleasant thought hit him. "There's a possibility that I don't know what a woman's for beyond house-keeping, and the obvious," Laredo said slowly. "I never thought about it before. All I remember of mom is her cleaning the house. She was happy about it. She sang a lot."

"She could pipe up on Dad a bit, too," Tex said wistfully. "Boy, he didn't like it when she was upset with him."

"No, he didn't."

"I just don't have her magic touch with roses," Tex said with a sigh.

"It hasn't felt like the Union Junction Ranch in a long time," Laredo said. "More like Malfunction Junction, just like the townfolks say. Seems more and more as if they're right."

Tex nodded. "Yep. That's what we are. Malfunction Junction."

Jerry didn't say a word as he drove. Laredo decided

there wasn't anything else to say. He was feeling melancholy and reminiscent. The Lonely Hearts ladies had shown him one thing—life at the ranch was pretty stale. He'd been ready to scratch his itch a long time ago, and head out to see the world, starting in the Appalachian mountains, maybe head up the Eastern seaboard.

It would be hard on Mason, what with Frisco being off his leg for a while. But there was no time like the present for a man to do something big with himself, and as soon as winter lightened up a little, he was going to leave.

ANNABELLE GAVE EMMIE her last bottle for the evening, then put her in a pretty white sleeper. "You're such an angel," she told the baby. "I love you."

Emmie seemed to nuzzle her back. Annabelle knew it was too soon for her daughter to really react to her, but still, it felt good. And she looked forward to the future, when Emmie would recognize her instantly.

For a moment, she thought of Tom, and what he'd chosen to miss out on. She felt sorry for Emmie, who would never know her daddy. "I had a wonderful daddy, your grandfather. You would have been the apple of his eye."

That made her sad, so she tucked her baby onto her chest and headed up the stairs to put Emmie to bed.

"It's about time," Frisco complained as soon as she entered. "Don't you think Emmie should get to bed earlier?"

"I beg your pardon? Are you trying to tell me you know what's best for my daughter?"

"No. I missed her, though. Come here, little bit, and let me hold you."

Frisco stretched out his arms to take the baby, and it

was all Annabelle could do not to let the tears she felt stinging show. She surrendered the baby, watching her tiny daughter be engulfed by two big hands.

"I heard you're leaving tomorrow," Frisco said.

"From who?" She felt surprised and embarrassed. She'd wanted to slip out without him knowing.

"You said goodbye to Delilah. She was pretty shook up about it, and she told all the girls so they'd know to say goodbye to you tomorrow." He laid the baby down beside him, tucking a blanket around her, before giving Annabelle a full-on stare. "I figured I'd say my goodbye tonight."

"I see. Well, it's a bit awkward." It was a lot awkward.

"Were you going to say goodbye to me?"

She avoided his gaze. "Not necessarily."

"That would have hurt my feelings."

She still didn't look at him. "That wouldn't have been my intention."

"Maybe not. I'm just telling you that I wouldn't have liked that at all."

"I'm sorry."

"Please look at me."

It was hard, because she wanted to—and yet, she was so afraid. There were things she wanted to see in his eyes, and yet, those same things she didn't want to see. How could she explain to him what she really didn't understand about herself?

"Annabelle."

Slowly, she turned at the command in his tone. "Yes?" she whispered.

"Kiss me."

"I can't."

"Because?"

She could barely hold his gaze. Even her hands were trembling. "Because I'm... It's not the right thing to do."

"Can't take advantage of a man with a broken leg?"

He was trying to lighten the mood, but when it came to the idea of kissing him, she couldn't take it as a simple matter of swapping saliva. "Why do you want to kiss me?"

"Because I have the strangest feeling that I'll always regret it if I don't. You...pull me to you in some way I can't quite explain. And I think you feel that pull, too."

"I don't."

"Not at all?"

She lowered her gaze.

"I understand about Emmie's father, Annabelle. I know it's too soon for you. I'm not trying to rush you. It's like having the answer to a question, and I guess I want the answer."

"You scare me," she murmured.

"In a good way?"

"Is there a good way to scare someone?" She stared at him, curious.

"Well, you scare me a little, too. But I think it's called attraction. And I understand you want to leave. But I'm more scared that you won't kiss me." He caught her fingers in his as she stood beside the bed. "I really, really got scared when I found out you were leaving tomorrow. Tell a man who's got a busted leg that the woman he's been mulling over kissing for two days is leaving. That's almost cruel. I couldn't come find you; I couldn't run you down and grab you like I wanted to. I had to wait, and hope that you'd come upstairs to put Emmie in my bed. It was torture, Annabelle."

She hadn't meant to torture him. She was tortured enough for both of them. He'd been the one to turn away last night, which had hurt more than she could have imagined.

And yet, she was touched that Frisco had wanted to come to her for this kiss he wanted so badly. He'd admitted to feeling some of the pain she was feeling, which made her feel much less alone. "I felt abandoned," she whispered.

"I know. I thought about it later and knew I'd screwed up. But you were gone this morning before I could tell you, and then I heard you were thinking of leaving...."

Neither of them were certain of the proper steps in the dance. He hadn't meant to make her feel deserted—it was just too soon after Tom's abandonment, and she'd felt that painful feeling again. Her father's death had left her feeling alone and shipwrecked, too.

A kiss, nothing more. As Frisco pointed out, he was in no position to chase her down if kissing made her more nervous than she could handle.

A kiss. Swapping saliva. Sucking face. No need to make more of it than it was.

And Frisco was basically promising her that he wouldn't leave her out there by herself. If she was ever going to move forward with her life, she had to get over being afraid of every lonesome shadow.

Slowly, Annabelle moved her face toward his, startled when Frisco removed his fingers from hers to cradle her face in his hands as gently as if she were Emmie. She nearly sighed with the pleasure of it.

He touched his lips to hers, and she sank onto the bed beside him, every fiber of her body relaxing toward him.

Ever so unnoticeably, he increased the pressure until he was no longer just touching her lips, but a part of her.

It felt so good.

He pulled back, and her mind cried out, *Don't stop!* "All right?"

All she could do was nod. Beside them, Emmie's soft breathing hung in the room.

This time, Annabelle moved toward him, placing her lips on his, trusting, wanting, seeking. His hands tightened on her face, pulling her toward him. Her knees went limp, so she drew her legs up onto the bed. Facing him, she leaned into him more, and when his arms went around her, it was as if her whole body sighed with recognition.

Heat and passion and warmth. All the things Tom had never given her spun through her mind. Closing her eyes, she reveled in the magic of the moment.

And when Frisco pulled away from her and moved her head down onto his chest, she leaned against him, relaxing as her hammering heart slowed, content to take the shelter he was offering.

Nothing had ever felt so good in her whole life.

And yet, it was the worst thing she could have discovered. Real passion. True heat. Something that came along maybe once, twice in a lifetime, with a special person.

She might never know it again in her life.

WHEN SHE AWAKENED the next morning, she found herself still tucked up against Frisco's chest. Fully dressed. He couldn't be comfortable like that, especially with his broken leg.

She hadn't seen him take any pain pills since the

first night. Couldn't blame what happened on happy tablets.

"Time to go?"

She turned at his deep voice. "After I feed Emmie."

He was silent for a long moment. "You're special, Annabelle. Don't forget it."

She had forgotten it, and more, after Tom had deserted her. "Thank you, Frisco. You are, too."

He made her feel good about herself. He made her feel special.

She couldn't wait to get out of his room, and out of his house.

"Promise me you'll call if you need anything. Anything at all."

She nodded. "I will."

She wouldn't.

Last night's kiss hung between them. She couldn't look at him. Without a glance, she picked Emmie up and hurried to the door.

"Goodbye, Annabelle."

"Goodbye, Frisco."

She left with a stolen glance at him. With two days stubble on his face he looked rakish, especially with his shirt off and his long body obvious under the white sheet. She'd lain quite happily on that broad chest.

Oh, my Lord. If I don't go now, I'll beg him pitifully to keep me and Emmie forever, she thought.

Hadn't Frisco said he wasn't interested in children or settling down? That he had all the family he needed?

Whatever was between them had to be attraction. She could live with that. Attraction could be recovered from, like a case of head lice.

Becoming dependent on him, when he'd clearly outlined his life, was not what she was going to do. She'd already been dumped once, and she had no intention of putting herself in that position again.

But there had been one really good thing about Frisco that made her see her life in a new light. She could live through anything: colic, grouchy cowboys, single parenthood. Cooking. Ice storms.

Now she had known kindness from a man besides her father. And real passion.

She felt herself changing, like sun moving shadows away from rocks.

Instead of continuing her old habit of moving on, she was going back to the Lonely Hearts Salon. Not to work, but to cross that damn street and walk right in the door of the Never Lonely Cut-n-Gurls. With Emmie.

She was going to ask to speak to Tom.

He was going to meet Emmie face-to-face. Emmie was not a monster. She was not at fault. If an ornery cowboy could take a shine to her little baby, then Emmie was bound to catch the heart of the most hard-hearted male.

Maybe not Tom's heart, but that was to be determined. Annabelle accepted this might be the case. But Tom was by golly going to see Emmie. Emmie was going to have her chance with her blood father.

And if Tom refused to see her—and Emmie—that was fine, too. She would slap him with a paternity suit so fast it would make his sunshine-blond head swim. She didn't need the money. It was something she hadn't thought of before, because she'd been running from rejection.

Frisco had taught her that she had no reason to run from Tom's rejection. Frisco was better-looking, more successful—and unless she badly miscalculated what had been under that sheet before she'd tossed the blanket on him, had about four inches on Tom in a very manly place.

And Tom couldn't kiss worth a damn.

Frisco had found her desirable. He gave her confidence. She'd fight for Emmie's chance to know her father. Paternity suit, visiting rights, whatever.

Like Marvella, Annabelle could be a pain. She'd simply be a boil under Tom's behind he couldn't get away from. Until he saw his daughter, Annabelle wouldn't rest.

And if he didn't want her after that, so be it. But she'd do her duty as a mother. It wasn't revenge she was seeking and she didn't want Tom back. So far from it. Child support was the minimum Emmie should get from him. Acknowledgment at the maximum. A father's love only a prayer.

It took two to tango, and she was ready to dance.

Thanks to Frisco.

An hour later, when she'd packed herself and Emmie into Jerry's truck, she hugged and kissed her friends. "I'll see you in a few days," she told them. "I've changed my mind about leaving town for good. I've changed my mind about a lot of things."

"That's my girl," Delilah said. "I always knew you had grit."

Annabelle glanced up toward the upper story of the house. If she hadn't known it was impossible, since Frisco couldn't stand up by himself, she would have thought she saw his shadow in the window, behind the curtain.

Just in case, she waved.

The shadow didn't move.

Wishful thinking. "Tell Frisco thanks for everything.

Funny that none of us ever laid eyes on Mason, since he was the reason we came out here in the first place."

"Ah, well," Delilah said. "We never know what the future holds."

Jerry closed the cab door. Annabelle buckled herself in, with Emmie in a car seat between her and Jerry. Glancing back up at the window, she saw that the shadow was gone. But the sun had moved, as well, and if she'd learned anything on her time at the Union Junction Ranch, it was that she'd never chase shadows again.

CHAPTER ELEVEN

FOUR HOURS AFTER Annabelle had left, Frisco's room filled with the rest of the Lonely Hearts ladies.

For his part, Frisco, unused to having women in his room, decided to pull the sheet as high over his waist as he could. There was some appreciative eyeing going on, and while he once upon a time would have eyed appreciatively back, he was feeling a bit more unfriendly than usual.

He missed Emmie in the bed beside him. That little short-term carpet-grabber had been quite a comfort, once she'd stopped griping about her stomach pains. He sure hoped those cramps didn't return.

He wasn't happy about Annabelle leaving, but women were known to be notoriously headstrong about whatever they decided to do. A mental shrug and a curse was all he was going to spare on that.

Besides, he had all these women in his room, and he wasn't sure what they wanted. It felt rather as though a jury had assembled at the foot of his bed, catching him out when he'd been scrolling the TV channels hoping for a glimpse of a better football game or Pamela Anderson to take his mind off his leg, the missing baby and the woman he'd kissed last night.

No big deal.

"What's up, ladies?"

"We're leaving," Delilah said.

"Any particular reason?" He didn't think he could handle pounding his brothers if they'd gotten out of line. On a good day, he would enjoy the exercise; today, he just wanted to lie still and debate the world's existence as it centered in his leg.

"All good things must come to an end," Delilah said with a grin. "We've got to get on to the next leg of our journey."

Talk of legs at this point only brought a wince. He tried to concentrate on being a good host. "I thought you were on vacation."

"A vacation should be a journey, if possible, while being a fun trip."

He squinted at her. "Am I getting a lecture? I should know, so I can pay attention."

She smiled at him. "You've had your mind on other things."

Oh. Possibly she was pointing out his interest in Annabelle. Could be she meant he was mainly focused on himself. He wasn't sure where she was heading with this, but he looked at her with alert, careful eyes. "Good luck on your journey. I take it you're looking for something. Maybe you'll find it."

Her gaze, and seventeen others, focused on him as he lay helpless in the bed. The sensation made his scalp crawl. They were smiling at him.

These women wanted something. And he didn't think they wanted the biggest ménage-à-plenty Texas might have ever seen. "Ah, Delilah, why are you smiling at me like you've got a secret only recently unclassified by a rogue feminist group?"

"We'd like to give you a parting gift," Delilah said. "Something to make you feel better."

"I feel fine—"

"When we get through with you, you're going to feel better."

One of the ladies closed the door.

He resisted the unmanly, unexplainable urge to shout for Tex and Laredo. These women looked way too happy about whatever they were going to do.

Four approached the bed. He clutched the sheet.

"Hold still, Frisco," Delilah practically cooed. And she pulled out the biggest pair of pointy scissors he'd ever seen. On the opposite side of the bed, the buzz of an electric razor punctuated his apprehension.

He was trapped with women whose goal was to whip him into shape.

And there was nothing he could do about it.

TWO HOURS LATER, Frisco closed his eyes in relief. They were done, finally satisfied. Every pore of his body was warm with relaxation. He'd been cut, clipped, trimmed, massaged; in short, totally tamed. Hair styled, stubble gone, nails buffed. His cast was signed in colorful pens by all eighteen women. The sheets had been changed. He'd been lifted from them by Tex and Laredo, whom Delilah called to the scene.

Tex and Laredo had left—the traitors!—laughing at him as if he were a prize poodle getting a blue-ribbon grooming.

Even his room was clean, not a speck of dust anywhere. Katy and Delilah had taken down the blue-checked drapes in his room and washed them. Lemon-oil permeated the air, mingling with the smell of clean sheets and body lotion.

"Ah-h-h" was all he could say. At this point, if they'd wanted to put beads in his hair or a tattoo on his back, he probably wouldn't argue. "Thank you. Thank you. Thank you."

"You're welcome," Delilah said. "Thank you for having us out."

"Oh, it was no trouble at all," Frisco said, feeling less like a prisoner and more like a prince. "You just come on back anytime. Anytime at all."

His eyelids closed. He couldn't help himself. Reaching up, he felt where the hair used to brush his collar. Neck shaved nicely. And his hair no longer fell into his eyes.

Those ladies certainly knew what they were doing.

A sudden itch hit his leg, and he reached down to scratch it without opening his eyes. His fingers contacted something not part of the cast. Opening his eyes, he pulled it out.

It was a business card. Pink, with purple lettering.

Lonely Hearts Beauty Salon.
Let us take care of you.

Well, he wouldn't be driving that far for a haircut every three weeks.

His eyes snapped open.

But he might for another reason.

MIMI HEARD THE SOUND of her father opening the front door. She listened, wondering who would be visiting. Probably the deputy, or some of the other officers, as they knew her father was at home today. The flooding had required his attention around the clock, and he was tired. He seemed to get tired more quickly lately, and it worried her.

He was not the young man he'd once been, and he worked darn hard.

After a few minutes, when she didn't hear the sound of men's deep voices, she went downstairs. To her surprise, all the Lonely Hearts women were talking to her father.

"Hi," she said to the room at large. "Is there something wrong?"

"We just came to say goodbye," Delilah told her. "We didn't want to leave without letting the sheriff know we were going."

"Oh." Mimi supposed that was fair enough. She couldn't say she was sad. Mason was due back soon, and if all this crew was cleared out—particularly the too-cute Annabelle and her precious bundle of joy—Mimi wouldn't mind. It would make matters less complicated, because Helga was supposed to be here tomorrow. Helga, not Olga.

Mason would be so pleased. Julia said she'd sent the perfect woman to fit Mimi's description of what Mason needed.\

Delilah, her dad and the other women looked at Mimi, obviously waiting for something. She quickly reviewed her manners. Uh-oh, lacking, once again, in her pursuit of Mason's happiness.

"All of you did so much for Union Junction," she said sincerely. "I know my father has probably said it, but the shopkeepers said many times that if you ever decided to move your beauty salon here, they'd welcome you with open arms and help you make a success of it. And in this town, that's saying a lot. They don't often offer welcome with open arms."

Particularly to a bunch of pretty women, Mimi thought.

"We were proud to assist. We've enjoyed being here. It felt like our own town," Delilah said.

"I'm sorry it didn't work out. The housekeeper's position, I mean." She tried to look sorry and might have made it, since her father's gaze was approving.

"Oh, that's all right. That's part of the interviewing process. There's no guarantee of being hired. But we had a great time with the men over there. Sorry we missed Mason, though."

"Yes, well, he won't be back for a few more days," Mimi said hurriedly. "I'll tell him all about what nice ladies his email advertisement brought to town." Although when *she* told the story, none of *them* would be man-magnets.

Storytelling license, the discretion of the teller.

"We owe the first wonderful days of our vacation to you, Mimi. In a way, if it hadn't been for you, we might still be adding up vacation days," Katy Goodnight said.

"We'd like to do something for you," Delilah added. "To thank you."

"No need. We should be thanking you," Mimi said, her manners now silver-shiny for her father's sake. "Truly."

He nodded at Delilah. Delilah turned to look at Mimi. Uh-oh, secret signals.

"Our only way of thanking anyone is to give them a makeover," Delilah continued. "And since your father mentioned you have a date tonight—with a lawyer fellow, right?—we'd like to give you the works. If you'd let us."

Mimi's jaw sagged a bit. Her father beamed.

"Uh—" she stammered.

"A few highlights, some pretty makeup, a little

sparkle on the fingers and toes...what do you say, Mimi? You're beautiful already, but we'd love to make tonight really special for you."

Glancing down at her blue jeans and boots, Mimi didn't have to reach up to feel that her hair had long since grown out of any type of style. It was cowgirl-casual. Her makeup was Maybelline-over-my-dead-body. Her perfume was eau-de-pasture, and her skin was best described as cat-tongue rough.

She didn't give a flying cow patty about the lawyer coming to see her father tonight. But Mason would be home soon—and if these ladies thought they were miracle workers, who was she to stand in the way of the great white light?

"You know, Delilah, that sounds wonderful," she said. "I'd really, really love to take you up on your oh-so-kind offer."

Wouldn't Mason be surprised?

THE MIRACLE THAT THEY wrought on her was nothing short of well, glamorous, Mimi decided. "Your shop must stay full of customers," she told them, looking at herself in awe. "You must have a waiting list a mile long. Thank you so much! I never dreamed I could look like this."

Delilah gave her a pleased once-over as she packed away a large cosmetics case, rollers and nail polishes. "We don't have as many customers as we like."

"Well, I second the invitation from our community, then. Come here and open up a shop!" She twirled her skirt in front of the cheval mirror. A skirt! Twinkly red sequins adorned the seriously short skirt, black sequins adorned the heart-shaped bodice, and a long black lace length of fabric with more sequins lay across her shoulders and hung delicately to her hands, keeping the ensemble from looking scandalous. Sexy, but not scandalous. Just right for an evening with someone her father wanted her to entertain.

"We can't come here," Katy said. "We're going to stay and fight."

"Fight?" Now there was a word Mimi had some passing acquaintance with. "What kind of fight?"

"Oh, metaphorically speaking. Never mind that," Delilah said, brushing off the question. She smiled at Mimi. "We have to go now, but have a good time."

Mimi hugged Delilah. "You're like my fairy godmother."

"I hope the mystery man is a prince, then."

"Oh. Him. Yeah, maybe he will be." Too bad Mason can't see this dress. It would knock his boots off!

Of course, there was no need for drastic measures. She didn't even know why she cared about what His Highness the Hard-Headed thought.

"Goodbye," she said, walking the ladies to the door. "Stop back by some day." Not too soon, of course, because Helga was due to come tomorrow, and she didn't want anyone's feelings hurt. "Bye!"

"Bye!" the group called back. It was like watching a camp retreat, Mimi mused, as the ladies put their suitcases on the porch and went outside.

Thirty minutes later, they loaded up into various trucks, driven by the Jefferson brothers, and headed out. For the bus station, likely.

The phone rang, and she jerked it up, still amazed by the woman staring back at her in the mirror. How did those women get her hair to curl like that? So sexy and feminine! It was almost like not looking at herself, but someone soft and gentle and desirable. "Hello?"

"Mimi, Frisco."

She frowned at his growl. "So?"

"So you remember when you said you weren't helping us out while Mason was gone?"

Her lower lip stuck out. "Yeah?"

"Well, you done a fine job of keeping your word, but now you're going to have to come over."

Not in these heels, buster. Delilah's crew had talked her into pantyhose—disgusting!—and high heels. The dress and heels were to be shipped to the Lonely Hearts Salon after tonight. She wasn't going to risk ruining this get-up just because Frisco had been careless. "I can't. Can it wait until…tomorrow?" When Cinderella will be wearing jeans and boots again and not borrowed girlie glam?

"There's a woman here—in my room, I might add—who seems to think she's applying for a job," he said tersely.

Mimi blinked. It couldn't be any of Delilah's girls—they'd all just left. Annabelle was long gone. "You shouldn't let strangers in the house, Frisco. Anyway, there's no position to apply for. I thought we settled that a few days ago."

"We did. This lady says—in very broken English—that you sent for her. Her name is Helga."

"Oh! Helga! Why didn't you say so? I'll be right there. You be nice to her, Frisco. Just because you've got a broken leg is no reason to be a sourpuss."

She hung up, gave herself one last glance in the mirror—and a fluff under her long, curly hair just for fun. She called to her dad that she was leaving and decided that this once she'd drive next door.

"WHAT TOOK YOU SO LONG?"

Mimi glared at Frisco, prone in the bed with a very

large, very old woman sitting next to him on a chair she'd moved quite close to the bed—almost as if she were afraid he might escape.

"Why are you dressed like that? You look like a showgirl," he complained.

"A showgirl?"

"Yeah, the kind that—"

"Shh! I'm sure you have wide experience in the different varieties of showgirls, Frisco. We need not hear about your downfall." She pinched the big toe of his bad leg surreptitiously and smiled at the grim-faced woman tucked right up beside Frisco's bed.

"It's *so* nice to meet you," she said with a sugary smile. "Welcome to Union Junction, Helga."

"Tank you," Helga said without smiling.

She was *perfect.* As nice as Delilah's crew had been, this was the housekeeper Mason needed.

"You're hired," she said.

"Tank you," Helga replied, her eyes gleaming as she looked down at Frisco. Mimi pinched his toe again, enjoying his smothered curse.

That would teach him to call her a showgirl.

CHAPTER TWELVE

"I'M HOME!"

A man's voice from downstairs brought a gasp from Mimi. "Mason!"

She tore downstairs, fluffing her hair one last time before bursting from the stairwell. He was looking through the mail.

"Hi, Mason," she said.

He glanced up, did a double take.

Mimi's heart soared.

"What happened to you?" he asked.

Her heart crash-landed. "What?"

He stared at her, his gaze taking in the oh-so-short skirt, the high, strappy heels and then the curls. Scratching his head, he said, "Let me guess. Costume party?"

Drawing herself up tall, she forced herself to act as if she didn't want to kick him in the shin. "Not tonight. Maybe in October, though. Mason, the housekeeper is upstairs with Frisco."

"Great." His head swivelled as he glanced around the den and kitchen, his gaze much more interested and approving than he'd been to her. "New curtains. Flowers. Mmm, and something's in the oven."

Delilah and her crew must have put something in for the guys before they left. Mimi stood statue-still as Mason looked at his feet. "And vacuumed, even." He looked up at her, his eyes full of…surprise. "You were right," he said, not bothered at all to have to make the admission. "We did need a housekeeper around here. She's awesome, Mimi."

Her heart crumbled; she wasn't about to tell him that Helga wasn't the cause of his newfound contentment. He looked too happy, and it was so great to have one of her plans go right instead of backfiring like a bad firework.

"I'm glad you…think she'll work out for you."

"Well, if she did all this, then yeah, it's going to be great!"

His enthusiasm was heartening, yet it was killing her. Why not that glow in his eyes for her?

"I've got to go," she said. "I'll see you later."

"What's the hurry? Stay and have dinner with us. It smells great."

Stay and have dinner with me and the boys, she wanted to mimic. She looked down at her sparkly nails and her gleaming red toenails. "I can't. Thanks, though, Mason. Good night."

She went to the front door, turning at the last moment. He was looking through the mail again.

"By the way, her name is Helga."

"What? Oh, okay."

He nodded, as if it mattered. But now she knew it didn't. Mason didn't care who took care of his hearth and home. She was his friend, and she always would be.

She left, her heart broken.

MASON COULD HARDLY WAIT until the front door closed behind Mimi. He'd nearly dropped his teeth when he looked up and saw her! His heart thundered and his blood felt as if it was going to pound out of his ears.

It had been totally obvious that she had a date, and he wasn't about to let on how much that bugged him. She'd never bothered to get all babed up for him, though. Whoever it was, he had to be someone she was set on impressing. He'd never seen her in high heels. Not even at the prom, damn it. She'd worn a long dress and her boots underneath.

His brow furrowed. In fact, if they hadn't swum in the swimming hole over the years, he'd never even have seen her toenails. And there she was, with some red glittery paint peeping out of shoes that looked as if they belonged on one of Laredo's dates.

He didn't want Mimi giving another man glittery toes and heart-shaped cleavage.

Damn and blast. More had changed around here than the curtains.

"Mason? Is that you?" Frisco called.

He sounded edgy. "Be right up," Mason answered.

Needing it bad, he grabbed a beer to keep him company. He'd swallowed half of it before he crested the stairwell, and it was a good thing, too, otherwise he would have spewed it.

Frisco had what looked like a busted leg—surely there was a costume party Mimi and Frisco weren't telling him about—and an elderly female warden was frisking his brother.

"What's…going on?" Mason asked weakly.

"She—Ms. Helga—wants me to change the channel. She doesn't think watching *Sex Slaves from Outer Space* is good for a man with a broken leg."

"Why not?"

"Hell if I know!" Frisco finally gave up and surrendered the remote. The channel was changed to a cooking show.

"Do something," Frisco pleaded.

"What the hell happened to you?" Mason demanded, frowning at the leg cast.

"Ch-ch," Ms. Helga said.

"Uh, sorry." Mason looked at his brother, who looked imprisoned. Maybe Ms. Helga was only efficient like this because Frisco was laid up. All the other changes he'd seen in the house so far were positive ones. If they had to tone down the swearing, that would probably be best for all of them.

"Do something," Frisco implored.

"I think…I'll go get another beer." He headed downstairs, his brain too twisted by Mimi's get-up to deal with Frisco's moaning right now. Ms. Helga was obviously very conscientious about her work. Conscientious wouldn't kill Frisco.

Besides, dinner smelled *heavenly*.

AN HOUR LATER, MASON thought he was going to heave his dinner; he was outside counting calves and a red Ferrari pulled into Mimi's driveway.

He ducked behind some big-bodied heifers to spy unashamedly. Ten minutes later, out she came in her red dress, with a big lunkhead opening the car door for her. "Dressing to match the car. I'll have to remember that," he muttered to himself.

Since he had a white truck, she'd have to wear something white to go out with him. Very white. With white shoes. And white pantyhose, he told himself in a very smart-alecky, discontented inner voice. No, make that white stockings, garter belt, and thong. Gotta have the thong. Waited a long time to have the thong.

He heard Mimi's delighted giggle float on the wind as the Ferrari roared past.

Would like the thong between my teeth, he told himself. *What am I thinking?*

This was practically his little sister he was thinking pornographic thoughts about. This was his best gal pal, his comrade-in-pranks. She could date if she wanted. It shouldn't throw him. That was it. She'd just thrown him with the new look and the Ferrari.

Then he sighed. He'd known for a long time that Mimi was restless. She was only staying in Union Junction because of her father. If her mother hadn't deserted them for the bright lights of Hollywood—an act for which Mimi despised her mother—Mimi herself would have been a disappearing act only rivaled by the great Houdini.

"Damn, damn, damn." He kicked at a fence post that had a lean to it, righted it and worked it farther into the ground.

Then he stopped, horrified.

He had no idea what she was wearing under that dress.

It could be the white thong of his fantasies.

The skirt was undeniably short. A woman wouldn't wear granny panties under something that delicate.

Or…or…

It could be not a damn thing at all.

"Mason!" his brother yelled out an upstairs window. "Mason, help!"

He saw Frisco wrestling with his jailer, back-lit by the light in the room. But he had much bigger problems than Frisco's sense of injured independence. "Shut up, Frisco! Do you want the whole damn countryside to hear you?"

"Yes!"

The window closed with a crack. Mason shook his head and went inside the house.

Surely Mimi wouldn't fall for a man who drove a wimpy car like the one she'd gone off in. "City dude," he muttered. "Mimi'll never fall for that scarecrow-dressing."

And if she did—which she wouldn't—he'd be the first one to throw rice at her wedding.

Wedding dresses were white. *That would match my truck,* he thought, mulling over the startling complexity of his undiscovered feelings for Mimi.

But knowing Mimi, she'd probably wear black just to be different—or annoying, depending on how one saw it—so he could sit in the front row and smile at the sad sack who eventually got duped into marrying her.

FRISCO WAS READY TO KILL Mimi Cannady. Helga had made him her special project, and though she meant well, he was sleep-deprived and hallucinating. He didn't trust the woman. No, that was too strong a word. He wasn't comfortable with the woman manning his room. Oh, occasionally she left to clean or cook or do whatever. And Mason seemed as happy as Mason could seem. Tex and Laredo said they preferred to stay out of it and remained unmoved by his complaints.

But he missed Emmie, and all the spoiling he'd got from Annabelle. Now that was how a man should re-cover. Little Emmie relaxed him, and Annabelle had made him believe there was life with a broken leg.

Helga made him wish for the kind of conscience that would allow him to slip his pain medication into her water glass. She could sleep peacefully until his leg healed—and he could tell Mason that Mimi had hired a cadaver for a housekeeper.

It was all Mimi's fault. They didn't need a damn housekeeper.

He said as much to Mason when he came up to visit the next day. Helga was off getting him some lunch, so Frisco took the opportunity to make his case.

"There's plenty of changes around here, all for the better, I might add. No one would call this Malfunction Junction anymore," Mason said with pleasure.

Yeah, they could. It was. Likely it always would be. "Mason, I think Mimi pulled a fast one on you," Frisco began.

"Like what?"

"Like…this Helga."

"Favorably recommended by Mimi's friend, Julia Finehurst from the Honey-Do Agency."

"Yeah, well, remember the ad you posted on the internet? It said over forty or something like that, right? Not forty times two?"

"Are you discriminating against the elderly?" Mason asked with surprise.

Mason's shame-on-you tone grated on Frisco. "No. But, okay, what about the 'must not be offended by swearing' part? Every time one of us drops a minorly offensive word, even something so simple as *bird crap,* we get 'Ch-ch.'"

"It's just as well to say *bird doo* when Helga's around."

If Frisco's leg wasn't broken, he'd have slapped his elder brother with the sense he was badly lacking. "And the part about not minding big animals? She saw that bull get loose to try to jump up on the new red cow and nearly lost her dentures."

"She thought that he was going to hurt the female.

She was just trying to point out something she thought was going wrong. Wouldn't you want to know if something bad was happening? Frankly, I find a pair of sharp eyes around here comforting. Besides, who's going to look after you? We can't lose a man to babysit you."

"I was in *better* hands," Frisco said, surly-toned.

"What?"

Frisco shook his head, unwilling to bring up Annabelle and Emmie.

"You know, Frisco, it's past time you and I cleared the air between us." Mason put a boot up on the foot of the bed, leaning forward. "You've been at me like a bad-tempered jackass for months. It's worse than ever since I got back. What's eating you?"

"I can't imagine."

"I can't, either. But I'm about tired of putting up with it."

"So shoot me and put me out of my misery."

"Don't think I wouldn't if I had a tranquilizing gun. The next time I'm at the vet, I may borrow one. I'll tell him we've got a big ornery jackass that won't simmer down."

"You wouldn't."

Mason cocked a brow at him. "Get off of Helga's back. She's done a lot around here."

Then he left the room.

"Oh, brother."

Frisco had two options open to him.

He could become a babbling idiot from sleep deprivation and hallucinations.

Or he could lock Ms. Helga into his bathroom and call a taxi. He could get the hell out of Dodge City and go somewhere where he could curse when he wanted to, watch *Suntanned Girls from Borneo* when he felt like it and eat all the candy he wanted.

Mostly, he could sleep.

He pulled the card from his cast that Delilah had left him. Lonely Hearts Salon.

Somehow, he had to arrange a jailbreak.

Flipping the card over, he saw a penciled phone number, and a name: Jerry Wallace, Independent Truck Driver.

Jerry must have meant to give Delilah his phone number, and she'd accidentally put this card inside Frisco's cast.

"Hallelujah!" Frisco yelled. Jerry was the only person Frisco knew who was big enough to help him down the stairs. Plus, he had his own transportation.

And Jerry would understand that Helga, nice as she might be in one of her previous decades, was no Annabelle. A man could die without the basics of life: Air. Food. Beer.

A beautiful woman.

A pretty baby that slept beside him.

Of course, Annabelle might not have him. She was at a crazy point in her life.

It didn't matter. All he wanted was her bed—and that wasn't too much to ask considering he'd shared his with her.

He dialed the phone.

"Jerry Wallace, independent trucker."

"I need an independent trucker like nobody has ever needed you before. Jerry, it's Frisco Jefferson, and if you come bust me outta here, I'll pay your next month of fuel for that damn rig of yours. It'd have to be a reconnaissance mission of sorts…."

CHAPTER THIRTEEN

DEEP BREATH, Annabelle told herself. She hugged Emmie to her a little tighter. The baby was dressed in her prettiest outfit, and she smelled like the sweetest baby soap. If Emmie couldn't charm the socks off a man, they simply couldn't be removed by any means.

Of course, this was Tom. A father wouldn't have to be charmed, would he? It would be a spontaneous, natural bond between father and child?

In Tom's case, maybe not. All he'd been interested in was Dina.

Before Annabelle could muster her courage to step across the street, the door to the Lonely Hearts Salon opened. Her mouth fell open as Tom strolled in, all golden-haired and brightly smiling as always.

"Tom," she said, going weak in the knees from surprise.

"Hello, Annabelle." He approached the carrier slowly, then said, with more determination than she'd ever seen in him, "Is this my daughter?"

"This is Emmie." Unless he didn't know the difference between a hand puppet and a baby, he knew this was his daughter.

"She doesn't have any hair."

It was probably not best to point out that his was thinning on top, and he was only the south side of forty.

Possibly Dina was a bit too vigilant with the scissors. "It will grow one day, Tom."

He looked closer, checking Emmie out. Possibly for defects he couldn't possibly have chromosomed?

Done with his fatherly—or not, as the case certainly had been—perusal, he glanced up at Annabelle. "You're looking well."

She didn't say anything because there was no need. A man who dumped the mother of his child for another woman wasn't interested in what she looked like, before or after. And she certainly wasn't returning the compliment, if that's what he was fishing for.

"I think we should get married," Tom said. "For Emmie's sake."

At that moment, Emmie returned to true form. She let out a bloodcurdling cry that had Tom reeling a good two feet away.

That's one nay vote. "Uh, Tom, could you hand me that diaper bag, please? I need to get her a bottle."

He did, quickly, though he didn't reach in to get the bottle or reach to hold his wailing infant. Frisco would have already had the situation under control, she thought, but that was a useless memory.

A few seconds later, she had Emmie situated with the bottle in her mouth and a pretty bib under her chin. Normally, a burp diaper would have sufficed, but this was her first visit with her father.

"Glad that's over," Tom said. "She's loud, isn't she?"

"She's healthy."

"If she'd been a boy, would she have been as loud?"

Annabelle ground her teeth. "All babies cry," she told him. "When they're hungry, wet or cold."

"So she does that often?"

"Yes, she most certainly does," she affirmed, just so he could have a chance to change his mind about his ridiculous proposal. What had she ever seen in him?

"Back to what I was saying about getting—"

"How's Dina?" she interrupted.

His gaze slid away, a crawling-under-a-rock impression. "We're not seeing each other anymore."

"Really?" She raised her brows. "May I ask why?"

"She just wasn't my type." He glanced down at the baby uncertainly, as she sucked on the bottle.

"It took you eleven months to figure that out? Quick study, huh?"

"I really don't like sarcasm in my women," Tom told her.

Annabelle held back a snort. "I'm not one of your women, Tom."

"No, but you were. Before you got all clingy and marriage-hungry."

She blinked, wondering if she dared bean him with Emmie's bottle. Now that would be sarcasm, or maybe black-humored justice, but then Emmie would be upset and there was no reason to make her cry just because Tom was a louse. "Clingy and marriage-hungry. Well, now that is a reason to dump a woman you've made a baby with. Very valid."

She nodded at him as if he made perfect sense, which he didn't, but he seemed to think he did, and she was still in an incredulous humor-him moment. The mood probably only had a few more seconds before it hit expiration.

He narrowed his eyes. "About getting married, which I think is the right thing to do, considering—"

The door swung open, and the rest of his pompous diatribe was lost. To her amazement—and quite possibly delight, she acknowledged—Frisco limped in, with Jerry's arm supporting him heavily.

The cavalry had arrived. Saved by the bell. And any other cliché she could throw.

She had never been so glad to see a man in all her life. And he looked really *good,* clean-shaven and not shaggy anymore and just overwhelmingly manly in general.

"Frisco!"

"Hey, Annabelle. Don't get up. Emmie needs her bottle. Thanks, Jerry." Obviously worn out and in pain, he propped himself against a rinse bowl. "Nice place."

"What are you doing here?"

"I was going a little stir-crazy. Decided to do some traveling. Jerry was coming this way, and I decided to hang a right with him."

"I'm so glad." She smiled at him.

Tom harrumphed.

"Oh, this is Tom. Tom, this is Frisco Joe Jefferson and Jerry Wallace."

The men didn't shake hands. The explosive glares in the room could have sent shrapnel thirty feet.

"I'll feed Emmie," Frisco said. "Come here, little angel," he crooned, taking the baby into his arms.

Annabelle's heart blossomed.

"Who is this, Annabelle?" Tom asked.

"My fiancé," she lied gracefully, with a mental apology to Frisco. But he'd heard about Tom. He wouldn't mind the little fib. She hoped. Frisco puffed up his chest, not looking exhausted anymore, and Annabelle decided he hadn't minded the lie at all.

Tom started laughing. "I don't think so. You can't make me jealous, Annabelle. You'd never fall in love with a broken-down rodeo has-been. Frisco Joe, indeed.

Sounds like an old-time bank robber, and you're far too blue-blood for that."

"Blue-blood?" She turned to stare at him.

He shook his head. "Never mind. Listen, buddy— Frisco Joe—I was just in the middle of proposing to Annabelle. And as that is my daughter, I'd say you're butting in at the wrong time."

"Proposing?" Frisco cocked a brow in that smart-ass manner Annabelle fully recognized. "Where's the candles? The flowers?" He gave Tom a thorough once-over that seemed to shout, What have you done to make her consider a loser like you? "Why aren't you down on one knee?"

"Because I'd get my pants dirty, which isn't sensible at all. And Annabelle's a very sensible girl. If you knew her better, you'd understand that." He looked back at Annabelle, gloating. "Aren't you a sensible girl?"

"Well, hell," Frisco said. "I really didn't want to have to do this, but seeing as how you're making a mess of the whole thing, I'm just going to have to go against my good breeding and cut in line." He handed Emmie to Jerry. The baby made the transition easily, and the truck driver beamed.

Painfully, slowly, Frisco bent his bad leg to the side, gingerly making his way down on one awkward knee. He put his hand over his heart. "Annabelle, belle Anna, you would make me the happiest man on the earth if you'd take me up to your bedroom."

She held back a giggle. Tom's jaw dropped so fast it had rocket propulsion, and Jerry turned his whole body in order to keep from snickering. But she could see his shoulders shaking.

"Come on, Frisco," she said gently. "You need to rest. My bed is perfect for resting."

"Oh, yes, I'm totally exhausted. Just plumb worn out. Completely on my last legs and with one of them in pieces, that's not saying too much," he said dramatically. "See you around, Tom. Thanks, Jerry."

Jerry tipped his cap, a big grin on his face. Annabelle said, "I'll take good care of him, Jerry." Then she helped Frisco from the floor up the stairs, one slow step at a time.

"Thanks for not ratting me out about the fiancé thing," she whispered to him.

"Thanks for not ratting me out about the bedroom thing. I figured I was riding on slim rails with that one."

Annabelle shook her head and tucked her body more firmly under his shoulder. Because he was so tall, she wasn't as much support as she wanted to be. He was gripping the wooden rail tightly as he basically pulled himself up the staircase. "You were perfect. Talk about arriving just in the nick of time."

"I hate for you to leave Emmie in the same room with him." Frisco tried to glance down the stairs but it was too much to twist and stay upright. "I don't think she likes him."

"How could you tell?"

"I don't know. It just seems like she hesitated when you left the room, almost as if she were saying, 'Oh, well, I gotta do what I gotta do, I guess. But I've got Uncle Jerry to protect me at least.' Didn't you notice?"

"Ah, no."

Turning into her room, she helped Frisco to the side of the bed, where he promptly collapsed into it with all his considerable weight and length.

The springs of the bed screamed in protest, and

Frisco managed to bounce himself up and down on his back just enough to keep the springs screaming.

"Sounds like we're *really* glad to see each other, doesn't it?" he asked above the squeaking.

Rolling her eyes, she said, "I'm going to get Emmie, so you'd better stop."

He slowed down. "I need another five minutes to be convincing. At least."

"Five…minutes?" She blinked at him.

"You know." He stopped bouncing altogether and stared at her. "To make it sound like real lovemaking."

"Oh-h-h. Real lovemaking." She nodded as if that made perfect sense.

His gaze narrowed. "Annabelle—"

Emmie's wail hit a high note. "Oh, my goodness!" Annabelle tore down the stairs. "Let me have her," she said to Tom, who was now holding the baby.

"I didn't do anything!" Tom protested.

Jerry shrugged. "He said anyone could feed a baby and he wanted to give it a go. I thought surely he couldn't mess that up. Unless he pinched her—"

"I did no such thing! She just started crying for no reason!" He glared at the baby as if she'd done it on purpose.

"It's all right. Tom, listen. It's been…interesting, but you'll have to excuse me. I'm real busy right now."

"Okay. I guess. But we need to talk later, Annabelle. That *is* my daughter."

The glance he gave the shrieking baby illustrated his feelings for his daughter. Annabelle guessed those feelings were better expressed, *That is my hemorrhoid.*

"Jerry, can I do anything for you?"

"No. I've got some local runs to make between here

and the panhandle. I'll stop back in and check on you two. Call me when you're ready to get rid of Romeo Joe."

"I thought his name was Frisco Joe," Tom said.

"Not tonight," Jerry told him kindly. "After you, son," he said.

Annabelle sighed, swiftly locking the door. She hurried back up the stairs and walked in the room. Frisco instantly put out his arms. "Bring her here," he commanded. "Plainly this is a woman who knows what's good for her, and she's missed me something fierce!"

"NOW THEN, YOU JUST fall asleep for your Uncle Frisco," he said sweetly. "Watch how I do this," he told Annabelle. "It's like a massage, only at a real reduced level. See how she's putty in my hands?"

He put the baby next to him, tucked up against his body. Then he proceeded to touch her neck with two fingers, slowly, down her shoulderblades. Each arm received a delicate caress. He was careful not to press too hard, because women didn't like that. Slowly, gently, soothing. Emmie'd had a hard day—as far as he was concerned he'd gotten here in the nick of time—and nothing felt better to a woman than a foot massage.

But not yet. She had to have the full treatment, because that twerp of a father-come-lately had gotten her all worked up.

After he finished with Emmie, he was going to work Annabelle out of the lather the twerp had put her in, too.

Definitely a foot massage for Annabelle.

"There you go," he whispered to Emmie. "You just let it all go. Breathe in the butterflies. Blow out the bees.

I learned that from *Saturday Night Live,* which we may watch together if you're of a mind to stay awake." He kept his voice soft and hypnotic. "Now I'm going to massage these hammy little thighs of yours," he told her, "and you're going to let go of the stress. That's right."

The baby was just about prone now. Her thumb had gone into her mouth, her eyes were barely open. Now for the final phase of the seduction. The feet.

"Trick or treat, I've got your feet, now you go to sleep, good and sweet," he murmured, rubbing her heel. It felt like a little ball between his fingers. Then he moved toward her arch, working it lightly, his fingers finally underneath her toes where he rolled them like early peas between his thumb and forefinger. "Good night, sweetheart," he told her, laying his head down next to hers.

And before he realized it, he'd fallen asleep, too.

ANNABELLE SMILED AT THE big man slumbering next to her child. He'd put both of them to sleep, and nearly her, too, with his mesmerizing voice. Her skin had prickled from imagining Frisco's fingers soothing her the way he was doing Emmie.

The man simply knew his way around her child. Probably women in general, the rat. And he was proud of that fact.

As much as she wanted to join them for a quick nap, she couldn't. She had a proposal to answer, which, caught off guard, she hadn't been able to think about. There was no time like the present to talk to Tom, while her baby was safe with Frisco. She'd leave him a note, even though she didn't plan on being gone long.

And anyway, she didn't figure she had far to go to

find Tom. He'd looked awfully slimy about his Dina-wasn't-my-type story.

She shouldn't have any further to look for him than across the street.

CHAPTER FOURTEEN

"HEY, MIMI," said Laredo when she blew through the front door. His non-welcoming tone caught her attention and she halted, counting ten of the Jefferson males sitting in the den watching TV.

Well, now they were watching her.

All ten appeared displeased. "Where's Mason?" she asked, not sure what gave them such disgruntled faces. Maybe Mason was out of town again.

"He's not here right now. Checking some equipment in the barn. But we've darn sure got a bone to pick with you," Tex said.

"What?"

He pointed to the ceiling. "The housekeeper from hell."

"That's not nice, Tex." Mimi frowned at him. "Mason says she's doing great."

"Because Mason got here after the Lonely Hearts women were here, and he thinks Broomhilda—"

"Helga."

"Precisely. H-e-double-l-g-a." He stared at her to make certain she understood his meaning. Hell-ga. "He thinks Helga is the reason the houses look so nice."

"Isn't it?" She glanced around the room. "It certainly seems tidier in here."

"We don't want it tidy," Fannin told her ominously. "We like living in some fashion of disarray. The remote belongs beside the easy chair. It's always been that way." He gestured to the table where they liked to sit and play cards or dominoes. The table held a pretty, bright finish, instead of dull fingerprints.

"What's wrong with it?"

"We're not allowed to touch it," Ranger said. "How the hell can we play cards if we can't touch the table?"

"It's your table. Do as you like."

"If we do, she'll dust around our elbows while we play. It's quiet warfare between us," Last said. "And I pride myself on being easygoing, but if I have to eat cabbage and sausage one more breakfast, I'm going to have a permanently puckered face."

"Tell Helga what you want to eat," Mimi said reasonably.

"She got upset and went to Mason, telling him we didn't like her cooking. Since he's enamored of the cabbage stuff, he told her that whatever she fixed, we'd eat." Archer was outraged.

Crockett shot her a dirty look. "Of all the tricks you've played on us over the years, Mimi, this one stinks at the lowest level."

"It wasn't a trick! I was trying to be helpful!" She couldn't figure out what they were complaining about, anyway. Didn't they want to have a clean house and hot food?

"It's either me or her," Bandera said.

"You don't even live here, Bandera."

"Yeah, but we eat here and crash here after work to relax. We can't relax like this," Calhoun said. "I've never felt so jumpy in my life. It's like having fleas in my boots."

Navarro shook his head. "Mimi, you've brought good men to their knees."

"Oh, brother. What a bunch of whiners! If you don't like her, have a family council and tell Mason what you've told me. It's ten against one—where's Frisco?"

"It's eleven against one, but Frisco left without casting a vote. He couldn't handle being jailed by Helga the Horrible. She watched him like a hawk, in her version of nursing. But he felt like he was living in a psycho movie, where any minute he was going to open his eyes and find a gray-haired drag queen standing over him, preparing to take a butcher knife to some parts of himself he prizes," Laredo said. "Not that Helga's mean or anything, but she watched him pretty good and it made him crazy, and he got sleep-deprived so that he was starting to hallucinate a bit. Frisco fighting off dream spiders in the night is not much fun to listen to."

"Poor Frisco! Where did he go?"

Tex shrugged. "No one knows. He had Jerry come get him when we were all busy. He left a note saying he was going on a long vacation where he could sleep like a baby. Said if he could just get forty-eight hours of undisturbed sleep, he'd be ready to rock."

She reminded herself that these were grown, if not one-hundred-percent mature, men. They could handle themselves—and Helga—if put to the task. "Listen, I didn't come over here to listen to y'all bellyache, though I'm sorry you're not happy, but it sounds like your beef is with Mason, since he likes Helga."

They murmured darkly at that.

"I just wanted for all of you to be the first to know." She took a deep breath. "I'm engaged to be married."

AT NEARLY THE SAME TIME Mimi made her announcement, Annabelle was making one of her own. "I'd like to speak with Tom, please," she said to the receptionist of the Never Lonely Cut-n-Gurls Salon.

It was true what she'd heard. The chairs *were* red, the lights *were* dim. The infamous slogan *was* on the wall in gold letters. Every mirror had a lavish sign with a woman's name painted on it: Dina, Lola, Sapphire, Ruby, Silk, Emerald, Marvella, Satin and Valentine. Every chair had fresh-cut flowers beside it; the towels were purple. Fragrant candles burned here and there. In the back of the salon, a raised spa bubbled away, big enough for ten people to fit into.

It was all Annabelle could do not to gasp. And no telling what secret pleasure grottos awaited upstairs. No wonder the men brought their business to the salon!

"Tom's not here," said the receptionist, who happened to be Valentine, according to her tight red T-shirt lettered with the name.

"His car is around back," Annabelle said, expecting the excuse. "And either I see him now, or I call the police and let them know you've a lice infestation of biblical proportions. The police and health department will be out on the double, and they may not find lice but from the looks of things, they'll find something else to cite you for."

Valentine snatched up the phone, staring at Annabelle rebelliously. "You're just jealous because Tom left you. And we're putting your salon out of business."

"We don't conduct your kind of business. And as for Tom, I've got a cowboy asleep on my bed, waiting for me, who makes Tom look like the Pillsbury Doughboy with an itty-bitty jelly roll, if you get my drift." She snapped her fingers. "Either you make a call, or I do. Your choice."

Valentine punched the button. "Tom's got a visitor," she said into the phone. "No, I don't think *she'll* wait."

She hung up, her eyes snapping sparks at Annabelle. Examining her long fingernails, she said nonchalantly, "How's the baby?" in the tone of someone who thought babies were living hell.

"Going to grow up to be a lady," Annabelle shot back. "You'll have to look that word up in a dictionary. Tom, thanks for sparing me a moment of your time," she said, as he came down the stairs, his light hair awry and his trousers unzipped, though buttoned.

Dina followed behind him a second later, bearing a furious expression and no lipstick, since Tom had it on his fly. *Note to self—red lipstick shows big-time on khakis.*

Thank heavens Frisco preferred blue jeans, one-legged as they were right now due to his cast. Red wouldn't be quite as startling on denim—although as Tom had said, she was a sensible girl. She knew where to leave her lipstick, and it wouldn't be on the fabric.

"What happened to you not wanting to get your trousers dirty proposing?"

"Huh?" he asked, clearly hoping to play dumb.

Well, that wasn't too hard for him. "I've thought over your marriage proposal," she said to Tom, "and I—"

"Marriage proposal?" Dina demanded.

Tom's guilty expression gave away the wrong answer. Dina slapped the guilt and maybe two layers of skin clean off his face. "You slimy turd!" she screamed.

"Oh, that was painful," Annabelle said sympathetically, silently applauding Dina. Now Tom's cheek matched his crotch, and it was all good in her book. "I can't accept the proposal, of course. But my lawyer will be contacting you to arrange the paperwork for visitation, should you want it, and, of course, for child support payments."

"Child support payments!" he howled. "You've got a lot more money than I have, Annabelle. Millions! I'm going to sue you for...palimony or something! I have rights in this, too."

"How do you know about my financial situation?" She hadn't expected him to want to pay—that had been a bonus jab for fun—but she was curious as to why he thought he deserved palimony. Ridiculous, since no court would consider such a stupid claim, but all the same, she wanted to know.

"You're Annabelle Turnberry of Turnberry Wines, and you just came into your father's entire fortune and estates." He shook his finger at her. "I don't have to pay you a dime."

"You're not paying me," she said quietly. "You're living up to your responsibility by seeing to your daughter's future. If you choose not to do that, I'm certain that my lawyer could work out a deal with you. No child support, no visitation."

He glared at her. "I don't want to see her anyway."

For Emmie's sake, her heart broke, but she'd expected no less. She'd been prepared. The truth was, she'd fallen for Tom when she was in pain from her father's death. She'd thought he was someone he wasn't, but her innocence was spent. She wouldn't make that mistake again.

Emmie had her, and that was enough.

"I'm sorry to hear that, Tom. I'll have my lawyers send you the paperwork—to this address, I guess?"

"Hell, no!" Dina shrieked. "You get out of here, you two-timing, lying, bellycrawling shyster! And you'd better pay me the thousand dollars you borrowed, or...

or—" She glanced at Annabelle for inspiration. "Or you'll be hearing from *my* lawyer!"

He stared at both of them, his mouth gaping open.

"Tom, your fly is open," Annabelle said.

MASON SHOOK HIS HEAD like a big bear, trying to clear it from what Laredo had just said. "Mimi's engaged? Who would marry her? I didn't even know she was dating anyone."

He was babbling. He certainly didn't want to hear any more than he just had. "Maybe you heard wrong."

"No, she came over to tell us first, she said. And she was wearing a huge rock, though none of us recovered fast enough to ask who'd given it to her."

"Maybe it's a fake," Mason said.

Laredo shrugged. "I doubt it. It sure was catching the light. Anyway, why would she fake having an engagement ring?"

"Fake engagement," Mason clarified, the last hope available to him sounding odd even to his ears. "Don't think she would. She seemed very serious. Like I've never seen her this serious."

Mimi had clearly been swept off her feet by the Ferrari city dude. "Well," he said slowly, "I wish her all the best. Guess I'll get to meet him sooner or later."

"Probably not until the wedding. And after that, she's moving to Houston with him. At least that's what Sheriff Cannady said."

"Houston!" Mason thought that sounded highly unlikely. "Mimi doesn't belong in Houston."

"Well, she's been here all her life. I think she's probably ready to move on. Raise her own family and all. She'll be a good mom, although I have a hard time seeing her driving a van in car pools and dragging snacks to soccer games. Sitting on the sidelines with the cheerleaders and doing booster club stuff. Actually, I don't have a problem seeing that at all," Laredo said thoughtfully. "Mimi will do awesome. She's got all that energy she's never known what to do with."

"Mimi...raise a family?" Mason's heart slid somewhere below his boots, right into the very ground he stood on. He couldn't imagine her pregnant, had never thought of her in that manner. "What for? I mean, why would she do that?"

Laredo smirked at him. "Because everybody who doesn't live at the Malfunction Junction usually wants one, bro."

"I suppose." He didn't. He'd thought she felt the same way. For some reason, he felt a bit betrayed. "I never knew she wanted children."

"Don't worry about it." Laredo slapped him on the back. "You'll make a great uncle."

DELILAH HUNG UP HER cell phone with a smile. "Jerry said he dropped Frisco Joe off in town to visit Annabelle," she told her staff. She was happy about that, because she had a funny feeling those two had something to talk about and maybe a little more, but she had something sad to tell the rest of her girls: Beatrice, Carly, Daisy, Dixie, Gretchen, Hannah, Jessica, Julie, Katy, Kiki, Lily, Marnie, Remy, Shasta, Tisha, Velvet and Violet.

She was going to miss them.

"There's something I have to tell you all. This week has been a vacation of sorts, or at least that's what I told you. Actually, it was my last chance to be part of a big family. I'm going to have to cut back, girls," she said softly. "I'm sorry, because you are all like daughters to me. Unfortunately, I'm not making what I was at the salon, and now I'm barely covering the rent."

The women sitting and drinking coffee with her in the highway-side coffee shop stared at her with trepidation.

"Cut back?" Katy Goodnight asked. "How much?"

"I'm going to have to reduce my staff by fifty percent."

A gasp of dismay met that announcement.

"I couldn't feel worse about this. But since my sister opened her salon across the street, my life has changed in many ways, and I don't think I have to tell you that."

Kiki nodded. "We understand, Delilah. You took most of us in when we had no place else to go, and we've been grateful for that. When will you tell us who has to go?"

"I'd as soon know now," Shasta said.

Delilah nodded. "Fair enough. Was anyone planning on turning in their notice to me any time soon?"

No one spoke up. She hadn't expected them to. They'd been a family for a while. Most of these women had no place else to go. Or they chose not to. Sighing, she tore paper strips off the place mat. "I've thought about this every which-a-way. I could go on a seniority basis. I could go on a most-earned basis. None of these ways strikes me as particularly fair, because I love all of you, and that's not a business emotion. They say not to mix business and pleasure, but you girls have been my pleasure, and without you, I wouldn't have had a business. So. I'm going to draw names."

Her heart bleeding, she wrote each name on a paper. Every stroke of the pen made her hand shake more. She didn't think she'd be able to write the last name; the pen felt as heavy as an executioner's blade. "I'm so sorry," she whispered.

"It's all right," Kiki said. "We know you did your best, Delilah. We all did."

Delilah nodded, taking a deep gulping breath. She put the papers all together in a pile she'd rather have burned than use for its intended purpose and covered it with her hands, prayer-like, with her eyes closed. "Ready?"

"As we'll ever be," Shasta said.

"All right." Behind closed eyes, she held back tears. Her business, these women, were all she'd ever had in her life that gave her pleasure. These were her sisters the way Marvella never would be; these were the daughters she would never have; these were the friends who shared her happiness and tears.

These girls were pieces of her soul.

"Annabelle," she said, reading the first piece of paper she pulled from underneath her other hand. The other girls gasped and some began to sob. Annabelle had a baby and a broken heart. It would kill her to tell her she had to go.

"Beatrice, Gretchen, Jessica, Lily, Marnie, Tisha, Velvet, Violet," she read, pulling names as fast as she could to get it over with before she broke down and cried.

"Carly, Daisy, Dixie, Hannah, Julie, Katy, Kiki, Remy, and Shasta remain employed at the Lonely Hearts Salon. Now, if anything should change, anything at all, I—I—" She couldn't hold back any longer. Putting her head down on the Formica table in the roadside restaurant, she cried as she'd never cried in her whole life.

Except maybe when Marvella had accused Delilah

of stealing her husband. That had been the knife driven into her heart.

The wound had never healed, and today, it started bleeding all over again.

CHAPTER FIFTEEN

IT WAS NEAR EVENING when Frisco awakened—evening of the next night. "I think the winter weather is making you and Emmie hibernate," she told him.

"Have you been in this bed?" he demanded.

"Yes, and Emmie's been up for feeding and playtime. You never moved."

"Jeez. I'm so sorry." He sat up, running his hand through his hair so that it stood straight up.

"I think you were very tired," she said with a smile.

"I was more tired than I've ever been in my life. Did I tell you about Helga, the hellish housekeeper Mimi hired?"

She shook her head, jealous already, especially if she was the cause of Frisco not getting any sleep. Although *hellish* didn't sound like he was that crazy about her.

"She nearly drove me out of my skull. Imagine having someone staring at you 24/7, waiting for you to move, trying to give you pills, cleaning your room—you'd think a seventy-year-old woman would want to sit down occasionally, wouldn't you?"

"Seventy." Annabelle nodded as if she'd automatically known that, but warmed to the core that Mimi hadn't hired some sweet young thing. "Maybe she's overcompensating. She could really need the job."

"I don't know. I just knew I had to get out of there

or I was going to jump out my window. Hope you don't mind me running to you. But this was the only place I knew where there'd be some serious sleeping going on. Emmie sure does like her snooze time. And so does her Uncle Frisco," he said, looking down at the baby who was too asleep to care about Uncle Frisco at the moment.

"Jumping out your window would be bad with your busted leg," Annabelle reminded him.

"Don't I know it. Jerry is a man of principle, honor, duty and integrity, you know it. And any other complimentary word you can think of."

"That about covered it," she said. "Can I get you something to eat?"

"My treat. What's in this town?"

"Whatever you want. Prepared questionably."

"What's the local specialty? That can be delivered? No cabbage, though."

She shook her head. "I hate cabbage."

"Wait a minute. I want to see what's across the street." He staggered to his feet, hopping over to the window. Staring out at the Never Lonely Cut-n-Gurls Salon, he whistled. "Bet I know what they cook over there. Look at those T-shirts walking in, would you?"

She went behind him and snapped the blinds down. "T-shirts are cheap."

"Uh, yes. Yes, you're right about that. A dime a dozen." He gave her the most mischievous grin she'd ever seen on a man. "I just wanted you close to me, Annabelle. Gotcha." He reached out and snaked an arm around her before she could protest, pulling her tight against him. "Now, that's worth a two-hour drive and an Italian dinner, complete with candles. What do you think?"

"That I love spaghetti," she said, loving the feel of him holding her in their first real embrace. "It might be akin to sauerkraut in visual effects, though."

"No. Trust me, they are not even distant cousins. I missed your cooking, Annabelle."

"You did not. I'm not a good cook."

"But you tried hard. That matters." He looked at her, his eyes gleaming in the moonlight streaming in from behind the blinds. "In fact, I'm beginning to think just about everything about you matters."

She held her breath, surprised. So he kissed her, and she didn't move anything except her lips, until her body took over her fears and she slid her arms around his neck, pulling him close the way he'd done her.

This time, there was nothing about their kiss that was friendly. It was hot and hungry and passionate.

"This is just friends," she gasped. "Right?"

He propped her against him so that he bore her weight as he leaned against the wall, and she leaned into him, willing to move with him.

"What else would it be?" he asked between searching kisses.

"Nothing that I can think of." Her hands moved across his chest, back over his shoulders to slide under his Western shirt. "Except maybe best friends. You shouldn't sleep in all your clothes."

"The very best of best friends. I had to sleep in all my clothes. We're alone together in this big salon. You might get wild ideas about my cowboy body."

He nipped at her earlobe, and she tilted back her head, sighing. "I never had wild ideas before. I think I like it."

A groan escaped him as her hands wandered. "I saw you going into the competition's den over there."

She leaned her head again to look at him. "You couldn't have. You were asleep."

"I have acute hearing. The sound of unfamiliar doors opening and closing had me peg-legging to the window."

She smiled at him, pulling his face down so that she could nuzzle his chin. "I'm sorry. If I'd known that, I would have told you."

"Not that it really matters, because we're just best friends, but—"

"The change in Tom was due to discovering that I had money of my own."

"I should whip his hide."

She shook her head and ran her hands around his waist. "Dina already did."

"Dina? Good woman."

"Probably not, but it was okay by me if she did the dirty work. So, you already knew who my family was?"

"A little birdie told me. But that's not why I'm here."

She laughed low and husky, moving her hands from his waist down inside the back of his jeans. "I didn't think so."

"I just think we should get that straight. I'd rather cut off one of my appendages than be a kept man, and even if we didn't need to get that drastic, I'm not hurting financially."

"I know." She kissed his chin. "You wanted to shack up with me so you could sleep."

"Yes, but I'm wide-eyed and bushy-tailed now."

She slid her hands from the back of his jeans to the front. "Something like that."

"Annabelle, honey, you're heaping flames onto an already raging fire."

Her gaze went to his eyes. "I want to be so sophisticated about this, Frisco, but it's just not in me."

"I know." He kissed her forehead.

"Um, remember what you said about needing five minutes of squeaking my springs to give Tom the impression that we were making love properly?"

"Yes." His eyes were patient, waiting.

"And you know what I told you about the sign painted on the wall across the street that said Save A Horse; Ride A Cowboy?"

"Yes, babe."

"Cowboys try to stay on for eight seconds, right?"

"Mmm. If they want to win."

"My experience at the rodeo ended before the bell. Or the buzzer, or the gong, or whatever it is that—"

"Annabelle." He pulled back to look into her eyes. "Honey, you're not saying what I think you're saying, are you?"

"It was my first and only time," she said miserably.

"Whew." He glanced from her to Emmie. "You must be one fertile lady. Holy Christmas, and we've got three sets of twins amongst my siblings alone. You could be the gift that keeps on giving."

She tried to smile.

"So...no sweethearts before Him-Who-Had-No-Staying-Power?"

"No. My father had Alzheimer's for ten years. I was his sole caretaker because I wanted it that way. I don't regret it for a minute. But it left me without a social life, the usual flings and break-ups and drama that are part of normal learning. And then, when my father passed away, I was shattered," she said quietly. "I think I just wanted someone to care for me for a change. You can see why I don't want any more children. At least not right now."

He hugged her to him, close and sheltering. "I completely understand. I don't want any except Emmie. I mean, you know what I mean. Best friends and all that. Uncle Frisco."

Her blush felt like it was all over her body. "I was afraid you'd be disappointed."

"Because you don't want more children?" At her nod, he said, "Annabelle, you can't even begin to know how relieved I am. Count the brothers around my house and tell me we need more bodies to fall over."

She lowered her gaze. "And you're not disappointed about…the other?"

"The other what?"

"My lack of experience in pleasing a man?"

He laughed out loud. "Annabelle, you please *this* man. As far as I can see, I'm getting the best of all worlds here. I get a sexy lady, a best friend and a virgin all wrapped up in one, plus a sweet baby to hold that's mine in spirit. Where am I lacking?"

"Frisco, you see me in a light I've never seen myself," she said shyly.

"Well, that's because I can see in the dark," he said confidently. "And right now I'm going to see you, and feel you, and hold you, and take you. And before the night is over, you're going to know what it means to be really loved. I've got plenty of those things you found in my drawer—"

"I remember. Striped with fluorescent colors," she said. "Stars and an interesting device on the tip for maximum pleasure."

"And I can hang on well past the bell, Annabelle. I would never let you down."

"Oh, my gosh," she said on a moan, as he opened her shirt and suckled her breasts.

Then he kissed her lips before moving back to lick each nipple. "Tonight, we're going to test just how sound Emmie can sleep. Because I won't have done my job unless they hear you come across the street. Can you count to eight, Annabelle?" he murmured against her skin.

"Yes," she whispered, her whole body beginning to tremble at the possessive, meaningful promise behind Frisco's words.

"Then let's see about saving some horses."

He slid her blouse to the floor.

THE ONLY THING THAT could move Annabelle to leave her bed the next morning was Emmie urgently requesting a feeding time.

"I'll get her," Frisco said, kissing Annabelle on the lips before he swung his bad leg to the side of the bed. "Come here, little princess. Let's me and you go hunt big game bah-bah. Where's the kitchen, pretty mama?"

Annabelle practically cackled into her pillow, loving Frisco's ridiculous chit-chat with her daughter and his silliness in general. "At the end of the hall is a mini-fridge and microwave. Eight," she said on a groan. "I stopped counting, but I'm pretty sure it was eight." Frisco had loved her until she screamed, laughed, cried and sometimes was torn between which she should do. It was the most amazing thing that had ever happened to her.

And he still got up to feed her baby. "I don't know, Frisco. If I'd met you first, I'm sure I would have fallen in love with you. I never would have even seen another man," she muttered facedown in the pillow.

"What's that?" he said, coming back into the room with a bottle and Emmie.

"Nothing. I was just saying how glad I am that we're best friends."

"What'd I tell you. There's men who know how to be friends to a woman, and then there's men who give other men a lazy reputation. The few of us who know what we're about become legends."

She rolled over, laughing at him. "It's been a while for you, too, huh?"

"At least a year," he replied, sheepish as he sat down. "But it wasn't for lack of willing victims."

"What was it then?" She sat up against the pillows, pulled the sheet up over her breasts and stared at him.

"I'm discriminating. Only the best." He jerked the sheet to her waist with the hand that wasn't holding Emmie's bottle. "That's what I like to see in the morning. Your navel," he teased.

She blushed as her nipples tightened from the brisk temperature in the room—and his very interested perusal. He was no more looking at her navel than she was looking at his, though it was attractive as a man's navel went. Trying to ease the sheet back up when he wasn't looking was futile—he held it in a knot.

"Don't deprive a man of one of the few joys in his life. Especially take pity on me because of my broken leg. I need a visual focus while I feed this child for you."

"It's hard," she protested.

"It most definitely is." He leered at her.

"I've never been a man's visual focus. I've never been this naked around a man." He was practically eating her alive with his eyes. "I've got to take a shower." She leapt out of bed before he could grab her ankle, though he tried. "Frisco, I couldn't make love again even if I wanted to. Trust me."

To her surprise, not three minutes later, he joined her in the shower, with Emmie, cast wrapped.

"I'm not going to make love to you in the shower—not today, anyway," he teased. "But this is a moment I can't pass up." He held Emmie against his chest, and Annabelle against Emmie's back and against his shoulder, and the three of them stood under the warm spray, enjoying the feel of each other. Not seductive. Just close.

Necessary.

It felt like a real family: a mother, a father, a baby. All happy. She loved it.

She was falling in love with Frisco Joe Jefferson.

In fact, she was long past falling.

CHAPTER SIXTEEN

AN HOUR LATER, as Annabelle and Frisco sat in the kitchen eating breakfast, pounding on the downstairs door sent Annabelle jumping to her feet. "I'll go see who it is."

"Tom, most likely."

"I don't think so. He'd call at this point, since he knows you're here."

"Or slither under the door. A snake could slither under the door, right?" He kissed Emmie's forehead while the infant gazed up at him adoringly. "I shouldn't talk badly about your father," he told her. "I should teach you to love your mother and father. Your mother, that's a piece of cake. Your father is a whole other matter in spiritual charity."

"Frisco," Annabelle said on a laugh. "I'll be right back."

Hurrying to the door, she pondered how much her life had changed—for the better. She was no longer sad; she no longer mourned her father. She would always miss him, of course, but now she felt as if she could move on and live a happy life. She and Emmie.

It was all turning out so much better than she had ever dreamed—thanks to the man who'd taught her everything about herself she'd needed to know.

Jerry's red nose and cheery blue eyes were peeking in the glass pane. She opened the door, motioning for him to come inside. "Hello!" Giving him a big hug, she said, "It's a cold wind that blew you back here, Jerry. Can I get you some coffee?"

"I'd accept that offer."

"Great. Frisco, Jerry's here!"

The two of them went into the kitchen, and Frisco stood to shake Jerry's hand. "Got your haul taken care of?"

"That I did," Jerry said, seating himself. "Thought I'd stop here on my way and see if you wanted a ride back to Union Junction."

Her hand froze over the coffee pot. It made perfect sense that Frisco would return with Jerry. He couldn't stay here forever.

"Did I ever tell you that you look like Santa Claus?" Frisco asked.

"Actually, yes, you did." Jerry's eyes twinkled at him. "It's a compliment to me and my red Kenworth sleigh, hauling goodies. 'Course, last time you called me Santa, you'd just busted your leg and were jabbering like mad."

Frisco frowned. "I don't remember."

Annabelle set coffee in front of the two men. "Here you go," she said, taking Emmie from Frisco. "I'll hold her so you can get your things."

"I didn't say I was going, did I? Did I say I was leaving?"

He looked at her, and Annabelle smiled. "It's okay. I'll be all right now, Frisco."

Hesitating, he looked at her and then the baby. And then her again. "Annabelle, I—"

They were just friends. She didn't want more from him than that because it wasn't right to expect more. Though Tom had called her marriage-hungry and clingy, that had been him making himself feel better. She didn't want Frisco to think he had to prop her up forever.

And besides, what were they going to do? Stay here and make love until they got sick of each other? Follow him to Union Junction and be his housekeeper? That wasn't the way she wanted Emmie raised. She owed it to her daughter to set a stable, loving example of motherhood. "It's for the best," Annabelle said.

"I guess you're right. I'll get my things and join you in a moment, Jerry."

"Take your time. Lemme hold that little toot. You go say goodbye."

Handing the baby over, she went up the stairs with a heavy heart. It would be a difficult goodbye, but she was getting used to those. "Frisco," she said, entering her room, "thank you for coming to see me. And Emmie."

He shook his head at her. "You sound like we'll never see each other again. I kind of hear it in your voice. You know, Delilah says you don't stick in one place for long."

"Well, I didn't. But I'm going to now. I owe it to Emmie."

"Oh." He smiled at her. "You're a good mother, Annabelle." And then he hugged her, and Annabelle hugged him back, with tears in her eyes she wouldn't let him see. "Goodbye, Frisco."

"Bye." He kissed her, a sweet goodbye kiss, not on the cheek like friends but on the lips like best friends and a bit more. "Miss me a little, okay?"

"I will."

Nodding, he went down the stairs. She followed, taking Emmie from Jerry.

"I'll see you soon, no doubt," Jerry said. "Now that

I know where the salon is, I might as well get my hair trimmed here. On my way through."

"Me, too," Frisco said.

Annabelle nodded, not saying a word.

"Bye, gal. You mind yourself," Jerry said.

Frisco kissed Emmie on the forehead. "And you mind yourself, sweetie. Mind your mother."

They walked out, waving in the cold winter air. Annabelle waved back, then closed the door and locked it.

The salon seemed dark and silent without them. She'd never noticed the lack of light and laughter before.

The sisterhood was the best part of the salon. She'd miss it, but she was strong enough now to leave the sisterhood and forge ahead. She had a responsibility to Emmie—and to herself. "Come on, sweetie," she said. "Let's go pack up. It's time to go home."

FRISCO KNEW THE MINUTE he stepped out of the salon that he was making a mistake. The feeling followed him from Lonely Hearts Station halfway to Union Junction.

What had that friends stuff been all about? Maybe he still had some screws knocked loose from when he broke his leg, because he sure didn't feel "friendly" about Annabelle.

It had seemed like the wise, self-preserving description of the relationship at the time. Mainly because he hadn't wanted to rush her.

But damn it, he felt like he'd just walked out on the best thing he'd ever had.

Best friends, his foot. He sounded like he'd had his head slammed in a psych textbook and forgot to have feelings of his own. He should have swept her off her feet. Maybe she wasn't quite ready for a long-term relationship, but he had a big broom. He could sweep her so that she liked it.

"Something on your mind, friend?" Jerry asked.

"Not really. Yes, actually. I'm wishing I hadn't left without saying something to Annabelle."

"I got a cell phone."

"Thanks, no, I've got one, too." He scratched his head. "What I want to say can't be said on a cell phone. I'd have to be holding her in my arms."

"Kenworth hanging a U-ee," Jerry said. "It's gonna be wide and short, so hang on."

"Wide and short?" Frisco asked with some alarm. "What are you doing?"

Jerry pulled to the left side of the highway, where there was a spot to turn around. "We're going back to Lonely Hearts Station."

"You don't have to take me back."

"How else you going to get there with a busted spoke?"

"I don't know."

"And didn't you say it had to be said in person?"

He'd poked fun at Tom for not putting enough effort into what he was saying to Annabelle. "Yes, it does."

"Then back we go."

"Jerry, you are more than a friend to me."

"Nah, at this moment, I'm tacking on freight charges for you and your cast. I'm adding it to the month's worth of fuel you promised to pay." But he chuckled, and Frisco knew the big trucker had a soft spot for a good love story.

"You're great to help me out."

"I'm a trucker. I like the road, and it likes me. Sit

back, close your eyes and compose your speech. I want it to be worth it when we get there."

Frisco grinned, leaning his head back and closing his eyes. Finally, he'd found a woman he cared enough about to hang a U-ee for.

THE LONELY HEARTS SALON was dark by the time Jerry pulled into a parking space on the town square. "Did she have a light on before?"

Frisco frowned. "Seemed like she had some lights on."

With a bad feeling inside his suddenly racing heart, Frisco jumped down from the truck. Going to the door, he pounded, all the while peering through the glass, trying to see inside.

"I'll try to raise her on the cell phone," Jerry called from the truck cab.

After five minutes, when Frisco knew she wasn't in the bathroom, and she wasn't busy with the baby, and she wasn't going to open the door, a voice at his elbow made him nearly jump out of his boots.

"She's gone," a petite redhead said.

"Gone?"

"Left town. Went back home."

"How do you know?"

The redhead gave him a saucy once-over. Frisco realized she was wearing a Never Lonely glittered T-shirt. She batted long eyelashes at him coyly. If he hadn't been in love—yes, damn it, in love—he might have been interested in the game she was offering. As it was, he just wanted her to spill info.

"My name's Valentine," she said. "I work over there."

"I got that. Why would you know what Annabelle was doing?"

"Because she came over and left a message for Tom with me. Tom used to see Dina, until she found out he was trying to snake her with Annabelle." Valentine's tone was outraged. "The two-timing skunk."

"Ah, yeah." Valentine had twisted logic, but her shirt was cut short enough to show her midriff, and even in winter, he had to think a woman like her could get cold enough to stop thinking straight. "So, can you share the message with me? That she left for Tom."

"I could, cowboy, if you were nice to me."

He gulped. "How nice do I have to be?"

"Come into our salon," she said, in the voice of the spider luring the fly. "We've been looking for customers all day."

On another day, such an offer might have been worthy. Today, he just wanted to track Annabelle. "Listen, I'm in a big hurry, so maybe… Would you be interested in a crisp Ben Franklin?" He took out the money Annabelle would never take back from him and held it up.

Valentine snatched it like it might blow away any second. "She went home to the family winery. With Emmie. She told Tom that she was having her lawyer send papers to arrange for sole custody, there was no money involved for him and if he messed with her, she'd make certain the bank foreclosed on that fancy car he recently bought."

"Well, I'm sure he talked a good game. Now, listen to me, Valentine, because this is important. Do you know where the family winery is located?"

"No. I don't drink wine," she said with a sniff. "Only sexy drinks."

"Sexy drinks?"

"You know. The kind you have to shake." She leaned against his arm, bouncing a little for illumination.

"Er, thank you for all your help. It's been great talking to you," he said, being nice as he backed away in case he ever needed to use her for an info source again. "Goodbye!" Jumping into Jerry's truck, he slammed the door and locked it. "Gee whiz!"

He could hear Jerry sniggering into his sleeve. "What are you laughing about?"

"That little gal didn't care about your broken leg. She was gonna crawl right up you and eat you alive."

"Yeah, well, she'll have to go hungry a while longer. No wonder Delilah's having trouble keeping clientele."

Jerry sobered instantly. "Damn shame, that."

It *was* a shame because Delilah was a nice lady trying to do right for women who had no other place to go. He sighed. "All right. Do you know where Annabelle's family home was?"

"Somewhere in central Texas."

This was harder than he'd anticipated. Trust Annabelle to throw up a challenge he couldn't meet by himself. He couldn't drive there with a broken leg, he couldn't fly because he didn't think he could get his leg to fit in the tiny space in front of an airline seat.

"I need to go home and think about this," he said. "Maybe the best thing for me to do is give Annabelle some space." His heart had sunk the instant Valentine had told him Annabelle was gone. She'd wasted no time lighting out of Lonely Hearts Station after he'd gone.

"I'm sorry you wasted a trip on me, Jerry," he told his friend. "While my first inclination was to go after her, my second is that…she has my number if she wants to call me. She knows where I live."

"If you say so." Jerry looked as confused as he did.

"I wouldn't have thought she'd light out that fast. But I told you what Delilah said—"

"I know. I know. Annabelle's a rolling stone." And he wasn't so sure she hadn't just rolled right over him. Dang. "If you don't mind taking me home, I'd surely appreciate it," Frisco said.

Home to Helga the Horrible.

H-e-double hockey sticks-g-a.

He was going to take up window-jumping.

CHAPTER SEVENTEEN

"THIS PLACE SUCKS!" Last told Tex and Laredo two weeks later. "I'm praying for March and some good stiff winds to blow out the bad aura around this joint."

"It's the same as it's always been at the Malfunction Junction," Laredo said. "Quit yer bitching."

"It's not," Last insisted. "Mason doesn't say a word. I think he's forgotten what his lips are for. And I won't even discuss Frisco. He's forgotten what his heart is for, and he sold his soul to Oscar the Grouch."

"He'll look good in green fur," Tex said without much sympathy.

"Speaking of looking good in fur, did you see the one Mimi had on the other day? I realize it was simulated, but it wasn't cheap-simulated. She said her fiancé gave it to her as an engagement gift!"

Last's voice clearly communicated his disbelief. Laredo cocked a brow at him. "So?"

"Well, it's Mimi we're talking about. What's she gonna do with a full-length fur? Feed her goat?"

"It's really none of our business," Tex told him sourly.

"Well, don't act like you're not depressed as hell."

Tex pounded his hand on the table, which brought Helga running with a cloth. They all waited politely until she was done wiping up the fist print, but as soon as she left the room, Last leaned forward to whisper urgently,

"Everything has gone cockeyed around here and you know it. We've got to *do* something!"

Laredo was of half a mind to agree, but he'd been busy hatching his plan to hit the road. All he had on his mind was a merciful escape. "Talk to Ranger."

"Ranger isn't going to do anything. He's been so buggy over his military books he pays me no mind."

"There's half a dozen more of us. Go bother them."

Last drew himself up. "If you don't care, why should I? If no one cares, then fine. You can all just steep in your misery."

"What do you want us to do? Tell Mimi that Mason misses his playmate? Tie Helga up and ship her back to Europe? Find Frisco a woman?"

"That was the original plan, if you recall. We said a woman would take care of his bad temper. And it did."

"For a while," Tex agreed. "Now he's blacker than night. I think it had the adverse effect."

Last shook his head. "He's in love, stupids."

"What does that have to do with us?" Laredo wanted to know.

"You could offer to help him," Last suggested.

"It's really, really bad to try to help other people's love lives. Haven't we gotten burned on that one?"

"Isn't doing something better than nothing?" Last asked.

"No," Tex and Laredo said in unison.

"Well, fine." Last backed away from the table. "The problem here is, no one remembers that this used to be a happy home."

"Last, listen. You were the baby. You had life easier than the rest of us. Of course you remember it with lollipop-colored vision," Laredo told him.

Tex snickered and looked out the window.

"Hey, that's not true. Mom was a good mom."

His brothers didn't say a word.

"You know it's true. And Dad was crazy about her. When she passed away, he lost all his heart to go on without her. Can't you see that's happening to Frisco?"

Laredo rolled his eyes, but he was beginning to realize that Last was serious. He was a serious pain in the keister, one that wasn't going to be relieved until he got what he wanted.

And maybe, partially, he had the story right.

"You're so sensitive," he told his youngest brother. "What the hell do you want from us?"

"I think you should offer to drive Frisco to find Annabelle."

Laredo raised his brows. "How do you know he'd go?"

"I don't think he would, willingly."

"So we kidnap him and force him to be happy with Annabelle? And you say I've got problems," Tex griped.

"He doesn't know how to win Annabelle. He's afraid she won't have him. But I say, he who chickens out, never wins his feathers."

Laredo snorted. "After we make this ridiculous offer to chauffeur our brother, and he eats our head, will you shut up and leave us alone about it? Or go write a romance novel in the privacy of your own room?"

"I promise I will."

"All right. If this is what it takes to get you to go bother someone else, I'm on my feet." Laredo looked at Tex. "Are you going with me? Two of us should be able to subdue Frisco."

Tex grinned. "What the hell."

Slowly, the three of them ascended the staircase. Laredo tapped on Frisco's door.

"Go away," he called impatiently.

"Frisco, can we talk to you a minute?" Laredo called.

The door opened. "Is Helga nearby?"

"No," Tex said looking over his shoulder.

"Come in, then. Hurry!"

The three brothers jumped into the room. Frisco slammed the door and locked it. "I've started leaving by the window when I want to get away. Just like the old days."

"Really? You're going to break your other leg," Laredo said, peering out the window. "Drain pipe or sheets?"

"I reinforced the drain pipe and keep a tall ladder hidden behind the crape myrtles down there."

"Good thinking. Hey, me and Tex were thinking about taking a drive. Wanna go with?"

"Where you headed?" Frisco asked, perking up.

"Texas wine country," Tex said nonchalantly.

"Oh. No, I think I'd better stay here."

"Don't be such a coward, Frisco. What's happened to you?" Laredo demanded. "You used to be so hellfire and brimstone but now you're too quiet. I liked you better the other way. At least you had *cojones*."

Frisco was silent for a moment. "Maybe."

"Why are you taking it so personal, bro?" Tex asked. "You knew she had a life of her own."

"Yeah, but that doesn't mean I thought she'd leave me out of it. I mean, I shared my life with her."

"You did? I find that hard to believe," Laredo told him.

"Well, I shared my bed, and my room, and—you

know, she didn't say goodbye. I mean, that brings up all kinds of insecurities."

"Yours, apparently. Call her, then. Ask if she would like to see you."

Frisco brightened. "I could do that. I could call her."

"Sure. You just put your finger on the phone and push some buttons. No problem." Tex handed him the phone.

"Um. Okay." He held the phone as it if were ticking. Then he took a deep breath and dialed Information. "Annabelle Turnberry, please, in Austin or the suburbs," he guessed. Tex shrugged, Laredo nodded and Last scratched his head.

"That number is unlisted, sir. Can I try another number for you?"

"No. I don't think so. Thanks anyway." He hung up and glared at his brothers. "That was a really dumb idea."

"Why didn't you ask for Turnberry Wines?" Last asked.

Frisco shook his head. "I can't just call her, guys. It's not the way I feel. A phone call is for friends."

Laredo sighed. "I'll get my truck keys. Last, pack us a cooler."

Frisco limped to grab his already-packed duffle. "Thanks. I really appreciate this."

"Hey! Why are you already packed?" Tex demanded.

"Because I was about to succumb to paying taxi fare all the way to the Turnberry Winery." He grinned at his brothers. "But since you've graciously offered, I'd much rather take up the backseat of the double cab."

"Great," Laredo grumbled.

"You guys are the best brothers."

"Great," Tex echoed. "Last, we're going to tie you up and leave you for the roadside pick-up if you open your mouth between here and Austin!"

ANNABELLE WALKED UPSTAIRS to her father's study, entering on quiet feet. It had been nearly a year since she'd been back in their home. The housekeeper and groundskeeper had done a nice job of maintaining it.

That was a comfort to her.

The house was lined in dark wood with delicate floral rugs, elegant hanging chandeliers. In every room, she could hear the laughter of happier times.

She could also feel the moments Alzheimer's had stolen from their lives. She closed the door of the study.

"Well, Dad," she said out loud. "I miss you more than I knew I could miss someone. It's really, really difficult." Swallowing hard, she sat down in the leather chair behind his desk. Here she'd played under his feet as a child, while he conducted business calls; here she'd read many a book as a teenager, while her father met business associates. As a young woman, she had been an active hostess for her father and had discovered the business aspects of the winery came easily to her.

"I've really let you down, Dad," she whispered. "You said I was a stable one, and I went clean off the rails."

That was the hardest thing. She had let her father down.

"But you'd love Emmie," she said. "I'm not certain, but she seems to have your knack for getting what she wants." Her breath was deep as she drew it in. "And I'm finally stumbling out of the wilderness. I won't let you down anymore. But I wish you were here," she said. "I met a man I fell in love with. You'd really like him,

I know you would. You'd say he was full of crap and molasses, and that's what you often said got you past your competitors."

She spun his chair to look out the window to the grounds below. "I'm sorry to admit I was too afraid to do anything about it."

A truck moved up to the monitored gate. She leaned forward, watching to see if the housekeeper would buzz for the truck to enter. The truck doors opened, and three men got out, staring over the wrought-iron security gate at the house.

One of them was wearing jeans with one leg missing. Like Frisco.

Frisco. She jumped to her feet, and went tearing down the spiral staircase. "Open the gate, Mrs. Dawson! Open the gate!"

And then she flew outside, across the wide lawn, making it to the gate just as it opened wide enough for her to run through and jump into Frisco's arms.

He kissed her on the mouth, and she hung on in a manner that would make any rodeo rider proud. Way past eight seconds.

And then slowly he put her down.

"Well, that was worth the drive," Tex said.

"A plus," Last said, "if you ask me."

Which no one did.

She gazed into Frisco's eyes, unable to stop holding his hands. "I can't believe you're here."

"Next time you decide to roll, could you at least leave a trail of bread crumbs? I was scared to death I wouldn't find you."

Annabelle smiled. "I'm home now. No more rolling."

Frisco looked up at the big house. "Well, it's impressive and all, but too big for one woman and one tiny baby."

"Oh? What do you think I should do about that?"

"We could spend the night here," Last suggested. "I think I see a golf course out back. A big, snakey-looking one with dog legs and tricky rough. I've always wanted to play on a course like that."

"Shh," Tex said, knuckling him. "Go get back in the truck."

"What I think is that we should develop our friendship," Frisco said to Annabelle, ignoring his brothers' conversation.

Slowly, he edged down, his bad leg bending to the side, so that he could rest on one knee. Annabelle held his hand tightly, trying to help support him, her heart blooming so big she didn't think she could breathe.

"I'd like you to be my best friend, Annabelle Turnberry, in all moments in our lives, good, bad and ugly. Through ice storms, broken limbs, Never Lonely Cut-n-Gurls and babies who cry in the night." He stared up at her, with love in his dark brown eyes. "But mostly, I'm asking you to be my wife, because I love you, and goodness knows, you and Emmie grabbed my heart right out of my chest when I wasn't looking and I'm praying you'll keep it. And me."

"Awkward, but the best he could do," Last whispered to Tex. "For a man unused to expressing himself, he's doing all right, doncha think?"

"Shh," Tex said. "I can't hear."

But there was nothing else to hear, because Annabelle got down on her knees and whispered something for Frisco's ears alone, and then she slowly helped him to his feet. She fitted herself up under his arm, and supporting him, they walked through Turnberry's monitored gate.

Frisco reached out as they passed the brick columns supporting the gate and pushed a button, never looking back. The gate slid shut behind them.

"Hey! What about us?" Last called. "What about the golf course?"

Laredo laughed. Tex pulled his younger sibling away from the fence.

"That was the point," Laredo said. "They just left us behind. Be happy, bro," he said to Frisco with a last glance at the big house. "You and Annabelle and Emmie deserve that happy-ever-after."

ANNABELLE LAUGHED AS Frisco tried to carry her over the threshold. "You're going to hurt yourself."

"I'm not. I'm a big, tough, strong cowboy."

"I love my big, tough, strong cowboy."

"And I love you, whoever you were, are and turn out to be."

For a woman who had just discovered who she was in life, his words were powerful. "You have no idea how much you mean to me, Frisco Joe Jefferson."

They kissed, long and sweetly—until they heard Emmie let out a little cry.

"She must know you're here," Annabelle said with a smile.

"True happiness is when a man walks in the house to have his wife and daughter cry out for him," Frisco said, putting his arm around her. "Take me to my demanding daughter—and then we're going to have a treasure hunt. How many rooms does this shack have?"

"I don't know. More than twenty," she said, laughing at the meaningful expression on his face. "Why?"

"Can you count to twenty, Annabelle?"

"If you give me a week," she said, leaning up against him, her heart full of happiness.

"I'm giving you a lifetime."

Annabelle turned to look up at her father's portrait in the stairwell. "See, Dad? I told you you'd like him. Crap and molasses. Big promises, sweet talk and sticking power."

The recipe for success.

EPILOGUE

ANNABELLE SMILED at her husband as he lay in a hammock on the grounds of the Turnberry estate. Emmie snoozed in the hammock beside him, which made Annabelle's heart warm in every corner. "I worried that you'd have trouble settling in here, Frisco. I was so afraid you'd miss your brothers. And Malfunction Junction."

"Worry not, lady love." Without joggling Emmie, Frisco snagged his wife, pulling her down on top of him. He kissed her, slow and long.

It had only been a month since the wedding, but every time Frisco grabbed Annabelle and kissed her like this, Annabelle felt certain no woman was as lucky as she. "You make me tingle all over," she told him.

"Then I'm not doing something right. You should be feeling sparks, lady. That's what I feel when you walk into a room. And I don't even want to put a name to what I feel when you walk into a room naked."

She laughed. "Have I done that?"

"Not often enough. But we've got plenty of time. And I'm a very patient man. I'll be around for any nudity twitches you suddenly develop."

She smiled up at him. "And if I don't?"

He kissed her forehead and then her lips. "I know how to work a zipper. Buttons, bra straps, none of that can stand in the way of a man determined to hold his beloved."

"Am I? Your beloved?" she asked, knowing full well the answer but wanting to hear it anyway.

"Nah," he said.

She giggled. "Frisco!"

"Kiss me and maybe I'll rethink that."

She kissed the teasing smile right off his face.

"Wow," he said when they finally pulled apart. "You're my beloved and then some!"

"Did you feel sparks?" she whispered.

"I felt sparks, and I felt magic, and I felt love, Annabelle. I love you so much."

Frisco laid Annabelle's head on his chest. Quietly the three of them swung in the hammock, enjoying the gentle breeze. The warm afternoon sun. The happiness and peace of being together.

And being in love.

You were right, Dad, Frisco thought, closing his eyes as he held his new family. *Home is what a man feels in his heart.*

And Frisco's home was with Annabelle.

* * * * *

LAREDO'S SASSY SWEETHEART

Many thanks to my readers!
There is never enough I can say to thank you
for your support and your generosity.
This series is for you. Here also I wish to extend
special mention to the following wonderful people:
LaJoyce Doran, Shadin Quran, Nicole Christoph,
Jeanette Bowman and Beth Reimer. More than ever,
my gratitude goes to the editor angels at
Harlequin who watch over my career—thank you
to Melissa Jeglinski for your many kindnesses and
Stacy Boyd for your calm guidance and patience!

And extra-sloppy, noisy kisses to Lisa and Dean. I adore
you and need the light you bring to my life~~Mumzie.

CHAPTER ONE

"A man only fights for the good, boys, not to impose his will on others. Believe in yourself. No one can do that for you. But a real man learns to fight with his brain, not his fists."

—Maverick Jefferson to his sons when they asked him if they could give Sammy Wickle a black eye in kindergarten.

LAREDO JEFFERSON had seen a lot of madness in the past month. The neighbor the twelve Jefferson brothers had known all their lives, Mimi, had become engaged, a startling situation in itself, since the engagement was to someone other than his big brother, Mason. Mason hadn't pulled his head out in time to realize he was going to lose someone who mattered a lot to him—or, at least, Laredo was pretty certain Mimi and Mason meant a lot to each other. Sometimes it was hard to tell if all the preening and poppycock was prideful love or just the wear and tear of a brother-sister relationship.

Frisco Joe had married a fine woman, another surprising development, since, of all twelve brothers, Frisco was the darkest horse, being possessed of an ornerier-than-most nature. Amazingly, Annabelle had certainly sugared him up a bit, and baby Emmie kept Frisco in a constant state of cockeyed grinny-ness. It had been a pleasure to watch his sour brother get mowed down by a little mama and her no-bigger-than-a-chickpea baby.

But he was not about to be caught in the same net.

After all the years of drought on their ranch near Union Junction, they'd had a veritable shower of charming female visitors. And it was all he could do to resist paying court to every one of them! Nine new women had come to town from Lonely Hearts Station, a neighboring town. After helping out during last month's terrible storm, the women had decided they would stay.

A lot of bachelors in Union Junction, Texas, had been real happy about that.

Laredo hadn't asked any of the women out on a date. Fidelity was something to be avoided, at least in his opinion. If you were dying of thirst, and someone offered you a huge jug of water, wouldn't you drink as long as you could? he'd reasoned to Mason.

Mason had grunted and told him to go fill the water troughs for the horses. Laredo thought the house was going to be plenty empty without Frisco, and plenty full of Mason and his bad temper. Without Frisco Joe, life wouldn't be the same! Mason had ridden Frisco, Frisco had bucked Mason—without Frisco, Laredo might be next in line to be ridden, and he didn't have Frisco's ability to deal with Mason. Laredo's brothers called him a dreamer, but they usually gave him a pass and picked on his twin, Texas, more, since Tex's passion was growing roses that never bloomed. Budus-interruptus, Frisco had told Tex, that was his problem. Tex had been really steamed, but Laredo had snickered under his sleeve, his face turned from his twin.

Maybe his brothers were getting on his nerves. Maybe they'd lived together too long. Which got him thinking about traveling east—something he'd been thinking about long before the madness of love had hit the ranch. He was in the mood for adventure, a change of pace. Love wasn't going to hit him, he vowed, and picked up his packed duffel bag. He was not about to settle down.

He wanted to do something big.

Without another glance back he left the only home he'd ever known to venture out into the warm March morning. First stop: paying a visit to the Lonely Hearts Beauty Salon, just long enough to say hello to some ladies who'd made his life a little more fun last month. *There* was a place for a troubled man to find a sympathetic ear.

Three hours later he was standing outside the salon, amazed by the hubbub inside—it sounded more like a general meeting place—when suddenly the door flung open. His sleeve firmly grasped in two desperate female hands, he was hauled inside.

He remembered Katy Goodnight, the woman who now had him in her determined grip. He remembered thinking that a man could spend many good nights with a girl like her.

"This is him!" Katy announced to the room at large, which was filled with elderly men, a lot of women and even a pet chicken in a cage on one of the back counters. "This is the man we can enter in the rodeo as the champion for Lonely Hearts Station, Texas. If anyone can ride Bloodthirsty Black, it's Laredo Jefferson. Ladies and gentlemen, pay homage to your champion, and the man who can whup the daylights out of our rival, the Never Lonely Cut-N-Gurls and their bull, Bad-Ass Blue!"

Voices huzzahed, hands clapped, Katy released his shirt so she could clap, too, and even the chicken uttered a startled squawk. But no one was more startled than Laredo to be picked as some kind of bull-riding savior.

He'd never ridden a bull in his life.

Katy whispered, "You got here just in the nick of time. You're my hero!"

He swallowed, and decided to keep his mouth shut. After all, he'd been looking for a little adventure—and it wasn't every day a man got to be a hero to a woman named Goodnight.

KATY KNEW that desperation had just opened the door and sent her a man—a man who looked as if he could solve her problem. Laredo was big enough to hang on to an ornery, few thousand pounds of irritated horns-and-hooves. He was strong, judging by the muscles in his forearms and the biceps not covered by a short-sleeved red T-shirt. That area below the leather belt and covered by nicely fitted blue jeans looked healthy, as well—guaranteed to fit in a saddle and keep a seat well past the eight-second horn.

He was sexy as all get-out, too—a strong chin, square face and simmering dark eyes under a summer-weight Western hat set her heart to jumping just like mad Bloodthirsty Black when he shook off lesser handlers. But sex appeal had nothing to do with her mission.

All she needed was a man who could hang on for eight seconds. Was that so much to ask?

Maybe hanging on wasn't what Laredo wanted—by the look on his face, she'd completely startled him with her announcement—but matters being what they were, she'd have to take the chance that his gentlemanly instincts would overcome his shock.

Their last bull rider had backed out after the Never Lonely Cut-N-Gurls sank their claws into him, filling his ears with stories. Katy had a vague idea what stories might be told in the salon across the street. Remembering her ex-fiancé, Stanley, wrapped around her ex-best friend, Becky, in the bridal changing room in the church, she had an inkling they were *bedtime* stories.

She eyed Laredo with eyes that missed nothing, and realized that if the Never Lonely girls had set an all-out campaign for the previous rider the Lonely Hearts girls had sent into the arena, Laredo had about a sixty-minute shelf life before he was discovered by the enemy.

And lured away.

Temptation must be avoided at all costs.

Because Miss Delilah, the owner of the Lonely Hearts Salon, really, really needed a champion. Katy's boss—and rescuer—Delilah, was looking for something big, something miraculous to happen for her salon. It housed the closest thing to real family Katy had ever known. So unless he turned her down, something big and miraculous was what Laredo Jefferson was going to be, Katy determined, staring up at him as he stared down at her, apparently rooted to the floor in his big boots. If she weren't so desperate, she'd have time to appreciate the scenery, but as it was, time was limited.

Please let him say yes, she prayed, gazing up into those beautiful, stunned eyes.

Or at least don't let him shrug her off like the crazy woman she knew she must seem to be. She'd never had much luck with men—in fact, her ex-fiancé was right now enjoying her ex-best friend's thong in the south of France on a honeymoon *Katy* had planned—but she wasn't really frigid. She was certain her heart was warmer than an ice cube, no matter what Stanley said. Being a virgin wasn't a crime…naiveté was unfortunate, perhaps, but it wasn't prissy, uncaring virtue she'd

been wearing like a steel-plated hymen. It was just…
innocence.

Or maybe, she thought suddenly, as she dimly realized Laredo had gorgeous dark-coffee-colored eyes that
were dilated and focused on her with a heat matched
only by the sun outside, maybe it was uncertainty that
had kept her a virgin.

Uncertainty may have frozen her once, but today was
a new day, and Laredo was not Stanley. She took a deep
breath and forced her best cajoling tone. "So, what do
you say, cowboy?" she asked softly.

"Little lady," he finally said, finding the voice she'd
shocked out of him. "We have a problem."

Her throat dried out. A problem. That didn't sound
like a yes, did it? She could feel all her sister stylists
watching them, could feel their breath held as tightly in
their chests as hers was. "Problem?"

His eyes softened as he nodded. "Would you care to
talk about it, maybe outside?" he asked.

Slowly she released his sleeve, which she'd been
clutching since she'd dragged him inside the salon. "All
right, Laredo." She glanced around at everyone in the
salon. "I'll be right back."

Not towing a hero, maybe, and minus her paltry self-
confidence. Not that her self-confidence was the main
thing, of course. If Laredo couldn't be the hero they
were looking for, then time was paramount. They'd have
to find another hero.

The rodeo was in four days, and someone had to ride
their bull. Lord only knew she'd fantasized about riding
it herself, to save Delilah from her sister, Marvella, who
owned the competing salon across the street. Marvella's
salon had just about finished off Miss Delilah's honest
way of work.

Because, rumor had it, it wasn't just a close shave being sold across the street by the Never Lonely girls, which left Miss Delilah with very few clients indeed. She'd had to let half her staff go last month. Fortunately, Union Junction had welcomed the nine newcomers. Yet, how cruel of Marvella to deliberately set out to ruin her own sister!

Not yet, Katy told herself, as Laredo closed the salon door behind them. Not if she had anything to do with it.

Outside, the sun shone brightly on the pavement. If it was possible, Laredo looked even more handsome in bright light.

Flirting skills. Enticement. Clearly, she was lacking in some womanly fundamentals, she decided. Because Becky, her ex-best friend, who even now was no doubt having her thong removed by the apparently lusty Stanley Katy had never known, would have roped, tied and thrown Laredo to the ground, all without doing much more than smiling. Rolling her hips. Showing pretty knees beneath her daily miniskirt parade.

Becky would have had a yes out of Laredo before he'd even drawn another breath.

That didn't mean she was sexless or frigid, Katy assured herself. It just meant she hadn't ever tried flirting. She didn't get an F just because she didn't take the course.

She took a deep breath, marshaled up her best Barbie smile, widened her eyes and sucked in her stomach so her breasts would at least marginally appear through her linen ankle-length dress—a move she was copying straight from the Never Lonely Cut-N-Gurl handbook. Her posture thrown off by the sudden stiffness, Katy placed a hand on Laredo's forearm for support, which he gallantly covered with his other hand, as if she truly were a doll worth holding! Maybe Becky had been onto something with all that gooey a-man-is-made-to-be-adored stuff. "You were going to tell me about a teensy little ol' problem, Laredo?" she asked, so sweetly she was certain sugar drizzled out of her mouth. "I'm just positive a man like you never lets a little ol' bump in the road stop him."

He nodded, frowning, seemingly flustered by her full-force display of flirt-go-ditz.

"I've never ridden a bull," Laredo said.

THE EXPRESSION on Katy's face was no longer hero worship, and Laredo felt as if all the air had been let out of him. Bam! Just like that, he was an ordinary mortal again. And here he'd been dreaming of doing something big with his life.

"Never ridden a bull," Katy murmured, as if she couldn't believe her ears. "But you live at the Malfunction Junction Ranch. All your brothers bull ride. I saw the ribbons and trophies. There must have been hundreds."

He shook his head. "Not me, though. Mason figured I was the one most likely to have a wandering foot that'd take to the rodeo lifestyle permanently. It's one of the very few things I would admit that my brother guessed right about me. And Last never has, either, but that's because he was the baby and Mason didn't have time to teach him to ride much of anything except a horse. Actually, Last never really did learn to ride a horse very well." He realized he was babbling, trying to fill in space so he wouldn't have to finish letting Katy down.

"Wandering foot?" Katy repeated. "What does that have to do with staying on a bull?"

He ran a gentle finger along the curve of her chin. God, how he hated disappointing her. She really was a cute little thing in her sandals and long dress, just like a girl playing dress-up in her mother's clothes. He liked the fact that she had little or no makeup on. Her hair was a bit ruffled, which he wouldn't have expected for someone who worked in a beauty salon. Everything about her seemed somehow fresh and innocent, from her big blue eyes to the dark bangs that framed them. "Mason was determined to keep our family together. It's a long story, but it has to do with the fact that our father left when most of us were young and Mason got stuck with the details of parenting. He made decisions the best he could. Sometimes he was wrong. But most of the time, he was dead-on."

"So you're a restless type."

"That's right."

She pulled her chin away from his finger. "I wouldn't know the feeling."

He eyed her, knowing that she wouldn't find that adjective attractive in a man. But that was okay, because he wasn't trying to suit himself up to be attractive to her. "I don't suspect you would."

"So you never got to ride a bull?"

"I could have sneaked around. Last wasn't supposed to, either, but he did just the same. Mason didn't want the baby of the family busting himself up."

"Of course not," she murmured.

"But Last has always done whatever he pleased."

She glanced up at him. "But you obeyed your brother."

He shrugged. "I couldn't quibble with his logic. I didn't want the family separated myself, and I wouldn't have been the one to do it. No one else seemed to have a hankering to leave the ranch like I did."

"You've left now," she said.

"Yes."

Hope flared in her eyes. "Maybe now is the time to disobey Mason about bull riding!"

He laughed. "I don't have to obey him anymore. But I wouldn't be any good at riding, Katy. I never learned. And there's more to it than getting on."

She looked as if she might cry any second.

"Here," he said gently, "let's take a walk. Tell me what's going on, and maybe I can help you resolve your situation."

"I need a hero," she said stubbornly.

He placed a hand dramatically over his chest. "I promise I think better than I ride. Come on. Walk and talk."

She sighed, not liking his offer one bit, but clearly seeing no way to refuse. "There's a lot at stake."

"You don't look like the kind of girl who hangs around rodeos, Katy." He eyed her curves underneath her long dress with appreciation. She'd look mighty fine in blue jeans—

"I'm not," she said as they began to walk side by side. She glanced up, almost catching him eyeing those curves. "Until last week, I'd never even seen a bull up close."

"What happened last week?" He couldn't resist asking since her head had drooped, her pretty sable-colored hair swinging forward as she spoke. "Tell Uncle Laredo."

She shot him a wry look. "You are not my uncle, cowboy."

"Oh, that's right. I'm supposed to be the hero. Only I got shot off my horse."

"Bull, not horse." She sighed. "Every year Miss

Delilah buys a bull from one of the local FFA kids. The kids raise their bulls, usually from the time they were born, until they auction them at the fair. This pays for college and other expenses. Then Delilah enters her bull in certain events, such as riding, and best hoof painting."

"Hoof painting?" He put out a hand to slow her determined gait. "You act like you're marching on the enemy yourself. What's best hoof painting?"

"It's sort of a paint-your-nails-for-bulls event. Only it's the hooves that get painted as pretty as they can possibly be. Flowers, doodles, Indian sunsets, you name it. On an animal that won't stay still. It's a mental and physical challenge."

"I've never heard of that."

"Miss Delilah thought it up."

"Of course." It sounded like a beauty salon owner's idea.

"Don't sound so snickery. Miss Delilah raises a lot of money for charity with her contests. People come from miles around to enter. And then, when the fair comes to town the following year, she sells the bull to the restaurant in Texas that bids the most for it. By then, everybody's seen her bull for that year, in several events, and they bid it pretty high. With this money, she's been able to keep her salon open." Katy shook her head sadly. "Everyone wins, you know. The student who raised the bull, Lonely Hearts Station charities, a lucky restaurant and Miss Delilah's favorite charity, taking in women who need a helping hand. But not since the Never Lonely girls opened up their salon."

She tossed her head in the direction of a business no one could miss—almost the red-light establishment of beauty salons with a neon sign sure to light up a dark sky and all manner of lip prints painted on the windows. "Rivals, huh?"

"Delilah's sister, Marvella, runs that shop, and she wants nothing more than to put Delilah out of business. And her weapon of the moment is a bull named Bad-Ass Blue."

Laredo would have laughed, except, by the serious stiffness in Katy's back, he knew he'd better swallow the laughter fast. "So, how does a bull ruin Miss Delilah's shop?"

"By getting more attention. By having a rider that knows how to showboat. By luring our rider into missing his ride," Katy said bitterly. "Bloodthirsty Black never even got out of the chute because we didn't have a rider."

Laredo was afraid to ask, but he had to know. "And the best-hoof-painting contest? How did Bloodthirsty Black fare in that?"

"Not at all," Katy said. "Someone slipped a baby mouse into his stall and he darn near broke it down trying to crush the poor thing. After that no one dared get near him."

Laredo shook his head. "No one plants a mouse. They just hang around livestock areas."

"Not this one. It still had the price tag on it."

He couldn't help a chuckle now, which earned him a rebuking stare from Katy. "They don't put price tags on mice, Katy."

"This one was wearing a red price tag on his back. Two dollars and ninety-eight cents," she said definitively.

Laredo was positive she was giving him a tall tale. "A marked-down mouse, I guess."

She instantly halted, putting her fists on her hips. It

was a gesture he kind of thought looked good on her, even though any sane man shied away from a ticked-off female. "There is nothing funny about Miss Delilah's dilemma. If you were truly my hero, you would know that this is a serious matter."

That stung, far worse than it should have. So much for doing something big—he couldn't even pass a small hero's test like not laughing at a story aimed to make him look like a patsy. "I'm sorry," he said earnestly.

"You certainly should be. It's not gentlemanly to laugh at people's livelihoods."

He hadn't thought of it that way, and Katy was right. In silence they began to walk again, more companionably now since he'd proffered an apology. "Okay, say the price tag on the mouse was a coincidence. Maybe it had run through a bag and picked it up accidentally."

"Maybe, but I don't think so. It was from a store in Dallas."

"But it could have been something someone brought to the rodeo," he insisted. "What's the purpose of leaving a price tag on a mouse? It basically alerts you to the fact that there's been cheating and sabotage."

"But that's the intimidation factor. They have never cared that we know what they're doing. Who's to stop them? All the younger men in this town go to that salon, including the sheriff. We get the wives, who want no part of what goes on over there."

"And that's another thing. Have you ever been inside the salon? Tried their services?"

"No."

"So how do you know that this is all deliberate?"

"They lured our cowboy into their salon, they got him drunk—and possibly more—on the day he was supposed to ride. What assumption would you draw from that?"

"That he was a lazy cowboy, and maybe not even a real bull rider, Katy. Did you ever think of that?"

"He had a buckle and all kinds of pictures of him with other trophies."

Laredo sighed, knowing any of that could have been bought or finagled. Katy, as earnest as she was, seemed the type people might take advantage of. She was so sweet and trusting and open. A marked-down mouse, indeed. Why would a rival salon go to the trouble of bringing in a mouse with a red tag when they could have spooked the bull any number of ways? "So, if the rodeo is already over, why do you need another rider?"

"Because Miss Delilah raised a huge stink and called Marvella and told her that she knew she'd cheated and that if there wasn't a rematch, she was going to burn the Never Lonely Cut-N-Gurls Salon to the ground."

"She did that?" This didn't sound like the woman who had come out to Malfunction Junction with twenty women and one baby, who had taken care of eleven cowboys and a truck driver during one of winter's worst storms. That woman had seemed very sane and practical. "I'm having trouble with Miss Delilah being a lawbreaker and an arsonist."

"We'll never know, because her sister agreed to a rematch. The thing is, though, I think it's a setup," Katy whispered, stopping to gaze up into his eyes. Laredo felt his heart go thud and then boom as he tried to inhale. Then exhale. Katy's eyes widened, drawing him in. "I think a red-lined mouse was child's play to Marvella. Call me gullible if you will, and trusting, but I was recently duped by a girl who was just like a sister to me."

"You don't say," Laredo breathed, trying real hard to sound surprised.

She nodded. "So I know what women are capable of."

"I'm sure you do."

"And I know Miss Delilah's getting set up on this."

"What could Marvella do?"

Katy's gaze swept over his shoulders and then across his chest. "I don't know. But she will send her girls to steal my hero."

His mouth dried out at the thought of a bunch of women coming after him with their feminine lures. It wasn't an altogether unhappy vision.

But the words from Katy's mouth had perked up his heart. He could be her hero. He could do it. He was not the kind of guy to make a promise and then cut and run.

"You can count on me," he said.

"You'll ride Bloodthirsty Black?" she asked on a gasp.

"I'll probably get stomped by his brightly painted hooves, but then at least everybody will know about the hard-wired bull Miss Delilah's got for sale. Then the charities will be happy, and a restaurant will be happy, and some FFA kids will be happy—"

"*I'll* be happy." She threw her arms around his neck by launching her small body up against his chest, leaving about twelve inches dangling between her feet and the sidewalk. "Thank you, Laredo. I knew I could count on you!"

He would call Mason tomorrow, he thought, and get some tips on how to stay on a beast from hell. Right now he was just going to stand here and smell Katy

Goodnight's perfume, and try not to think about how sweet a girl like her would be in his bed.

And then again, maybe thinking about how sweet she'd be in his bed was exactly why he'd said he'd ride her darn bull. He hadn't been kidding when he said he'd probably get stomped.

"So," he said into her hair as he held her against him, "what happened to the mouse?"

"I rescued her," Katy murmured. "When Bloodthirsty kicked in the stall, she ran out, and I scooped her up before she could run into another stall to get crushed by a different bull."

"Her?"

"There are only girls in our salon. We named her Rose, and she sleeps in a little box beside my bed."

Oh, boy. "Lucky mouse," he muttered.

"What?"

"Nothing," he said quickly. "I just can't wait to ride that bull," he fibbed.

"Think you can stay on eight seconds?"

He squeezed her to him, breathing in deeply. "I'm positive I have much longer than eight seconds in me."

"Really?"

"Well," he said hastily, switching gears from sexual to realistic, "I don't expect I'll be that good."

She smiled at him luminously. "Since it's your first time and all."

He swallowed, his Adam's apple jerking in his neck like a double knot on a child's tennis shoe. "Yeah."

"Do you have a place to stay for the night, Laredo?"

His throat tightened. Was he about to receive an invitation of the best sort? "No."

"Then you can sleep in my room."

Heaven! Hallelujah! Doing something big in his life

was turning out to be so easy. Why hadn't he been adventuresome sooner?

"And I'll sleep with Miss Delilah," she continued.

His enthusiasm withered like day-old soda pop. He set her down on the concrete. "I'd hate to put you out."

"It's the least I can do for the man who's going to single-handedly save our salon."

He nodded jerkily, trying to look appreciative.

"And we're fixing wilted lettuce and greens for dinner."

He pasted a smile on his face, thinking that if the menu was always so green and healthy, he wouldn't have to ride Bloodthirsty Black. He'd just gnaw the steak-on-the-hoof to death and chalk up an easy win that way. "Thank you," he repeated.

"Let's go back and tell everyone what you've decided," Katy said, delighted.

"Oh, yes. By all means," he agreed reluctantly. Longingly he glanced across the street, where a stunning blonde was deliberately trying to catch his gaze through the window. She was wearing a red shirt tied at the waist, and, even at this distance, he could tell she was a very healthy girl. To his surprise, she held a sign to the window that read Free Meal to Travelers in bold red, glittery letters.

Beside him Katy floated along, oblivious to the exchange. To be polite—because he'd only heard one side of the story, after all—he tipped his straw Western hat to the blonde and then shook his head in the negative.

Fair was fair, and no matter how bright the invitation across the way—even if they served steak and mashed potatoes—he was going to be a man Katy could trust.

CHAPTER TWO

"So what exactly was the big problem?" Hannah Hotchkiss asked as she walked into Katy's bedroom.

"Problem?" Katy asked, eyeing her best friend and companion stylist warily.

"The one Laredo mentioned. By the time the two of you returned from your walk, you had a yes out of him, and he was wearing a distinctly cattywhumpussed expression."

"A minor detail," Katy murmured. "Nothing that was truly a problem." She wasn't about to share the worrisome detail that their knight in shining armor lacked experience in the saddle.

"I think you've caught that man's eye."

Katy glanced up, horrified. "Do not say that. He is not my type at all."

"What is your type?"

Stanley came to mind, but Katy tossed that thought violently out of her brain. "I haven't figured it out yet. But I'm certain I'll know it when I see it." She blew her bangs away from her forehead. "These bangs will not grow fast enough to suit me."

"Why are you letting them grow out? They suit your face and showcase your eyes."

"I look like a little girl. I don't want to look like that anymore." She handed a picture to her friend of a model dressed like a ballerina, her hair pulled away from her face in a severe topknot. "That's the way I want to look."

"Like you haven't had a good meal in a month?"

Katy snatched the paper back. "Elegant. Sophisticated."

"Like you don't give a damn."

"Exactly." Katy nodded. "I don't."

"Now you just have to convince yourself."

"Right."

"What a bozo that Stanley must have been." Hannah sighed and got to her feet. "Listen, pulling your hair back until you look like a scarecrow isn't going to give you the mature edge you're looking for."

"You have a suggestion for maturing a permanent baby face?"

"No. The baby face is not the problem—and, by the way, it's called a cute face. There's nothing baby about you. Your challenge is to become more daring. *Daring*. Remember that word."

Katy raised a brow.

"You're masking your real worry by making it a hair issue, something all women do, and sometimes men, as well. The key is to face the issue dead-on, and pin it on the body part where it actually belongs. It's never a hair issue. Could be the brain, could be the breasts, could be your—"

"I don't need a body catalogue," Katy interrupted.

"So, where's your real issue?"

"My heart."

"Not possible. Choosing the heart is a stall tactic. It means you're still transposing and referring your denial. The heart is not part of the equation, as it is only a label for people's emotions. A visual, if you will."

"I don't know if I will or not." Katy groaned, unwilling

to go down the path. "My womanhood," she finally said. "If I'd been more of a woman, even Becky couldn't have gotten Stanley away from me."

"That's a myth, you know. Women successfully steal men all the time. It doesn't take much effort."

"I will never believe that. There are a few men out there who have antitheft devices on their hearts."

"Yes, but we're not talking about their hearts, and I have it on good authority that antitheft devices do not fit on a man's p—"

"All right!" Katy interrupted. "So any man is ripe for the picking. Then what's the point of me trying to overcome *my* issue if *their* issue is unsolvable?"

"Because once you develop more confidence, your chance of a man ever straying from you is dramatically diminished. You put a certain amount of color on a lady's hair to diminish her gray, don't you?"

"Yes," Katy said uncertainly.

"Well, you have to wear confidence to attract and keep someone you love. Become a bright, new color. Remember our new word—*daring*."

"Lack of confidence was not why Stanley married Becky."

"He did that because he was already at the church, the guests had flown in, his mother was wearing Bob Mackie, and you, my sweet gullible angel, had footed the bill as the bride. Plus, he still had a smile on his face from what had occurred in the bridal changing room. Strategically, if he couldn't wait another five minutes or so to enjoy your virginity, I'm thinking he didn't have much staying power for the long haul. Not that I'm judging him, exactly, since I have never met him. However, sometimes actions speak louder than words, and I sincerely believe your wedding day was one of those loud action moments." Hannah examined her nails casually. "By the way, you *are* going to send his parents a bill for the wedding."

Katy gasped. "Maybe Stanley and Becky, but not his parents!"

"No way. His parents are filthy rich and worried about impressions. You got the shaft and they'll be anxious to make certain you don't pay for their son's cruel indiscretion, lest you tell someone important like... Dear Abby. Oprah, even. The whole matter sounds very Jerry Springer to me. That'll hit Stanley's parents where they panic, and they'll certainly cough up what you're owed."

Katy flushed, hating the humiliation she'd suffered that day. "I want to keep it quiet. Forget about it. Move on."

"You are *not* as confident as you could be, Katy," Hannah said softly. "And under the circumstances, I understand. But by the time I'm finished with you, confidence will radiate from you!"

She wondered what Laredo saw radiating from her. Messy ponytail and no lipstick—probably all he saw was a dull aura. "Okay, do your darnedest. I guess."

Hannah lifted Katy's ponytail and ran it through her hand; Katy could practically hear her friend's creative brain whirring away.

Sighing, she reminded herself that she'd come to work at the Lonely Hearts Salon for just this reason. She needed the emotional support of women to help her get over her deepest fear: that she was sexually dysfunctional. Truth was, it hadn't been all that hard to keep her virginity. She had never felt a point-of-no-return reason to surrender it. But her best friend was talking about men as if they were as easy to pick as a dessert from a menu, and for Katy that would never be the case. It would take a kind and gentle man eons to teach her any differently. "I'm like Rapunzel. Locked in my own ivory tower."

"I think you should experiment on Laredo Jefferson, Katy. I believe romancing that man could knock a few bricks out of your tower. Rattle the foundation a bit."

Katy shook her head. "The last person who could ever save me from myself would be the freewheeling Laredo Jefferson. I've been to his home at the Malfunction Junction Ranch, and his family is wild and woolly. Fun, but too much for a girl like me." She shrugged. "Anyway, someone once told me that an ivory tower is really a phallic symbol—in Laredo's case, I'd believe it! And right now, this is just a stop on his eastward hunt for adventure, so I'd never dream of allowing him to scale my walls. Even if he wanted to."

"See, there you go again. *If.* Of course he does!"

"Do you really think so?" Katy asked doubtfully.

"A man does not agree to ride a bull unless he's fairly sure there's a helluva prize waiting for him once he's hit the dirt, honey."

Katy straightened. "I don't think of myself in those terms."

"Wait till I'm done with you. You'll be thinking Scarlett O'Hara by Saturday. I promise."

"Scarlett O'Hara was a flirt, a maneater," Katy protested.

"Exactly."

"YOU'RE DOING WHAT?" Mason shouted in Laredo's ear over the phone. "Have you clean lost your mind?"

Laredo pictured Katy's concerned face. "Not lost it,

just temporarily misplaced it, maybe. Mason, I need some tips."

"You want a phone course in killing yourself by stupidity."

"Someone has to do this, and it's going to be me."

"Obviously," Mason muttered. "This is not what I thought you meant when you said you were heading back east for adventure. You've barely left the county!"

"You know what they say about one's own back-yard."

"Oh, hell." There was an audible sigh from the other end of the line. "I guess I'll send Tex over with the gear you're going to need."

"Tex won't want to be torn away from his roses right now," Laredo warned. "He's right in the middle of pre-paring for the oncoming spring season."

"I'll hire Martha Stewart to babysit his buds," Mason growled. "In the meantime, Tex can come out there and share his vast knowledge with you."

Somehow, the idea of his twin coming out and spending time around Katy wasn't altogether appeal-ing. "Well—"

"I can't give you pointers by phone, if you're deter-mined to do this. What's the name of the bull, by the way?"

"Bloodthirsty Black."

"Is he a first-night bull or a marquee bull?"

Laredo scratched his head. "He's an unknown quan-tity. The last cowboy who was supposed to ride him had a change of plans."

"Maybe he was smart."

Any man who chose having sex over bull riding prob-ably had some sense. Laredo squinted around Katy's room. Her bed was unrumpled and covered with a clean, white cotton bedspread. There were white lace curtains floating at the open window. Beside her bed, Rose the mouse stared up at Laredo, her pink-flesh ears and tiny paws quivering. She was smaller than his little finger, and for a mouse, quite adorable. Her red price tag was stuck on the side of her wire-covered box as a pretend welcome mat. Katy had drawn a door above the welcome mat, and placed paper lace cutouts around fake windows. Laredo sighed to himself, then sat straight up as he realized something white and lacy was poking out from under Katy's pillow.

Gingerly, he tugged the lace. It left its hiding place with a smooth, gliding flash of froth. Holding it up, he realized it was sheer, it was very short, and Katy slept in this at night. His pulse raced as he glanced toward the door. He was pretty certain Katy wouldn't appreciate walking in and finding him with her nightgown in his hands and very little room left in his jeans.

"Laredo?" Mason's voice asked in his ear. "Laredo!"

Having sex or riding a bull.

He hadn't been offered sex. But occasionally a lucky hero got gifted with such a prize. Shoving the nightgown back under the pillow, he said, "I'm riding that bull, Mason, come hell or high water."

"DID YOU GIRLS NOTICE the new man in town?" Marvella asked as she stared out at her sister's salon.

"Did we ever!" her girls chorused.

"Looked like a *real* cowboy to me," Marvella said. "I so love cowboys! I do wonder how Delilah keeps coming up with these timely miracles."

"I've got first dibs," a stylish brunette called. "It's my turn for a new customer."

"Honey, he's not a customer till you convince him he is," someone corrected her. "And all's fair in love until the moment one of us closes the bedroom door."

"I wouldn't say it's over just because the door closes," someone said. "If I recall, one of you managed to be in the bed waiting, while you had a fake phone call downstairs for the girl he thought he was going to be spending the night with."

A few giggles went round the room, and a redhead in the corner blushed uncomfortably. "I should have known it was a trick. Extra points for creativity, especially since he didn't seem to mind the switch," she said.

"Well, this cowboy isn't going to get his eight seconds onboard Bloodthirsty Black. If Delilah wants to be humiliated twice, we can accommodate her," Marvella said. "But we can't be obvious, because I can guarantee you, he's been told in detail how truly mean, unkind and positively sex-starved we are. Delilah will be extracautious this time." She tapped long fingernails against the windowsill. "In four days. I don't want him to even lay a leg over Bloodthirsty Black. This calls for sweetness and light, dainty coincidence."

"Dainty?"

"Did you see that he was escorting Katy Goodnight on a walk? That's dainty as powdered sugar on a doughnut," Marvella pointed out.

"If her fiancé ditched her at the altar and married her best friend, she's got something missing in her sugar bowl," someone suggested. "Dainty is not always delightful."

"Okay," Marvella said with a snap of her fingers. "I've got just the plan."

"Is it dainty?"

She smiled as she watched the lights coming on inside her sister's salon. "No," she said. "It's a doozy."

CHAPTER THREE

THE NEXT MORNING Laredo met his brothers at the arena so they could get an eyeful of Bloodthirsty Black in his holding pen. The bull looked as if he had only ten more seconds before he busted out another perfectly good stall. Stepping back so they wouldn't irritate the bull more, Tex and Ranger shook their heads in unison.

"You're a nut," Ranger said. "You're going to need spine replacement if you ride him."

Laredo glared at him. "Tex is the one who's coaching me. You just came along for the laugh."

Tex shrugged. "He came along to keep me company on the ride, and mainly to try to help me talk you out of getting yourself killed. How's your health insurance, by the way? Both physical and mental? Maybe you should see a head shrink before you do this, 'cause I think you may have left your brains back in puberty."

Twin or no, Laredo was duty-bound to argue. "If I was deranged, I wouldn't be calling for reinforcement. Now, shut up and start coaching."

"Let me ride him for you," Ranger offered. "The Lonely Hearts girls just need a champion. They don't care who it is."

"It's gonna be me," Laredo said stubbornly.

"Why?" Tex demanded. "Ranger has the most wins besides me."

"He's too old. That was ten years ago."

"Excuse me?" Ranger said. "I'm thirty-two. You are thirty-four. How am I too old?"

"Because you've always been old. Me, I'm just now trying to find myself. This is my midlife crisis," Laredo said proudly, staring at Bloodthirsty Black. "All two to three thousand pounds of it."

"Sheesh. Other men want a pretty woman. My twin wants a head-and-neck rearrangement from an animal born to hate him. Makes perfect sense to me."

Ranger chuckled. "If Laredo's suffering a crisis, does that mean you are too, Tex?"

"Just because Archer's spending all his time writing to a Nicole Kidman look-alike in Australia, does that mean you're burning up the stationery with Byronic sonnets?" Tex jutted his chin. "Pull your head out, Ranger. Being twins does not mean we're split halves of the same person, as you very well know!"

Bicker, bitch, battle. For a moment Laredo thought his whole big fantasy of being a hero might go flushing downstream, until Katy Goodnight rounded the corner, bearing a basket with a cherry-printed cloth napkin inside. Instantly his whole day brightened. "Hi, Katy," he said with a big grin he couldn't control.

"Hi, Laredo," she said with a smile, before turning to his brothers. "And another Laredo," she said to Tex. "I'm sorry, I shouldn't have forgotten your name since I met you only a month ago, but I do remember your face," she said to Ranger.

"Well, that's all that's important," he said gallantly. "If a pretty gal just remembers my face—"

"Howdy, fellas," said another female voice.

They all turned as Hannah Hotchkiss came into view, carrying a basket decorated with blueberry sprigs. "This is Hannah," Laredo began, then ceased his introduction when he realized Ranger had nearly swallowed his teeth as she smiled up into his face. "Ranger," Laredo said sternly, "this is Katy's best friend."

"We brought you a snack," Hannah said. "We didn't know you had company, Laredo. But we have plenty."

Ranger took the basket from her and peeked inside. "Mmm. Cookies and strawberries. My favorite." He pulled Hannah with him until they were off by themselves.

Laredo rolled his eyes at Tex. "Did you have to bring him?"

"Oh, well. He can amuse himself now." Tex smiled at Katy. "How've you been, anyway?"

"Just busy. What brings you to Lonely Hearts Station?"

"We came to give Laredo some tip—"

"They just stopped by to say hello," Laredo said.

"It's nice of you to check on your twin. Is it true that twins are really close?" Katy asked.

"No," Laredo said.

Tex laughed. "We're fraternal in mind-set, you might say. I'm the settled one, Laredo is the wild one. If one of us was ever in a fistfight at school, the teachers didn't bother to check which one of us it was. They just automatically called Mason and said, 'Come get Laredo.'"

"It wasn't quite like that," Laredo said, getting more annoyed with his twin by the second. "I wasn't a hooligan."

"I grow roses," Tex said.

"Oh, I love roses," Katy replied.

The dreamy tone in her voice as she stared into his twin's eyes was almost more than Laredo could stomach. Her reaction was the same as every other woman's when Tex mentioned those stupid roses. Clearly, the roses were a conversational prop Tex employed just to get a woman's attention—he probably grew the stupid things just to get on women's good sides. "Okay, enough with the flowery stuff. Can we get on with the lesson?"

"Lesson?" Katy repeated.

"Yeah, I'm teaching Tex everything I know about bulls."

"I thought you didn't know anything," Katy said, her voice innocent.

Tex snickered, and Laredo made a mental note to punch him later. "I know a few things," he said, trying to hang on to his bravado. Something about Katy just got him so mixed up and confused! He wanted to brag in front of her, wanted to strut his stuff just a little, but somehow he kept goofing it up.

"What Laredo means," Hannah said, as she and Ranger moved back to the circle, "is that he knows more about Bloodthirsty Black. He's filling Tex in on the history."

"That's right." Laredo straightened with a grateful glance at Hannah. "History's important."

"Yeah, we all remember your report card," Ranger said.

Silence descended. "Excuse me," Tex said. "I'm going to go find a gents'."

He left, and the conversational void stretched. Laredo frowned at Ranger, who sighed.

"Now, just what is it about this bull we need to know?" Ranger said, clearly deciding to leave off the sibling rivalry and let Laredo get his neck broken if he was determined to do so.

"He pulls to the left," a voice said. "And then, just when you lean, he jerks to the right with a mean midair kick. Every time."

All four of them whirled to look at the woman who'd spoken. Laredo felt his jaw go slack, and heard Ranger's jaw hit the pavement with a resounding thunk.

This woman was simply stunning. As fresh and cute as Katy was, as punky-funky cute as Hannah was, this woman would set records for head-snapping stares.

Beside him, he could feel Katy stiffen.

"Hell-oo, there," Ranger said. "Thanks for the tip." He tipped his hat to her, and grinned.

The woman smiled back, one hand on her hip, the other casually resting against Bloodthirsty Black's stall. "You're welcome."

Laredo glanced at Katy for an intro. Hannah didn't seem too happy about the woman's presence, either, especially since she and Ranger had just spent a cozy five-minute chat together.

The woman ignored the female frostiness and extended a delicate hand to Ranger. "Staying in town long?" she asked softly, her voice full of hints.

"He's leaving in a couple of hours, actually," Laredo replied.

"And you?" she asked smoothly, looking back to Laredo.

He probably shouldn't tell what he was up to, Laredo thought. Katy probably wanted him to be the surprise weapon. "Uh, a guy can't hang around beautiful women in a quaint town forever, I guess."

"That's too bad. We're real nice to strangers here in Lonely Hearts Station." The woman smiled, and imperceptibly tightened her posture so that her breasts thrust forward in an invitation even the greenest male could understand.

Laredo thought he could see Ranger's eyes spinning

around in their sockets. Wow! He didn't think he'd ever seen his hard-edged brother so...softened up.

"This is Cissy Kisserton," Katy said reluctantly. "Cissy, meet Ranger and Laredo Jefferson."

"Real cowboys?" Cissy asked.

"Born and bred, ma'am," Ranger said. Hannah rolled her eyes, which Laredo thought was appropriate.

"Well, I don't want to keep you," Cissy said. "Just wanted to be friendly to the visitors in town. You send them over our way for a cup of cocoa, Katy. We'll make sure they're well taken care of."

"It's a bit chilly in here, after all, isn't it?" Ranger said. "I'll take you up on that cup of cocoa right now, Miss Cissy," he said, following after the beautiful woman like a lovestruck puppy.

The two of them disappeared around the corner, but not before Laredo saw Ranger slip his arm around her. Laughter floated over the stalls to them. Laredo groaned to himself. Ranger was the most steadfast of the brothers! Certainly he had his share of wild hairs— he'd been bluffing about going to do some military service for nearly a year now...of course, he'd never leave Malfunction Junction Ranch, but he'd sure been trying to put action where his big mouth was. He'd actually started hanging around the police station, trying to act civilized.

But nothing like a beautiful woman to make a man's mouth run away from him. Laredo looked at Katy, who appeared dumbfounded; Hannah seemed disappointed down to her very orange toenails, peeping out of cut-open tennis shoes.

The expression on Hannah's face told Laredo that Cissy wasn't the only woman around who thought Ranger was a hunk.

Oh, boy.

"Where's Ranger?" Tex asked, coming back to join them.

"He went off with a woman," Laredo said. "Cissy Kisserton. You should have seen her."

"You should have seen *him*," Hannah said. "It was like watching a giant tree get felled by one termite."

"Oh. I apologize for my brother's behavior," Tex said.

"Is Cissy a Never Lonely Cut-N-Gurl?" Laredo asked.

"Obviously," Katy said.

"Whoa." He'd have to be very careful to avoid that Venus fly trap. There was a real sensitive issue between the two salons for certain, and it clearly wasn't all about who gave the better haircut. "By the way, Tex, Cissy was awfully helpful. She says Bloodthirsty Black pulls to the left. And when you lean, he jerks to the right with a midair kick every time."

"Does he, now?" Tex eyed the bull speculatively. "And why was the competition being so helpful?"

Laredo looked at Katy and Hannah. "I guess she just wanted to be nice to the strangers in town."

Katy and Hannah made disgusted sounds, gathered up their baskets with the food in them and marched off without a word.

The parting looks they shot the men spoke loudly, however.

"You just blew it," Tex told his twin.

"What did I say?"

"First rule of girlhunting—never let a woman you like believe another woman has anything to offer you. Anyway, I'm supposed to be giving you tips on Mr. Bloodthirsty, here, not love. It's unseemly for a brother to have to coach his twin in things any freshly minted teenage boy knows."

Laredo's heart sank. "Cissy was awfully friendly. I thought she was nice. And she didn't have to tell us about the trick this old bull plays."

"True."

"Ranger stuck on her like glue. He didn't see anything wrong with her, either."

"There, then. You don't have anything to worry about."

Laredo frowned. Nothing to worry about except he'd upset Katy, and that was the last thing he wanted to do.

"Pulls to the left, huh?" Tex said. "When I went to the gents', I noticed the arena was empty. There's no one around. Let's sit you up on Bloodthirsty and see exactly how hard he kicks."

"Have you lost your mind? I'm not getting up on him." Laredo eyed the bull, who was pawing at something in his stall as if he were sharpening his hooves for the kill. "Don't we need about four other men helping us hold him?"

"If we were loading him in a chute, yeah. But you're just gonna get up on top of this bull and get used to the feel of him underneath you."

Laredo shook his head. "I'll wait till Saturday."

Tex sighed. "Look. It's not that hard. Watch me."

He pulled on his glove and looped a rope around the bull's neck. The animal snorted, demonstrating his displeasure by slinging his head. Tex jumped up on the top rail, squared himself up, jumped and landed briefly on the bull's back.

There was silence for an infinitesimally split second, and then all hell broke loose.

"I DON'T THINK the Jefferson boys are the men we thought they were," Katy said to Hannah as they walked home. "Laredo brags, Tex is a ladies' man and Ranger's off with the enemy."

Hannah nodded. "For a minute I thought Ranger might have liked me. He sure seemed to."

Katy's heart melted at the sound of sadness in Hannah's voice. "It's just that darn Cissy Kisserton. She knocks men down at their kneecaps."

"But if he'd really liked me, he wouldn't have even seen her," Hannah said. "You notice Laredo didn't so much as shake her hand."

Katy brightened a little. "I suppose he didn't." Then she faded again. "But he's still a braggart. If I were to fall for another man, I know I'd want one whose actions match his words."

"That may be the impossible holy grail, Katy. All men pad their résumés. So do women."

"*I* don't."

"You *do*," Hannah insisted. "I've noticed that since Laredo hit town, you're trying to stand like our competition does. Tush out and breasts stuck forward."

Together, they walked up the back-stair entrance of the salon and went upstairs to Katy's room. "It's true," Katy said. "That's exactly what I was doing. But if I don't shift things around, I'll never stand a chance against a girl like Cissy. She's got all the moves. And it's only a matter of time before those girls set their aim on Laredo. I just don't want to be around when they score a bull's-eye."

"Now, now." Hannah sank onto the bed and stared down at Rose the mouse. "Courage. Laredo seems loftier in morals than most men."

"I don't know. I noticed a marked decrease in loftiness

when Cissy came by. We brought picnic baskets, and Cissy brought a tight skirt and high heels."

Hannah frowned slightly. "I thought I might like Ranger, but it was one of those moments where you look at someone and see someone they're not because you want them to be something else. I must be in a needy phase. I'll have to be more careful."

Katy sat beside her, and patted Hannah's hand. "What happened to daring?"

"That's you, not me." Hannah perked up. "Katy, stand up," she said.

Katy complied, her eyes widening when she saw the scissors Hannah picked up from the table. "Not my hair, Hannah," Katy protested. "I know you've been itching to cut it for a long time, but it's unwise to give up an inch for a man. Truly, short and sassy isn't me."

"It is when you've got nice legs you never show," Hannah said, picking up the hem of Katy's long dress. She decisively cut up to Katy's knee.

"Hannah!"

"Hold still, I'm gauging your siren potential. I think another two inches," Hannah murmured, continuing to cut.

"I'm too short for short dresses," Katy protested. "I'll look even more like a baby-faced doll than I do!"

Hannah tossed the red fabric aside. "Nope," she said happily. "Now that's enough to give Laredo whiplash."

"Hannah." Katy knelt down to look into her friend's eyes. "Listen to me. Laredo Jefferson is the last man I need. He doesn't fit the description. In fact, in some ways he reminds me of Stanley."

Hannah cocked a wry brow. "In what ways? Stand back up so I can gauge the hem length."

"Laredo's ogle-meter. And that's enough to tell me that he's not even remotely close to…date material."

"Did Stanley ogle Becky before the two of them met like ships passing in the bridal chamber?"

Katy wrinkled her nose. "Not that I ever noticed. I think that was why I was so shocked."

"Something doesn't add up about that. What made those two suddenly jump in each other's arms?"

"My virginity."

"No." Hannah sighed, pulled out a needle from a drawer in Katy's nightstand and threaded it with red thread. Industriously, she went to work turning up the hem of Katy's dress by an eighth of an inch. "Linen's hard to sew by hand," she murmured. "I'm going to take tiny stitches, so stand very still."

"Don't you need a chalk or tape?"

"This will do for the lunch hour. I need you to concentrate. Did you ever tell Becky anything about Stanley?"

"I told her everything! She was my best friend, my maid of honor."

"Did you tell her anything personal? Like, oh, that you two hadn't slept together?"

"Everybody knew that, even my mother. We had a nine-month proper engagement. Stanley used to say he was proud to be marrying a virgin." She wrinkled her forehead.

"Don't do that. Your face will look like a race track," Hannah instructed.

"I told Becky everything a girl tells her best friend. Just like I tell you. She also knew that Stanley didn't like to kiss me."

Hannah stopped sewing. "What?"

"Stanley didn't like to kiss me. Why are you looking at me like that?"

Hannah shook her head. "Why didn't he?"

"He said it was too much temptation, since we couldn't…um, you know."

"And Stanley's family is wealthy?"

"Right. Stanley Peter St. Collin III, of St. Collin Faucets and Hinges."

"Oh, of course. Naturally." Hannah grimaced. "And Becky's family was where on the social register?"

"Well, way below ours, if you must use social register terms. Her mom and dad divorced a long time ago, when she was a child. And her mom worked as a waitress at night to make ends meet. Becky worked two jobs, too, after we graduated from high school."

"And your parents were the Goodnights of Goodnight Protective Arms, starting with well-heeled British immigrant parents and going back three pedigreed generations in your hometown. And you dutifully and impressively went to college and obtained a degree in chemistry."

"Well, it was the easiest thing to do," Katy said. "Chemistry is much easier than economics or something." She shuddered. "Columns of figures and business principles, or putting cool stuff like hydrogen chloride into test tubes and seeing what blows up. Protons. Dissection. No contest there, huh?"

"Oh, yeah. I can see where chemistry is the easy answer. Miles and miles of chemical configurations." Hannah went back to sewing.

"After I sort myself out—and I'm just about done, thanks to Miss Delilah—I'm going to teach chemistry at Duke in North Carolina in the fall. Of course, my original plan was to marry Stanley and become a perfectly manicured Mrs. St. Collin III. Luckily, I'd sent out lots of applications after I graduated from college and *before* Stanley proposed. He didn't like me interviewing at Duke. Did I tell you that I was invited to interview at Cornell, too?"

"Peachy. Turn." Hannah moved the needle in and out without glancing up. "These pretty legs are wasted on a chem prof.

"So, Duke in the fall."

"Yes." Katy sighed. "I should never have given up chemical calculations for a man."

"Not Stanley, anyway. But you can't throw marriage overboard and closet yourself in a lab."

"Look at me, Hannah, please."

Hannah complied, and Katy smiled at her friend.

"You have all been wonderful to me. But it's time for me to strike out on my own and realize my true potential. I'm not man savvy. I'm not sophisticated. I spent too many years studying while my girlfriends were hanging out at frat houses to have learned the feminine ropes. If life is based on sexual chemistry, I got an F in the sexual and an A plus in the chemistry. But being smart means I can take care of myself. I think I might have gotten a little nervous about my life, and when Stanley proposed, I jumped at it. Maybe I didn't want to be the smartest virgin spinster." She sighed, looking down for just a moment. "In a way, Stanley dumping me at the altar was the best thing that could have happened. It made me realize I'm much safer if I just rely on myself."

Hannah shook her head. "I think if you hadn't told Becky that Stanley didn't like to kiss you, she still would have stolen him. She needed a way out of her life, and you only thought you did. I think you subconsciously gave her the invitation to steal him."

Katy stared into the mirror, seeing the miracle Hannah had wrought with her dress. She looked like a different person. Sexier. Hipper. "Maybe I had some unconscious motive I didn't recognize, but I wouldn't have picked my wedding day to be dumped."

"That was unfortunate, but she was probably plagued by guilt, which caused her to wait until the last minute to act. She's probably not enjoying her honeymoon at all, thinking about you crying your eyes out." Hannah stood. "I haven't seen you cry at all, Katy. And I think all this talk of sexual dysfunction is a cover-up. Maybe you just wanted to keep men on the periphery of your life."

"If I didn't then, I do now. It's humiliating when the maid of honor marries your fiancé, wearing the hot pink dress you picked out for her. It's like, here's hot and sexy and here's plain and virginal. Which do you think most guys want? *I* don't know," Katy murmured. "You sure have a lot of insight into people, Hannah. How did you develop that?"

"I'm a hairdresser. I've heard lots of stories over the years. Be still." Gently she took hold of Katy's below-shoulder-length hair, slicked it into a smooth, high po-nytail, then took one strand which she wound around the rubber band and pinned down. "Now a touch of red lipstick," she said, applying it to Katy as she spoke, "and whammo! Instant femme fatale."

Katy inspected herself in the mirror. "Maybe it's fatal femininity."

"Think confident. Be confident. *I'm* confident that you're a woman not to be overlooked. Anyway, the plain-vanilla you is all but a memory." Satisfied, Hannah put

away the needle and thread and the hairbrush and lipstick, glancing with cool smugness at Katy's dress. "See
how easy it is to be daring?"

"This is daring?"

"For you? Yes. It's a start. Let's go have lunch at the
cafeteria, Virginity Barbie. All this thinking's made me
hungry."

LAREDO HESITATED outside the door of the Never Lonely
Cut-N-Gurls Salon. If Katy saw him going in here, he
was toast. Unfortunately, he needed Ranger, and he
needed him *now*.

Glancing guiltily across the street at the Lonely
Hearts Salon, he pushed open the door.

KATY GASPED as she saw Laredo go inside the enemy
camp. She and Hannah stepped back inside the door
quickly, staring at each other in surprise.

"Whoa," Hannah said. "I have to admit to being
caught off guard."

Katy's heart felt as if it bled a drop as red as her newly
short dress. "I told you. It's a dysfunctional thing. Those
girls have allure—and I do not." Why should she even
care? she asked herself. She didn't like him anyway.

Did she?

"Boys will be boys, I suppose," Hannah said. "You
could go rescue him from himself."

"I'd rather join Marvella's payroll. Come on. Let's go
eat at the cafeteria. Only, we're taking the back door. I
wouldn't dream of allowing Mr. I'll-Ride-That-Bull-For-
You to know we saw him slinking into the competition's
bunker."

CHAPTER FOUR

"HOLD STILL, TEX," Ranger said, his teeth gritted, slightly annoyed at being dragged away from Cissy to tend his brother in Delilah's barn. Tex was writhing a bit dramatically on the hay-covered floor, and Ranger had been far more impressed with the shoulder massage Cissy had been giving him back at the salon atop a satin-covered chaise lounge. "I've got to check your shoulder good because if it's broken, it'll set crooked. What were you thinking, anyway?"

Tex tried his hardest to lie still while Ranger none too gently probed his back and shoulder. "I wanted to test this bull and see if what Cissy said was true."

Laredo stared at his prone twin. "You couldn't tell a darn thing with that bull in a pen."

"I can tell you he's got a helluva liftoff. But I don't think he cranks left. No, I don't."

Ranger stopped what he was doing to look at his brother. "You don't think he cranks left?"

Tex shook his head. "I don't."

The three men studied the bull through the rails. Bloodthirsty seemed satisfied to have flung Tex into the stall across the aisle. For the moment he was quite a bit calmer.

"He does have a spring-loaded midair jump, though," Tex said. "Either this bull's changed his mind about how he tries to kill people or you were getting set up, Laredo."

Ranger shook his head. "Cissy's a nice girl. She wouldn't deliberately tell someone wrong."

"And bulls don't change their mind," Tex said stubbornly. "If they start out kicking left, that's usually the way they always go. Bloodthirsty didn't hesitate. Then he bunched himself up in the air and tossed me over the pen."

Laredo wasn't certain what to think. "Why would Cissy give me a bad tip?"

"So you'd lose, dummy," Tex told him. "She's a woman, and she's a rival, and she's sucking Ranger's face to make certain all her bases are covered."

"She didn't suck my face!" Ranger protested.

"Your lips are pink," Laredo pointed out. "Did you borrow some tinted chapstick, maybe? Drink a strawberry pop? Borrow a sun lamp and use it on your lips?"

"It was just a friendly peck," Ranger said. "Nothing more." But his face and neck turned as pink as the lipstick, and Laredo frowned.

"Why are you lying?"

"I'm not." Ranger shrugged and gently helped Tex to his feet. "I think your shoulder's fine. Just don't test him again anytime soon."

"Why? So we won't interrupt your friendly pecking with Cissy?" Tex asked. "What's gotten into you?"

"What's gotten into you?" Ranger shot back. "Since when have you cared who I talked to?"

"Since we're supposed to be here helping out a woman who rescued us last month, Ranger," Laredo stated. "Have you forgotten whose girls helped us and Union Junction through the big storm? Who helped with sandbagging, and cooking and mopping up a creek's worth of water? Who hung curtains in our house and cleaned and generally kept the town from getting washed under?"

Ranger stared at his brothers, speechless. He shook his head as if his ears were buzzing. Then his shoulders drooped. "I don't know what came over me," he said, his tone apologetic. "It was like…it was like the call of the wild, and I couldn't shut it off. Like being in a dream I didn't want to wake up from." He looked at them sheepishly. "For a minute there, I was almost totally hypnotized by a woman. Whew!"

"Oh, boy." Tex shook his head. "Listen, we've got to keep our heads on straight. Our brother has signed on to ride one of the worst bulls I've ever come in contact with, and he has no idea what he's doing. We've gotta have a plan."

"My plan is to get on and stay on," Laredo said. "I'm going to be more stubborn than this bull."

Bloodthirsty Black cared little for Laredo's announcement. He gave a round-nostriled snort, reminding everyone he was in the business of tossing cowboys as if they were hay.

"Maybe you should just give money to Miss Delilah's charity," Ranger said doubtfully.

"It's a man thing." Laredo glanced toward the barn exit. "In Spain, they run from bulls. Malfunction Junction Ranch cowboys laugh in the face of danger."

"And get gored," Tex said narrowly. "Are you falling for Katy Goodnight? Did something happen last month we don't know about?"

"Nope. Nothing went on between us except some mopping and some curtain hanging."

Ranger and Tex looked at each other. "Oh," they said in unison.

"What? What does that mean?" Laredo asked suspiciously.

"Keeping house," Tex explained. "The two of you were trying on domesticity. And you must have liked it."

"We were not! And I didn't!" He glanced around to make certain Katy hadn't decided to return unexpectedly—although, he figured that was hoping for too much. He lowered his voice. "But when she mops, she really moves her tush. Man, oh, man. That's what I remember most about her!"

Tex and Ranger groaned. "I'm sure she'd love to hear that," his twin said. "We'll pull together and buy her a bottle of Mop & Glo for a wedding gift."

"She can mop up your blood when this bull's done with you," Ranger said, equally disgusted. "You dummy."

BOTH HIS BROTHERS had called him a dummy, but Laredo didn't care. Something was telling him that this was the right moment in his life to do A Big Thing. This was his time to shine. And he couldn't wait.

His brothers left in disgust to go find a hamburger, but he wanted to find Katy. He headed over to the Lonely Hearts Salon, only to be told she'd gone to the Lonely Hearts Station Cafeteria with Hannah.

Waving his thanks, he loped off in that direction, quickly passing by the Never Lonely Cut-N-Gurls Salon without a glance.

The blinds snapped back into place in an upstairs room when he strode by.

"THAT'S THE COWBOY you were supposed to bring back, Cissy. Not that Ranger one."

"I wasn't expecting there to be two cowboys, and they both fit your description," Cissy explained. "But Ranger's a good kisser. It certainly wasn't time wasted."

"You wasted my time," Marvella insisted. "Three days before the rodeo. We need to turn Katy's cowboy to our way of thinking. I want you to try again."

Cissy smiled. "With these men, it's a pleasure. But he seems to like Katy very well. What if he won't be lured into our salon?"

"You are my magic potion, my dear. No man has ever looked in your eyes and said no. I'm confident you'll be up to the job."

She peeked at the cowboy, who was heading at a near jog toward the cafeteria. "But what *if?*"

"If the *what if* happens—and I don't believe you have a failure rate anywhere in that man-magnet body of yours—we'll simply kidnap him the night before. Just like we did the last cowboy."

Cissy laughed. "That was so much fun. It was like having our own cowboy toy for the night."

"If you're hungry, Cissy, I'll buy your lunch at the cafeteria."

Cissy put out her hand, palm up. "I'm always hungry."

"DON'T LOOK NOW, but here comes your cowboy," Hannah said. "Be nice to him, please, Katy? He looks anxious."

Katy gave Laredo a brief smile as he sat down next to them.

"Hi, Katy," he said.

"Hi, Laredo. I forgot to ask you how you slept last night? Good?" She was all prepared to act as if she'd never thought about liking this cowboy. Stiff and for-mal—and nothing more than acquaintances.

"I did. Thanks for letting me sleep in your room. How did you sleep in Delilah's room?"

"Very well. Thanks for asking."

And that was all she could think of to say, because she really wanted to ask him why he'd gone over to the Never Lonely Salon. That would break the acquain-tances' rule of no prying, though.

"Hi, Hannah," Laredo said.

"Hey. Get your bull all figured out?"

"I think so, but I missed getting to eat what you two had in those picnic baskets."

He looked at Katy when he said this, and she felt herself flush because she'd flounced off in a snit over Cissy Kisserton.

"So…were your brothers any help?"

"Tex is. He knows more than just about any of us about bulls."

"I can't tell the two of you apart," Hannah said. "Do you ever have trouble when you go places?"

"Nah. I'm nicer than he is. More outgoing. People notice."

Katy stared at him. "I don't know if I agree that you're the more outgoing of the two."

He smiled and slid his hand over to snag a French fry off her plate. "Tex is always thinking about ratios of manure versus fertilizer composition, et cetera."

"Ratios?" Hannah perked up.

"Yeah. And the chemical configurations of fertilizer and exciting things like that. Real exciting."

"Maybe you set your sights on the wrong twin," Hannah murmured, but Katy kicked her underneath the table. Then, embarrassed because Laredo had heard, she excused herself to go get another glass of lemonade.

For the first time in her life, men's heads turned as she walked to the soda fountain. She hoped Laredo was watching. She hoped he realized she could be as sexy as a girl like Cissy—she'd just needed a little coaching— and she walked a little more slowly to give him time to notice, in case he was slow on the uptake. She smiled at a stranger in a pair of jeans and what looked like an expensive Italian shirt. Why anyone would wear an Italian shirt in Lonely Hearts Station, she didn't know, but his ponytail was as long as hers, only not so high on his head. To her surprise, he got up from his table and began walking toward her.

Uh-oh, she thought. She'd gone and done it now! Her sexy short dress was one thing, but piling on confidence she didn't have and a big smile might have—

"Excuse me," the man said as she busily tried to get the soda fountain to work. For some reason it wouldn't pour the lemonade!

"Yes?" she asked nervously, forcing herself to look at him. After all, Laredo was watching, and he'd just been in the enemy camp, and two could play at that game. Right! If only she could get through this moment, she'd go home and take her silly ponytail down and put on one of her long dresses.

"I'm Lars Van Hooven from *Playboy Magazine,*" he said, handing her a card, which she hesitantly took from him. "Photographer. We've been combing the United States for small-town girls for our magazine."

"Playboy Magazine?" Her head was spinning. Why would he be giving her a card?

"Yes," he said with a smile that definitely wasn't wolfish. It was a smile meant to comfort her. "We're going to do a pictorial on small-town girls, and you've definitely got what we're looking for."

"Oh, thank you," Katy said, not certain exactly what she had.

"If you want to try out for the magazine, we'd fly you to our offices, all expenses paid."

She tried to hand the card back. "Well, Mr. uh, Mr. Lars, I'm not really—"

"I know," he said with another easy, winning smile. "It's okay. Keep the card. Think it over. Call me if you have any questions. Maybe you'll change your mind. I live for girls who change their minds."

"I see. Okay, well, thank you."

"You're welcome." He reached above her, flipped the lemonade switch, and, magically, her cup filled. In her nervousness, she hadn't pressed the switch properly.

She felt her face flush. "Thank you," she said, her smile shy and embarrassed.

"Magical," he said, staring at her. "Please change your mind about calling me."

And then he walked away. Katy looked back at her cup, which now sparkled with lemonade. *Never,* she thought. *No way.*

But she *was* going to have Hannah cut off every dress in her closet!

She tucked the card into her purse when she sat down.

"What did that guy want?" Laredo asked.

"He just helped me get the lemonade working," Katy said with an innocent smile. "Laredo, you haven't told us about your family. How are they doing?"

"Well, we still have the housekeeper from hell. Helga keeps everyone on a rigid schedule and drives us all nuts, but Mason would get rid of us before he got rid of her. He believes she hung the curtains you hung, and stocked his freezer with casseroles, so we're stuck with her. And he's too torn up to notice any different, because Mimi's getting married to a city slicker, and Mason's too proud to hunt her down and make her change her mind."

Hannah ate some Jell-O. "Maybe it's a family trait. Those are the worst to break. So…where's Tex?"

And Ranger, Katy knew she wanted to say.

"My brothers went to get a hamburger. I came to see how y'all were doing."

He gave Katy a smile that said, *See? I'm different from Mason. I'm not too proud to hunt down a woman.* "I like your dress, Katy."

He'd noticed! And after he'd been to the opposing camp, too. Actually, he hadn't stayed long, now that she thought about it…and he wasn't wearing any lipstick stains. He hadn't backed out of riding Bloodthirsty Black. And he didn't smell like perfume, just warm male. Slowly she smiled back at him, feeling her whole face relax as she decided to forgive him for taking a detour.

Across the cafeteria a camera whirred, snapping up pictures of a small-town girl on the verge of falling in love with her cowboy.

CISSY WALKED into the Lonely Hearts Station Cafeteria, seeing the same beatific, early-crush smile the camera was enjoying.

She had to work fast, that was for certain. Marvella never fired anyone, but when things didn't work her way, she could be a witch on a broom and make a woman's life miserable for weeks.

She ran a quick hand over her platinum, show-stopping locks and smoothed her miniskirt. Then she started walking, the way a woman walks when she's got a destination in mind.

"Hello, Laredo," she said, leaning over to move in between Katy and him. She gave him a fast kiss on the cheek he couldn't get away from. "We really enjoyed seeing you at our place. Come on by…anytime."

Stunned into a grin, he looked up at Cissy, not missing, Katy noticed, her full-size breasts on the way to her eyes.

"We'd invite you to sit down," Laredo said, his manners in full effect, "but there's no room."

"Oh, I'd lo-o-ove to sit with you all," she said silkily, and nudged Katy over with a hip. "Katy, honey, scoot over. You're hogging the bench."

CHAPTER FIVE

CISSY SANK ONTO the bench between Laredo and Katy, giving him a dazzling smile and an eyeful of cleavage as she sat. She sure smelled good—and her platinum locks brushed his bare arm. His mouth dried out.

What was it Ranger had said? He'd suddenly heard the call of the wild? Blinking to chase off the pea-soup inertia taking over his brain—which curiously came accompanied by a sound like horns warning ships to stay clear during dense fog—Laredo tore his gaze away from Cissy. He looked across the table at Hannah, who was staring at him curiously, her spoonful of quivering red Jell-O halfway to her mouth. Like a drowning man, he focused on Hannah's direct gaze and her wild and tousled hairdo and pulled his brain out of the drowning swirl it was caught in.

He might not have ever ridden a bull, but he knew when he was set directly on the horns of a dilemma. "Hannah," he said, slowly and carefully, shutting his ears to the call of the wild, "would you mind keeping Miss Cissy company? I'm going to walk Katy back to the salon because she needs to feed Rose."

"Feed... Oh, oh, sure," Hannah said, catching on. "I'll be happy to, Laredo."

"Please excuse us, Miss Cissy," Laredo said, nodding to her as he took his tray and Katy's. "We'll be seeing you around."

Katy said goodbye to Hannah and Cissy, seeming more than happy to leave.

"I hope you don't mind," Laredo said as they walked out into the bright sunlight. "You looked like you were done eating."

She smiled up at him. "I was happy to go."

"Good."

"Rose was an inventive excuse."

"It was the truth. Since I slept in your room last night, I didn't figure you'd had a chance to feed her. I picked her up out of her box, and she told me she wasn't the kind of girl to be handled before she'd had her breakfast."

Katy smiled, and he looked at her appreciatively. "You look real nice, Katy."

"Thank you." She hesitated before glancing up at him. "Laredo, are you sure you're all right with riding Bloodthirsty Black?"

"I want to do it. It's a personal issue for me, a goal I've set for myself."

"Goals are good."

"What are your goals?"

"To be a first-rate chemistry professor at Duke in the fall," she murmured.

"Chemistry. I like chemistry," he said, cupping her face with one hand.

"Really?" she asked.

"Unless Tex is talking about it. Then it has something to do with flowers and is annoying."

"Some women like flowers," she said on a breath as he stroked her cheek and then her chin.

"Tex's flowers never mature," Laredo told her. "They never get from bud to bloom. I prefer a more direct process for my goals."

"Like, get on mad beefsteak, get neck broken by mad beefsteak?" she asked with a smile.

"Something like that."

"You're doing this out of a sense of responsibility. If I hadn't dragged you into our salon, you'd be halfway to— Where were you going, anyway?"

"Anywhere," he said, leaning down to place his lips gently on hers. "Somewhere," he murmured, as he felt her still beneath him. "Probably nowhere as fun as Lonely Hearts Station."

Then he kissed Katy the way he'd been wanting to since he'd first noticed her tush when she was mopping.

And when he felt her unstiffen, felt her relax against him and then felt her lips move under his, Laredo decided Katy was even better at kissing than mopping.

"SORRY THAT DIDN'T WORK OUT for you," Hannah said gleefully. "Guess your sexual grenades don't get Laredo's attention. Maybe he's more the subtle type. You know, sparklers instead of incendiary devices."

"I wouldn't say that. He ran out of here for a reason." Cissy smiled with surety. "A man only runs when he's afraid."

"I'd be afraid of you, too, Cissy."

Cissy tapped Hannah's tray with a fingernail. "Pay attention here, country girl. He's afraid of being *tempted*."

"Oh, was that what made him run?" Hannah finished up her Jell-O and licked the spoon with smug contentment. "Temptation. Hmm. Remind me never to try that on a man."

Cissy leaned forward. "Hannah, you may think you were working a direct angle with your little blueberry napkin-lined basket, but you saw how quickly *Ranger* did whatever I wanted."

The smugness left Hannah's face.

"Yes, Hannah, dear, one of us has kissed him, and the other has not."

Hannah sat very still, watching Cissy with big eyes.

"So if I were you, I'd not be too quick with the congratulations to Katy." Cissy stood. "I have only just begun. Besides, I melted Ranger easily enough. Why shouldn't his brother be just as easy?"

"Is there a reason you can't confine yourself to Ranger?" Hannah said, though it hurt like heck to say it.

"There is a reason, and it's really none of your business," Cissy said, her voice biting enough to make Hannah sit up straight.

"Can't your salon win without cheating?"

"It's not cheating if your cowboys always fall apart at the last second."

And yet it would take a man of iron not to fall for Cissy and the Never Lonely girls. They just knew what it took to wind a man's sex drive into full gear. Poor Katy didn't have a chance against them. "Why does Marvella hate Delilah so much?" Hannah asked.

"I'm only an employee," Cissy said with a toss of her beautiful hair. "I do what I'm told, and I make a good living. Can you say the same?"

"Well, we're not performing the same tasks," Hannah retorted. "So I don't think we can compare paychecks. Cissy, do you think, just this once, you could leave a man alone? I think Katy really likes Laredo, and she's just getting over a broken heart."

"One never pulls back just when they're about to win the war."

"Excuse me, ladies," a man's voice interrupted. "Lars Van Hooven, photographer for *Playboy Magazine*."

"Playboy Magazine!" Cissy said, lighting up like morning sunshine. "I'm Cissy. How do you do?"

"Fine, thanks." Lars glanced away from her to look at Hannah. "I met your friend over by the soda fountain, and I gave her a business card in case she decided to try out for our small-town girls pictorial. But I forgot her name. Can you tell me what it was?"

"Katy Goodnight," Hannah said with a pointed smile for Cissy. "Although I hate to dim your hopes, but I don't think you'll be hearing from her. Katy's a shy, innocent kind of girl. A real diamond among bad fakes."

Cissy stuck her tongue out at Hannah. Hannah winked back.

"Thanks for the info." He tapped Katy's name into a Palm Pilot, missing the byplay between the two women. "She's exactly what we're looking for."

"Need a blonde?" Cissy asked, all her charm on display.

Lars shook his head as he put his organizer away. "Sorry. Thanks for offering. But what we have in mind is freshness, and that country sweetness. The world is really looking for innocence right now." He nodded to them and left.

"Well, well, well," Hannah said. "Totally immune to you."

"Only because he's gay, Hannah. I never said I could work miracles," Cissy snapped.

"Freshness and country sweetness. Can you say *defeated,* Cissy? This war is lost."

"We'll see on Saturday, won't we?" Cissy gave her a shriveling glare and stalked away.

THE SENSATION of being thoroughly kissed by Laredo had Katy turned inside out. Everything in her body felt weak and somehow shaky, feelings she'd never felt before.

It was too much, too powerful, too soon. Her heart had been betrayed last month, by her best friend and her fiancé. Nothing that felt this overwhelmingly hot and passionate could be taken slow and easy.

She felt as if she was standing square on the point of no return, and in serious danger of falling over the edge. Parts of her body she'd never known could react felt as if they were filling with liquid fire.

Before she could help herself, she pulled away from Laredo, blinking up at him in wonder.

"What's wrong, sweetheart?" he asked.

"I...I don't know," she said on a gasp. "I've never been kissed like that before."

He smiled. "Then let's do it again and go for two."

But this was no light matter for her. Pieces of her had flown out of their usual reserved place, like glass chips missing from a window. She felt fragile in his arms, when she needed to be getting stronger. *Sweetheart?* Not her. "I'm sorry," she said quickly. "Laredo...I'm not the girl for you."

And then she ran into the Lonely Hearts Salon.

Laredo scratched his head as he watched Katy flee. Not the girl for him? Of course she wasn't the girl for him. He wasn't looking for a girl to be right for him. He was passing through town on his way to big things, whatever it was that he could pit his strength and his smarts against.

This stop in Lonely Hearts Station was just Big Thing #1.

Of course he liked Katy, liked her an awful lot. Wouldn't want to hurt her.

And yet, he understood what she was saying. She didn't want to be played fast and loose. She wasn't available for a good time.

Fact was, she was right. Neither he nor any of his brothers had ever itched to be settled. Frisco Joe getting caught was a weird thing, but it had shown all the brothers that extra caution was called for or they'd all end up with a wife and a wailing baby.

Of course, Frisco was pretty dang happy.

Laredo thought about his father, who hadn't been seen in years. He thought about his mother, whom he remembered mopping, cleaning, cheerfully making a home and a family with a rough man who'd adored her.

His dad hadn't been able to stand it when the only gentle, sweet flower in his life died. He'd left Mason to raise a houseful of rowdy boys because the pain had been too great.

And that could happen to him if he wasn't careful.

Katy was right: she wasn't the woman for him. There would never be a woman for him.

He should never have kissed her.

He stepped off the curb to head toward the barn to find his brothers, whistling "On the Road Again."

"Hi, Laredo," he heard Cissy Kisserton say as he reached the middle of the narrow street.

"Hey, Cissy." Now there was a woman who wouldn't ask for more than he could give. Nor did he particularly care to give her anything, but there were girls one played around with because they understood the game, and other girls one married.

The kind of girl who understood the rules was eminently more fun, or at least had been before he met Katy. Not the girl for him? In spite of his agreement with her tidy statement, he was puzzled. Somehow Katy had hurt his feelings, and he briefly wondered if he was talking bravado through his cowboy hat.

"Laredo," Cissy said with sweetly downcast eyes as she stood close to him, putting one hand on his T-shirt, "I have a confession to make."

"A confession?" The hairs on the back of his neck seemed to stand up. Something about this woman had a very strange effect on him. It was like watching lightning dance across the sky and wondering if it might strike you if you stood in a wide-open field. He'd not seen Cissy when she wasn't one hundred percent *on*, but right now she had her switch on low wattage, no radiance, dimmed to pleasing supplication.

"Yes," she said softly, finally looking up at him with huge aquamarine eyes, "Laredo, I'm afraid I lied to you about Bloodthirsty Black."

CHAPTER SIX

AT MALFUNCTION JUNCTION RANCH, there were also some untruths being suffered. All the Jefferson brothers seemed painfully aware of the sidestepping, reality-avoiding situation—except one.

Mason sent a glance around the table, eyeing his younger brothers. All present and accounted for, except Frisco Joe, who was in the Texas wine country with Annabelle and baby Emmie, and Laredo, Tex and Ranger, who were goofing off, best as he could tell.

Laredo and his crazy something-big plan. All Mason needed now was another catastrophe to hit, and he'd move out himself.

The front door opened and Mimi Cannady blew in, wearing jeans, a fluffy white sweater and a bright smile to match her new engagement ring. "Hey, everybody!"

Mason instantly lost his appetite. Diamond engagement rings seemed to have that effect on him, or maybe it was just Mimi's two-carat princess-style cut, as she'd described it to him. She'd seemed delighted with it, but he'd been unimpressed. What was he supposed to say: Gee, that's the prettiest ring I ever saw? "Hi, Mimi," he muttered along with his brothers, carefully avoiding glancing at her and her ring.

"Brought you some frozen key-lime pie." She laid it on the table. "Where's everybody else?"

"Gone to make jackasses of themselves," Mason said sourly.

"More so than usual?" she asked, seating herself at the table in the seat that Laredo would have occupied, which just happened to be next to Mason. He could smell her perfume, and it smelled different to him than it had before.

No. It *was* different. "Did you change perfumes?" he demanded.

Mimi and his brothers gawked at him—and then Mimi smiled, bigger than he'd ever seen her smile. "I wouldn't have thought you'd notice such a thing, Mason."

"I noticed because I don't like it," he said hurriedly, though he really did.

Her smile flew off her face, and all his brothers scowled at him.

"You look real nice, Mimi," Calhoun said.

"And you got a new sweater," Last offered. "White looks nice on you, and it's so soft."

"Thank you for the pie," Bandera said. "We're not gonna share with Mason 'cause he's a horse's patoot."

She laughed. "So, where are the Jefferson boys who are making donkeys of themselves?"

"They're in Lonely Hearts Station. Laredo's entered in a rodeo this weekend. He's going to ride a bull named Bloodthirsty Black," Archer said, to a round of chuckles.

"A bull? Laredo can't ride," she said, glancing at Mason.

"He's making a fool of himself for a woman, on the pretext of noble intentions," Mason said.

"Remember the Lonely Hearts ladies who helped us out so much?" Last said. "They needed a cowboy for a charity ride, so Laredo offered. But we think he's really trying to impress Katy Goodnight."

"Oh, that's so sweet!" Mimi glanced at Mason. "That's not being a jackass, Mason. That's *romance*."

He shrugged.

Last sighed. "I'll get a knife for your pie, Mimi. Stay and have a bite with us, will you?"

"No, I've got to get back to Dad," she said, quickly standing. "You *are* all planning to come to my wedding next month, aren't you? It wouldn't feel right not to have all my brothers there."

Every head nodded—except Mason's.

"We wouldn't miss it, Mimi," Last assured her.

"Mason?" she asked softly.

He held back the sigh that begged his chest to heave for release. His jaw locked to keep the words inside him, whatever they might have been. But this was no time for spontaneity. This moment called for…realization.

Things had changed. Everything around him was changing, and it was all out of his control. The days when he was the captain seemed to have evaporated.

Still, a man went down with his ship.

"I'll be there," he said, a lukewarm response that was more a grunt than a promise.

"Thank you." She glanced at him one last time, but he didn't look at her. "Goodbye, fellas. I'll stop by, maybe tomorrow, and check on you. You all are going to see Laredo ride, aren't you?"

They seemed perplexed by that.

"He is your brother. And he very well may need last rites, for heaven's sake," she pointed out. "Of course, love is a wonderful cause to throw caution to the wind for."

The brothers sat silently, although Mason became very interested in the seal on the pepper shaker.

"I reckon we'll go," Last said. "Wanna go with?"

She beamed. "I thought you wouldn't ask. I will, thanks!" And then she left, the wind catching the door as she blew out, causing a noisy slam.

Silence descended after that. Mason could feel his brothers' gazes on him. They didn't need to tell him he'd been cantankerous and mean. He knew it. He just didn't know how else to be around Mimi. Her getting engaged had stopped him cold, shocking him beyond words. In his mind, she'd always been *his* best friend. She was his troublemaker, his life of the party. If there was some fun to be had, she knew how to find it, while he had no more clue about absurd hijinks than a schoolteacher. In a life that had early met hard responsibility, Mimi's spirit had been his let-off valve.

He'd never imagined another fella in the picture.

But suddenly there was, and he was torn. Worse still, though he'd been prepared to dislike the city-slick lawyer in the fancy red sports car, Mason had found that he liked Brian O'Flannigan. He seemed just right for Mimi, a fact that annoyed Mason but which he also admired, when he forced his conscience to be objective.

His brothers got up to leave, taking the pie with them. Mason barely noticed. He sat at the head of the table, staring at nothing, thinking about things he really didn't want to think about, mainly abandonment.

First his mother. Then his father.

Now Mimi.

It was, for reasons he couldn't fathom, the deepest cut he'd ever suffered. No fun at all.

"HI, DAD," Mimi said to Sheriff Cannady as she walked inside the kitchen of their home. "You're up now."

"I am." He smiled at his only child. "You look pretty, honey."

"Thank you." She kissed the top of his head and pulled out another refrigerated key-lime pie. "Your favorite."

Her father smiled, but his skin seemed grayer than it had yesterday. She was worried about him, more worried than she would tell him or anybody else. There was nothing that could be done about it, of course. Her father needed a liver transplant, and the list was long, the chances slim to none. They'd told no one in Union Junction, specifically because her father wanted to go out being the strong sheriff the people had elected for nearly twenty years running. She thought he had a right to that.

They had faced tough odds before. It had always been the two of them against the world.

She couldn't face the thought of losing her father.

Time had run out for her, forcing her to grow up. Mason wouldn't understand that an hourglass didn't have forever to be turned over and over again, keeping the sand pouring continually, infinitely.

If it had been up to her, Mimi knew she would have waited forever for Mason.

Yet even she knew that forever was exactly how long she would have waited—because Mason would never have asked her to marry him. Mason didn't love her. In his mind she would always be the ragamuffin next door, the little girl in ponytails who hung around him like a fun, colorful pest.

Her father's illness had changed her priorities. She couldn't wait any longer for a dream that would never come true. Like the best of fortunes, Brian O'Flannigan had come to help her father with some legal work and fallen head-over-heels in love with her.

It had felt so good to have someone fall for her, someone to want her so much that they were willing to give her half of themselves and so much more. Still, she loved Mason, even though she knew he wasn't capable of loving her the way Brian did. A choice had to be made: she could be happy, or she could be sad.

Strange how her father's life had made her choice easy.

Because if she was going to lose her other parent, the one who'd raised her and loved her with all his heart, she was determined that he was going to see his only child happily married.

And, if God heard her prayers, she was going to make her father a grandfather before he died. He was going to know his grandchild.

She was not prepared to let him go without seeing him hold her baby.

These were the odds she was up against, and Mimi had a well-deserved reputation for being a fighter. This was a battle she meant to win.

"MAYBE IT'S TOO MUCH to ask of Laredo," Delilah said to Jerry the truck driver, who stopped into the salon every time he was near Lonely Hearts Station. They'd become friends and a bit more, in the last month, since he'd driven her and all her girls home from their trip to Union Junction.

Delilah enjoyed having a man around to talk to. Heaven only knew, her sister, Marvella, had stolen every other man in town. But Jerry was more than just male company; he'd become a champion in her corner, and she desperately needed that right now. Picking stubbornly at the letters on a western shirt, Delilah pulled out the name of Lonely Hearts' last champion who'd never even worn the shirt. "Maybe we should let Laredo off the hook and find another cowboy. Laredo barely knows the right end of the bull to hang on to."

Jerry shrugged. "He offered."

"So did you, but I turned you down." She smiled sweetly at the man who reminded everyone of a jolly Santa Claus.

"Because I'm old and fat. That bull wouldn't be able to lift his weight with me on him." Jerry winked at her. "I say turnabout is fair play, anyway. They shanghaied our rider. What do you say we do the same to theirs?"

Delilah laughed. "I don't think I can bring myself to cheat, no matter how much fun it would be."

"Did you know that Cissy Kisserton's out in the middle of the street talking to your cowboy right now?" Jerry asked, staring out the window.

Delilah jumped up from her chair and flew to the window. "That she-devil!"

He shook his head. "Of course, Marvella figures it worked so well last time, why not give it a go again."

"Well, I'll be!" She looked at Jerry. "Gosh, it's not like we have the best of chances since our cowboy's unproven!"

"Our own virgin cowboy," Jerry agreed. "Does seem like Marvella works just a little too hard at what should be a friendly way to benefit charities."

"Maybe I'll change my mind about cheating!"

He chuckled and kissed her cheek. "No one could blame you if you did, but I'd rather see you stick to the honest side."

She was silent for a minute, weighing her doubts.

"Jerry, I've already let half my girls go. They were lucky. They're settling in Union Junction and opening their own shop. Katy and these other ten gals might not be so fortunate if I have to close up totally. Then how am I going to feel?"

"Like you did the best you could, honey. No one's guaranteed a cakewalk in this life. You gave them fresh starts. Gave them what you had to give. If we get beat, me and you, we're going ice-fishing in Delaware. Or Canada. For good."

She heard the "we" and felt so much better. And yet—

"Jerry, this shop is all mine. It's all I've ever had. When my husband died, I scraped for every penny. Then Marvella's husband left her and we fell in love and got married. I did not steal him," Delilah said with a steely eye. "Marvella has made me the scapegoat, but it was two years after they split up before I even saw her husband." She sighed, the memories hard. "And then he passed away. After that, I was tired of burying husbands. I opened this shop, and it's given me everything I've needed for the past ten years. More than anything, I've enjoyed the girls. They come here sad and hurting, and they get well, and they go away healed. And I'm darn proud of that."

"But you wouldn't want to kidnap some hapless bull rider just to win."

"I think I would!"

He laughed and tweaked her nose. "We'll find another way. Come on. I'll help you finish picking the letters off that shirt so you can put Laredo's name on it. At least we can count on *him*."

CHAPTER SEVEN

LAREDO STARED AT THE beautiful woman in front of him. "Lied to me? Why?"

Cissy gave him a sweet smile. "All's fair in love and war. At least that's what I always heard. But now I don't think that's right anymore. I want to be on *your* side, Laredo."

He wasn't buying this act for a second. "Why?"

"I like you," she said, her tone innocent and shy.

Hmm. Still telling lies, but at least the kind he liked to hear. "Thought you liked my brother Ranger."

"I like him, too," she said earnestly.

Double hmm. "You just like men in general."

"You might say that." She curled a finger down the buttons of his shirt. "But I like you *best*."

This girl was a bad'un, and he wasn't in the mood for a reform fantasy. "Listen, this is serious, Cissy, for a lot of people. I can't play games with you. I have to beat your salon's bull, and I aim to do it."

She pursed her lips at him. "You need me on your side, Laredo, giving you inside info, if you know what I mean."

"You'd rat out your own salon?"

"If there was something in it for me," she said silkily.

Uh, yeah. Economics 101—there was no such thing

as a free lunch. Laredo shrugged. "What's the something?"

"A ride out of town."

He stared at her. "Bus, plane, train. They're all transporting, I hear. Especially trains, since this town is still a working station."

"I'd rather someone I know take me where I want to go."

There was a trap being laid here. Laredo just hadn't sprung it right. "Where do you want to go?"

"Anywhere, as long as you're taking me."

He stepped back from her shirt-roving hand. "Cissy, I wouldn't dream of driving off with you. People would be looking for my body for months."

She laughed. "We're not *that* determined to win."

"No, but you're working me for some reason. I suspect you're supposed to lure me out of town and then knock me out until the rodeo's over."

"You're so suspicious!" She smiled at him. "Are you always like this?"

Since he'd met her? "Yes."

"Oh, piffle. You're just letting that crazy Katy Goodnight make you nuts."

"Crazy?"

"Sure." She blinked at him. "Everybody knows she wouldn't let her ex-fiancé kiss her. So he dumped her. Big surprise, huh? I mean, virginity shouldn't be a remote-control trap, should it?"

Whoa! His mouth instantly dried out. "Virginity?"

"Well, if she won't let her fiancé kiss her, she sure wasn't going to get to normal relations."

"How do you know this?" He couldn't see Katy confiding in Cissy.

She laughed. "Laredo, this is a very small town. And

we make it our business to know each other's business. Delilah and her girls act like unblemished Southern ladies, but they keep tight tabs on us just like we do them." Cissy stepped between his legs so she could stare up at him with big eyes and a sultry mouth. "Depriving a man is cruel, Laredo. A man could lose his mind that way."

Wind blew through his brain in tunnel-like fashion. Cissy was standing too darn close to him. There was nothing remote-control about her trap. She was all about hands-on ambush. "Thanks for the tip on Bloodthirsty," he said, turning to head in the opposite direction. "If you'll excuse me, Miss Cissy, I've got to go."

If indeed Cissy was telling the truth this time, he had to tell his brothers. They had some major strategy revising to work on.

After that, he had to move out of Katy's room. A virgin? His tongue felt as if it had turned into a dry sponge. The first thought he'd ever had about Katy was that a man could spend many good nights with a girl like her!

He'd been way off the mark. No wonder he'd had trouble sleeping—he'd been in a virgin's bed. And he had two more nights to go!

He'd never make it. Sleep was going to be a thing of his past until he left Lonely Hearts Station, or until he vacated Katy's room. Every time he looked at Katy he thought about sex. Now, if he *could* get to sleep, he'd probably be dreaming about making love to her.

Being the first man in a woman's life was a load of responsibility.

It would also be a rush of major proportions. He'd never let that little gal out of his sight if he were her first….

That would not fit the doing-something-big plan.

Glancing up and down the street, he saw he had two choices for lodging: his truck and Miss Delilah's. As their champion, they felt it proper to put him up. He'd kissed Katy—and she'd virtually run away. Without sleep, he'd be mush by Saturday, and they'd have to pour him onto Bloodthirsty, and that bull would throw him to kingdom come. He'd wind up sleeping in a hospital.

Slowly he walked back into the Lonely Hearts Salon and climbed the stairs to Katy's room, where he knew he'd find her.

KATY TURNED as Laredo walked into her room. He looked different, worried. "What's wrong?"

Silent for a moment, he finally said, "I'm sorry I kissed you."

She only kept her lips from parting in surprised disappointment by the greatest effort. "Sorry?"

"I shouldn't have forced myself on you." Laredo rubbed his chin and then the back of his neck. "You were right to...reject my advance."

"Oh," she murmured. How much could words hurt a heart? Hannah said the heart was only a symbol, but it sure felt like her symbol was breaking. She'd been wishing she wasn't such a chicken when it came to Laredo; she'd been envying Cissy, who could throw herself at men with such confident ease.

Yet Laredo was sorry he'd kissed her. And Stanley hadn't liked to.

There *was* something wrong with her. It was some kind of weird spinsteritis. Men sensed it as soon as they touched her.

She had hoped it would be different with Laredo. She

had hoped *she* would be different. "It's all right," she murmured. "Kissing's not that big a deal."

Of course, it was to her, but she wasn't going to make Laredo feel bad over her lack of sex appeal.

He looked surprised at her statement. "It's not?"

She shrugged. "Not really."

"Well…I'm surprised to hear you say that. You practically set a record running away from me."

A blush burned across her cheeks. "I was caught off guard."

"You said you weren't the girl for me. But I'm not looking for a girl for me."

She blinked. "What are you looking for?"

"Adventure. And that's just about it."

Kissing with no strings attached. That certainly took all the pressure off. "I like to be adventurous."

He grinned at her, knowing at once that she was fibbing, she supposed. "Well, I'd like to be adventurous," she added.

"I don't have any plans tonight," he said.

"Are you asking me out?" After she'd run away from him like a scared rabbit, why would he?

"Friends can go out, can't they?"

"Friends?"

He nodded. "I promise not to kiss you again."

Her heart sank. "Okay," she said, trying to be a good sport.

"If that's what you want."

"Oh, yeah, yeah, sure. It's what I want." Well, not really, but she was in a bit deep here, and he was standing in her bedroom. Laredo didn't really stand, he lounged, or maybe it was *loomed*, because he towered over her. She'd never been alone with him like this, and never in such close proximity to a bed, and if they started kissing again like they had just a few hours ago, the virgin part of her might unfreeze and she'd jump him and then where would they be?

In bed.

She wasn't certain that would be such a bad thing.

On the other hand, he'd just said he wouldn't kiss her again. That didn't sound like a man who could be jumped.

Strange. She'd never thought about jumping Stanley.

"What kind of friendly date did you have in mind?" she asked.

"Tell me what's in this town."

"Um, lots of unmarried women."

"One woman per date, I always say."

She rolled her eyes at him. "We could go riding."

"We could go for a walk and see what kind of trouble we could find," he suggested. "Seems there's always something brewing here."

"We could go lay pennies on the train track. The eight-thirty will come through tonight."

"Katy," he said suddenly, "what kind of dates have you been on lately?" He went around the fiancé issue, not wanting Katy to know that he had been filled in on her broken heart.

Or maybe not-so-broken heart. She didn't look all that broken-up to him.

She way-too-casually studied her fingernails. "Oh, you know, the usual."

He thought about that for a minute. "I haven't dated in a while. I'm rusty. What's the usual?"

"Mostly watching TV at my folks' house."

"I've got an idea," Laredo said. "Let's go for a drive."

"Where?"

"Nowhere. Out in the country, with some blankets

and some beer. We'll lie in the truck bed and count the stars."

Her eyes got round. "That almost sounds…romantic."

No way was he going to let her get scared off again. If he knew anything about Katy Goodnight now, it was that she didn't know what a really good night was.

And he wasn't going to be the one to show her.

"Nah," he said, "it's the cheap man's entertainment. Beer and a truck bed for stargazing."

"All right," Katy said. "We can drive down to the creek. Let me change into some jeans and grab my blanket. You get the beer."

"Do you want to invite Hannah along?" he asked, hoping she'd say no but wanting to make her more comfortable. It was so hard to be considerate when it was far more appealing to be alone with her!

"Oh," she said, her tone surprised.

Belatedly he realized he'd given her the wrong impression. "No, I mean that—"

But she'd already gone to the door. "Hannah!" she called down the hall.

"What?" Her friend poked her head around the doorway.

"Do you want to go for a drive with Laredo and me?"

"Sure!"

Katy looked at him. "She wants to come."

"Great," he said. "Just great."

In Laredo's truck Katy made certain Hannah sat between them. It had surprised her that Laredo had wanted Hannah along, but it made sense, along with his promise not to kiss her again.

She wasn't about to show how hurt she was. This was almost an instant replay of Stanley and Becky. She always seemed drawn to men who wanted her best friends, she thought. She was definitely sending off the wrong signals.

She had to get this problem figured out.

Surely she wasn't such a rotten kisser. If she was, she was looking at possibly being rotten in the lovemaking venue, as well—and that was a thought she could barely contemplate.

Maybe she had it all wrong! It wasn't celibacy she needed. It was practice! Practice made perfect, she'd always heard—and from this moment forward, she would resolve to practice with enthusiasm. In fact, she was going to throw all caution to the wind and become a Cissy Kisserton type of girl! "I've made up my mind," she told her two companions.

"What?" Laredo and Hannah said, both glancing her way as the truck bumped over tall weeds and rutted road to get to the side of the creek.

"I'm going to become free and uninhibited. A virtuoso mantrap."

Laredo swerved on the road. *"What?"*

Hannah stared at her. "Virtuoso? Aren't you already?"

"No," she said, with rolled eyeballs for Hannah's benefit. "That's something else, which I aim not to be anymore."

Laredo perked up. "As your very good, extremely fond friend, I hereby put my services forward in *any* way I can to help you."

Katy blinked. "You don't even know what kind of help I need."

"Well, I…still resolve to help my very good friend," he said, looking past Hannah at Katy.

The light in his eyes had changed from *I'm driving* to *I'm driving toward something,* and Katy was suspicious. "Since when am I your very good friend?"

"Since we kissed and agreed we weren't going to do that anymore."

"You two kissed?" Hannah said.

"Not very well," Katy said.

"What?" Laredo looked outraged. "I didn't hear you complaining!"

"You kissed me, actually. I didn't kiss you back. And it was too short of a kiss to tell, really. Didn't you think?" Katy stated earnestly.

"Well, I don't know. I've never had a play-by-play called on my kissing skills." Laredo scratched his head. "Possibly you weren't engaged in the moment. But I can work on that, as I help you achieve mantrap status."

"I don't need a coach," she snapped.

"No, no, no. I see myself more as a *partner.*"

"Why are you so anxious for our Katy to become a mantrap?" Hannah asked.

"I was wondering the same thing." Katy gave him a suspicious glare. "You know, don't you?"

"That you're…you're…special?" Laredo said, carefully choosing his words. "That you're a discriminating female?"

"That I'm a virgin," Katy said flatly. "Who told you?"

"If I tell you, it's a breach of confidence," he said, sidestepping.

"Hannah?" Katy stared at her friend.

"Not me." Hannah raised her hands. "I only advise from the sidelines. I don't coach from the middle of the field."

"Who?" both women demanded, turning to stare at Laredo.

"Cissy Kisserton," he said, his face pinkening a bit.

"Cissy! How does she know?" Katy demanded.

"She says everybody in town knows." Laredo cleared his throat. "It's not a CIA-encoded secret, apparently."

Katy leaned back against the headrest. "I see. And so now you're offering to help me achieve my goals because…"

"Because he wants to go where no man has gone before," Hannah intoned.

"I'm just being a good friend," Laredo insisted.

"Shut up," both women said.

"What was in it for Cissy Kisserton? Why did she tell you this?" Katy asked. "Just so I can understand why she was discussing my personal business. This couldn't have had anything to do with riding our bull this weekend."

"I think it did," Laredo said, confused. "Actually, I can't remember how we got onto the subject. Something about you driving men crazy because you deprived them."

"What?"

"Yep. That's what she said," Laredo said with satisfaction. "You had an ex-fiancé who took exception to your, um—"

"Okay. I've heard enough. Take me home," Katy demanded. "At once."

"Hey, I didn't ask her to tell me any of this. And trust me, I left as soon as I realized nothing good was going to come of the conversation. She just wanted me to know that she'd lied about Bloodthirsty Black's crank out of the chute, and the chatter went downhill from there."

Katy glared at him. "Is that why you asked me out tonight on a poor man's date? Isn't that what you called it?"

"No. I like driving around. I like hanging out. Frankly, you're not the kind of friend I feel I have to take to a hundred-dollar restaurant to make happy, since we agreed that you're not the right woman for me, and I don't want a woman, anyway. But I will take you to a hundred-dollar restaurant, if you'd prefer that. It's just, then we won't be friends, we'll be nuts."

She sat back again. "One of these days, Cissy is going to open her mouth too wide and find herself in big trouble."

"I couldn't agree more," Laredo said cheerfully. "But I don't think you should become a mantrap unless you allow me to be the one to spring your hinge. Practice on me, Katy."

She looked back at him. Hannah giggled. "It is so weird being in the middle of this conversation. Katy wants practice, Laredo wants to give it to her, and I'm tagging along as mediator, I think."

"Thank heaven," Katy said.

"Yeah," Laredo agreed, "because I don't think I would have been brave enough to bring this up without a witness to my good intentions. We haven't gotten along very well up to this point. Have you noticed that?"

"It's pent-up sexual attraction," Hannah said with a nod. "We should have brought your brothers. At least then we could have double-dated. Or would that be a triple date?"

"This is not a date," Laredo and Katy said at the same time.

"It's not if the definition of *date* is individuals engaging in simultaneously pleasing activity, but whatever,"

Hannah said. "Let's play strip poker at the creek edge."

Katy stared at her. "Strip poker."

"It's my favorite game," Hannah said, pulling cards out of her duffel-shaped purse. "Remember, I told you that."

Laredo put the truck into gear and rolled forward a few hundred feet to park beside the creek. "It's gotta be my favorite game, too, but only when I win. And when I'm with beautiful women." He gave a mock leer at Hannah and Katy. "I should warn you, I cheat."

"We know," Katy said. "It shows in the company you've been keeping."

"Actually, I don't admire Cissy at all for lying to me. Even though she was trying to undo what she'd done," Laredo said self-righteously.

"I think there's a difference between cheating and lying," Hannah said. "Cheating can be honorable if the game rules allow for it. Then it's creative competition. But a lie is just smarmy."

"That's it," Laredo agreed. "Cissy must have been covering something up, or she wouldn't have come clean about the lie. She's working on two tiers, is what I think."

"What else could she be doing?" Katy asked.

"Trying to throw me off track. Exactly what was it they did with the last cowboy?"

Hannah shuffled the card deck on her knees. "They lured him."

"Okay. I'm not the kind of guy who can be lured."

Both women stared at him incredulously. Then Katy shrugged, opening the truck door. "Come on. Let's spread out in the truck bed where we can think this through better."

"A beer will definitely help my thinking process," Laredo agreed cheerfully. He pulled down the truck gate and they piled in, each grabbing a blanket to sit on. They pulled beers from the cooler, and then the cooler became a table for the cards.

"This night sky is gorgeous," Hannah said. "And that will help *my* thinking process. Don't take your shoes off, Katy. You need them for the game."

"No, no," Laredo disagreed. "Remember, she wants the practice of being a mantrap. I'm willing to let her practice on me, and she can start by being near naked."

"That's assuming you win," Katy said frostily, "and I don't intend for that to happen. You eliminated yourself from practicing with me when you discussed me with Cissy."

"Picky, picky," he said. "Take your shoes off if you want."

"I'll keep them on. All night, more than likely." She gave him a level stare, but Laredo grinned at her.

"All right, back to the plan," Hannah said, dealing hands. "You're not the kind of guy who can be lured, you say. But sex is their great weapon, and hey, we all know a guy can't pass that up."

Laredo cleared his throat as Katy's gaze stayed on him. "Well, it is a lot to ask, but sacrifices are necessary at times. And the Lonely Hearts ladies did a lot for my family last month. I can refuse luring."

Hannah put down one card, while Laredo and Katy asked for three.

"If you're the dealer, aren't you supposed to go last?" Laredo asked.

"This is just a friendly game of poker," Hannah said. "Just something to help me concentrate." They all turned up their cards, drawing a smirk from Hannah. "Choose your article of clothing, cowboy."

Good-naturedly, he pulled off a boot and tossed it over the edge of the truck. "Opening-round bad luck."

Katy raised her brows. "If Laredo continues to resist Cissy, they'll try another tack."

"Right." Hannah nodded as she dealt another hand. "And you've got the *if* handled?"

Laredo nodded. "The *if* is not even a problem. I'm pretty certain that sex with Cissy would be one of those trips into the phantasmagoric wonderland of excess a man tries diligently to avoid."

The women stared at him.

"Right," Hannah said, her brows raised. "Then we have to be prepared for sabotage, I suppose."

"Sabotage!" Katy dropped another three cards. "You don't mean our bull?"

"It's possible," Hannah said. "It's either our stud or our bull. That's sort of how Marvella thinks."

"Hey!" Laredo exclaimed.

"Her steely mind adds up our weapons. But I still think Marvella would never believe that Cissy couldn't pull off enticing Laredo," Hannah continued blithely.

He finished a beer and tossed the empty into the cooler. "You girls make it sound like I'm so easy," he complained, grabbing another beer. "I'm not like other guys."

They turned over their cards.

"I lost again," Laredo said, disbelieving. "Are you cheating, Katy?"

"Me?" She shook her head. "But speaking of cheating, who is the Never Lonely Cut-N-Gurls cowboy? Does anybody know?"

"That might help us, if we knew that in advance," Hannah said.

"Would you steal him?" Laredo asked. "Isn't that a lying, cheating combination? *And* copying the enemy's game plan?"

"Shh," Hannah told him. "I'm going to call Cissy and ask, since she's such a blabbermouth these days." Pulling out a cell phone, she punched in some numbers. "Of course, she's probably busy on a Thursday night," she said snidely. "Laredo, don't forget to remove an article of clothing. Hello, Cissy? Hannah. Sitting here playing strip poker with Laredo and Katy. Yes, I am. Laredo's losing. He's down two boots." She held up the phone. "Say 'Hello, Cissy,' you guys."

Laredo and Katy dutifully called, "Hello, Cissy."

"So, Cissy, we were wondering, what cowboy do you have riding Bad-Ass Blue this weekend? I was talking to the copywriter for the *Lonely Hearts Station Dispatch* today, and I couldn't remember for the life of me who you'd told me it was. And they want it for their article, you know," she said, holding up two crossed fingers to show that she was fibbing through her teeth.

She listened for a few moments. "Oh, I see. Okay. Well, good luck. Bye." Turning off the phone, she stared at Laredo for a moment. "They don't have a rider yet," she said, amazed. "That's the second tier."

"What is?" Laredo and Katy asked in unison.

"You. That's why Marvella pulled out all the stops and sicced Cissy on you. Marvella's obviously hoping Cissy can change your mind so that you'll be *their* rider instead."

Katy gasped. "They wouldn't stoop that low!"

"Why else would Cissy make certain Laredo knew

about your…um, lack of experience?" she said tact-fully.

Katy and Laredo stared at each other. "To make me look bad," Katy said. "Not as worldly and sophisti-cated."

"She was saying, Here's something and over there you get nothing. So ride our bull, because there's benefits to it you never even dreamed of."

"Okay." Laredo sat up straight. "Listen to me care-fully. I'm going to ride Bloodthirsty Black this weekend, and then I'm leaving town."

Katy looked at him. "If he leaves now, then neither of us has a rider."

"I'm not leaving," Laredo said. "Are you saying you think I should leave?"

"No, but if they think you're gone, maybe they'll settle down," Katy pointed out.

"You're kind of crafty," Laredo said with admiration. "I don't think you've shown me this side of you yet."

Katy gave him an arch look. "I haven't shown you any sides of me."

"They've got to find somebody by Saturday morning." Hannah put the cards down. "They have one day."

"I don't know," Laredo said. "Maybe Cissy was lying again."

"And that could be, too," Hannah said. "Okay, it's hot, and I vote we swim. Then we'll think some more."

"Swim in what?" Katy asked doubtfully.

"Anything you want to." Hannah hopped out of the truck. "Last one in the creek is a cow patty!" She pulled off her top and sprinted a few yards away from the truck. Katy and Laredo followed, peeling clothes as they ran.

"Whee!" Katy yelled, feeling free and uninhibited and

fun for the first time in a long time. In white cotton bra and panties, she jumped into the creek, hearing the giant splash Laredo made behind her. They sprayed water at each other madly for a couple of seconds, and then the sound of a truck engine halted their horseplay.

"See ya!" Hannah called from the truck, joyfully waving Laredo's jeans out the window. "I left you a blanket over there, and the cooler. Be back in a few hours, kids!"

And then she drove off.

Leaving Katy alone in a creek with Laredo, and neither of them wearing more than underwear. At least, she hoped Laredo had underwear on…she glanced nervously toward the water's edge, but she didn't see anything that looked like underwear on the bank.

Hopefully he still had it on, she thought, gazing at his hard chest and muscular shoulders.

And that dark intense look was back in his eyes as he stared at her chest the same way she'd stared at his. Then his gaze met hers, pinning her, it felt, with heat.

"Practice makes perfect, Katy Goodnight," Laredo said. "I think we should start your lessons tonight."

Then he put his arms around her, drawing her against him.

She glanced up at him. "Laredo, maybe I haven't decided that you're the most credible teacher for me."

CHAPTER EIGHT

"WHY NOT?" Laredo demanded, surprised that Katy would sound so indifferent to him. He certainly was not indifferent to her. In fact, he was afraid that despite the cold water, he might do serious injury to himself by bursting a muscle somewhere in his groin area if she didn't hurry up and say yes.

At this moment, her tone was more truculent than he liked. *Truculent* was a word he'd never heard anyone use except on a *Peanuts* cartoon he'd watched once when his brothers were younger, but at this moment, staring down into Katy's blazing eyes and soft, pouty mouth, he knew he was looking at truculence personified.

"You're too cocky," she said. "Which is good in a bull rider, but not in a kiss mate."

"Cocky," he repeated. "I am who I am."

"Yes," she said on a sigh, "I realize that. While I can accept it, that doesn't mean I have to like it."

"Katy," he said in some desperation, "a kiss isn't forever. I swear my lips aren't cocky. If you just stand still a moment, I can clear up all your doubts about your kissing skills."

She shrugged enticingly bare shoulders at him, rounded skin that gleamed above the dark water and hinted at the sweetness bobbing just beneath.

How he wished it was daylight so he could see her better!

"A kiss could be forever," she insisted. "If it's done right. Not like that little peck we shared yesterday. You're already telling me you're not going to do it right this time. And why should I participate in that?"

"Katy, no one kisses for forever."

"But that's my problem, Laredo," she said. "Stanley didn't kiss me with his whole heart. Although Hannah says that the heart is not really involved, that it's basically an allegorical muscle, I don't buy that."

"What?" Laredo had serious heat beneath the waist, and she was trying to fry his brain with deep thoughts. "Hey, I just want to taste you, Katy Goodnight. You know, between friends."

"Nope." She kicked toward the shore and got out, streaming water down her long ponytail, running droplets down her back, into her panties, which showed a wonderful delineation of well-rounded bottom—

"There's no such thing as a real kiss between friends," Katy called over her shoulder.

"Wait, wait, wait. You're going about this all wrong." He got out of the water, walked up the bank, picked Katy up and strode back into the water with her.

"Laredo—"

"You said we'd think better when we were wet, and I'm certain this water is easing my thought passages. Like soda bubbles need syrupy water to get through a straw. Now, listen, Katy, you're going about this mantrap business all wrong. I offered to let you practice on me. You're supposed to use me and abuse me."

"I am?" Her glare turned to question.

"Oh, absolutely. Most definitely. Take advantage of me. Lay your lips on me and then say goodbye. Kiss and flee, leaving me crying."

"Oh, I wouldn't want to hurt your feelings—"

"Katy, I swear, I won't cry in front of you. Now, pucker up. Please."

She cocked a brow at him. "Stanley never said *that* to me."

He squinted his eyes at her. "Stanley clearly didn't know all the magic words. I'm going to teach you how to be the best mantrap in town. Man-magnet of the century. Cissy Kisserton won't be able to touch your talent. You practice on me, and we'll both get so good, we'll open up a kissing booth at the next rodeo. We'll make a fortune for charity."

She wound her arms around his neck, and he looked down, enjoying the view of flat tummy and puckered nipples through a cotton bra sticking to all the things he wanted it stuck to.

"Okay, Laredo," she said softly. "Let's practice."

Thank heaven. Yee-haw! All his smooth-talking had gotten him just what he wanted. He was going to kiss this little girl; he was going to dazzle her until there were stars in her eyes she couldn't shake out….

Holding her closer, he placed his lips against hers, making certain he gentled her, like a rider with a new mare.

To his surprise Katy locked her lips onto his, sucking and pulling, and then changing pressure as she moved her lips to a different position. Her breasts snuggled up against his chest as her hands clasped the back of his head. Her lips and tongue did a sex dance all over his mouth. The heat in his groin exploded into a raging fire.

Suddenly she pulled away and stared up at him with big, blue innocent eyes. "Was that right?"

His legs were trembling from the afterburn. "Uh, yeah," he said, "I think we've got something to work with."

"HEY!" Hannah called, interrupting Tex and Ranger as they stood eyeing Bloodthirsty Black. The brothers turned around, and she tossed Laredo's truck keys at them.

Ranger caught them with a deft hand. "You look like a windblown daisy. What have you been doing?"

"Playing strip poker with your brother and Katy."

Tex stared at her. "If you're here, does that mean you won?"

"It means I think quicker than them. It's hard to get those two to cut to the chase. They just dance around the whole issue like Baryshnikov's ballet—"

"What issue?" Ranger demanded.

"Sex," Hannah said. "Love. Rock 'n' roll. You know."

Ranger stared at her, somewhat bemused. "Are they having sex? Or rocking 'n' rolling?"

"I doubt they're doing either. Or anything other than swimming. Last I saw them, they were nearly naked in Barmaid's Creek, which for most people would be encouraging." She sighed heavily. "But not for Katy and Laredo. They're probably still arguing about who's going to make the first move tonight. Or ever, for that matter."

"My brother's pretty slow on the uptake," Ranger said.

"And Katy's too smart for her own good. Can do bio, organic, almost any kind of chemistry you care to name, but she has no sense when it comes to the sexual kind."

"I don't care to try to name any of them," Ranger

said. "Although organic sounds like it'd be right up Tex's alley."

"Not right now," Tex said. "I'm focused on Malicious Bull Riding 101."

"So you left them in the creek?" Ranger asked.

Hannah nodded. "Do you mind fishing them out in a couple of hours? They'll be too mad at me, and I'm afraid they'll take their revenge by sending me down the creek-fall in nothing but my bra and underwear."

"Sounds vengeful but inviting," Ranger said on a rough breath. "Maybe you should accompany me to pick up the lovebirds."

"Oh, make no mistake about it," Hannah said with a patient expression, "they are far from lovebirds. They'll peck each other's feathers out before they admit that they might like each other."

"It's a Jefferson curse," Tex said on a long-suffering sigh. "We never settle down, and then when we do—"

"When we do?" Ranger interrupted. "The only one who has is Frisco, and he was a freak case."

"Why?" Hannah asked.

"Oh, it was that storm or something. All that rain diluted his brain." Ranger turned his attention to the bull in the stall. "It all went south when he broke his leg, in my estimation."

"Yeah, Helga trapped him, and he darn near went mad with the daily emotional trauma of her caring for him. So he was ripe for the picking. But as you can tell, Laredo is in fine physical and emotional shape," Tex said. "He may not be very sua-vay at dating, but he's definitely on target to avoid falling in love."

Hannah stared at the two of them. "You're both full of wind, but I suppose you're harmless enough. Please

don't forget to pick your brother and Katy up in a bit."
And she walked away.

"Hey! Don't leave," Ranger called. "You should ride
out to the creek with us."

She waved and kept on walking. A few more strides
and she disappeared.

"That's one crazy lil' ol' gal," Ranger said with
wonder. "Leaving my brother in nothing but his Calvins
in a creek somewhere."

"That sounds like a Mimi trick," Tex said, his tone
just as impressed. "And we thought only Mimi had that
type of superspunk."

"Good thing we're not interested in a woman at this
time," Ranger said, his gaze turning to his brother.

"Yeah, man. Let's get back to this bull," Tex agreed.
"He has just a little less crank to him than Hannah."

"True," Ranger murmured, his gaze bouncing back
to the exit Hannah had used. "Just a little less crank.
But a helluva liftoff."

"WHAT I WANT TO KNOW," Laredo said, as he placed a
beer bottle cap on his bare stomach to show Katy that he
could roll just as well as she could, "is why you agreed
to marry that Stanley guy in the first place. If he didn't
like to kiss you, that is. Isn't sucking face a basic building block for a successful marriage?"

Katy lay very still on her back on the blanket Laredo
had laid down for them. She focused her stomach muscles to move slowly, so that the beer cap on her belly
made a guided flip, flip, flip motion up her stomach. "I
fell in love with Stanley, not with his sexual prowess."

Laredo grimaced. "I guess not."

"Did you ever fall in love with anyone?" Katy asked,

taking the beer cap off her stomach and resettling it lower.

The question interrupted his successful rolling of the beer cap. "I was up to two rolls until you asked me that," he charged. "You should never ask a man about love when he's trying to align his stomach muscles into the perfect gyration for beer cap rolling."

She put two beer caps on her stomach and began crunching her muscles so that the two caps moved upward in unison. Laredo sighed and sat up. "I'm not going to be able to beat you at this game. How about we try one of mine?"

"Answer the question," she told Laredo, putting a third cap on her stomach.

"No. I've never had a hankering to fall in love."

She frowned. "One doesn't always get a hankering. Sometimes love just hits."

"Did you have a hankering? Or a hit?"

"A hankering. Actually, I'd studied so long to be good at my chosen profession that I think I really wanted a fling. The kind the other girls had when they went on spring break."

"Katy," Laredo said, "when your friends went to the beach for spring break, they were not going to find a husband. Subconsciously you picked stability."

"I know. Well, marrying Stanley felt as wild and crazy as I could be. However, after living around Hannah for a while, I've decided to change. I'm going to up my footloose meter."

"Excellent. Can I make a swimsuit top for you out of beer caps?" Laredo asked.

She stopped rolling her stomach, which made him feel slightly less hypnotized. On the other hand, if she could move her muscles that well, imagine what other muscles she could utilize—

"Laredo, I said, go ahead."

"Oh." His mouth watered as she accepted his invitation. Of course, he hadn't been serious. He'd been teasing, certain of a *No!* "Well, to make a proper swim top," he said, trying to sound knowledgeable, "you'd have to take off the one you're currently wearing."

She sat up, turning her back to him.

"What?" he asked dumbly.

"Unhook me."

His fingers started gently trembling. Maybe he'd drunk too much beer. That was it! He didn't have enough caps for a proper beer-cap top. He counted three Katy had rolled on her stomach, and two on the ground beside him. There was an old one someone had tossed away; he could use that one. It would be an even number, he thought, his mind hazy with rapid-fire counting. He could cover her decently with six caps. One each for her nipples, which left four caps, two per breast…

He was going to lose his mind in the process.

"Laredo," Katy said, turning her head to glance at him, "maybe you are all bull and no consummation."

"Ahem." He cleared his throat, reaching a tentative hand toward her back.

But then he pulled his hand away. If Katy thought kissing was forever, then making love to her would be lifetimes into infinity. If not infinity, at least into googolplex, a word he thought Miss Smarty Pants might be impressed that he knew.

"A googol is ten to the hundredth power; a googolplex is ten to the googol power," he said, wishing desperately he was brave enough to accept her invitation. The thought of seeing her bare breasts was enough to scissor his brain in two. "A googolplex is the largest named number. Bet you didn't think I knew that."

Her eyes widened. "Do you always delve into mathematical jargon when you're undecided?"

"I was trying to get my mind off my hormones. It's not working."

She let her gaze roam downward. "So I see."

Taking a deep breath, he said, "Katy, I think I'll rescind my creative offer of a beer-cap top."

"Because?"

"Because I won't be able to stop there. I'll want to make you a beer-cap thong—"

"And then we'll be drunk..."

"And then we'll be drunk, and then...then I might make love to you but neither of us would remember it, and your first time should be special," he said on a rush, happy to have found reasoning that sounded sane.

"I want to," Katy said softly. "I want you to be the first."

"Why me?" Laredo had never heard such sweet words, but he truly was not the man to act upon them.

"Because you're sexy. And macho. And I'm going to Duke after the summer, and I'll probably fall for another of my own kind—"

"Your own kind?"

"Some studious, boring, tenure-bound professor, and I'll have missed the opportunity to have a hot cowboy take my virginity. That sounds like a woman's dream fantasy come true, don't you think?"

He wasn't sure about a woman, but he knew the fantasy sure as hell had him standing straight up. "Katy," he rasped, "you've got to quit talking like that. I can only take so much."

"Uh-uh," she said, turning all the way around and

situating herself between his legs so that she faced him, "This is the new me. Remember?"

"I like the old you," he said desperately.

"Yes, but the old me lived in her fears. She was a shell without adventure or fearlessness. I don't want to be a chem prof with no sinful side explored."

"The right man is out there," Laredo said, hanging on to *no* with all his might. "The one who'll stay around and give you children and a secure house and a solid marriage. The one who'll take you to church on Sunday and give you an iron for Mother's Day and—"

"Laredo, you're more afraid of making love to me than riding Bloodthirsty Black," Katy murmured against his neck.

Goose pimples exploded on his body. "Fear is a healthy emotion."

"It kicks the fight-or-flight mechanism into gear," she whispered into his ear, before nibbling on it.

"I'm flighting," he said.

"I think you're the right man for my adventure," Katy said. "Of course, if you don't want to—"

It was all a man could bear. It was endurance beyond expectation. He rolled Katy onto her back, pinning her beneath him. "Katy Goodnight," he said, "you have driven me past no."

She actually laughed at him. "Good. I'm working on that vixen side of my personality."

He tore her little cotton bra straps down with his teeth, until he revealed each breast. "Oh my God," he murmured. "You are perfect."

A door slammed somewhere up the bank. "Hey, Laredo!" Ranger called. A loud, annoying moose mating call erupted from Ranger as his footsteps seemed to head their way.

"Are you down there, bro?" Tex yelled, his voice cutting through the darkness. "Your rescue crew has arrived and is reporting for duty!"

Katy stared up at Laredo with huge eyes. By the moon's light, Laredo could see her hard nipples topping sweetly rounded breasts only inches from his mouth. "I'm going to *kill* my brothers," he growled. "The biblical Cain had *nothing* on me."

CHAPTER NINE

IT WAS A VERY QUIET ride back. Laredo had dropped the blanket over her shoulders to protect her body from his brothers' inquiring gazes. They were trying to be gentlemen, but of course, they were curious as to why she only wore a blanket. Not that they verbalized the question, but the expressions on their faces were priceless.

"Uh, Hannah didn't say anything about you not having clothes," Tex said.

"I'm sure she didn't," Laredo bit out. "Come on, Katy." He helped her into the back of the extended cab, covering her with an extra blanket from the truck bed.

Katy's hair was wild and matted from swimming, and her heart was disappointed. She'd been so close to being a femme fatale. Or at least an unmade maiden.

"That was it?" Hannah demanded once Katy made it into her room.

"That was it. We didn't even say a proper good-night, because Tex and Ranger dragged him off with them." Katy was totally dejected.

"All my planning for nothing. I really thought I'd worked it to where you two had no reason not to manage the miraculous."

Katy crawled into bed beside Hannah. "Apparently not. He was babbling about googolplexes at one point, so I'm pretty certain he was relieved when the cavalry arrived."

"He'll be asleep in your room tonight. Just crawl in bed beside him. Maybe even on top of him. Trust me, he won't kick you out."

Katy sighed. "Yeah, but I've had time to think about it. Laredo's right. We shouldn't do it."

"Because?" Hannah's voice was incredulous in the darkness.

"He doesn't really want to. I mean, the body is willing but the spirit is very reluctant."

"You could change his mind if you wanted to."

Katy thought about that and then closed her eyes. As easygoing, available, macho as he'd tried to make himself sound, she'd figured one thing out: Laredo wasn't a man to womanize. He didn't fall in love easily or willingly. And she couldn't just take advantage of him as he'd suggested.

He *was all* bull and no consummation.

Bull rider, in this case. And nothing more than that.

RANGER AND LAREDO SAT in the Lonely Hearts Cafeteria, stewing. "You'd better be careful," Ranger said. "I think that bull is gonna whap you upside the head, 'cause you're not thinking straight."

It was true. Laredo's mind was still in a twist over Katy in a wet bra and pair of panties. It had taken all his strength to keep her pure, and he'd just about not made it. "I'm in no condition to ride a bull," he admitted. "Specifically since I don't know how."

"Well, the competition doesn't know that." Ranger forked some steak and chewed.

"The competition doesn't even have a cowboy riding yet."

Ranger brightened, then his face fell. "No, a forfeit is too much to hope for."

"Besides, I should ride. I owe it to myself to ride," Laredo said. "It's my first Big Thing on my list of Big Things To Do."

"And after this? Then what?"

"Then I'm continuing on my trek. Searching out opportunity and adventure." He thought about Katy for a second. There was opportunity and adventure in abundance, but not really the kind a man could boast about. Not like riding a bull, or collecting yak hair in the Andes. "Are there yaks in the Andes?" Laredo asked.

His brother stared at him. "You dope. Do I look like a reference point for Yaks-R-Us? How the hell would I know?"

"I don't know." Laredo scratched at his neck. "I just always had the idea that our family was smart. Above average, intellectually."

Ranger put down his fork. "We work, and we do all right. We've all got some talent at something. We drink too much beer, and sometimes we let women chase us around town. That's above average, I'd say."

Not enough to measure up to a whiz like Katy, though. "Remember Joey Forrester?"

"The science geek you rolled up in a carpet and set on top of Mrs. Fisk's desk? You called him the human enchilada for your science project. What was the theme again, anyway?"

Laredo rolled his eyes. "Something about digestion. I can't remember now. Do you know what happened to Joey?"

"Yeah. He married some science geekess and they gave birth to lots of Einsteinian tots. He teaches at Harvard, and she teaches at the equivalent, while breastfeeding on the three-year plan while she crusades for women's issues. I think they're both up for some kind of academic recognition." Ranger ate a roll with butter on it. "Boy, they sure know how to cook in this town. And it is a change from Helga and her sauerkraut. I may never go home, either. I have been thinking about joining the military, you know."

Laredo nodded, not really hearing his brother's kibitzing. That was exactly the future he could see for Katy: she'd marry some really smart guy, and they'd have extremely Mensa-qualified ankle biters who had their own Kappa keys given to them at birth by the latest Nobel Peace Prize winners. "Yeah," he said, "But Helga's sauerkraut is home."

"You're not homesick yet, are you? You haven't even left the state."

"I know," Laredo said miserably. And when he did finally get out of the state, he had a funny feeling it wasn't going to be the sauerkraut he missed.

It would be Katy.

CISSY SMILED as she crept into the barn, stealthily moving up on the lone cowboy staring at the bull. Hannah had lied! And Cissy had been too quick to fall for that bait. Of course Laredo wasn't playing strip poker with Hannah and Katy. Like Katy would ever let her hair down, anyway. Strip poker?

Oh, Laredo had been around…but he hadn't been with Katy.

And now Cissy had her chance at having him alone, with no prying eyes anywhere around.

"Hi," she said softly.

He turned around, settling his hat back from his forehead. A big smile grew on his face. See! She'd known

Laredo hadn't been immune to her. He'd just been too gentlemanly to put the moves on her.

Fine. She could play candy and cream just as well as Katy G. "Got that bull figured out?" she asked, standing next to him.

He stared down at her with eyes that didn't miss a thing, not her low-cut, waist-tied top, nor her long and shapely legs. Nor, by the appreciative sniff he gave her hair, her perfume.

"I don't know about the bull," Laredo told her, his eyes gleaming, "but maybe I'd rather figure you out."

"I promise, I'm a-b-c simple," she cooed.

He laughed and picked her up off her feet, settling her onto his waist. "I'm sure you are, darling. I'm sure you are."

Whew! He was more man than she'd bargained for. If she wasn't careful, Laredo was going to make her forget all her sugar-and-spice planning.

Before she realized what he was about, he was planting kisses in the opening of her blouse, between her breasts. She shivered, loving every second of it.

He popped the snap on her jean shorts and kissed her belly. She writhed, feeling herself come alive in a way she hadn't in a long time. Not for any man who'd come the Never Lonely Cut-N-Gurls' way.

Then he kissed above her knee, sliding his tongue along her inner thigh to the edge of her frayed shorts. Cissy tried to hold in a moan and wrapped her fingers in his hair, her mind swimming.

"How do you feel about hay?" he asked her.

She didn't care if the bed was made of rock salt. "Fine," she said on a gasp. "Just hurry."

Laredo grinned at her and carried her into a freshly

filled stall. Tossing a clean blanket onto the ground, he lowered her to the floor.

This time, Cissy thought, the conquest was going to be so worth the chase.

AN HOUR LATER Cissy's knees were shaking and her body was melted sunshine. "You're a cutie," Laredo said against her breasts. "I could spend all night with you."

"Why don't you?" she asked, her body heating up again. "I've got a real soft bed."

He grinned. "Why don't I just? Show it to me, cutie."

Marvella was going to be so proud of her! Once he was inside the Never Lonely Cut-N-Gurls Salon, he was theirs for the keeping.

He would be her love slave.

He would be her bull rider. He wouldn't be able to say no to her feminine wiles.

Silently she took his hand and led him home. When she opened the door, all the girls who were sitting around the main area quieted.

"Good night, everyone," was all Cissy said, unwilling to share her catch. These girls were tricky, and she didn't dare let go of her prize for an instant.

Hurriedly, she pretty much dragged Laredo up the stairs and into her room. "Make yourself comfortable," she said.

"I plan to," he said, tackling her on the bed so that he landed beside her. Then he caught her lips in a lingering kiss that stole her breath.

When she could speak again, Cissy stared up at her lover. "I have to admit, I didn't think you had this much potential." Any man who was interested in Katy Goodnight had to have cold little pebbles for a brain!

He laughed at her. "You never know about a person, do you? It's us quiet ones that have all the attitude." Sliding her on top of him, still fully dressed, he situated her on his stomach. "You are a pretty little thing. When I go back home, I'm going to send you a week's worth of roses."

She smiled. "Actually, I have something else in mind you can give me."

RANGER AND LAREDO LEFT the Lonely Hearts Station Cafeteria. Ranger squinted up at the lights on the top floor of the Never Lonely Cut-N-Gurls Salon as they went out.

"So, what's up with that place, anyway?"

Laredo shrugged. "Don't know. Have no interest in finding out. Anyway, you were in there. What did you think?"

"That Cissy Kisserton is a wonderful kisser."

"Are you interested in her?"

"Nah. No more than she was in me."

Laredo eyed his brother. "Now, see, Katy isn't like that. She just isn't the type of girl to understand that a kiss can be just a kiss and nothing more."

"You're not that kind of guy, either. Get over it."

They walked past the Lonely Hearts Salon. Laredo sent a longing glance toward it. "I'd bet Katy's in bed by now."

"Tuckered out after a long swim." Ranger chuckled. "Bet you wish you were in there with her, but it wouldn't do any damn good. Sort of the sexual *Twilight Zone,* complete with the do-do-do-do, do-do-do-do background music. Scary, and with a twisted ending every time."

"Shut up." Laredo didn't feel like being teased about Katy, or their swim, or their nonlovemaking potential.

"Hey, no problemo." Inside the barn they went to Bloodthirsty Black's pen, which was empty. "Out to pasture, I guess. Nightly roam."

"Wonder where Tex is?" Laredo asked.

"Probably got tired of waiting for us and decided to bunk in for the night."

Laredo nodded, not too worried about his twin. "Guess I'll hit the sack myself."

Ranger grinned. "You do that. I'm not ready to turn in yet."

"All right. Good night." Actually, he was glad to leave Ranger and head back to the salon. Maybe, if he was lucky, he'd get to see Katy.

But the salon and the halls were dark. There were some cookies on the kitchen counter with a note with his name on it, written by Miss Delilah.

He carried the cookies upstairs to his dark, empty room. Switching on the lamp beside his bed, he stared down at Rose the mouse. "Miss me?"

She twitched her whiskers at him and ran into her tube.

"I'm the reserved type, too," he said.

The door closed. He turned, his brow raised, and Katy floated over to the bed in a long, slinky gown that looked like something a movie star would wear to bed.

"I thought I'd tuck you in," she said.

"Good idea," he said.

"That would be crossing the bounds of our friendship."

He was salivating for more than the cookies. "Yes, it would."

"And I wouldn't want to sap your strength before your bull ride."

"That's day after tomorrow. I recover quickly." She looked so pretty in the long white gown. Pink ribbons were tied around the neckline, and he itched to undo them with his teeth.

"I had a good time swimming with you, Laredo," she said. "I just want you to know that."

"I still owe you a beer-cap bikini top." He could see her nipples through the satiny fabric. "One day I'll make you one."

"Good night," she said.

It was all friendly banter with no twist. Ranger was wrong. There was no background music; there was no *Twilight Zone* where they fell into an alternate reality and made love. Katy wasn't going to get in his bed. He really couldn't blame her, not after he'd given her the speech on not getting tied down. And he wasn't going to get into hers, not with the virgin reality hanging on his conscience.

Whoa, boy.

She looked at him, and he looked at her, and they both became uncomfortable. Then she was gone, and he was alone with Rose. The mouse didn't seem all that interested in him.

Stuffing the cookies in a napkin, he decided to eat them while he took a long walk to get rid of the sudden surge of energy running through his body.

"BACK SO SOON?" Hannah asked.

"Scoot over." Katy slid into bed, completely dejected. "We're both all bull and no consummation. I couldn't get my nerve up to whisper anything seductive. It was pretty obvious he'd changed his mind."

"He was probably too shocked that you were in his room to grab you and divest you of your gown. Give him time to get used to the idea."

They heard the door down the hall open and close. A few seconds later they heard boots on the stairwell. Then the front door shut. Both girls flew to the window and peered out, to see Laredo walking down the street.

Katy sank back into the bed. "He probably thinks I'm chasing him. That is not a man who is dying to get me into his bed."

Hannah pulled the covers up to her chin. "You know, the right guy is probably waiting at Duke for you."

Katy tried to be happy about that, but the problem was, she couldn't be. It would be so bad to fall for a man who didn't like her, especially after her disastrous nonmarriage. "Do you think he's going to the enemy camp?"

"Nope."

Of course, that was where men went when they needed to get some…peace of mind. Still, Laredo had told her he wasn't interested in Cissy. She believed him.

And yet…

"Is it wrong to follow a man?" she asked Hannah. "Does that fall under the heading of spying? Stalking? Prying?"

Hannah jumped from the bed. "I wasn't going to suggest it, but since you mentioned it, I think late-evening walks under any heading are healthier than lying awake. Hurry and get dressed!"

CHAPTER TEN

"SEXUAL TENSION is very bad for the brain," Laredo told Ranger as they met at Bloodthirsty's pen.

Ranger nodded. "I think I'll drink all day tomorrow. You should, too. That's the best way to train you for riding this beast, I do believe. Let's go get a case, and we'll both go at it. That way, when you finally do ride him, you won't remember how stupid you looked when Bloodthirsty flings you into the next county, and I won't remember the shame and embarrassment of my brother's unfortunate rendezvous with the dirt." He grimaced. "So much for Jefferson pride."

"We gotta find Tex." Laredo glanced around, frowning. "Where do you think he is? He wasn't back at Miss Delilah's."

Ranger shrugged. "Think he's across the street."

"Why do you think that?"

His brother jerked his head toward an empty stall. Suspiciously, Laredo went to peer inside.

There was a pair of pink panties lying in the straw that said "Make My Day" in silver-studded letters. In fact, the tiny stud letters were about all that made the panties classify as a garment; there wasn't much fabric to brag about.

Laredo blinked. "They're kind of see-through."

"Yeah. You have to kick them over to read the back.

It says 'And My Night Too.'" Ranger laughed. "That scalawag."

"Hmm." Laredo felt a little sad. Tex didn't have any conscience, no guilt. He knew how to eat from the Garden of Good and Evil without repercussions. Katy had been in Laredo's room, looking like sweet heaven—and all Laredo had done was stand there like a goon.

"Don't feel bad," Ranger told him. "You and Tex are total opposites. You only look alike. But inside you're so different, you'd probably be schizo if you hadn't been split into twins."

"Yes, but he's the settled one, the gardener, the grower of buds. I'm the rebel, the James Dean. But I've never had trouble with women before," Laredo said, worried. "They like me, and I like them."

"Well, Katy's got you spooked. It's because you like her for serious."

"I do not like her for serious." Laredo shook his head. "She…she's too smart for me."

"One day you'll get it together, maybe," Ranger assured him. "You'll find the moment, and you'll get it right, and when you do, I don't want to have to hear you babble about it for weeks on end. Just enjoy it, and don't screw it up."

"Screw it up?" Laredo went pale. "I don't know if I can enjoy it if I'm worried about screwing up. I think you just gave me my first case of performance anxiety, and I don't even know what I'm performing."

Ranger grinned. "For your first performance, you're going to hang on to this bull for eight seconds, or at least long enough to make yourself a winner in Katy's eyes. Then you're going to let her reward you for a job well done."

Laredo followed his brother out of the barn. "And if that's not how the performance goes?"

"Then you don't get a curtain call. You get to move onto the next Big Thing."

"That's right." Laredo told himself he felt better about that, but strangely the thought made him feel something altogether different.

Performance anxiety had just kicked up another notch.

"SEE?" HANNAH SAID. "I told you Laredo wasn't going over to the enemy." They watched as the two men got into Laredo's truck and drove away. "Don't be such a fraidy-cat."

"I'm not." But she was, Katy acknowledged to herself.

"Okay, here's the deal. When he's done riding on Saturday, you take him back down to the creek and you finish what you started before the wild boys rode in to the rescue," Hannah instructed. "After that, you can plan your future."

"Future?"

"Whether this is a spring fling for you or something serious. Whether it's Duke University, or the cowboy for you." Hannah smiled, pleased with her advice.

"I'll miss you when I go, Hannah," Katy told her. "I never had a real best friend before, and it feels good. You're so much like a sister to me."

"Hey," Hannah said, her funky-punky hair totally awry. "Don't get mushy on me. The way I see it, I'm going to lose you, either to Duke or to Malfunction Junction. It's to my benefit to do everything I can to help you and Laredo break through this barrier of reluctance you've built. Both of you. I've got to tell you," Hannah said with a sigh, "you're both so prickly around each other, it's starting to jangle my chi."

Katy followed her friend back inside. "Rest your chi. I'm going to sleep in my own bed," she said. "I have a feeling Laredo and Ranger will be gone for a long time."

WHEN KATY AWAKENED, she had the unbearable sensation of being smothered. Something was crushing her, and it was huge, and no matter which way she tried to wiggle, it had left her no room to escape.

Her mouth was open for air, so at least her trachea wasn't squished, she rationalized. It was dark in her room, too dark to see anything, but her panic subsided when she recognized Laredo's scent. Macho. But still on top of her.

"Laredo!" she whispered urgently. "Get off!"

He snored in her ear.

She tried to push him.

He didn't budge.

It wasn't all bad having the cowboy in her bed and on top of her, but this wasn't the way she'd dreamed it would happen. With a muffled grunt, she managed to pull one arm free.

"Laredo," she said, tapping on his shoulder.

Bare shoulder, she realized.

He snored again.

She moved her hand below the sheet and tapped at the bottom of his spine. "Laredo," she said more softly, not really wanting him to wake up now.

It gave her an excuse to tap just a few inches lower, just enough to tell whether—

She squeezed her eyes shut, prayed for bravery and traced a few inches lower to his buttocks.

He was buck naked. Lying on top of her.

And from the feel of frontally aligned matters, he was now fully awake.

Laredo didn't move, keeping his face buried in the pillow. Katy's tap-tapping had awakened him in every sense of the word. He knew it was Katy because no one else would be sleeping in her bed.

He just hadn't realized he'd laid himself on her when he'd crashed into bed like a falling tree. Surely he'd lain *beside* her and then rolled over on her.

His heartbeat seemed to triple. She felt so soft and small underneath him. The gentlemanly thing to do would be to get off her right now…but he had a massive erection, which he was hoping would go away any second, before she noticed.

He really did not want her to notice.

Problem was, he was pretty sure she couldn't miss it, since it was pressing against her lower region. Her female anatomy. The place where "Make My Day" underwear would be, if she were the type of girl who wore such, but she wasn't, and that was his biggest problem of all.

Her breath caught in a gasp, and he realized he was busted. She *knew*.

He was pretty certain that no matter how far Bloodthirsty threw him, his embarrassment couldn't come close to what he was now feeling.

There were two options open to a man with an obvious predicament of desire: he could apologize, get up and vacate the room—and probably the premises—for good.

Or he could act like it was nothing out of the ordinary, roll over and go back to sleep.

They didn't have to discuss it.

Suddenly he felt her hand, the one that had been tap-tap-tapping its way down his backside, make its way around his hip and underneath, between them. His surprise made him arch, and she caught him in her small, delicate hand.

"Oh, my," she said on a whisper. "I had no idea."

He hadn't, either. He was going to die if he didn't get inside her quick. There was a Lonely Hearts train running on the tracks outside—no, the train was in his head, pushing all rational thought out of his mind. He couldn't bed Katy. She would regret it if he took her because he'd be her first, and he had no intention of being here past Saturday.

There wasn't a woman on earth who didn't want a man to hang around, even if she said otherwise. Especially not a virgin.

But her hand was gently squeezing, and the last of his sanity began to drain away. "Katy," he said on a groan.

"Yes?" she asked, somewhere near his ear.

It all felt too good. "Sweetheart, I want you real bad, and if you don't let go, I'm going to lose my mind."

And you're going to lose your virginity, he didn't add.

She hesitated, her hand relaxing. He tried to take a deep breath, to push back the demand his body was begging for.

"All right," she said. "I understand."

She released him, and he rolled away. She got out of the bed. Her retreat was so swift and so sudden he opened his mouth to complain.

But she was gone.

"Damn it," he said. "Damn it to hell!"

He'd only been mildly out of sorts when he'd gone to

drink a few beers with Ranger, but now he was really out of sorts. And a whole keg of beer wouldn't put out the fire engulfing him. Even his mouth had dried out from erotic heat. She'd felt so good underneath him! So pliable and warm and sweet…yet once again he'd let her slip away.

And she'd sounded so disappointed it nearly killed him.

"You bozo," Ranger said when he complained about it the next day. "Maybe you've forgotten what to do to a willing woman."

"That's the trouble!" Laredo glared at his brother. "She doesn't understand what she's willing to do!"

"Sounds like she does."

"I mean, she… Katy's special. She's different."

"Oh," Ranger said on an enlightened note. "She's—"

"Yes!" Laredo glared harder. "Yes, she is. And I think she should stay that way, seeing as how it's only me she's trying to give it to."

"Hmm," Ranger said thoughtfully. "That does muddy the waters a bit. I'd have to recommend that you leave that opportunity unexplored."

Laredo's heart sank as the voice of common sense jibed with his own gut reaction. "Me, too."

"After all, you have nothing to offer her."

"Nope," Laredo agreed, shaking his head.

"She could do much better, first off."

"I know," he said glumly.

"So forget about her," Ranger told him.

"I'm trying. She's just so darn cute, though."

"You know, once passion gets ahold of you, bro, it's gonna eat a hole in you big enough to fit itself into."

"I think I'm already there. I feel like Jerry could drive his rig through me."

"Listen." Ranger clapped him on the shoulder. "Go home. To Malfunction Junction."

"Why?" Laredo stared at his brother.

"You're in way over your head. You can't ride this damn bull, anyway. All they need is an eight-second guy, and that would be me. Or Tex. Not you."

His throat dried out; his stomach clenched. "I'm not a quitter."

"No, but you shouldn't have said yes in the first place. Only reason you did was to show off. But you didn't know you were going to fall for Katy, and you didn't know she was, you know—" Ranger cleared his throat delicately "—untouched. And so, it's best if you move on. If you don't go home, at least move on, and keep looking for that Big Thing you're wanting to do. This is not it."

Laredo closed his eyes, pressing his fingers against his eyelids. "I think I'm falling in love."

"I know it, you dope. Fortunately, Katy doesn't realize it. While there's still a piece of your heart that's ambivalent, get gone. Otherwise you're going to end up making love to that little gal. And you'll do something stupid after that, like get her pregnant—"

"I know how to wear a condom, thank you," Laredo snapped.

"Finer men than you have worn the raincoat only to find themselves at a shower nine months later. That'd be baby shower," he emphasized.

"I get it. I don't think you're right. I think I can stay here another night and ride that bull and stay away from Katy."

"And then?" Ranger asked.

"And then ride away and forget it."

"Not to doubt you, bro, but there are clues that tell me different."

"Name one," Laredo invited.

"You ran over here with your zipper unzipped, for one."

Laredo glanced down at his jeans, making a swift adjustment. "That doesn't mean a thing. It was dark on the stairwell, and I didn't want to turn on the light and wake everyone up as I passed their doors, and I was trying not to kill myself by falling down the stairs when I left."

Ranger laughed. "Whatever."

"Name another clue."

"Where did you sleep, if not in Katy's room? After the incident, I mean."

"In the upstairs den. Or TV room. Whatever you want to call it. I bunked on the sofa."

"Why'd you fall asleep on her in the first place? Just a question that leads up to clue number two."

Laredo thought about the softness under him he'd awakened to. "Guess I was tired, or I'd had too much to drink, and I got in the bed I'd been sleeping in. I didn't know she was there."

"But you ended up sleeping on top of her. Even in your subconscious, you want to be with her. Right on top of her, to be specific." Ranger grinned at him. "And anyway, all you have to do is say 'Katy,' and your nostrils flare. You look like you're going to explode any second." Ranger snickered, shaking his head. "I don't think I've ever seen anybody with the hots as bad as you've got them. You're radioactive, man."

When she'd held him in her soft, little hand, Laredo had felt positively nuclear. He rubbed his face, thinking over his choices. "I can't not ride the bull. You hellish beast," he said to Bloodthirsty.

"You're in hell, but it has nothing to do with any bull other than what you're spouting."

"I can do this. I am bigger than myself." Laredo brightened. "That's my new mission statement."

"Being bigger than yourself?" Ranger leaned against the rail. "Think of it this way. You won't be able to make love to Katy once this bull stomps your gizzards out of you, so it won't matter."

Laredo felt himself go chilly all over. "None of you became impotent from getting thrown."

Ranger laughed. "We knew how to land. You're a virgin at bull riding. She's a virgin at lovemaking. One brings you pain, and one brings you sheer joy." He shrugged. "Let me know if you want to back out. I'll make your excuses."

Laredo straightened. "A Jefferson never quits. If I did that, then I'd be...like Maverick." He couldn't bring himself to say "Dad."

"Yeah, well." Ranger sighed. "We're all running from those demons."

CHAPTER ELEVEN

"AND THEN?" Hannah asked with interest the next morning at the breakfast table.

"And then he disappeared like a puff of smoke, but I think even smoke hangs around longer," Katy said. "He vamoosed."

"After you massaged him." Hannah grinned like mad.

"You're not listening. I didn't really get to massage him. I tried to imagine what a Never Lonely Cut-N-Gurls might do if she were in my—"

"Bed with a hunky cowboy," Hannah said gleefully.

"I just tried to act like I knew what I was doing. Obviously, I don't." She scratched her head. "Maybe I squeezed him too tight."

Hannah wheezed and put her head down on her arms.

Katy couldn't eat. She hadn't been able to see Laredo's face when he'd hit the door, but any man who could sprint that quickly was setting a record for escape.

"I don't think you can squeeze a man too tight *there*," Hannah said. "I mean, maybe, but if he didn't say ouch, you're probably safe."

"Really?" Katy brightened.

"Oh, brother." Hannah rolled her eyes. "If I was a matchmaker, I have to admit I wouldn't try to pair the two of you up. I'd never make my commission."

"If you're trying to make me feel better, you're doing a lousy job."

"Didn't you ever have any boyfriends? Fool around at all? Back seat of someone's car? Anything?"

"I was caring for my parents. And studying. I studied a lot."

"Clearly not anatomy, Miss Brainiac." Hannah finger-combed her hair.

"What would you have done in my place?"

"Exactly what you did. Except…when he tried to move, I might not have let go."

Katy gasped. "Are you saying I should have just hung on to his…his—"

"He couldn't have left then," Hannah pointed out.

Katy was speechless. "I didn't want to hurt him. He wanted to leave. I wouldn't think it's ladylike to…try to keep him there by holding on to his— This is so confusing."

"I'm teasing. Relax." Hannah patted her hand. "There's a couple of positive clues here."

"Could you point them out? And hand me a magnifying glass?"

Hannah ignored that. "First, he had an erection."

"I heard men get those about fifty times a day. How is that special?"

Hannah shrugged. "I think that's a male-oriented myth. Their pants would look like they were keeping a jack-in-the-box inside their underwear if it were true. In Laredo's case, he has demonstrated that he clearly does not find you offensive."

"Can we get to clue number two? Because I don't think clue number one was all that decisive," Katy asked.

Hannah nodded. "Clue number two is pretty obvious, actually. He hasn't left town."

Katy stared at her.

"Well, he doesn't have to ride tomorrow, Katy. No one's paying him. He's not under a legal and binding contract. The only reason a newbie bull rider hangs around to get tossed off a bull is because there's someone he wants to impress. So I think Laredo wants to impress you." She took a bite of egg and then a drink of orange juice. "What I can't figure out," Hannah said, "is if he ever plans to make a move."

"I don't think so," Katy said dolefully. "He calls me sweetheart, though."

"Sweetheart's good," Hannah said, "but he's still gone tomorrow afternoon. Sweetheart."

Katy nodded. "He'll change, but I won't." She looked at Hannah. "He rides a bull for the first time. But I don't do anything for the first time. And I'll never know for certain whether I'm...sexually normal."

Frigid was not a tag she wanted to keep.

If she'd ever actually been frigid, she was pretty certain Laredo was the man to change her.

"I'd say you're toast on the lovemaking issue unless there's a miracle or a change of heart," Hannah agreed. "And I'd bank on the miracle before Laredo having a change of heart where your virginity is concerned."

She just had to talk to him, Katy decided. She would tell him how she felt about being with him. It wasn't as if she said, If you ride this bull, I'll sleep with you. What he needed to know was that...somehow she had the funny feeling that he was meant to be her first.

Of course, he wouldn't want to hear that she thought she was falling for him. That would get in the way of his plans for the big thing. He wouldn't lay a finger on her then—forget the virginity issue.

So she would tell him. No more hiding behind politeness. No more ladylike silence and waiting for him to make the first move.

It was now or a lifetime of redefining *frigid*.

But the next time Katy saw Laredo, it was Saturday.

And he was in the chute, slated to ride Bad-Ass Blue for the Never Lonely Cut-N-Gurls.

For the enemy.

CHAPTER TWELVE

KATY COULDN'T BELIEVE her ears when she heard Laredo's name and Bad-Ass Blue's called together. Beside her, Hannah gasped, as did the other Lonely Hearts women. The humiliation for all of them was fairly complete. Practically everyone who knew the Jefferson brothers had turned out to watch Laredo on his virgin bull ride. Even the ten women who'd gone to set up shop in Union Junction had returned for this event. Mimi was here, too, with her new fiancé, Brian O'Flannigan. They'd even brought Mimi's father, Sheriff Cannady, along for the charitable fun.

But now Katy felt like she couldn't pull breath inside her. Laredo riding for the Never Lonely Cut-N-Gurls? How could Marvella steal their cowboy—particularly Katy's cowboy? The bigger question was *how* had she? What allure would have been enough to make Laredo susceptible?

Sitting in the stands, surrounded by now-blurred people—even more people were attending this second rodeo than the first—Katy had been so nervous. She'd gotten Laredo into this; she'd been praying that he'd be fine. What were the stats on first-time riders? Did they stay on? Get broken and stomped?

She'd hardly been able to bear the thought of it.

But when the announcer had called Laredo's name, it was Katy who got broken and stomped.

Her heart was in shocked pieces, more pieces than when Stanley had dumped her at the altar for her best friend.

ON THE BACK of Bad-Ass Blue, Tex barely heard his twin's name called as rider. There was no time to correct anyone. Beneath him, the bull was bunching and trying to kick, just itching to get out of the stall where he could run free and do his damnedest to toss the cowboy on top of him.

He tightened the rope around his gloved hand, shoved his hat down on his head one more time, put his arm up and nodded.

LAREDO HEARD HIS NAME called for the wrong bull, but he was dealing with a bigger problem. Bloodthirsty Black had definitely gotten up on the wrong side of the pen this morning, and though his brother Crockett had come early to paint the bull's hooves, the bull had decided he wasn't going to put up with that nonsense, either.

This bull had gotten more ornery with each passing hour. They'd had a helluva time getting the hooves decorated for the contest. This was especially important to Laredo, because he was desperately afraid he wasn't going to win the bull riding contest, and he wanted to bring home a win of some kind. He and Crockett had argued over creative design—Crockett was on a nudes-only kick—but Laredo felt that was inappropriate considering the salon for which he was riding as knight in shining armor. Besides, he'd told Crockett, the type of detail with which Crockett liked to paint his nudes would probably lose some artistic power once translated onto a bull's hooves.

So in the process of arguing over the matter of nudes versus the roses that Laredo thought would be a blue ribbon winner, Bloodthirsty Black took a horn to the paint cans and Crockett's rump, neatly lifting him a foot into the air and scooping him out of the pen onto the concrete floor.

It was Bull-1, Cowboys-0, Laredo thought grimly, but no bull was going to get the best of him.

The bull was not appeased and sensed he was in the company of a greenhorn. After that, every time Laredo came near the bull, Bloodthirsty Black let out a bellow, which might have been a victory yell, and it might have been a warning. Either way, it was making Laredo more nervous than he'd previously been.

The beer he'd drunk the night before as part of Ranger's suggested training was no longer sitting comfortably in his body. Knight in shining armor, he reminded himself, staring at the painted bull. Unfortunately, his armor felt dastardly dull today.

Crockett did a swift, impressive press-on design of vivid bluebonnets, which was his artistic compromise to Laredo's suggestion of roses. "They remind me of nudes," Crockett told Laredo, "they're pear-shaped and lush and beautiful."

"What-freaking-ever," Laredo said, his mood totally sour. The bluebonnet renderings looked really cool on Bloodthirsty's midnight hooves, and Laredo had to take his hat off to Crockett's swift application of paint on waxed paper which he pressed onto each hoof the second Bloodthirsty decided to glare at Laredo. But they in no way looked like nudes to Laredo, and right now, he'd have given anything to be in a place with nudes and no bulls. "Miss Delilah should be real pleased with your work, Crockett."

Crockett beamed at the praise. "His hooves are going to flash as they fly through the air in the ring."

Laredo glared at Crockett as he shrugged into the shirt Miss Delilah had given him to wear. "Why did you drag everybody from Union Junction to the rodeo? I just wanted your artistry, not a convention."

"We wouldn't have missed your first ride, Laredo, even if we think you're brainless for doing it."

"Yeah, well. You must have looked like a convoy tearing over here with everybody. And what's up with Mason? He looks like some unattractive bug species just flew into his mouth." Laredo peered into the arena where he could see the Union Junction crowd taking up a full grandstand.

"Mimi's fiancé tagged along. It's not that we don't like Brian, it's just that he seems to have a rude effect on Mason."

"How so?" Laredo tightened his belt.

"Mason sees Brian, Mason gets ruder. Or annoyingly silent. We can't decide which is worse."

Laredo looked up. "It's not like Mason was winning any prizes for personality to start with."

"It's getting worse, bro. In the past couple days, Mason seemed to have come to grips with Mimi's engagement, but then we got the wedding invitation, and—"

Laredo held up a hand. "Don't tell me any more. I don't want my brother to be the last thing on my mind before I get squished. I'm going to the chute. How do I look?"

"Like you're about to die," Crockett said cheerfully. "And not too happy about it, either. Hey, you really like that little girl, don't you?"

"What little girl?" Laredo glowered at his brother,

arranging his steely game face for the upcoming show-down. If the game face worked on Crockett, maybe it would impress Bloodthirsty.

But Crockett laughed. "You're just like Mason," he said. "They say actions speak louder than words, but I never knew that the one who was acting could be totally deaf to themselves."

"Huh?" Laredo glowered harder. "Paint fumes get to you?"

"Yep, just like Mason," Crockett said on a sigh. "Show-ing your emotions through physical engagement."

"Whereas you paint your emotions, and since nudes are your favorite artistic topic, can I assume you're hornier than a mallard in May?"

The smile slipped off Crockett's face. "And that's just what Mason would have said. You're turning into him."

"No, I'm not." Laredo turned to walk away. "That's precisely why I left the Malfunction Junction."

"Good luck," Crockett said to Laredo's retreating back. "And not necessarily with you," he told Blood-thirsty. "Whew! Talk about deprivation. If anybody's got it bad, it's him. If you break something on him, I'm painting mating mallards all over his cast!"

WHY TEX HAD DECIDED to ride for the Never Lonely Cut-N-Gurls, Laredo wasn't certain. Nor did he have time to find out anything more than his twin's score of an eighty-nine.

Not bad, but not unbeatable, either. Of course, Tex had a lot of experience, and Laredo had none.

Bloodthirsty was brought into the chute, and he was helped onto the trapped bull.

Oh, hellfire. What was he doing here? Pull rope

tight around glove, mash down hat for good measure, be grateful to the four cowboys trying to keep this bull from breaking his legs against the chute walls, hope Katy's watching, hope he stayed on this stupid bull, he *was* going to stay on this stupid bull—

He heard his name called as rider—mix-up on the names, Jerry the truck driver explained as he played announcer—but a Jefferson was a Jefferson and how lucky was Lonely Hearts Station to have a pair of strapping twins from Union Junction here to help them out in their charitable endeavors?

None of that mattered to Laredo at the moment. The "Make My Day" panties had probably had a lot to do with his twin riding for the opposing salon. He wouldn't take offense to that, but if he lost to Tex, he'd probably have to thrash him later for the sake of his ego.

"He pulls to the left," Cissy's voice reminded him. "And then, just when you lean, he jerks to the right with a mean midair kick. Every time."

Tex had said he didn't think the bull pulled to the left. Laredo took a deep breath and leaned to anticipate the jerk to the right.

Why hadn't the damn gate opened? Laredo nodded, remembering at the last second that he was supposed to do so. The chute door swung open, and he was dimly aware of a rodeo clown clinging to the side of the arena before Bloodthirsty burst out, wringing hellfire from Hades and flashing bluebonnet-painted hooves.

KATY'S HEART LEAPED inside her as Bloodthirsty Black flung himself from the chute. He was an immense bull—and the rider on his back appeared to be Laredo. She clasped her hands together, praying harder than she'd ever prayed. Eight seconds—that was all the Lonely

Hearts Salon needed. Eight seconds—please don't let Laredo get hurt.

Two seconds later Laredo went flying off Blood-thirsty Black, landing gracefully for a man who was thrown boots-over-head. But the bull wasn't through with him, and having a taste for Jefferson brother butt after horning Crockett, elected to do the same to Laredo. Laredo went flying into a post, the bull was shooed away by the clown, and Katy was already running down the steps before the Jefferson brothers vaulted en masse from the grandstand.

"WELL," MARVELLA SAID with a satisfied grin, as the Never Lonely Hearts cowboy went flying. She was watching from the stands across the arena from her sister. "Who would have imagined twins? You stole the wrong cowboy, Cissy."

"I thought it was Laredo," Cissy said hotly, wondering why Tex hadn't mentioned in the entire night that they'd spent together that he wasn't Laredo. But now that she thought about it, their time together had been very silent, very passionate and very, very satisfying. She got shivers all over thinking about it. In her newly formed opinion, Tex was all man and no bull, and if she ever got the chance to make love with the wrong cowboy again, he wouldn't have to ask twice.

Of course, he wouldn't ask again. Men like that went for sweet girls, delicate untouched girls like Katy Goodnight. They liked their fun and adventure, but in the end they married a Madonna. The real kind. And she was no Madonna.

It didn't matter that she'd wanted a different life. It didn't matter that she wished she'd known about Delilah and her girls before she signed on with Marvella. She'd been desperate, and she'd reached out to take the hand that had saved her when she was drowning, and there was no turning back. She had secrets—eight of them—and she could never forget that.

She stared at Katy Goodnight rushing to Laredo's side, and the pit of Cissy's stomach turned with empathy. Inside, all she could think of was how glad and relieved she was that she hadn't stolen Katy's cowboy. No matter how wonderful the lovemaking had been, there had been a tinge of regret for what she was doing.

"It doesn't matter," Marvella said with delight. "Even if you didn't humiliate them by stealing their rider, you appear to have lured the only cowboy who *could* ride. And believe me, that's a job well done, my dear."

No, it's not, Cissy thought, watching as a doctor aided Laredo to his feet. Something was wrong with him. And it was all her fault. She had given him bad advice at first—though later she'd corrected it. But the nagging voice of conscience wouldn't go away.

THE GATE MONEY was considerable this time, almost double the first rodeo, money that Lonely Hearts Station desperately needed for the city coffers. Street repair and some renovations to the cafeteria were tops on the list the city fathers—and Mother Delilah—had in mind.

The prize money and the buckle went to the Never Lonely Cut-N-Gurls, again. But that wasn't the part that had Katy in tears. She'd gotten Laredo on the back of that bull—and now he had a concussion.

A slight one, the doctor at the hospital said. What could be termed level one, and thankfully the CT scan was normal. But he still had enough of a concussion that he needed rest.

He'd sure been talking stupid there for a while,

something that had straightened the hair on Katy's arms. Something about his dad. Where was his dad? Where was his dad? Over and over again, until Mason had finally barked at him to relax. But then Laredo had started babbling about the winning nudes. Did the nudes win? The blue nudes? Did the nudes win?

Tex finally told Laredo that a blue nude would win anytime, and would he please rest his mouth?

Katy had felt terrible for Laredo. It was all her fault. She'd wanted a win for Delilah so badly, wanted to be a help and thank her for all Delilah'd done for her that she'd risked this cowboy's life.

Fortunately, his head had cleared an hour later, and he never mentioned blue nudes again. Now they were all standing outside the hospital, deciding how to organize the going-home exodus. During the wait for Laredo to be examined, some of the Jefferson brothers had sneaked out to Laredo's truck and unearthed the beer out of the now-iceless cooler. Mimi and her fiancé had long since gone home. She said she needed to check on her father, who had left early.

"Laredo can ride back with me to Union Junction," Mason said.

It was probably for the best, though Katy's heart sank a little.

Laredo glanced at her, shaking his head and then wincing. "I'm staying here," Laredo said, "if Miss Delilah will have me."

"Of course!" Delilah replied instantly. "We should nurse you back to health!"

But it was Katy he was looking at while he waited for an answer. "I can find someplace other than your room," he said. "The upstairs den sofa is fine."

"Absolutely not. Hannah and I can bunk together for a few more days, until you're feeling better."

"I'm not the champion you were hoping for, Katy."

She looked into his eyes and saw the disappointment he was suffering. "Come on," she said. "Tex brought your truck. He can ride back with one of your brothers."

"Tex, give Katy my keys," Laredo instructed. "She's going to drive me ho— Um, she's going to drive me back to Miss Delilah's."

"Are you sure you don't want to come back with us?" Tex asked, handing the keys over, anyway.

"I've only started on the first leg of my journey to doing a Big Thing. So the leg has a small joint in it I wasn't expecting. It's not enough to make me put my tail between my legs and head home."

"You *should* head home," Mason interjected. "Helga can take care of you. Katy needs to be working, I'm sure, not playing nurse to a cowboy who shouldn't have tried to ride what he didn't know anything about."

Laredo scowled. "I'm fine, Mason. And let me be the first to inform you, since Frisco Joe didn't seem to enlighten you, I'd rather be nursed by Hitler than Helga. We all would."

Frisco Joe put his arm around Annabelle, who was holding baby Emmie. "Helga *is* Hitler, in woman's attire. Did you know he had a thing for cross-dressing? And that it's rumored he's not really dead? Look closely at Helga's face, and you'll see a striking—"

"Enough!" Mason cut in, his tone allowing no further argument. "Your manners are showing, both of you. Helga took very good care of you when you were dumb enough to bust your leg."

All the Jefferson boys rolled their eyes, knowing full well it was Helga's ministrations that sent Frisco Joe running to Lonely Hearts Station to seek shelter with Annabelle Turnberry, now Jefferson.

"Thanks all the same, Mason. I'm staying here," Laredo stated. "It's safer, believe me."

Katy's eyes were locked on Laredo. "If you're sure about this, let me get you back to the salon. The doctor says it's very important that you don't scramble your brains again for three months, and that you rest completely for forty-eight hours."

"I need it," he said. "Because I'm asking for a rematch in a week's time."

CHAPTER THIRTEEN

"You can't be serious," Katy told Laredo once she was behind the wheel of his truck. "The doctor told you not to hit your head again for at least three months. You'll end up with Troy Aikman syndrome."

It didn't matter, Laredo knew. Conquering Big Things had to do with bravery. Commitment. Grit. And not running out when things got rough.

"And our salon did win the Best Painted Hooves contest," Katy continued. "We blew them clean out of the water on that one."

Of course the prize money for that was smaller, but Crockett's rendition had brought him a lot of attention, which he totally deserved since his own brothers were the first to rag him on his artistic endeavors.

No matter how much they really were developing an artist's appreciation and a voyeur's eye for his nudes.

"But that was Crockett," Laredo said. "It didn't have anything to do with me."

"You asked him to paint for us. That's something."

Katy stopped at a single-light intersection, and Laredo put his hand over hers on the wheel. "Katy, you don't understand. I know I can stay on next time. And I aim to prove it."

"Well, any notoriety you bring to Miss Delilah helps the price of her bull," Katy said slowly. "Goodness knows the gate take was up, and we even had some regional photographers doing some articles, so our tourism will probably improve—"

"Katy, it's the least I can do."

"Why, Laredo?" She stared at him. "Why do you want to help us so much?"

"Because it's the right thing to do. Helping to save a small town in a struggling economy is worthwhile as far as I'm concerned. As soon as I get the chance, I'm going to tell Tex he's a rat for riding against me."

"He said that the Cut-N-Gurls didn't have a rider. Which makes sense, if you think about it, Laredo. All these people had bought tickets. They would have been disappointed if we hadn't had the rodeo with the headline event." Besides the marquee rematch, several lesser bulls had been ridden. There'd been a calf catch, as well as a table of cowboys playing chicken to see who would be last to vacate their seat before a bull charged them. It had been a huge success. "Maybe the Cut-N-Gurls weren't even being sneaky this time," Katy said.

"I may have seen evidence to the contrary. Hot pink with silver lettering, but never mind that right now. I just want to get in bed."

She felt her face pinken as she parked the truck in back of the salon. "Here we are."

They went upstairs, Katy leading the way. "Can I get you something to drink?"

"You can get me something," Laredo said, drawing her into his arms, "but a drink isn't what I had in mind."

"I don't think you should kiss me while your head isn't totally clear."

His arms locked around her. "I'm not suffering from temporary amnesia. I know full well that your name is Penny Calfcatcher."

She rolled her eyes at him. "Very funny, cowboy."

"I let you down."

"Not by half." Lifting her foot, she nudged the bedroom door closed behind them, and began to pull off the Lonely Hearts shirt Laredo was wearing. "Let's get you ready for bed."

"You're being very Helga-ish. I'm going to insist upon a winner's kiss, even though I didn't win."

She looked up at him. "Laredo, I can't. I'm too nervous. Too uncertain. When I thought you were riding for the Cut-N-Gurls, I nearly died a thousand deaths. I thought last month had repeated itself, with them stealing our cowboy. Only this time, you'd been stolen from me, just like my—" she drooped her head "—my ex-fiancé."

"Katy—"

He tried to tip her chin up but she shrugged his finger away. "You're braver than me, Laredo. Already you're itching to get back on and try again with Bloodthirsty. But I'm not a get-back-in-the-saddle girl, I guess. I want to keep both my feet firmly planted on the ground."

He stared at her, and she had to glance away from his deep, probing gaze. His expression was puzzled and disappointed and wistful. It made her heart turn over hard in her chest. "I'm sorry," she whispered. "I really am."

"No way would I have ever done that, Katy," he said softly. "I would never have ridden for the opposing team."

"I know. I knew that then, but seeing was believing, Laredo, if only for eight horrible seconds." She shook her head. "I had no reason to imagine that the announcer was wrong, or that your twin had gone over to the other side."

"It's not my fault," he told her, stroking her face. "Katy, you're going to have to learn to trust again one day. I propose that I'm the man you should trust."

"Why?" she asked. "You were supposed to leave today. Right after the rodeo. Nothing's stopping you but a concussion."

"I could leave now. But I haven't."

She turned her face slightly away. "Laredo, please don't press me. I have a thousand thoughts racing through my head, and I just don't want to…make another mistake. My heart can't take it." She took a deep breath. "Remember the fight-or-flight theory? Well, I want to stay on my flight plan. I'm finishing up my summer here, and then I'm going on to Duke where I belong. I'm going to teach science, be the best prof I can be and bury myself in academic pursuits. If I hadn't strayed from my plan in the beginning, I wouldn't have ended up a jilted woman. I'm not straying again," she said, her voice resolute as she turned back to look into his eyes.

"You really thought I would do that to you?"

"I didn't know." She couldn't look at the pain in his eyes. "I just really didn't know. The Cut-N-Gurls can be so tricky."

"Your confidence is down," he said comfortingly. "And I understand that. But, Katy, sometimes a man can't be taken in by a woman. They have to want to be. And I don't want to be taken in by those ladies. I like you."

The shell around her heart crackled a little, allowing hope to stream in. "I know you find Cissy attractive."

"Sure. Even Cissy finds Cissy attractive. But that doesn't mean I'd go there. And don't say anything about the Jefferson reputation. Tex may be my twin, but we couldn't be more different." He rubbed his chin, wondering about his brother's sudden penchant for the beauty queen temptress. "Actually, to be honest, I'm a little surprised by my brother. Tex isn't the type to fall for a girl like…well, never mind."

"See?" she said softly. "If you're surprised about Tex, why is it so unlikely that I would have misjudged you? The Cut-N-Gurls have a focal goal, they go for it, and rarely do they not achieve it."

"They didn't this time."

"Maybe they seduced Tex, thinking it was you."

"Jeez, do not even mention that around my twin. He would have a fit. His ego couldn't take it." Laredo laughed softly. "Even if they did, that should just confirm to you that I'm unseduceable."

"Completely?"

"Care to find out?" He nuzzled her nose.

"You have a concussion. Why don't you crawl into bed before you short-circuit something?"

"Maybe I will." He sighed suddenly, sounding tired, and sat on the edge of her bed. "Hey, Rose. What's going on in the mouse house?" Something on the nightstand caught his eye, and slowly he picked it up. "'Lars Van Hooven, photographer, *Playboy Magazine*.'" He turned his gaze to her. "Why do you have this business card?"

She snatched it from his fingers. "No special reason. And just because you're bunking in here does not give you permission to snoop."

He stared at her for a long moment. "You're not thinking of posing, are you?"

Starting to say no, Katy stopped herself. "I might. They're looking for sweet, unsophisticated, country girls—"

He sat up stiff and straight. "I don't think so."

She automatically bristled. Okay, so she'd gone into more description than was necessary just to jerk his chain, but his attitude made her want to call Lars Van Hooven on the spot. "Wait a minute, there, cowboy—"

"No, Katy."

A gasp escaped her. "Laredo, you can't tell me what to do."

"I'm not," Laredo insisted. "I'm expressing my opinion."

"You don't get one!"

"I do, too. I'm voting no. You won't be able to do it, Katy, and anyway, if you think you want to pose nude, you can pose for me." He leaned back against the headboard and crossed his arms. "In fact, you can start now."

"What?"

"Take off your clothes and pose for me. I want to see your smiles, both horizontal and vertical."

She frowned at him. "I'm not undressing in front of you. And may I add that I don't like your tone? It smacks of…possessiveness or something."

He raised a brow at her, which made her nervous.

"And besides, you're missing the point I'm trying to make."

"Which would be what, Miss July?"

She gave him a gimlet eye. "You rematch on that damn bull, and I pose."

"It's a matter of pride, Katy. I know I can do it. I'd just never felt a bull beneath me before, and I didn't know what to expect. Now I do. Experience counts."

"You're wearing your experience in the shape of a dented skull. Laredo, I got you into this, and I have to be the one to say it's not worth getting yourself brained over."

"Well, you can't just say you don't like my decision for a rematch—which, I might add, the Lonely Hearts Station city fathers and mother agreed to with great interest—you're only going to pose for *Playboy* because you don't want a rematch."

"I'm going to do something daring," Katy stated. "Not daring by some girls' standards, maybe, but certainly by mine. It's my Big Thing, Laredo."

His mouth thinned into a straight, compressed line. "You're going to make me say it, aren't you?"

"Say what?" She was curious, staring at the cowboy on her bed. Golly, but he was handsome. And yet so stubborn! Now that she thought about it, Stanley was not so handsome, and rather spineless. Just the opposite of Laredo. But she hadn't known who she was looking for before, just the what, which was a belated spring fling, which then turned into a marriage proposal.

But Stanley hadn't turned out to be a spring fling. She had the experience now to know better.

However, as she stared pugilistically at Laredo, she recognized that he was even less of a spring fling than Stanley. All that claptrap Stanley had given her about staying a virgin until after they were married had come down to him desiring not her but her family connections.

"You want me to say that I won't do the rematch. But I've already said I would, and I can't back out now, because that would be reneging on the Jefferson name."

"That's what you had to say? That load of turkey trimmings?" Why had she hoped he would say something romantic, like I'm only doing it to impress you?

"Katy!" Laredo swung his feet over the side of the

bed and stalked toward her. "You're making this very tough on me."

"I actually don't see why you should care, Laredo." Katy was only being honest. "It's my body. My life. My chance to be…uninhibited."

It appeared that he ground his teeth together. She could hear what sounded like crunching sandpaper in his mouth before he put his hands on her shoulders. "Katy Goodnight," he said, "you're far more ornery than any marquee bull. So…I'm going to go spend the night somewhere else."

SHE'D LEFT HIM with no choice, Laredo told himself as he stalked outside. For the first time, he began to feel a real headache coming on. Originally, he'd had a tender, bruised area on his head, but this went below the surface.

No one had ever infuriated him like Katy Goodnight.

For such a sweet-faced girl, she made him want to toss her down on the bed and kiss her until she said she'd do whatever he wanted her to. Mainly, not pose in a girlie mag! She was so innocent she didn't realize what men bought those magazines for. And if she thought he was going to allow her to let men see her and fulfill their sexual needs while staring at her—

"Whatcha doing?" Tex demanded from his truck bed.

"What the hell are you doing?" Laredo demanded, although it was obvious. Tex and Ranger were enjoying the brilliant starlit night, both of them sitting on top of barrels they'd retrieved from heaven knew where and drinking beer out of the still-packed cooler.

"Trying to decide if we should come in there and

drag you out and take you home," Ranger said. "We're debating the points in your IQ for saying you wanted a rematch. I've got you at about seventy, but Tex says you're closer to a hundred."

Which marked him from somewhat mentally challenged to pretty much mentally challenged, depending on whose scale he cared to use. "Is that beer still warm?"

"Nah. We got some ice out of Miss Delilah's freezer and restocked the cooler. Nice chilly brewskis now," Tex said with satisfaction. "How's your head?"

"Hurting, but not necessarily from Bloodthirsty's tricks." He climbed up into the truck bed, sat on the edge of the truck and took the beer Ranger offered him. "What made you ride for the Cut-N-Gurls, Tex?"

"Sex," Ranger said, though Tex shook his head.

"Not sex. Just wanted to do a little riding again, I guess. It was for a good cause, too, and that made up my mind. However, I had no idea you'd get thrown so easily."

"Don't go easy on my pride or anything." He took a swig of beer.

"I'm not," Tex said. "What I meant was that I figured it was all good clean fun. I figured you'd stay on come hell or high water to impress Katy, and I figured without a Cut-N-Gurl rider, you wouldn't get the chance to show off."

"So you did it for me?" Laredo asked.

"Not necessarily. I really wanted to ride again. I liked being a hero." He sighed deeply. "I'd rather have been a hero for this salon. I had to take my apologies to Miss Delilah, and I sure did feel like a rat."

"You are a rat," Ranger said with a grin, "but you meant well."

"Do you like Cissy?" Laredo asked.

Tex stared at both his brothers. "She's a nice girl."

"That's it?" Laredo probed.

"Well, how do you feel about Katy?" Tex asked defensively.

"Most of the time, confused. I want her naked, I want her pure, I want to spank her, I want to…I don't know. Marry her, maybe."

"What?" both his brothers yelped.

"Man, you hit your head harder than we thought," Tex said. "Marriage isn't a Big Thing."

"It is," Laredo said defensively. "It is if you intend for it to be forever."

Ranger put his hands behind his head. "Do we know anyone who's been married forever? Without any fooling around or trial separations? Just unending bliss?"

Tex shoved his hat back on his head. "I don't think we personally know of a documented case, but maybe they're out there. And Union Junction is so small that it's not really a representative sampling of the population."

Laredo rubbed his brow tiredly, just above where his head was throbbing. "We do know someone who's happily married. Think about it."

"Well, there's the Jenkins," Ranger offered.

"Only because the missus doesn't let the mister talk. Heaven knows what he would say if he could get a word in edgewise."

"Probably, 'Help! Help!'" Tex said. "What about the Smyths?"

"You can't count them," Ranger stated. "Mrs. Smyth was married to two men at the same time."

"She didn't know it," Laredo pointed out. "She thought one husband was dead in the war, and she remarried. But then she got divorced and married her first husband when he returned ten years later."

"Which was weird enough," Tex said with a grin, "except that then both the men remained in the house with her."

"They're wounded war vets," Laredo reminded him. "They both needed some assistance. It was a suitable arrangement all around." If a bit scandalous, he forbore to mention.

"I'll say," Tex agreed. "Maybe I'll find a wife who'll agree to let me have a second wife in the same house with us. I could dig being tended by two women."

"You'll be the walking wounded then," Ranger told him. "Plus the expense would be far worse than having two Thoroughbred racehorses, and there'd no doubt be hellacious bitching going on. Just concentrate on fertilizing your roses, Tex."

"So what about you and Hannah?" Laredo asked his brother.

"What about us?" Ranger's tone was unyielding.

"I thought maybe you liked her. Although you did go off with Cissy for a while."

Ranger shrugged. "I'm not going to like anyone. My life is fine the way it is. And I still say you should let your brains unscramble before you find yourself doing something stupid like getting married."

That's what it was, Laredo realized. He'd hit his head, and then Katy had mentioned posing nude, and he'd been attacked by paralyzing pain in his brain, and the word *marriage* had appeared as if Vanna White had turned the letters for him. The thing was, he wasn't the jealous type. Never had been. Nor had he been the possessive type. So, clearly, he *had* knocked something loose. "I think I'll turn in," he said suddenly. "The doctor said

I needed forty-eight hours of good rest. And I believe her."

Ranger laughed. "We've been meaning to ask you about that doctor, by the way. She had nice long legs and some other things. Did you suffer any amnesia? Because we want to know what kind of perfume she was wearing."

Laredo grunted. The doctor in question had been a Whitney Houston look-alike, a major babe in every way. He'd never have enough amnesia to keep him from noticing a woman like her. Plus her hands had been soft and cool when she touched his head.

What he really needed a prescription for was how, despite the doctor's beauty and soft touch, he'd kept thinking about Katy's worried face peering at him as he'd lain on the arena floor.

He didn't have amnesia. He had obsession, and best he could recall, there was no cure for that.

He jumped down from the truck bed and crawled inside the cab. Then he lay down, telling himself he'd be himself after a good night's rest.

"Nighty-night," he heard Ranger call, his voice all but grinning, if voices could. "Sweet dreams."

"Shut up," Laredo muttered to himself. If he was lucky, he wouldn't dream about Katy in front of a photographer's lens, showing her charms to the whole world. She was just bossy enough to do it.

"If you rematch, I pose," she'd said.

The thought made him groan.

Sweet 'n' sour Miss Katy Goodnight had two things she was about to learn: one, he never backed down from a challenge.

He *was* going to rematch.

Second, he never backed down from a challenge.

She had to be protected from herself. And he was just the bad-ass-in-the-flesh cowboy to do it.

TEX WATCHED through the back truck window as Laredo settled down in the cab. "Do we hang around for the final showdown or do we bail?"

Ranger shrugged and swigged some beer. "You're in it up to your hips, I'd say. Mason says he can give us a few more days off, especially if we come home in the middle of the week to lend a hand. Besides, you've got to ride again."

"Uh-uh. Not me. I only ride against my brother once."

Ranger stared at him. "You didn't ride against Laredo. He rode against himself. You were just a practice partner."

"Are you suggesting I should ride again?"

"Did Laredo ask you not to?"

"No." Tex rolled his shoulders and neck uneasily. "But I should think it would be obvious that family sticks together. And we're all behind the Lonely Hearts ladies." He shook his head. "I didn't mind subbing when the rodeo was too close to be called off. But they've got time to find another cowboy now."

"Thing is, Laredo needs to beat you just as much as he needs to beat that bull," Ranger whispered. "Otherwise, he'll never know."

"Never know what?" Tex whispered back.

Ranger sighed. "Well, think it through. You heard all that bull Laredo gave Katy about Mason not letting him ride rodeo, didn't you?"

"Yeah." Tex scratched his forehead.

"Well, think about why he didn't just tell her the truth."

"That Mason was less keen on Laredo riding than any of us, simply because he knew he'd never come home?"

"That's just it," Ranger said. "He didn't tell Katy that. And he didn't tell her that he loved playing soccer. He didn't tell her that while the rest of us were getting our heads cracked open, Mason was running him from field to field. He didn't tell her that he'd actually won a scholarship and gone to college full-ride. And he sure as hell didn't tell her the real truth, that he hated rodeo with a passion, and that bulls and broncs held no appeal for him whatsoever."

"Truth be known, he was always a little bit astonished by our interest," Tex agreed. "Couldn't understand why we enjoyed getting thrown off. And we couldn't understand why he enjoyed hanging about with a bunch of sweaty lads pouring Gatorade over each other and eating oranges."

"There you have it," Ranger said. "You see what I'm trying to tell you."

"Not really."

"He did the one thing he really had no interest in, and was even maybe a little scared of. It's his Big Thing. But he did it for Katy."

"Ohh," Tex said.

"So you have to ride. You're just about the best of the best, and if he can beat you this time—and his fear—then he's set himself up as a worthy knight for Katy."

Tex squinted at him. "How many beers have you drunk?"

"I don't know. Why?"

"Because you sound like you've drunk a case, yet somehow I'm hearing your reasoning clearly. Maybe *I've* drunk the case."

Ranger grinned at him. "Faint heart never won fair lady. Didn't you ever hear that?"

"I don't think so…. I've heard that you can't make a silk purse out of a sow's ear."

Ranger raised his brows at him. "Are you saying Laredo can't do it?"

Tex sighed. "I've got a lot of experience, Ranger. We can't hang around here forever riding a bull once a week so that Laredo can finally catch up and beat me to impress Katy."

"I know that. I don't think it'll take another week."

"And it's a really stupid, caveman, macho-guy way to woo a woman, anyway. That bodacious doc said Laredo wasn't to risk another head injury or he could really do damage. And then he'll end up at home with Helga, and then we'll have to keep him doped on smuggled prescriptions."

"He's not wooing the woman by riding the bull. He's wooing himself. He's got to do a Big Thing."

"You said he was doing it for Katy."

"I said he was doing what he didn't want to do for her. The choice of weapon is for her but the battle itself, that's all his."

Tex sighed. "For crying out loud. And say he wins. Then what?"

Ranger got off the barrel and lay down with his head against the side. Crossing his boots, he pulled his hat down low. "I only do analysis. To predict the future would make me a mind reader, and I'd have to be able to factor in Katy's mind set."

"No one can predict what a woman will do," Tex pointed out.

"I agree. Get some sleep. We're going to be very busy tomorrow."

"I'd rather sleep in a bed."

Ranger sighed. "Me, too. But Laredo's not sleeping inside, and that tells me something's not going all that well in the land of romance. So we gotta sleep out here and keep an eye on him."

"He won't sleepwalk."

"No, but someone might walk on him in his sleep."

Tex straightened. "Hey, the Cut-N-Gurls won't shanghai him. They're not that way. I think everybody's got them all wrong."

"Do you like Cissy Kisserton?"

"No," he denied. "Do you?"

"If I did, you'd never have had a shot at her. By the way, I was pretty impressed that you pulled an 89 after being up all night."

Tex stared at his brother's lowered hat suspiciously. "Who said I was up all night?"

"Just a hunch."

"Keep your hunches to yourself. I'm not interested. And," Tex said, hunkering down next to his brother, "don't even get started, because if I ever do have a grand romance, you're going to be the last to know about it!"

"I hope so," Ranger said mildly.

"So do I." Tex studied the stars for a moment. "Want to know a secret?"

"Not really."

"Marvella's bull isn't as mean as Bloodthirsty. In fact, he was a downright creampuff."

Ranger's hat moved back as he pushed it so that he could stare at Tex. "What are you saying?"

"I'm saying that there are bulls born to make a rider look good, and there are bulls born to make a rider look bad. Bad-Ass Blue made me look good. I really didn't have to do anything except hold on for eight. No trick shots, no low punches."

"Not a marquee bull?"

Tex shrugged. "Maybe Blue was having an off day. That bull's supposed to be meaner than mean."

"Says who?"

"Says everyone. Besides, the judges can tell when you're getting a good ride. He looks good. He looks mean. And he sure can run and kick with the best of them. But he doesn't have the lust for kill that Blood-thirsty has. Sure, he's mad and all. But he's lacking the fundamental tricks to be a nasty ride. Bloodthirsty's not a ride at all. He's a one-way suicide ticket."

"We could switch you," Ranger said quickly. "No one was the wiser when they announced the wrong riders this time. No one would notice next time."

"Nope. No way. Laredo would never allow it. You said it yourself, this is his Big Thing. Fact is, this is a holy war between Laredo and the same thing we're all grappling with."

Silence met that comment as they thought about growing up without parents most of the time. For some of the brothers it had been just about all of the time. It hadn't been terrible, but Mason was outnumbered and outmanned. He deserved a Purple Heart. Laredo had been the go-to guy when Mason had been funky.

Of course, the downside of this was that if Laredo was blowing a fuse now, then Mason was way overdue.

Tex sighed. "Nope, my twin's got himself set square on the horns of his own dilemma, and there are only two things I can see happening here. One, he wins. Two, he loses. Both are out of our control."

But with a trick bull and a woman who'd sent him to

his truck for the night, it seemed Laredo was in it up to his ears.

Tex was relieved he wasn't in his twin's boots.

CHAPTER FOURTEEN

DELILAH WAS MORE worried about the rematch than she let on. The calls from surrounding city papers had been gratifying. They'd even had a few offers of corporate sponsorship from some big-city restaurants. Bloodthirsty, it seemed, was garnering quite the reputation. For that matter, bookings for haircuts in her salon were up by twenty percent, and all from city folk interested in having their hair done by one of Lonely Hearts Station's infamous salons.

There was only one way to beat Marvella at her own game, and that was all that was on Delilah's mind today. It was past time she and her sister had a little chat. She could send someone in her place; Delilah being a town councilwoman, and it being town business, someone else on the council *could* talk to Marvella.

But this had become personal, now that Laredo had gotten hurt, and as far as she was concerned, the buck stopped with her. "I'm going to see Marvella," she told Jerry, who was sitting in the kitchen icing some cookies for her.

He never paused in what he was doing. "I'll send out the rescue squad if you're not back in an hour, but there's two things you should know."

"What?" She turned to him with a waiting expression on her face.

"One, it's a volunteer rescue squad. We don't pay

folks around here like the big city pays its emergency workers."

"Fair enough. Second?"

"Being that it's volunteer, the squad will most likely consist of me and those Jefferson boys asleep in Laredo's truck out there. I'm fixing to run them out some of these cookies."

"For breakfast?"

"They're just like doughnuts in my opinion," Jerry said cheerfully, "and they'll sit right fine on guts full of beer."

Delilah shuddered. "If you change your mind and decide to make breakfast for our champions, there are eggs and biscuits in the fridge."

"Delilah?"

"Yes?"

"How did you feel about Tex riding for the opposing team?"

"I felt rotten about it when I thought Laredo was on their bull, for Katy's sake. When I realized it was Tex, I felt fine. The Jefferson brothers are bringing business to my salon, Jerry, and to this town that I love. I can't complain about that."

Jerry grinned. "They sure are bringing in the women from far and away. Most of the reservations we took today were from women new to town, and all wanting to look beautiful for the rodeo. And all wanting to know who was riding this weekend."

"Ah." Delilah smiled and closed the door. She was a smart businesswoman. There was opportunity in a situation that had been out of her hands for too long.

It was time to start taking it back.

"Marvella," she called, throwing open the Never Lonely Cut-N-Gurls Salon door. About twenty employees and that many customers stopped everything they were doing, which, as far as she could see, was mainly inhabit a Jacuzzi and enjoy some masseuse attention. She was pretty certain all she had to do was send out a zoning committee to check her sister's permits—that Jacuzzi was not on any record she remembered seeing. No one could prove that Marvella's business was shady, but as a councilwoman, Delilah felt it was of the utmost importance to see that Lonely Hearts Station retained its promising reputation as a safe, wonderful haven for tourists with a yen for small-town appeal. "Sister, dearest, it's time you and I had a little heart-to-heart, so to speak."

KATY POKED HER HEAD in the kitchen, watching Jerry frost cookies for a minute. "Good morning," she finally said. "Would you like help?"

"No. Yes," Jerry said suddenly. "Take a dozen of these out to Laredo's truck, if you don't mind."

"Why?" She didn't mind, but why were cookies being sent out to Laredo's truck? Was he leaving?

"I'm sure he'll need breakfast eventually. Plus, you can make certain he's still breathing."

"Did he sleep out there all night?"

"And his brothers. I thought they might tie one on, but it was actually pretty quiet." He handed her a plate of cookies.

She looked at the plate in her hands. With a pretty blue napkin on the plate, it looked like a peace offering. That might be a good thing. "Thanks, Jerry."

"No problem." He went back to frosting, his face innocent of intention. After she and Laredo had argued, sugar frosting was likely a good idea.

"Here. Take these bottles of water, too. They can't

drink beer with their cookies. Well, they could, knowing them," Jerry said, "but we want to get a reputation for wonderful hospitality. Miss Delilah's thinking about leasing out the spot next door and opening up a bed and breakfast."

"Is she really?" That seemed like a wonderful plan.

"Yeah, but don't let the cat out of the bag. We wouldn't want Marvella messing her up in any way. Delilah got the idea because she's been putting up so many guests lately." He grinned at Katy. "People can't sleep in their trucks forever. And we're having all this interest in the rodeo. I do believe some ideas are blossoming in Delilah's brain."

"I'll be certain not to say a word." She went outside to Laredo's truck. Two cowboys were in the truck bed, snoozing like dogs on a lawn. One cowboy, the one she was interested in, was facedown in the back seat, with all the windows ventilating him.

"Laredo," she said through the window. "Laredo! Are you all right?"

"I'm fine," he said without looking up. "Go away."

"I've got frosted cookies."

He sat up. "Don't go away."

She handed him the plate. "You're supposed to share with your brothers."

He bit into a cookie and hid the plate on the floorboard. "In my home, we learned quickly that it was every man for himself. By the way, I've been thinking about our standoff."

"Our standoff?"

"Yeah." He licked his fingers. "Me rematching and you posing. It's not a fair threat, because I really want to do this and you really don't want to get naked. What would your parents say? And your ex-fiancé?"

She felt her face go pale at the thought of Stanley staring at her nude body. Just that image alone caused every reasonable argument she could conduct with herself to disappear. *Ugh. Never, never, never.*

But Laredo didn't have to know he'd just called her bluff. "We can talk about this another time," she said icily. "Please don't try to prey on my mind, either. It's beneath you."

"Not really." He snagged another cookie and stared at her newly shortened dress. "I like you in blue."

"Thanks. I like you when your eyes aren't red from sleeping in your truck."

"I didn't sleep well. Ranger bangs around like a bad drum in his sleep, and his boots kept crashing against the truck bed. I think Tex snores louder than Jerry."

She examined her nails. "Are you complaining or hinting?"

"Both."

She shrugged at him. "My bed is still available." And her body, but Mr. Big Thing had to make the first move.

"I may take you up on it. By the way, I've had a new idea."

Her brows went up.

"I'm going to call that nice doctor back, the one who treated me in the hospital, and I'm going to ask her to the rodeo this weekend."

Katy's blood pressure was going to need treatment if Laredo was going where she thought he was. "In case you hit your head again, you'll have your own personal medical team on standby?" she guessed.

"Nah. I'm going to invite her to bring the hospitalized kids out, the ones who are long-term but mobile enough to attend, to see the rodeo. They'd probably get a kick out of that."

Katy's mouth dropped open. "Laredo—"

"It's a charity event, after all. We should include the ones who would enjoy it the most."

She didn't know what to say.

"The tickets can be on me."

"I'm sure Delilah could wring one of her new sponsors for the tickets," Katy murmured. "What made you think of this idea?"

"My ever-present headache. I was feeling sorry for myself, and then I remembered those kids in the hospital, and I realized rodeo is for kids. I'm just a big kid, you know."

"I had figured as much," she murmured, touched by his idea.

"I want to be more than just a one-time thing," he said earnestly. "I want to be a gladiator. I want to matter. I want to do something with myself, something—"

"I know, I know," she said, "something big." Sighing, she gazed into his face. "Laredo, it's a wonderful idea. You need to mention it to Delilah and see what she thinks, but I believe she'll be delighted. And I'll bet Jerry would love to offer his driving services for the kids."

He perked up. "I hadn't thought of that. You know, me and you, we're an okay team."

She backed away from the truck. "I don't think so, actually. Just because a few of our ideas mesh doesn't make us interlocking pieces."

"Well, we haven't gotten to that yet—"

"And we probably won't," she said, turning to race back inside. Her heart beating hard, she ran up to her room and closed the door behind her. "Oh, Rose," she said to the mouse she'd rescued from Bloodthirsty's hooves, "I think I just lost my heart for good."

"LAREDO'S MIND revolves around doing something big," Katy told Hannah an hour later as they sat in Katy's room.

"And your mind revolves around him."

"Precisely. I feel like I'm trying to stop him from being on a path to himself."

Hannah shrugged. "All you want to do is hug him and kiss him and squeeze him a little. What's wrong with that?"

Katy stared at her friend. "You make him sound like a teddy bear, which he most certainly is not."

"So quit being such a chicken. He can take a break from being Sir Galahad long enough to rescue you from—what did you call it? The phallic tower you live in? And don't forget, you have a goal, too. To be the greatest chemistry professor Duke has ever seen."

She frowned. "I'm going from one tower to another."

"Yeah, but college can't really be considered a phallic symbol," Hannah pointed out. "I mean, can it?"

"What I mean is that I'm going from one cloistered, safe existence to another."

"I don't know that academics can be considered safe. At some universities it may be more of a political lion's den. Are you sure you know what you're getting yourself into?"

Katy closed her eyes. "Safety. Stay the course."

"That's right," Hannah soothed. "The well-proven path."

Katy opened her eyes when a knock sounded at the door. "Come in," she called.

Laredo walked in, and her breath tightened in her chest.

"Well, I must be going," Hannah said, quickly getting up and exiting. "Bye, Laredo."

"Bye," he said as she left. "Katy, can we talk?"

"Sure."

He closed the door behind him, which suddenly made her nervous, although she couldn't say why. Laredo hadn't made the remotest attempt to seduce her or even kiss her in days. Not since the day at the creek, in fact. And even that wasn't a serious attempt, or it would have happened.

"Katy, I've been thinking about this *Playboy* problem."

"Oh?" Not a good time to tell him it was no longer a problem, she supposed. Better to hear him out. Was it possible he was actually jealous of the thought of her being naked for other men?

"Have you called the photographer back yet?"

"Uh, no."

"Okay. Well, when will you?"

She shrugged, her mind moving quickly. "Tomorrow?" she asked. "Does that sound like a good time? It'll be Monday, after all."

He nodded. "Perfect. Okay. Bye."

And then he left.

She stared at the door he'd closed behind him. He'd sounded strangely as if he didn't care anymore, as if he'd been gathering remote information for a file. Of course, he was basically saying, "I'm riding, so you're posing. That's the gauntlet you threw down, so go ahead and do your deal."

And she had too much pride to tell him just thinking

of Stanley had illustrated how stupid her idea to get wild in that manner had been.

It was enough to make her cry. She'd never been so confused in her life. Part of her was positive she had no business falling in love since she'd just been burned, but the problem was, since Laredo, she'd realized she wasn't on the rebound.

She'd never loved Stanley. And Laredo had stolen her heart.

Yet he didn't seem to want it.

"I NEED Y'ALL to do me a favor," Laredo told his brothers when he went back out to the truck.

"Now what?" Tex demanded crustily.

"I need you to sleep in Katy's bed tomorrow night. One of you, at least."

Both of his brothers instantly raised their hands.

Laredo grimaced. "Not like that. I need you to be in her bed as a decoy."

"Where will she be?" Tex asked with interest.

"I'm taking her to Malfunction Junction. She'll be safe there," Laredo replied.

"Is she in danger?" Ranger sat straight.

"Only from herself. But I'll be there to protect her," Laredo said with satisfaction.

"Oh, yeah, that's great protection. She'll be glad to hear it, I'm sure," Tex said with a smirk.

"Actually, Katy isn't going to hear it." This was a detail Laredo had hoped to leave out, but it didn't seem as if that would be possible.

His brothers raised their brows and waited in silence.

Laredo sighed. "She's planning on posing for *Playboy Magazine*."

Their jaws dropped in tandem.

"What month?" Tex demanded.

Not for the first time, Laredo thought about doing damage to his twin. "She's not going to pose for *Playboy*. This is not the way she is going to become wild and crazy, which is her mission in life at this time."

Ranger whistled. "You're going to stop her?"

"Right. But I have to be careful about how I do this, because she's trying to stop me from my mission in life, which is to do a Big Thing, which is to stay on Blood-thirsty Black until the horn. So that I can save Miss Delilah's salon," he finished with a verbal flourish.

"Oh, yeah, the one-man cavalry. We forgot about that." Tex smirked. "Okay. Let us get this straight. You're going to girlnap Katy from under Miss Delilah's very wary nose and lock her into a tower at Malfunction Junction while you ride that bull until your heart's content."

"Right." Laredo nodded, happy that his family was so quick on the uptake.

"You are being a typical male, and I think it would serve you well to think over your plan for ruts," Ranger informed him. "I don't think Miss Katy's going to cotton to it."

"Are you recommending I should let her pose?" Laredo was outraged. If so, these were not the brothers he cared to claim.

"I'm stating that you can't have your cake and eat it, too," Ranger said mildly. "You can't do your thing and expect her not to do hers."

"Mine doesn't involve shedding clothing! Mine doesn't involve people gawking over my naked physique!"

Tex laughed. "That's presuming anyone would gawk."

"Well, they'll gawk at Katy, and I don't like it," Laredo stated stiffly. "You just figure out another way I can handle this matter, then, wisenheimers."

"No, no." Ranger held up a hand. "We don't interfere, we only participate when needed. It's your life, it's your funeral, 'cause she is surely going to kill you as you try to drag her off. But hey, we've always been a family for the rowdy choice, so I vote you go for it. I'll sleep in Katy's bed and do a convincing Katy voice when Miss Delilah does bed check."

"She doesn't actually do bed check," Laredo said stiffly, "but Rose the mouse will need to be fed and watered."

The brothers stared at him. "Oh, no," Ranger said. "I didn't agree to mother hen a mouse."

"Oh, hell," Tex said. "I'll babysit the damn mouse and play Katy in the night."

Laredo frowned at his brother. "I didn't particularly like the phrasing of your statement."

"I'm going to sit in my truck and laugh my butt off as you drag Katy kicking and screaming out of here," Ranger said. "Remember, the doctor said you were to suffer no further damage to your head, and that includes female inflicted. So when does this plan go down?"

"Friday night," Laredo said grimly. "I can keep her busy until then. After that, I'll be busy at the rodeo and I won't be able to keep a direct eye on her. Plus, she told me that if I rematched, she'd pose. So I have to get her out of here before I ride Saturday. Helga can keep an eye on her."

Because she was just prissy enough to take a train out of there Saturday afternoon after he hit the dirt. That was one lady who couldn't be trusted to let a man get away with living his life the way he chose.

He wasn't about to let her get away that easily.

Certainly not to display her charms to every Tom, Dick and Harry on the planet. He felt ill just thinking about that!

No way. If there was going to be a first in her life, she needed a winner. Not another loser like ol' Stanley.

That was the hero in him talking—the rescuer. The real underlying reason, as he would barely allow himself to acknowledge, was that he saw red when he considered the possibility of another man touching her, even on paper.

He wanted her all to himself. Not forever. Just long enough for him to figure out why he couldn't stop thinking about her. And wanting her enough to make him dizzy and desperate at times.

Dizzy. Desperate.

But not, he told himself, forever.

He'd seen what passed for forever, and he knew too well that there was no such thing. Like Santa Claus and fairy tales, he couldn't waste emotion believing in them.

It was all about trust. And he knew trust and forever didn't go together. Katy knew it, too, thanks to Stanley. She was looking for a second forever, though, like a sweet little lamb being led to slaughter. Oh, she denied it, but it was there in the hope in her eyes. Exactly what the *Playboy* photographer had seen. Vulnerability.

Laredo shook his head to clear the buzzing. If he didn't get Katy to himself real soon, he was certain he was going to go mad.

CHAPTER FIFTEEN

"HEART-TO-HEART?" Marvella asked.

Delilah nodded. The two of them hadn't spoken a direct word to each other in maybe fifteen years. Her sister had changed, her face leaner and perhaps more withdrawn than Delilah remembered. But she had been close to her older sister as a child, which made their emotional separation and Marvella's destruction all that much more heartrending.

"Go for it," Marvella said. "But make your heart-to-heart quick. My schedule is full. We've picked up forty percent from the rodeos."

"Which brings me straight to the point. Your schedule is full because of my cowboys."

"Your cowboys?" Marvella smiled and sat down, not offering Delilah a seat. "How do you figure? Your bull hasn't won in two separate weeks. I'd say it's Bad-Ass Blue that's garnering the attention. He's well on his way to being a superstar, I'd say."

Marvella examined her long, pretty nails. Even at her age, she was an attractive woman. If only her eyes held more love for mankind, she could even be called gracefully aged.

"All the better for his sale price. I love profit, don't you?" Marvella asked coyly.

Delilah shook her head. Maybe a few die-hard rodeo buffs were coming to see the winning bull, but the real magic lay in the charming town. The Jefferson brothers had added fairy dust. Of course, Marvella's salon would be pulling more extra business—Tex had ridden the winning bull.

"Marvella, I want this weekend's rodeo to be fair. No cheating, no dirty tricks. My cowboy has a concussion, and he shouldn't be riding at all. I think it would behoove us to let the best man win without interference."

Marvella shrugged. "I have no idea what you're talking about. Tex offered to ride Blue on his own."

Sure. After Cissy had softened him up. Delilah sighed. "Look. This is between you and me. It has nothing to do with our employees, the Jefferson brothers or Lonely Hearts Station. We should settle our differences like ladies."

Marvella's gray eyes suddenly glowed with heat. "How dare you suggest that I am not a lady? Who slept with whose husband, Delilah, dear?"

Delilah didn't answer. It was true that Marvella's husband had divorced Marvella to marry her. But the circumstances were not as Marvella cared to paint them. The trouble was Marvella seemed quite content to blame Delilah for the downfall of her marriage.

"Would you say that your behavior was becoming of a lady?" Marvella asked smoothly. "I mean, I wouldn't. I would classify you more as a…husband-stealing hussy."

Outrage bubbled inside Delilah. She forced herself to remain calm. "Name-calling isn't going to get us anywhere. I'm worried about Tex and Laredo and—"

"They're big boys," Marvella snapped. "Quit trying to mother everybody on the planet. It's annoying, it's manipulative and it bores me."

Delilah blinked. "Can I assume that you intend to remain busy with your bag of tricks?"

Marvella stared at her. "I have no idea what you're babbling about, but it sounds like poor sportswomanship to me."

The sisters held each other's gaze for several seconds. "You know," Delilah said suddenly, "I'm not certain that Jacuzzi or some of the other accoutrements of this room have a permit. Do you happen to know if your permits are up-to-date, Marvella? And could you swear in a court of law that your business is reputable?"

Marvella smiled thinly at her. "Delilah, don't try to use your seat on the council to threaten me. All the town fathers have been to my salon, my dear. They're not all regulars, but…" She let her words trail off.

Delilah stared at her sister, a sinking feeling inside.

"We do give good service," Marvella finished with a laugh. "And it's *all* about service. You know, I think that's the real reason you're here. You're going under, and you want a shoulder to cry on. Unfortunately, I can't stand poor sportswomanship in business, either. Did you care for my feelings when you stole my husband, sister?"

The look in Marvella's eyes was so determined and so cold. Involuntarily, Delilah felt a shiver go through her. She really had no defense against this much hatred. There was no recognition of warmth, of childhood memories. Marvella was locked in her own world of revenge.

"I'm sorry I came," Delilah said, completely regretting seeing how her sister had changed.

"Well, I'll see you on Saturday, Delilah, dear," Marvella said. "See you *lose*."

"I DON'T TRUST HIM," Katy said, busily picking the lock on the storage area in Laredo's truck bed. "He's planning to ride, and it doesn't matter what the doctor says, he's bound and determined to give himself the permanent stupids."

"Why do you care?" Hannah asked, squinting at Katy's handiwork and surreptitiously watching the street should any Jefferson brother happen to amble by.

"I care for two reasons. First of all, I got him into this. He's only doing it out of a sense of duty."

"I don't know. He seemed genuinely determined to ride Bloodthirsty again."

"Well, he's got hero syndrome. Bad, too, I might add."

"Are you going to cure him of it?"

"Nope." The storage bin popped open, and Katy gasped.

"What's in there?"

She'd been expecting to see his gear, which she planned to filch so he couldn't possibly ride. What she found instead was nothing. "It's empty."

"And his stuff isn't in your room."

Katy shook her head. "He's been sleeping in his truck with his brothers. Sometimes they drive off and don't come back until the morning. I thought maybe they've been going back to Union Junction at night, but I haven't gotten up the nerve to ask."

"Well, he has to have equipment."

"Yes." Katy closed the trunk and relocked the lock. "He's one step ahead of me somehow."

Hannah climbed up into the trunk bed. "Okay, his vehicle is here. He is not. But he could be someplace trying on his gear. He could be training to ride Bloodthirsty."

"Do you think he'd take that chance? He knows his brains are already scrambled."

Hannah shrugged. "I don't think we fully comprehend the minds of men. Don't waste your time. So, what was your second reason for doing this, before your plan went belly-up?"

"That I've fallen in love with him," Katy said slowly. "Stupidly, impossibly, in love with him. Which is really the dumbest thing I've ever done, up to and including trying to marry Stanley."

"Oh, boy," Hannah said. "You were just supposed to have him rid you of your virginity. You were supposed to remember that he has a wandering foot. You weren't supposed to stray from the course."

"I know. What makes it worse is that he doesn't care about me at all. He didn't even care about me posing for *Playboy*."

"So, are you going to?"

"No. I thought about Stanley looking at my naked body, and I felt genuinely ill. I'm not nude model material."

"You could tell him," Hannah suggested.

"Tell him what?"

"That you're in love with him."

Katy blinked. "And he would die of embarrassment. This is a man who is riding a bull out of an overinflated sense of duty. What do you think he does for a woman who burdens him with her emotions?"

"Says, 'Me, too'?"

She shook her head. "No. He hits the road in his shiny truck and he never even glances in his rearview mirror."

"Oh." Hannah sighed. "Well, if you can't steal his

gear, and you can't tell him the truth, then what have you got?"

"Nothing," Katy said miserably. "It's all about trust, and I forgot how to trust anyone. Then when I found somebody worth trusting, I blew it."

"You don't know that you've blown it yet," Hannah soothed.

"It feels blown like an old tire."

"Well, here he comes, so puff yourself back up."

Katy straightened, not able to help herself from looking too eager. "He's wearing his gear, the snake!" she whispered to Hannah.

"I know how you can steal it!" Hannah whispered back.

"How?"

"Play strip poker. You can borrow my cards."

Katy blinked as Laredo and his brothers neared. It was like looking at a mirage of the best-looking, toughest cowboys one could imagine simply appearing like magic in the middle of the dusty town street. Her mouth watered. "No strip poker. It's too risky. He'd probably win."

"Then just strip him, Katy. Like I stripped y'all the night we went to the creek. Be brave!"

"Be brave?" She had a mouse for a pet. She wasn't the type of girl to roar and break things and raise hell.

"Hey, ladies," Laredo said as they reached the truck. All the brothers tipped their hats, but Laredo's smile seemed to turn to a grim, determined line as he looked at Katy. "What are you doing in my truck? Stealing my beer?"

"Exactly," Katy said, trying to match his teasing tone. And yet, his eyes were not smiling for her.

"So, where have you handsome cowboys been?"

"We rode some horses over to the hospital and did some lasso tricks for the kids," Ranger said. "Laredo wanted to talk to the doctor who treated him."

Something burning seemed to lodge in Katy's heart, although she told herself it was silly to be jealous of the beautiful physician. "Did you tell her you were going to ride in a couple of days?"

"Yes, ma'am." He tipped his hat and looked at her. "And she said I was a fool, but that there was no prescription for that, so she would come to watch in case I needed a physician on hand."

"His own personal physician." Tex laughed. "None of us have ever had one of those."

"None of you have ever needed one, maybe," Hannah snapped. "Laredo's already hurt."

Katy couldn't take her eyes off Laredo. "She's coming to watch you?" That seemed medically sacrilegious on the doctor's part, which meant the jealousy spiking hot inside Katy's head would probably measure as a fever on a thermometer.

"Yep, and she's bringing a bunch of kids. Actually, she's organizing it, and Jerry's going to help out."

He looked so pleased with himself that Katy felt ashamed.

"So," he said, "called *Playboy* yet?"

Her mouth dropped open at the surprising change of subject. "No, actually I haven't."

He walked away, whistling. "Let me know what you find out when you do," he called over his shoulder.

"Guess we're heading to the cafeteria," Ranger said. "See you soon." He and Tex headed off after Laredo.

Hannah's eyes narrowed as she stared after Laredo. "That man is way too casual."

"What do you mean?"

"I don't know. I don't trust him."

Katy got down from the truck, her feelings totally blasted. "He doesn't care about me anymore, Hannah. Maybe he never did. Certainly after he took that whack on the head, things have changed. Either it's the doctor he met, or he knocked himself hard enough to forget that he ever wanted to make me a bikini top from beer caps. Or he wasn't that interested to start with. But I'm not going to moon around after a man who doesn't want me."

She headed toward the salon. Hannah hurried up beside her. "So, what are you going to do? Call *Playboy?*"

Katy winced. She wished she'd never thought that she could unleash her inhibitions in such a manner. The truth was, she was exactly what Stanley had said she was: less tempting than a day-old biscuit.

Frigid.

"I'm leaving," Katy announced. "It's time I took a leaf out of Laredo's book and headed out to do my own Big Thing. But you can't tell a soul."

LAREDO AND HIS BROTHERS crouched in the doorway of a nearby feed store, watching Katy and Hannah go inside the salon. "They're up to something," Laredo said. "What do you think they were really doing in my truck?"

"I don't know," Ranger said thoughtfully. "Hannah had so much mischievousness gleaming in her eyes, she looked like a raccoon."

"It's the hair," Tex said. "She's really cute."

"Raccoons are not cute," Laredo said.

"That one is," Ranger agreed. "Although she's a bit too tricky for my taste."

"Tricky?" If anybody was tricky, it was Katy. "At least she doesn't dream of taking off her clothes for major publications," Laredo stated.

"Well, hello, gentlemen," Marvella said as she left the feed store. "How are the famous Jefferson cowboys doing?"

Tex grinned at her, taking the package she was carrying. "We're fine."

"I've been waiting for you to tell me you're riding for me this weekend, Tex," Marvella said. "A repeat would be a wonderful attraction."

"You haven't hired anyone?" Tex asked eagerly. Then his face fell. "Actually, Miss Marvella, I'm afraid I can only ride against my brother once."

"Oh, dear," Marvella said. "I am so disappointed."

"Ride against me once?" Laredo sputtered. "You damn sure better be riding Blue this weekend! I have to beat you. Otherwise, I haven't achieved my goal." Or shown Katy that he could do it.

The brothers followed Marvella over to her salon. "Well, why don't you three come in and we'll talk it over?" she invited. "I think there's some fresh-baked banana bread and mint juleps just waiting for someone to enjoy them."

"I will," Ranger said.

"I sure can," Tex said.

With an uneasy glance toward the Lonely Hearts Salon, Laredo hesitated. But why be rude? This was the other half of the rodeo, which he was doing for Delilah, for Katy, for the sick kids, for Lonely Hearts Station and for himself. "I guess so," he said.

"Excellent," Marvella cooed. "Simply excellent."

CHAPTER SIXTEEN

WHEN MARVELLA WALKED in towing the three Jefferson cowboys, Cissy knew there was trouble in Texas. Marvella was up to her tricks, and someone was going to get hurt.

There was always an injury in Marvella's shenanigans. Cissy was afraid that if Marvella kept up with her attack, the injury this time was going to be Katy.

Why should she care? she thought. Katy had never been especially warm to her. Not that she'd ever given Katy a chance—and she did try to steal her cowboy.

Maybe that's why she cared. She hadn't felt right about what she'd tried to do to Katy. For some reason, once she'd made love with Tex, her heart had changed. If anything, she wanted to look good in his eyes. Oh, he'd never see her as anything more than a soiled dove, but…even soiled doves craved respect.

Without saying a word to anyone, Cissy slipped outside.

THE KNOCK ON KATY'S DOOR stopped her packing. It didn't sound like Delilah's tap or Hannah's bang. Certainly it wasn't Laredo's unannounced entrance. She supposed that since they technically were splitting a room, he didn't feel he had to announce himself. Then again, that's just how Laredo was. Unannounced.

But one never knew, and she didn't want her plans

brought to light. Quickly she pushed the suitcase under the bed. "Come in," she called.

Cissy Kisserton walked in. "Hi, Katy."

"Cissy?" Katy couldn't dampen the surprise in her voice. "What are you doing here?"

"I need to warn you about something."

"Whatever it is, I don't want to know." Uncomfortably she wondered if good manners demanded she offer Cissy a chair. No, she decided.

"You'll want to know this," Cissy assured her.

"Does it have anything to do with Lonely Hearts Station, cowboys or the rodeo?"

"It has to do with Laredo."

Spears of pain shot through her. "I definitely do not want to know about him."

"You don't?" Cissy's tone crept high with dismay. "Why not?"

"Because. It doesn't matter." It did, in a peculiar way she couldn't explain, but she couldn't let him matter to her.

"Oh. I beg your pardon. I shouldn't have bothered you, then."

Katy warily watched her prepare to leave. What exactly had been the purpose behind Cissy's visit? "He's… all right, isn't he?"

"Oh, yes. Healthwise, he seems very fit."

That was all the assessment she wanted from Cissy, thank you very little. "Then that's all I need to know."

Hannah walked into the room, her mouth gaping when she saw Cissy. "What do you want?"

"Relax, Hannah. This is just a civil conversation between Katy and me."

Hannah glowered at her. "Well, I'm here now. It's no longer civil. What are you up to?"

Katy held up her hand. "Hannah, it's all right. Cissy was just leaving. She came to tell me Laredo is all right."

Hannah raised a brow. "We know he's all right. Since when did you become the Good News Fairy?"

"Since Marvella just dragged him and his brothers into her salon," Cissy said. "But since y'all don't want to know—"

"Wait a minute," Katy said, grabbing hold of Cissy's sleeve. "Spit it all out, every bit of it, or Hannah holds you, and I take a hot curling iron to your hair. You'll look like the dippity-do-dog when I get through with you if you don't stop playing Miss Who-Me?"

"There's no need to get violent!" Cissy said, snatching her sleeve away.

"And you could be the Trojan horse. Spare us the melodramatics and get on with Marvella's hijinks," Hannah instructed. "I saw a curling iron downstairs that's been left on for three days and looks hot enough to brand cattle."

"I don't know what her plan is! I just know Delilah was there earlier, and the two of them had words. Exactly what words, I don't know, because when Marvella has a guest, we are not allowed to see or be seen. We all went upstairs and left the two of them alone. But the tone of it wasn't friendly, as anyone who knows Marvella would understand. And then Marvella walked in with Tex, Laredo and Ranger, and I thought Katy should know."

"Why Katy?" Hannah demanded.

"Because I owe her one," Cissy snapped. "Okay? Virtuous enough reason for you?"

"Guilt," Katy pronounced.

"Precisely," Hannah agreed. "Unless someone else is sucking up to Laredo right now and you want even."

Katy's heart skidded inside her. Could that be the case?

"No one's sucking up to anyone right now. Marvella's plying them with mint juleps and snacks."

"Then maybe she's just turned over a new leaf, like you," Hannah guessed. "After all, Tex did ride for her. He did make her a lot of money."

Cissy flipped her long, straight hair. "I've said too much. I'm leaving before I get seen in this salon. What you do with this info is up to you. And for whatever it's worth, while I do hope we win again on Saturday, I never wanted anyone to get hurt."

She left, her high heels clipping down the stairs. Hannah turned to Katy. "What do you make of that?"

"I don't know. She expects us to do a search-and-rescue on the Jefferson brothers," Katy said. "But I don't think I could."

"Nor me," Hannah said carefully. "I don't think men appreciate being dug out of their caves, do they? Isn't it kind of like roaches? They skitter away from the light and don't want to be disturbed?"

"Hannah," Katy said, laughing. "This is serious. Marvella is planning to shanghai all the cowboys this time, just to spite Delilah. That'll leave me to do the riding, and I'm not physically up to it. Nor emotionally, I might add. I like having my feet on the ground, not over my head."

"We *could* go save them from themselves," Hannah said thoughtfully. "But you'd think grown men would have more class. More panache. More common sense."

"Why would anyone think that?" Katy asked. "You just compared them to roaches."

"I was only trying to get inside their minds, and the only species I could think of that liked the dark and liked multiplying and liked not being disturbed was roaches." Hannah shrugged. "The point is, you'd think they'd know better."

"We could just let them suffer the consequences of their stupidity," Katy suggested. "It's not our fault if they louse up their chances of riding and winning."

But the cowboys didn't know Marvella like everyone else did. And like all men, they were suffering under some delusion that she was probably okay underneath all that faux charm.

What they didn't know was that the faux charm covered a layer of war paint so hard it was like a layer of steel sheeting.

"I don't know," Katy said with a sigh. "I can't always be rescuing Laredo. I've got to think of myself now. Back to packing." She retrieved her suitcase from underneath the bed.

"And I can't save the other two. In pairs, they're almost drawn to misadventure."

"So, that's that." Katy tossed some more things into the suitcase. "I'm going to do a little more packing, and then I'm going to sleep. It sounds as if I'll have my bed to myself tonight, and I intend to enjoy it for the last night it will be mine."

"I'm going to miss you, Katy," Hannah said softly. "I can't believe you're going to leave so soon."

"I'll miss you, too, but the truth is, I'm really looking forward to moving on with my life." Katy snapped the suitcase closed, putting it at the foot of her bed. She arranged her traveling clothes on top. "I'm ready for my own adventure."

SOMEWHERE IN THE NIGHT, Tex awakened aware of two things. He was alone, which was a relief, because he felt very stifled somehow. Two, the mint juleps he'd drunk weren't like lemonade, as he'd surmised, judging by the fact that his head felt two sizes bigger than normal.

Where were his brothers? Feeling around, he switched on a bedside lamp. And then he remembered! He was supposed to occupy Katy's bed tonight while Laredo girlnapped Katy! Holy smokes! He'd probably overslept the whole plan. No wonder he was here alone.

Sneaking out of the room, he quietly went down the stairs. Gently he worked the front door of the salon open, praying no one would awaken. How could he have ended up in such shape when Laredo needed him? Most times in the Jefferson household, it was every man for himself, but when it came to brotherhood, they stuck together like soles to boots. He didn't agree with Laredo's plan, necessarily, but he was going to help execute it and let the chips fall where they might.

Laredo's truck was gone from its parking place. Dang! He must have already left with Katy. Tex needed to get a serious move on. He didn't even know what the heck time it was, but he had a mouse to babysit and a voice to mimic.

Ever so silently, he took the key Delilah had given him and Ranger and unlocked the Lonely Hearts back door. He crept up the stairs with his boots in his hand, making certain not to make any noise, not even a groan, which he felt like doing. Damn mint juleps! Never again was he falling for some innocent-looking Southern libation.

Slowly and silently, he opened Katy's bedroom door. With cautious feet, he moved to the end of the bed, noting its outline by the light of the streetlamp shining through the window. So far so good. Now, to fall into her bed and sleep until Saturday.

Well, he might get up to swallow some aspirin tomorrow. And then he was hibernating until he knew for certain the coast was clear.

Something at the foot of Katy's bed caught his boot, and to his surprise, he toppled over like a great, drunken redwood tree. He fell right onto something soft—and shrieking.

"Aii—"

"Shh!" he told the shrieking thing, clapping a hand over its mouth. "It's only me!"

"Laredo?" Katy asked.

"What are you doing here?" he demanded.

"Sleeping, you dope! What are you doing here?"

Considering that he was Tex and not Laredo, nothing good. Dang! He was in big trouble now. Did he exit gracelessly? Or did he wait for Laredo to appear and help him bundle Katy off?

No, that would make him a girlnapping accessory, something he didn't want any part of. Bed-sitter was one thing; hands-on accomplice was something else. "It's Tex," he said, choosing the coward's option. "Go easy on me."

Instantly she relaxed. "Oh. Were you looking for Hannah's room?"

Ah! An easy out! "As a matter of fact—"

"Down the hall," she told him. "But I wouldn't fall on her the way you fell on me. She's been known to wallop men who've tried to sneak into her bed before. Try the gentle, romantic approach."

"I didn't mean to fall on you, Katy. Did I hurt you? I actually tripped over something at the foot of the bed—"

"My suitcase. I shouldn't have left it there. I wasn't expecting visitors—"

"Your suitcase? Why do you have your suitcase out?" Did she know Laredo was planning on sweeping her off her feet? Wouldn't that just jangle Laredo's nerves if he showed up to snatch Katy and she said, Hold the phone, cowboy, while I get my jammy bag?

"Don't tell anyone, but I'm leaving town," Katy confided.

He knew that already, but maybe it was best if he appeared ignorant. "Oh. Send us a postcard to Malfunction Junction," he said. "We don't often get anything except bills. Well, gotta run."

Trying to appear relaxed and focused, he got out of Katy's bed. He stood up straight, and with as much balance as possible, made his way to the door. "Good night, Katy."

"Good night, Tex."

He left, keeping his pride barely intact. Whew! That was a close one. Only he wasn't certain what he was supposed to do.

Best to leave that in his twin's capable hands. Laredo was the one with the screwy plan, after all.

With a glance at Hannah's door, he told himself not to borrow any more trouble and went into the upstairs den to find the sofa.

CHAPTER SEVENTEEN

TEX NO SOONER hit the sofa than he realized there was a bigger problem on his hands, one that the mint-julep haze had disguised. If Katy was in her bed and not girlnapped by his twin, and if his twin's truck was gone, then where the heck was Laredo?

Something had gone awry with the plan, and he wasn't sure how to cope with it. He checked his watch, seeing by the lit dial that it was now actually Friday morning. That, he remembered, was Katy-snatching day.

Getting up, he trudged down the stairs, as quietly as possible. Surely Laredo wasn't too far away. He shouldn't be, if he knew how soft Katy was in her bed. Soft and gentle. Although he hadn't gotten a good sense of her—she was after all his brother's desired, and he had landed on top of her with all the finesse of a sledgehammer—he'd been able to tell enough to know that Laredo was lagging behind when he should be barreling ahead.

"I have to show him everything," Tex muttered. "The dummy who said that twins are on some emotional wavelength was an idiot."

He went outside just as Laredo's truck pulled up. Ranger and his twin got out.

"Where have you been?" Tex demanded.

"We went for a drive," Ranger said.

"Without telling me?" Tex was totally put out. "Hey, am I in this plan or not?"

"You were at Marvella's. We didn't want to disturb you," Laredo said reasonably.

"Disturb me! I was sleeping off a Southern green buzz! Didn't you all feel the kick of those stupid julep things?" Tex demanded.

Ranger and Laredo glanced at each other. "Nah. I didn't drink mine."

"Me, neither," Ranger said. "I'm a beer drinker, though I didn't tell Miss Marvella that."

"Well, I must have taken a little nap." He frowned, thinking about Cissy. Where had she been, anyway? He couldn't remember having seen her but for a split second. In fact, if his memory served, she'd left the salon for a while. "Y'all haven't seen Cissy, have you?"

"Nope. We've been by ourselves since we snuck out," Laredo said. "Are you ready for the big moment?"

"Uh—" Tex tried to sort his scrambled thoughts. "I just came out of Katy's room and she's in there."

"Hey!" Laredo said. "I didn't give you the signal!"

"Sorry. It was the juleps. Anyway, she's already packed and ready to go."

"What are you talking about?" Ranger asked.

Tex shrugged. "Guess she's on to the plan. Or she's leaving Lonely Hearts Station. She definitely said she's leaving. I just thought she meant with you."

"That little minx," Laredo breathed. "She did call that dang photographer! She's leaving to pose!" He sucked in air. "Cover me, brothers. I'm going in."

He took off running toward the salon.

Ranger shook his head. "He's lost his freaking mind. She's going to kill him when he goes busting in her door."

"Yep," Tex agreed, thinking about how disagreeable a female who'd already been awakened and landed on once would be. "She's gonna slap him stupid. So much for avoiding further head trauma."

"Dude," Ranger said, "if I ever fall for a female, please, please, stop me. I do not want to be that insane. That bizarre."

"Hey, it's a deal. We'll commit emotional hara-kiri." They clasped hands, nodding solemnly over their pact, as Laredo came out the door bearing a screeching Katy in his arms.

"Put me down!" she commanded. "Put me down!"

"Go get her suitcase, Tex! She wouldn't let me carry both things at once."

Tex took off at a run, and Ranger started the truck. "Now, Miss Katy," Ranger said as Laredo put her into the truck, "you be sure and wear your seat belt."

Katy stared at him. "You have all lost your minds. You've been to Marvella's, and you've lost your minds."

"It was the mint juleps," Laredo said. "Never drink anything that sweet. It clogs the brain." He got behind the wheel as Tex tossed her suitcase into the truck bed. "See y'all tomorrow."

He sped away, thoroughly pleased with himself. So far, everything was going according to plan.

"Laredo," Katy said through steely teeth, "if you don't take me back right now, I promise to make your life so utterly miserable you'll think Bloodthirsty Black was a friendly sheep in bull's clothing."

Uh-oh. That didn't sound promising. "Katy, I'm doing what's best for you," he said, trying to sound soothing.

"What's best for me?"

"Yes. Now you just calm down. We'll be to the ranch soon enough."

"You're taking me to your ranch."

He nodded.

"Laredo, you are a dunce."

Wincing, he said, "Well, you and I are fighting, and this is the only way I know to win. It's because you're so darn stubborn, Katy."

"I'm stubborn?" She couldn't believe her ears. On the other hand, she was somewhat flattered that he cared enough to steal her. She had to admit it was much nicer than being jilted. "Why did you tell your brothers you'd see them tomorrow? Are you bringing me back in the morning?"

"Not exactly," he said. "I'm going back."

"You're riding in the rodeo," she said on a gasp. "You stole me so I couldn't leave to pose, but you're riding anyway."

There was no reason to lie. He shrugged.

Rational thought left her. She was trapped. He had played the cards all his way. Just like all the Jefferson men: their way or no way.

It was maddening.

He was watching her for her reaction, and she had one for him—the reaction of a woman who's been pushed to the edge.

She took off her top, and tossed it out the window.

"What are you doing?" Laredo demanded, sounding like something was pinching his throat.

She took off her bra and tossed that out the window, too.

Laredo's jaw dropped, and he slammed on the brakes. "I'll go get it," he said, averting his gaze. "It'll only take me a second. It's such a windy night, we should shut the truck windows."

She laughed at his babbling. "Laredo," she said, "I want you to make love to me. I want you to stop making up excuses. Be brave and make love to me."

"I…I can't."

"Oh, yes, you can," she said. "I always said you'd have to make the first move, but I know you'll never make it. And if you think kidnapping me so you could have your own way was a good idea, I've got a twist for your plan."

He was staring at her breasts, transfixed. "Yes, you do. I'm feeling very twisted."

"You cannot have your cake and eat it, too," she told him.

"I don't want any cake right now. I want you to tell me where you want me to make love to you. Name it, anyplace you ever fantasized about, and I'll get you there. Paris, Las Vegas, wherever."

"The creek," she told him. "I think the creek would be very nice."

He tried to think if that was appropriate for Katy's first time. Shouldn't there be satin sheets and wine and roses—

"Laredo," she said, "either you start driving or I lose another layer, and as you can see, that would be my shorts."

"Katy, I'm driving as fast as I can!" He floored the truck, turning down the road toward the creek. Never had he felt that his truck didn't have enough horsepower, but he couldn't get it to go fast enough. God, she was gorgeous. And she wanted to be his.

It was enough to drive him past sane thought. All his reasons for not making love to Katy flooded out of his mind. He had to stop her now from the foolishness of her plan, and the best way to do that was to keep her very near him.

His plan was foolproof.

He parked the truck at the creek's edge. It was dark and silent. The trees moved gently in a light breeze. Stars overheard flickered like tiny lights in an inky sea.

"You know, if I was a smart girl, I'd send you down to the creek to check for snakes, steal your truck, go back and collect my top and bra and leave you here," Katy told him. "You deserve it."

He stared at her suspiciously. "Maybe, but…you wouldn't, would you?" Unable to help himself, he drew her to him, touching her lips with a finger, then tracing down to her breasts. "I think I'd blow a fuse if I couldn't have you, Katy Goodnight."

She smiled up at him. "I was hoping you'd feel that way. You've stuck so hard to your plan it was hard to jimmy you loose."

"Well, I'm way loose now."

She opened the truck door. "Come on."

He was out his door in a flash and pulling down the truck gate. Grabbing the blanket from the back, he spread it onto the truck bed floor, then shaped another one into a pillow. Extending his hand, he pulled her up into the bed with him.

"Now, your shirt," she said, gently pulling his off him.

And somehow their lips met, touching, pressing and then pulling. Then all over again, until Katy found herself gasping. "Whew. I didn't know you could kiss like that. Why didn't you do it sooner?"

"I'm questioning that myself right now," Laredo said,

gasping as well. "But I'm trying not to think too much about it in case you change your mind."

"My mind! I'm the one who's been trying to get you to do this for weeks!"

"Very unvirginal of you, too, thank heaven," Laredo said, swiftly removing her shorts. "I should have listened to you sooner."

She tugged off his shorts. "You should have listened to me about a lot of things."

"We're not talking anymore," Laredo said, pressing her to the blanket. "There's been way too much of that. All we're doing is feeling. This," he said, rubbing his thumbs over her nipples, "and this," he continued, suckling each of them.

"And this," Katy agreed, running her hand down his chest, down the flat of his stomach, until she reached that part of a man. Taking him in her hands, she treasured the feel of him. "Laredo, I don't really know what I'm doing at this point."

"Argh," he said against her neck, where he'd rested his head when she'd taken hold of him. "What you don't know seems to be a good thing. Don't stop."

She giggled as he kissed down her breasts to her belly. He licked into her belly button, drawing a jerk of surprise from her, then he slipped his tongue inside her, and Katy froze. "Oh, my," she whispered. Any seduction she'd ever planned imploded as he stroked her, building magic feelings she couldn't even put a name to.

When he lifted her higher, giving him greater access to her, strange feelings she'd never felt seemed to freeze her. "Oh, oh," she murmured.

And then she slid over some mysterious brink, hearing herself call Laredo's name like she was afraid to lose him.

Gently he laid her back down, spreading her legs wider and settling himself in between. "Katy," he murmured, "I've dreamed of this for more nights than I can tell you."

He parted her, and slid inside, filling her past the point she thought she could take. She started to cry out, but he covered her mouth with his, taking her breath, taking her pain, and then he began to move inside her, and she mimicked his rhythm, wanting so much to feel his passion. It hurt, but nothing like the emotional things in her life had hurt. To Katy this pain was closeness, and it brought pleasure.

Inside her she felt Laredo growing. A sigh filled her, or least she thought it was a sigh, until the same brink built inside her. Wrapping her legs around Laredo, she buried her face against his shoulder. "Laredo," she murmured. "Laredo!"

"I've got you," he said, holding her tighter, moving deeper inside, penetrating her, driving her into his arms so that she would never want to leave. "Give it to me, baby," he told her. "Relax and let it go."

She trusted him to be there for her. With a surprised cry of rapture, Katy squeezed her eyes shut, feeling the sweet spasms take hold of her.

Her pleasure seemed to excite Laredo all that much more. "Katy," he whispered against her lips. "Oh, sweetheart."

"Laredo, you mean so much to me," she said, kissing him as she felt him beginning to tense. Recognizing that the brink that had claimed her was about to claim Laredo, she held him tighter, squeezing her inner muscles against him.

He moved inside her more fiercely, then suddenly cried out. Katy clung to him as he collapsed against her.

Over his shoulder she could see the stars in the heaven, and she knew that all her life she would remember her one night with Laredo.

CHAPTER EIGHTEEN

LAREDO FELL ASLEEP on top of her, sleeping like a man well satisfied. Katy smiled tenderly at her cowboy. The fantasy had turned into a wonderful reality.

She wasn't frigid. No way. She'd loved what he'd done to her.

But that was all sex, and she was a liberated woman now. It was time to break out of the rest of her shell.

No man, not even a cowboy like Laredo, was going to one-up her just because he thought he could.

Quietly she slipped his keys from his jeans, which were discarded nearby. She dressed, stealing his top for her own use. Knotting it at her waist, she crawled from the truck bed and got into the truck. When she started the engine, Laredo popped up.

"Hey!"

She locked the doors and floored the truck. Laredo sat down very quickly, realizing he had no choice.

Driving back to town, Katy parked the truck outside the salon. When Laredo jumped down to take possession of his truck, she backed out of the parking space quickly, leaving him standing in the middle of the street, his expression dumbfounded.

Well, maybe it wasn't the best of exits, but she couldn't have allowed him to drag her off to the ranch, anyway.

If he wanted to bust his head riding Bloodthirsty, she wasn't going to hang around to watch that, either.

It was time to move on with her life.

"THAT CRAZY GIRL stole my truck!" Laredo complained as Tex and Ranger ran to see why he was standing in the middle of the street with his arms in the air.

"Katy did that?" Ranger asked.

"Yes! Where are your keys? I need to follow her."

Ranger shook his head. "They're upstairs, but you can't use my truck anyway. It's not a good idea to go chasing after a woman with a hot head. You must have made her real mad about something."

"I didn't make her mad. I melted her bones," Laredo said thinly. "She's just so darn stubborn!"

"Where's she going?" Tex asked.

"I have no clue. But that minx stole my truck, and after I made love to her, too!"

That was the biggest insult of all.

Tex and Ranger were staring at him, their mouths open.

"Did you really?" Ranger asked.

"Yes, I did."

"And she drove off without you," Tex said in amazement. "Shew-ee. I hope you ride a bull better than you make love, 'cause clearly you've lost your touch. I never saw a girl run off from you before."

Laredo scratched his head. Hadn't she seemed happy? Satisfied? He shook his head. "She didn't like the kidnapping plan."

"Ohh," they said.

"She made love to you and then she left you holding the sheet," Tex said with some surprise. "That's your favorite trick."

Laredo scowled. "Not exactly true."

His brothers laughed, then walked away.

"Hey, where are you going? You've got to help me find her!"

Ranger waved him off. "You're on your own, Laredo."

This had all come about because of that stupid bull. First, she'd wanted him to ride, then she changed her mind. She wanted a hero, and then she wanted a stud. Who could figure that woman out?

And she'd already told him she wasn't interested in getting serious again, since her blown wedding was only about a couple months cold.

He'd told her he would never be interested in settling down.

It was true. Except then he'd fallen for her scrappiness, and her attitude, and her sweetness. He couldn't completely have her under his thumb. Just when he thought he had her pinned, she pinned him.

"So annoying," he muttered. "A woman should not be driving my truck."

Heaven only knew where she'd taken it. She might never return.

In fact, he knew she wasn't going to. And his heart contracted tightly at the thought. She could have the darn truck if she wanted, although he knew she'd taken it just to make her point. He was overbearing. He was cocky. He had thought he could control the relationship. He might as well have tried to control how hard Bloodthirsty would kick.

KATY WENT TO THE ONE PLACE she knew Laredo wouldn't think to look for her: Union Junction.

More specifically, she headed to her stylist sisters' new salon, Union Junction Style. Beatrice, Daisy,

Gretchen, Jessica, Lily, Marnie, Tisha, Velvet and Violet were the brightly painted names above the new hair-styling stations. And every chair was full, both with male and female customers. The salon was buzzing, but almost all talk ceased when she walked in.

"Katy!" they exclaimed. Whichever stylists weren't in the middle of a process rushed over to give her a hug. "What are you doing here?"

"I'm on my way to Duke," Katy said.

"You made up your mind to go," Violet said. She had been unanimously voted this salon's manager.

"Finally," Katy said. "It was past time."

"Can you stay with us for a while?" Marnie asked. "Before you go become a North Carolinian and we never see you again?"

Katy gulped. "I'd better not," she said. "I've dallied long enough."

Beatrice gave her a hug. "It's that Laredo, isn't it?" she said softly so her Union Junction customers couldn't hear.

"No, I really need to be moving on with my life," Katy protested.

"We heard through the grapevine—" Gretchen said.

"You mean from Hannah," Katy interrupted, knowing Delilah wouldn't gossip.

"The grapevine," Gretchen repeated, "that you and Laredo were engaged in an all-out battle of the sexes. We had our money on you. So what happened?"

Katy was confused. "Money on me? For what?"

"To rope him in," Daisy said. "You know. Marriage."

"Actually, no," Katy murmured. "Marriage was never on either of our minds. It's too soon for me to think of that again, and it will always be too soon for Laredo to think of it. He's got to do his Big Thing, and I needed to find myself. We're sort of on separate tracks that would never permanently connect."

"Oh." Sympathetic murmurs flurried around her.

"Why don't you go in the back and get washed up?" Violet said. "When we're done here, we'll take you to our farmhouse."

"Farmhouse?" Katy asked. "This isn't like Delilah's place?"

"Nope," Tisha said firmly. "It's as different as we could make it. Even down to the name. No more 'Lonely' anything."

"And all the Jefferson boys come to us for their cuts," Velvet said proudly. "We all get one apiece. Except for Last, because he's odd man out, so he rotates amongst us."

"I get him next," Lily said, "and I can't wait!"

"Who cuts Laredo's hair?" Katy murmured, for some reason needing to know silly trivia about the cowboy.

"I do," Violet said kindly. "He's a perfect gentleman, and he's got hair that doesn't want to lie down. Which is fine, because his hat keeps it mashed. And that's all I can tell you about your cowboy, Katy."

Katy flashed grateful eyes at Violet. "Guess I'll go see what you've done in the back."

THE FARMHOUSE was more like a home than Katy would have imagined. "Does Delilah know you've done this? It's wonderful!" she exclaimed.

All the women nodded. "She knows, but she hasn't had a chance to visit. We're pretty proud of it," Velvet said.

"The Jefferson boys helped us find financing, especially Mason," Daisy said. "Mimi actually found us the house. Union Junction has welcomed us with open arms."

"So you're better off here than you were in Lonely Hearts Station." Katy was amazed. "I remember when Delilah had to choose which of us to let go. At the time we thought it was the end of the world."

"We pulled together," Gretchen said, "although don't be fooled. At times we fought like cats and dogs."

They took her upstairs and showed her the bedrooms. "This is such a big farmhouse that we were able to convert extra rooms into bedrooms. Almost all of us have a separate bedroom, and bathrooms are generally shared between only two of us," Beatrice told her. "On the weekends someone usually stops by, either to fix something on the house or bring food."

"They'll never forget us helping them out during the big storm," Katy said. "And it didn't seem like we were doing all that much. Just pulling together."

"Well, we'll always be happy that the email Mimi sent accidentally came to us," Lily said. "Those were some of our darkest days."

Katy sat on a chair in the sitting room, a second-story screened-in porch. She instantly decided it was her favorite room in the house. "I think Delilah has a few more dark days ahead of her, though she would never let on."

"Hannah says that bookings are up," Tisha said.

"A little, yes. But Marvella won the real prize money, and since she's got the winning cowboy, she's getting more of the bookings." Katy sighed. "I thought the good guys always won."

"So what about Laredo?" Marnie asked.

Katy stiffened. "He's riding to the rescue tomorrow."

"So…what are you doing here?" Violet asked. "Don't you want to see him?"

"I don't want to see him get thrown again. I just can't. The doctor was very clear about no more head injuries, but Laredo doesn't listen to anything. He's so stubborn!"

Jessica nodded. "Stubborn. That's one of your traits, too, you know."

"Yes, I know, but…what crabs me is that he *could* let Ranger ride. Or someone in his family who knows what they're doing. But no. He's got to be the hero."

"For you, Katy," Jessica said. "He's trying to be your hero."

"But I don't want a hero. I want him healthy. I wish I'd never pulled him in off the street. I wish I'd never opened the door and seen him standing out there! I thought I'd seen a miracle, but he turned out to be just a…man," she said sadly.

"Why? Because he has no experience? You should give him a second chance," Velvet said reasonably. "Katy, life isn't cleanly cut into right and wrong. Tomorrow he may bust his head open like an egg dropped on cement. Or he could stay on. Who knows? You could admit that you're in love with him. You might risk getting your heart busted open again, or you may end up staying on. He's getting back in the saddle. Why aren't you?"

"Because I'm scared," Katy said. "In the end, I think I'm as big a mouse as Rose."

"So whose truck are you driving?" Gretchen asked, glancing out the window.

"Laredo's. I stole it from him. But I figure he'll be back here tomorrow night, and then he can pick it up."

"Uh-huh," Gretchen said. "That's a good idea. Except that he's out front writing on it."

"Writing on it?" Katy jumped to her feet.

With shoe polish, he'd written all over the truck sides, "Take my truck, but not my heart."

"Oh, my," Katy murmured. "He is one unstoppable cowboy."

"Are you going to go down there or not?" Daisy demanded. "That poor man!"

"He's not so innocent," Katy explained. "He was planning on kidnapping me and dumping me at Malfunction Junction so I couldn't leave town and pose for *Playboy*."

"Good for him," Violet said. "I like that man's way of thinking!"

"You are all against me," Katy said, realization dawning on her as they all waved at Laredo. He stood in the front yard, his hands on his hips, staring up at them.

"No, we're all for finding true love," Lily said.

"I think…I think I'll at least go congratulate him for outthinking me. And thank him for the use of his truck."

"You do that," Marnie said. "We'll be waiting up here for you."

HEART IN HER THROAT, Katy walked downstairs and went out to meet Laredo. "You found me."

"I knew where you'd go," he boasted.

"Hannah told you."

"Hannah gave me a couple of bits of insight," he admitted. "She said you probably wouldn't go far from your sisters."

She stared up at him silently.

"The kidnapping idea was a bad one," he said. "I

should have just told you that it killed me to think of your naked body in print. And now that I've made love to you, you leave me no choice. I know you hate to be told anything, but—"

She laid two fingers over his lips. "I wasn't going to, anyway."

"Never?" he asked, moving her fingers, his gaze lighting up.

"Well, I thought about it. I did need to break out of my shell and find out if I was frigid."

"You're not—"

"But," she said quickly, "once we made love, I knew for sure I couldn't do it. You satisfied that worry in me, and I'll always be grateful for that."

Laredo grinned. "I told you."

She sighed. "Laredo, you are too confident."

"I can have confidence for both of us. Until you get yours back, Katy. You just need someone to stick with you longer than eight seconds."

"You're still going to ride that darn bull, aren't you?"

"Darn tooting," he said. "Me and Bloodthirsty, we've got a date. But I'd like you to be there, Katy."

She thought about how frightened she'd been when he'd gotten tossed. And then Bloodthirsty had ladled out extra insult by horning him. She thought about how her heart had nearly dried up when he'd been lying on the ground, his expression dazed.

"I'm afraid of that bull," she murmured.

"I'm afraid of lots of things."

"You are not." She squinted up at him doubtfully.

"I was damn scared of you being naked for other men, Katy. That's far worse than taking a shot in the pants from a bull."

She shuddered. It was unbearable to think of it.

"By the way," Laredo said conversationally, "I went back and got your bra and top from the side of the road. To be honest, I was afraid when you shucked your clothes like that. I mean, I liked it, but you did kind of goose me, acting all uninhibited like that."

She didn't believe a word of it. "You didn't act scared."

"Well, it was kind of a buzz having you throw yourself at me with such determination. Who was I to say no? But I was afraid that you wouldn't like making love to me. That you'd always regret it. You're the kind of girl who thinks too much, Katy. You regretted nearly marrying Stanley, which was very wise of you. But then you regretted pulling me inside the salon and asking me to ride the bull—"

"I only regretted it after you nearly got your head split open," she disagreed.

"Irrelevant." He held up his hand. "The point is, then you might have regretted making love with me. This is every man's worst fear, that the woman in his arms will say, 'Gee whiz, I should have stayed home and washed my hair.'"

"Laredo Jefferson!" Katy stared at him. "You do not harbor any such doubts. Not behind all that cocky, strutting, everything's-my-way-or-the-highway attitude. Don't even try to sell me on that!"

"Well, I was reasonably certain I could make you happy," he admitted. "But you still crushed me when you didn't act like you wanted to hang at my bootheels when it was over. You know, follow me around like I was the best thing to happen to you since…you found Lonely Hearts Station."

She narrowed her eyes.

"Teasing," he said quickly. "Just teasing!"

He had confidence galore to tease her at the moment she most wanted to throw herself at him and beg him not to ride that stupid bull. Beg him to make love to her instead. What a ridiculous situation to have gotten herself into! This man was pigheaded and a little nuts, and here she had fallen for him. *Mental note: no more cowboys!*

Way too hard on the heart.

"Laredo, if I come watch you tomorrow, will you be happy? Because I really am planning on heading to Duke. And I don't want to keep you from your Big Thing, either. We can be friends, pen pals, even, but I don't want to make love again. Just in case that's what motivated your drive out here."

He shook his head. "That's not why I came here. Had to check on my truck," he said, shining it with the sleeve of his shirt. "No way. It was the last thing on my mind."

CHAPTER NINETEEN

"So, NOW THAT WE'VE gotten that out of the way," Laredo said, "can I take you out to dinner?"

He liked the way Katy stared at him. He'd caught her off guard for sure.

"Why?"

Shrugging, he said, "Why not?"

"Because I don't trust you."

"Well, I know that, and good thing you don't, probably." He squinted up at the windows where the new girls in town were staring down at them none too sheepishly. "I could order in chicken for the gang if you want to stay and visit with them."

She nodded. "They'd probably like that."

He smiled at her. "You staying here tonight? There's room at the Malfunction Junction if—"

"No, I think there's plenty of room here," she said. "Thanks just the same."

"You did like it, didn't you?" he asked, just to make certain. His pride was taking a beating, and he was trying to cover the heart on his sleeve, but he was pretty certain he just needed to be patient with Katy. She was like a wild doe that didn't want anyone to get too close.

He could be patient.

"I did," she said softly. "It was wonderful. Thank you for being my first."

No problemo, he thought, because he was darn sure going to be her last. "Fine, fine," he said cheerfully. "Shall I run go get that chicken?"

"If that's what you feel like for your last meal," she replied primly.

"All right, then. Hey," he called up to the girls framed in the screened-in porch.

"Hi, Laredo," they all called back.

"I was thinking about making a run for some fried chicken. Shall we have dinner?"

"Shall we!" Violet called back. "We'll rustle up some margaritas to go with it, if you'd like."

"Nothing better!" He looked at Katy. "Ride with me, pen pal."

She gave him the most suspicious glare he'd ever seen her wear. "Pen pal?"

"Isn't that what you said we could be from now on?"

"Sure," Katy said. "Pals is perfect."

He grinned. The definition didn't matter. He wasn't really a bull rider, and if he and Bloodthirsty worked things out, Katy wasn't really going to be his pen pal, either.

"SO, ARE YOU NERVOUS about tomorrow, Laredo?" Violet asked. The weather was perfect for an outdoor picnic, so they all sat on the screened porch, eating fried chicken and drinking margaritas. Katy put down her drink, waiting for Laredo's answer. She certainly was nervous.

"Heck, no," he said. "I think I've got it figured out."

"Is this your last bull ride?" Daisy asked.

He shrugged. "I don't think so. Now I see why Mason always wished we hadn't taken up the sport. I kind of wish I'd taken it up years ago."

Katy stared at him. "Why?"

"I don't know. It's a challenge. Maybe if I had done rodeo, I wouldn't be feeling this urge for a Big Thing now."

Clearly she was not a Big Thing in his life, which was something of a bitter fact for her.

"In fact, I'm going to talk to Miss Delilah about turning Bloodthirsty Black into a bounty bull. I'm pretty sure he might have the makings for it. We'd have to run several more cowboys on him, but if he keeps bucking like he did me, he'll be hard for anyone to ride."

Tight nerves crept inside Katy's stomach. "You know what? It's been a long day for me. I think I'll turn in."

"Come on," Gretchen said quickly. "I'll show you where you're going to sleep."

"Goodbye, Laredo," Katy said. "Good luck tomorrow."

He grinned at her, and her heart did a bellyflop. "Thanks, sweetheart."

All her friends' eyebrows shot up, but Katy paid no attention. He'd called her that before—and it hadn't meant a thing.

KATY RODE IN with her friends to see Laredo ride. She couldn't remember being this nervous last week. No doubt it had to do with knowing Laredo shouldn't hit his head, the beautiful doctor in attendance or maybe just knowing this was the last time she'd ever see him.

When Tex rode out on Bad-Ass Blue and rounded up another eighty-nine, the arena went crazy. It was triple-packed this weekend due to increased publicity, and the cheers were enthusiastic and loud.

Katy felt ill.

Then she saw Laredo loading into the chute, wrapping his hand. He gave a nod, and Bloodthirsty Black jumped into the arena, snorting fire and kicking flame.

Laredo lasted all of three seconds before he hit the dirt, but this time he landed upright and jumped onto a wall before Bloodthirsty could horn him.

Katy breathed a sigh of relief that felt like it came up through the soles of her feet. The arena cheered and clapped as enthusiastically as they had for Tex. Katy smiled as Laredo waved at the crowd. As he'd said, he liked rodeo, and apparently, it liked him. Even Bloodthirsty had to give up another second to Laredo.

It was a Big Thing to conquer one's fear.

Quietly she sneaked out. Her bag was already packed from the night before. She'd already said goodbye to Delilah and Hannah and the other girls this morning. Jerry was waiting to drive her into town to the airport.

She got on her plane and headed toward her new destination.

A MONTH LATER Katy was starting to settle in. She'd come to North Carolina and fallen in love with the town where the college was located. The staff had been welcoming, the people helpful, the alumni enthusiastic. She'd had an opportunity to take over for a chemistry professor who was on sudden sick leave, and she'd jumped at the chance to ease herself in this way.

It was all going so well, Katy thought. She felt very blessed to have finally found her path. It had taken her a while, but she'd met a lot of wonderful people, and she didn't regret a thing.

Except, perhaps, not seeing the smile on Laredo's face whenever she appeared. He'd made her feel different…and special. She did miss him.

And she missed her friends. And Rose, who was in Delilah's safekeeping.

But it was nice to be getting to know—and like—herself. Already she knew she could be a talented professor.

"Professor Goodnight," a voice said from the back of the lab, "I wonder if you could help me with this test result. It doesn't seem to be coming up the way it should."

She turned and saw Laredo smiling at her.

She should have been surprised, but she wasn't. "What are you doing here, cowboy?"

"Saying hello to a friend."

"You're not a very good pen pal," she told him.

"There wasn't a need. I was on my way here. I left right after the rodeo. My truck and me, we've seen a lot of history, and a lot of sights between there and you."

"Do any Big Things?"

He shook his head. "You?"

She shook her head as well. "Not really."

"Katy," Laredo said, taking her hand, "I'm not chemistry smart. But I do know about emotional chemistry, and you and I have got it in bulk. I think we could have it for the long haul. I'm thinking marriage is a really Big Thing, though, that I'd probably need a partner to help me with. I need you," he said, kissing her fingers.

Tears jumped into her eyes. "I've missed you. But I was mad at you, too."

"I know. I knew it the minute Bloodthirsty tossed me off. I got out of that ring thanking God I still had my head on straight enough to come after you. I knew I was going to do it. I just wanted to make certain you had enough time to follow your dream, the way you let me follow mine."

She took a deep breath that hesitated somewhere in her rib cage. "I thought you wanted to keep riding rodeo. They say all men do."

"Not this man. Ranger's riding next. It's turning out to be quite a cash cow for Lonely Hearts Station, if you'll pardon the pun."

A slow smile lifted her lips. "For my partner, anything."

"Anything?"

"Mmm."

He pulled her into his arms and took a jeweler's box out of his pocket. "Turn this lump of carbon into a diamond, Professor?"

She opened the box, gasping at the two-carat emerald-cut diamond lying inside. "Oh, Laredo," she said, "you're going to make me break down and say it, aren't you?"

He kissed her, taking her face between his hands so he could hold her as close as possible. "Yes."

"I love you," she murmured. "I have since the day I met you."

"I've loved you since the day I saw you mopping up water in Union Junction. I fell in love with your butt."

She smiled as he slipped the ring on her finger. "I fell in love with yours when Bloodthirsty tossed you. You looked so cute going head over heels."

They looked at each other and laughed. And then

he picked her up and carried her outside into the North Carolina sunlight.

"We're going to love it here," Laredo said with a smile. "Professor Sweetheart."

* * * * *

In Tina Leonard's new miniseries,
CALLAHAN COWBOYS, six bachelor brothers compete
for ownership of the family ranch. The winning cowboy
must get married—and have as many babies as possible!

Here's an excerpt from
THE COWBOY'S BONUS BABY, available July 2011,
only from Harlequin® American Romance®!

Aberdeen stared at the sleeping cowboy's handsome face. *Trouble with a capital* T. "Did he tell you his name? Maybe he's got family around here who could come get him."

"No," Johnny said. "He babbles a lot about horses. Talks a great deal about spirit horses and other nonsense. Native American lore. Throws in an occasional Irish tale. Told a pretty funny joke, too. The man has a sense of humor for being out of his mind."

"Great." Aberdeen had a funny feeling about the cowboy who had come to Johnny's Bar and Grill. "I'm going to see who he is," she said, reaching into his front pocket for his wallet.

A hand shot out, grabbing her wrist. Aberdeen gasped and tried to draw away, but the cowboy held on, staring up at her with those navy eyes. She couldn't look away.

"Stealing's wrong," he said.

She slapped his hand and he released her. "I know that, you ape. What's your name?"

He crossed his arms and gave her a roguish grin. "What's *your* name?"

"I already told you my name is Aberdeen." He'd said it not five minutes ago, so possibly he did have a concussion. "Cowboy, I'm going to look at your license, and if you grab me again like you did a second ago, you'll wish you hadn't.

So either you give me your wallet, or I take it. Those are your choices."

He stared at her, unmoving.

She reached into his pocket and pulled out his wallet, keeping her gaze on him, trying to ignore the expanse of wide chest and other parts of him she definitely shouldn't notice. Flipping the wallet open, she took out his driver's license. "Creed Callahan. New Mexico."

He grabbed her, pulling her to him for a fast kiss. His lips molded to hers, and Aberdeen felt a spark—more than a spark, *real* heat—and then he released her.

She stared at him. He shrugged. "I figured you'd get around to slapping me eventually. Might as well pay hell is what I always say."

*Find out what happens next
in THE COWBOY'S BONUS BABY,
available July 2011,
only from Harlequin® American Romance®!*

And be sure to watch for more CALLAHAN COWBOYS, *including a bonus Christmas novella, throughout 2011.*